Domestic Arts

Sisters of Stella Mare Book 2

Annie M. Ballard

DevonStationBooks.ca
Books to bring life to your life

DEVON STATION BOOKS

Domestic Arts, Sisters of Stella Mare

ISBN: 978-1-7782367-1-6

Published in Canada. Canadian copyright applies.

Copyright © 2022 by Leslie Ann Costello writing as Annie M. Ballard.

Cover design by Claire Smith of BookSmiths Design, Sydney, AU. Editing by LZ Edits. Orlando, FL, USA

Published by Devon Station Books, Fredericton, NB, E3A 2Z8, Canada.

All rights reserved. No portion of this book may be reproduced in any form without written permission from the publisher or author, except as permitted by U.S. & Canadian copyright law.

Contents

1. Chapter 1 — 1
2. Chapter 2 — 26
3. Chapter 3 — 32
4. Chapter 4 — 47
5. Chapter 5 — 57
6. Chapter 6 — 66
7. Chapter 7 — 72
8. Chapter 8 — 85
9. Chapter 9 — 97
10. Chapter 10 — 103
11. Chapter 11 — 116
12. Chapter 12 — 135
13. Chapter 13 — 146
14. Chapter 14 — 159

15.	Chapter 15	165
16.	Chapter 16	176
17.	Chapter 17	184
18.	Chapter 18	204
19.	Chapter 19	216
20.	Chapter 20	226
21.	Chapter 21	239
22.	Chapter 22	248
23.	Chapter 23	258
24.	Chapter 24	269
25.	Chapter 25	282
26.	Chapter 26	292
27.	Chapter 27	303
28.	Chapter 28	315
29.	Chapter 29	325
30.	Chapter 30	340
31.	Chapter 31	349
Gratitude		364
About Annie		366
Also By Annie M. Ballard		367

Chapter 1

"My life is a cliché," Evie muttered as she struggled to haul the heavy suitcase up the steps to her father's front porch. "Ugh." Dropping the case at the top, she gave it a shove with her foot. Glaring at the box, she kicked it hard. "Ouch!"

Shaking her foot, she headed back toward her car.

"Evelyn! Evie!"

Evie stopped dead. Oh, no. Mrs. Lewis. Pasting on a smile, she turned toward the voice. "Hi, Mrs. Lewis. Nice to see you." She waved toward the neighbour's porch.

"Home for a visit?" Mrs. Lewis asked cheerily.

Evie's smile weakened. She nodded energetically and moved briskly toward her father's house. She'd get her other stuff later.

Pushing the door open with her shoulder, she called out, "Dad! I'm here." The house was quiet. She tiptoed down the hallway to the sunny kitchen. Peering into the living room, she saw James in his recliner, afghan over his knees. She heard a gentle snoring, and then there was a scrabble of nails on tile and a couple of big, curly haired dogs pushed through the open sun porch door and headed joyously toward her.

James startled awake and Evie squatted down to receive canine kisses and hug the furry necks. She giggled a little.

"Evie! I didn't hear you come in." He started to get up.

"Stay there, Dad. I didn't want to disturb your nap, but I guess the dogs had a different idea." She stood up, and Custard and Mallow each gave a shake and a final sniff. She leaned over her father and kissed his cheek.

"Mrs. Lewis was very curious," Evie noted wryly as she perched on the sofa.

James scoffed. "She has to keep up with the neighbourhood. Other people watch TV, but Janelle watches people. Gives her a hobby."

Evie sighed. "I'm embarrassed enough about being here. I don't need Mrs. Nosy to air my business all over town."

"Oh, Evie. No need to be embarrassed. Your old dad needs you at home, that's all," James said.

"Ha. I appreciate the support, Dad, but we both know who is the one with the problem here."

"I'm glad you're here." He got up heavily. "I'm going to make a cup of tea. Have one?"

She nodded. "Yes, thanks. I'll go get my stuff. Mrs. Lewis should be back in her own kitchen by now."

She hauled her suitcase up the steep stairs to the room she'd shared with her younger sister. It wasn't her old room really, because Dorie had only recently moved out. Instead, it felt like Dorie's room, with her duvet, some old clothes in the tiny closet, and odds and ends in the dresser drawers. Evie sat on the bed to look around.

She recalled massive fights with her baby sister. It was so unfair, she'd complained to her mother, so unfair that she had to share with the baby, while Helen and Loretta—Rett—got to be together. Teenagers didn't want to have babies in their rooms, she'd said heatedly. Teenagers needed space. When she'd suggested moving into the big bedroom with Helen and Rett, she was nearly scorched by their disdain. Stuck, that's what she was, lacking the privilege of the oldest two sisters, and stuck in a space with this baby. Dorie really was the baby, being nearly twelve years younger than Rett, and a full fourteen years younger than Helen. Evie had to share her space with that baby sister, and the bigger sisters got to have a teenage space, with posters and their music, and makeup and talk. Evie's room had Legos and dolls. Though sometimes, at twelve-plus, Evie had been happy to play dolls with Dorie and ignore all the teenage drama going on down the hall.

But drama, tears, scary things, all of this had been okay because of Mum. Mum was the center.

Atop Dorie's dresser was a framed picture of the four girls and their mother, Agnes. Evie remembered the occasion: Helen's graduation from university. Helen, with her beautiful long hair and blue eyes, wore her graduation robe, and Rett, built on the same lines, had her light hair pulled back and wore a happy smile, Dorie, the baby and only little at the time, clearly was cut from the very same cloth. Their mother, Agnes.

Evie leaned forward to pick up the photo. There was Mum, glowing with pride in her daughters. Her hair and eyes were imprinted on each of the three, though Agnes wore her hair shorter, as befitted a middle-aged mother of grown and nearly grown daughters. Evie's face crumpled; her eyes grew hot. No hint there of what was to come. She went to set the photo back on the dresser but hesitated.

She gazed down at the fifth person in the picture. Oh, she was good at skipping over this part, but she was already crying, so why not?

There was this other person, short and sturdy where Agnes and the girls were long and willowy. A big mop of dark curls; deep brown eyes, with a faraway look. Everyone else was focused on the photographer (James, as Evie recalled) but no, this strange-looking girl wanted to be elsewhere, looked like she belonged elsewhere. Felt like she should be elsewhere.

With a shake of her head, Evie set the photo back on the dresser. Then she tipped it face down and dumped the contents of her suitcase on the bed. Enough of this emotion stuff. Feelings all over the place. She didn't remember having a day like this, even after finding out her mother had cancer and was probably going to die. *I can't believe I feel worse now than I did when we were losing Mum. Okay, not really worse. But more confused. Just crappy.*

A door slammed downstairs, and running footsteps heralded her sister Dorie.

"Evie? Evie, where are you?" she called out, and Evie heard her leap up the stairs. Evie stuck her head out the bedroom doorway. *Great. Just what I need. Youthful enthusiasm. I never felt older.*

"Here. I'm in here," she said, turning back to the pile of clothes.

With a gust of energy, her baby sister flung herself into the room and grabbed her for a hug.

"What?" Evie laughed in spite of herself. "What's this?"

"Dad said you were coming, and I just couldn't wait to show you." Dorie pulled back and looked in Evie's face. Suddenly serious, she said, "Hey, are you okay? What's up?"

Evie turned away from the look of concern. "I'm fine. I'm always fine, you know that." She looked back at her sister, glowing skin, bright green eyes, long light hair. "You look wonderful. What's with you?"

"Thanks!" Dorie bounced over to sit on the edge of the bed. "I kind of feel wonderful. You know Chad and I are getting a big grant for the old dogs' home, right?"

"Yeah, I heard that from Dad. I'm happy for you. That's wonderful."

"So, because we're going to have jobs and not be scrambling to try to feed a pack of old dogs and pay for their vet bills and barely having enough money to feed ourselves, we decided..." Dorie stopped suddenly. "Just look." She held out her left hand. Sunlight sparkled off the diamond ring.

Oh, no. Not this. Not today. She suppressed tears.

"Oh, my," Evie said reverently as she took her sister's fingers in her hand. "What a beautiful vintage piece. You're buying jewellery now?" She raised her eyebrows.

"Evie!" Dorie protested. "Don't play dumb. We're engaged!"

With an effort, Evie laughed. "Congratulations. I'm sorry to tease you. That's wonderful. When did that all happen?"

"Well, really just last night. We just found out about the grant. So that's why you didn't know yet about being engaged. We only told Dad and Alice, and we're going to make a more general family announcement on a Sunday video chat. But you're here, so I get to tell you in person!"

Evie felt that pain in her chest again. She pushed it away and said, "Chad's such a good guy. I'm very happy for both of you."

Dorie smiled happily on the bed. "I really didn't think it would happen so soon, but things change and then, you know, things change." She held out her hand and gazed at it admiringly. Then she looked back at Evie. "And what about you and Jase? I imagine you'll be making an announcement soon too. Right?"

Evie's breath caught in her throat. "I'm not thinking that, no." She looked away from Dorie's puzzled stare. "But let's talk about you. Do you have a date or anything?"

Her sister laughed. "Nah. I'm not in a rush, but the change in status makes Alice happier to have me and Chad living together in her house." Alice was Chad's grandmother, his only family.

"She's a little old fashioned, I guess," Evie suggested. "I bet that applies to Dad too."

"Maybe. But he hasn't said so, and I've been mostly living there since last fall. Only now we have a real plan." Dorie sounded jubilant.

There it was again, that feeling. Not jealousy, but a pang nevertheless. *Just pain, I guess. Who knew emotional pain could be physical?*

"How long are you staying?" Dorie asked, surveying the pile of clothes on the bed.

"The weekend or maybe more," Evie said vaguely.

"More? Don't you have to work?"

"Yeah, well, you know, work. One perk, maybe the only perk, of the artsy-fartsy life is that you have some flexibility about work."

"That's what Mum used to call it, right? Evelyn lives the artsy-fartsy life."

Evie gave her a dark glance. "I hated it when she said that. But now I kind of get it. Making a living in the arts isn't easy, but when you can pull it off, you get to do the thing you love best every single day."

"I get it," Dorie said, getting up off the bed. "I get living from grant to grant, after this past year with the dog sanctuary. If the work is your calling, you don't have a choice, but sometimes eating would be good, too."

Evie chuckled. "My, my, how my baby sister has grown up." She slung an arm across Dorie's shoulders, and they headed downstairs.

DOMESTIC ARTS

Stephen was whistling as he trudged away from the fish house. He shrugged deeper into his jacket. June and it was still freezing, he thought, looking back over his shoulder at the harbour. Comes with the territory. The harbour waters looked still, with fishing boats on moorings, and even one pulled up to the dock of the big fish market. After three months in town, Stephen knew the stillness to be deceptive, really just an indication of slack tide, that moment when the tide shifts from incoming to outgoing. The harbour basin was full now, but in six hours some of those boats would be sitting on mudflats. Three months in and he never failed to marvel at the extremes of the tidal changes.

So, cold or not, things were pretty good. He considered the contents of the bag over his shoulder. New stories, new people to talk to, and best of all, new wood carvings made by fishers old and young. With satisfaction, he thought about the two carefully wrapped artifacts now in his possession. Old Joe Wellington was willing to let him borrow his grandfather's hand-carved right whale and dory. Not that Joe had seen them as having any importance at all until Stephen showed an interest, he thought with an internal chuckle. He made Stephen practically sign his life away to carry them off to the gallery for a couple of weeks.

A good day overall, he mused. *Maybe I'll celebrate.*

The kilometre-long walk from the working harbour to the gallery didn't warm him at all, though he moved briskly. He stopped in to drop off his new finds. Stepping into the bright, warm gallery space felt good, but he walked through it to the office door without slowing to look at the art. He'd seen all the displays anyway, and he had helped hang the latest show.

He rapped at the door and pushed it open. "Hi, honey, I'm home," he called out.

Leonard looked up from his desk and smiled. "Right. You look happy."

He nodded. "Cold but happy. Yes, I got a couple of new pieces to look at and some good story leads."

Leonard clicked his tongue in satisfaction. "I thought old Wellington would be a good source for you," he said smugly. "Aren't you glad you decided to come here?"

"You need continuous reinforcement, don't you? Yes, Leonard, you gave me a good tip, and yes, Leonard, I'm happy to be in Stella Mare, and yes, Leonard, thank you for letting me stay here at the gallery."

Leonard snickered. "Okay, maybe I do like a little acknowledgement."

"A little!"

"But it hasn't been easy to try to get a foothold in this little village. I'm just happy that you can benefit from what I already experienced."

Stephen sat in the chair in front of Leonard's desk. "What do you mean? I've found people here to be just as hospitable as folks at home. Kind, welcoming, invite you over to dinner, that sort of thing."

Leonard looked askance. "Well, you're a handsome American guy from North Carolina with a cool accent, and you're only here for a visit. Me, I'm an upstart from Toronto trying to make a buck. Not as welcome as you, maybe."

"That's too bad," he said. "Things are good now though, aren't they?"

"Mostly," Leonard said. "Actually, having you here is probably good for my reputation in town."

"What?" Stephen laughed. "That's crazy."

"No, really," he insisted. "People like you. They think you're really interested in their old family treasures."

"I really am interested."

Leonard brushed that off. "They don't understand about getting some of these artifacts into gallery spaces, or into private collections. What I do doesn't make sense to them. But telling you stories about their ancestors, well, that's a local pastime. You fit right in."

"Interesting," Stephen said. "I'm pretty happy with my morning haul, as they say around here. I'm going out to celebrate. Want to join me?"

"Celebrate? What did you have in mind?"

"Don't get excited. Coffee and a cinnamon roll at the Sunshine Diner."

Leonard snorted. "Some celebration. I'll pass. You could bring me a cappuccino when you come back though."

"Done."

Ten minutes later, Stephen was walking down Water Street farther away from the harbour, hands tucked into the deep pockets of his Nordic sweater, purchased since coming to the Canadian Maritimes. *Oh, nobody really told me to expect summer to be cold.* On the plus side, it was nice to sleep without air conditioning.

Lunch rush was over and Cassandra was wiping down the front counter where she'd been filling sugar jars. "Hey, Cassie," he said, sitting on a stool.

"Stephen," she smiled. "You missed the big crowd."

"S'okay today," he said. "I got my stories direct down at the shore."

"Excellent!" She had a wide smile. "So now you're celebrating."

He chuckled. "I'm not mysterious at all, am I? You already know my routine."

"Well, nobody is immune to my uncle's cinnamon rolls, so I completely understand. Coffee too?"

"Yes, please. I tried to get Leonard to come but he was unimpressed with my plan."

"I bet he asked you to bring him a cappuccino though, didn't he?"

"You know it." They smiled at each other.

Then she said, "I'm off here in a few minutes and heading to the gallery anyway. If you like, I'll take it with me so you can take your time."

"That's so nice, Cassie. Thank you. How is it for you, holding down both jobs?"

She shrugged. "Oh, well, you know. This one pays the bills and that one, I dunno, I see it as my future. Somehow."

He raised his eyebrows in an unasked question.

"That whole curation thing really has me excited, you know? I just have to figure a few things out."

"You're young. You'll get it figured out," he said comfortingly. "When I was in my early twenties, I had no idea that fifteen years later I'd be doing what I'm doing. In fact, I can safely say that I had no idea that anyone did what I'm doing."

She looked at him curiously. "Really? So you didn't know you could be a professor?"

"Well, I didn't think I wanted to be that, but what I meant was I didn't know anybody studied the art and stories of people in their locales. I guess if I had started out in anthropology I would have known, but I started out in art."

She looked pensive. "Well, I tried to start in art, but I ended up starting in the Sunshine Diner, and now I've discovered the whole idea of digging into an artists' catalogue and motivation and context and all the things. And even just the science of hanging art. It's way cooler than I expected."

"That's how you know it's for you. When things are way cooler." They grinned at each other for a moment.

"Okay, I'm out of here," she said, Leonard's cappuccino in hand. She called to the kitchen, "Sonny, I'm leaving. Nobody here but Stephen." Sonny's assent was barely audible, but Cassandra flipped a wave and headed out the door.

Stephen picked up his plate and cup and headed for a booth. Popping in his earbuds, he opened the audio file from the morning interview. *Leonard is wrong. This place is totally welcoming.*

Dinner with her father James, plus Dorie and Chad, entertained Evie for the evening, but then the guests went home, James settled in to watch a movie, and Evie decided to take the big dogs for a walk.

"You guys are huge," she said, looking at their hopeful faces as she untangled leashes in the kitchen. They were unarguably big dogs, with Saint Bernard and Newfoundland ancestry, but they were family members from way back. Hairy, slobbery, and large, they were a fixture at the house.

"Hey, Dad," she called back toward the living room. "I thought Dorie would take these guys when she moved in with Chad."

James appeared in the doorway, leaning against the jamb. "She offered. But I like having them around. They remind me of your mother, and besides, they make me get out for my walk everyday." Mallow wandered over to James for a scratch on the head. "Yeah, you heard me say 'walk,' but Evie's going to take you." Mallow returned to monitor the leash activity.

"They remind you of Mum?" Evie asked. "How so?"

"You must remember when she brought the first one of these guys home," James said, sounding reminiscent. "We'd just lost, oh, I don't even know which one, but she was determined she'd never have fewer than two dogs at a time. Good company for each other, she always said." His eyes grew misty.

Evie reached to hug her father, leather straps still in her hand. Holding him tightly, she murmured, "Has it been hard being here without Dorie?"

He sniffed a bit and patted her on the back. "I'm okay. Really." He pulled away a little. "Sometimes it is very quiet here and then I'm glad to have these guys. But don't tell Dorie. I'm also so blessed glad she's grown up enough to be on her own. I don't want her thinking I need her here."

Evie shook her head. "No worries. It's a big change to be here alone after always having a full house."

He smiled at her, patting her shoulder. "And you're here for a visit and we'll have video chat on Sunday with your sisters and it's fine."

She nodded. Fine.

A few minutes later, she was out in the late spring night with the dogs. The sun had just set despite the hour. These pre-solstice days, Evie's favourite, were the longest. She led the dogs down the sidewalk toward the village center, first checking her phone. Nope. Nothing from anyone. Not Jase, not anyone.

Beautiful downtown Stella Mare. All the right trappings for the tourists. She noted the elegant streetlights, the carefully restored storefronts, the ocean-themed window decor in the shops. Two new seafood restaurants, plus, of course, old faithful, the Sunshine Diner, where the locals knew they could find the best coffee in town. The Sunshine probably didn't appeal much to tourists, or at least Sonny didn't go out of his way to make it appealing. She and the dogs continued to wander through the lengthening shadows toward the village center, where the old dock held more shops and amenities for the pleasure boaters who would be thronging them in the summer. What Evie considered the "real dock," the docks where the fishing boats unloaded their catch, was far across the harbour, too far to walk tonight, but this one was just fine. She breathed in the salt air, noted the tide (just past low), and heard the gulls squabbling as they settled in for the night.

Walking at big dog pace was meditative. Custard and Mallow padded along beside her, stopping occasionally for a sniff, but mostly just ambling. Her mind drifted away from Stella Mare to her home in St. Stephen. To her partner, Jase, and the conversation they had Friday morning, just before she threw her things in the car to leave town. Her chest tightened.

The quiet downtown of the village wrapped around her, but she barely saw it. Instead, she saw the inside of their loft/studio/home and Jase's face, surprised and angry.

"No," he said. "How can you think about that right now? I've got an opening in four weeks, and I just got confirmation of the funding for the Peninsula Festival. We've got a lot of work to do."

Tears prickled in Evie's eyes. "How can you not think about it? We've been living together for years, Jase. Twelve years this month, and I thought we'd be married long before now. But there's always something in the way." She tasted the bitterness in her mouth.

"That's right. It's just not the time."

She slapped her hand on the table. "It's never the time." She set her jaw. "When? If not now, then when?"

Jase took a long breath, gazing at her. She could almost see his brain working to change gears. Change gears but not the content. "Evelyn."

She narrowed her eyes. He didn't often use her given name.

"We're both under pressure right now. It's just not a good time to make a big change."

"Jason." Two can play this game. "I am now thirty-five years old. I'm not getting younger, and neither are you."

"Obviously. Nobody gets younger." He smiled at her. "What's the deal with now? I don't get it. We can get married now, get married later, never get married. We're together, right? That's what matters." He reached for her hand across the battered pine table.

She softened, feeling his strong hand holding hers. Softened but didn't cave. "Jase, I'm thirty-five. Older means something to women, even if it doesn't to men."

He leaned back in his chair and smiled at her, the warm glossy smile that he always wore when he got his way. Still holding her hand, he said, "Evie, you know I'll love you when you're old and wrinkled and grey."

She grimaced. "While you're distinguished and wrinkled and grey, right?"

He leered at her and brushed his hair off his forehead. "Well, of course. I'll make a handsome old guy, won't I?"

She smiled, almost by reflex. "You'll always be photogenic."

He dropped her hand, got up, and turned away.

"No, Jase. I'm not done."

He turned back, irritation making frown lines on his boyish face. "What?"

"A baby. Jase, I want a family. That's not something that can wait. Getting older means it's harder to have a baby."

He stepped back, gazing at her with wide eyes. "No."

"What do you mean, no?" She stood to follow him across the room.

"No," he said, and reached for his jacket. "No. Not that. I never signed on for that."

"What?" Shocked, she asked, "You never thought that someday we'd have kids?"

Shrugging into his jacket, he shook his head. "No. No kids. No way. I can't believe we're having this conversation. I thought you were on board, Evie."

Stunned, she gazed at him. "Why? We never talked about it. Why wouldn't I want a family?"

He came toward her and grasped her wrists. "Evie, we're artists. I've got some things I need to do in this world, make a mark, have a name in this world. You've always helped me, supported my art."

She pulled her hands away. "What did I get out of that?" she asked bitterly. "Your art, your life, your professional standing. I never ask for anything, Jase, but this is something I want. For me. For us."

Evie could hardly look at him, but she glanced up to see hurt and, oh, anger, playing across his boyish features. "What are you mad about?" she demanded. "You've got everything you want."

Turning away, he shook his head. "You have no idea. There's a lot more I want in this world. Married with kids isn't on the list." He reached for the door.

"Right, Jase, take off," she sniped. "Something doesn't go your way and you're out the door."

"We're hardly having a productive conversation, Evie," he snapped back. "I'm leaving before I say something regrettable."

"Regrettable! Like this whole thing isn't regrettable." She'd never felt this fired up before. "If you leave, Jase, that's it. If you can't even talk about this, then I'm out."

His face sagged a bit, but he sighed and said, "Then that's that, Evie. If you're willing to let all these years go just like that." He slid the big barn door open and stomped down the wooden stairs, leaving the breeze to blow up the staircase and into the loft.

She had gazed after him, feeling the coolness wash over her before she slid the door shut.

With a start, Evie noticed that the streetlights had come on in Stella Mare. What a difference a few hours and a few miles can make. *He's right. Do I really want to let go of so many years of being together?* Her chest pained her again. Losing Jase. It seemed almost unimaginable.

But look at what he wants me to give up, she argued with herself. *Oh, frig. Who can I talk to about this?* She looked at her phone.

Jase. He's the one I want to talk to. But I can't. Putting her phone away again, she and the dogs picked up the pace toward home. Maybe Dad would still be up.

On Saturday morning, Evie and James visited the farmers market, Evie heavy with worries. Dad had been asleep when she returned with the dogs, and she'd thought better about hitting her father with her personal problems. He had some health concerns that he wasn't talking about, and she didn't want to burden him with her stuff.

The late spring market was held on the downtown pier, the dock where Evie had walked the night before, but this morning it was wrapped in sunshine. Cool breezes came in from the harbour and there was the pleasant sound of vendors setting up booths, espresso hissing into cups, and a plethora of early greens and baked goods.

"You still know everybody," Evie commented to her father, as he waved and greeted more people.

"Oh, yeah, well, I've been here since forever, you know," he said, gazing at her fondly. "You'd know everyone too, if you'd stayed in Stella Mare."

"Yeah, I guess. Maybe I appreciate the privacy of a bigger town."

He chuckled. "Everybody knows your business in a place like this, that's true. There's no such thing as being anonymous."

"Evelyn!" A woman with bright red hair called her name.

"See what I mean?" Dad said to her, sotto voce.

"Oh, hi, Ginny," Evie said. "How are you?"

"Gosh, I'm great. You look good. Visiting?" Ginny gestured as she spoke. James murmured something and edged away. Evie gazed after him, with fire in her eyes. *Right, Dad. Desert me in my time of need.*

"Yes, visiting," Evie agreed.

"I haven't seen you since high school," Ginny bubbled. Then she was off to the races, sharing pictures of her babies, giving a recital of her social activities and her husband's accomplishments.

Evie's head spun. *How do I get out of this?* She looked at her watch. "I have to get going," she said.

"Oh, that's too bad. But are you here in town for a while? Maybe we could have coffee or something. My mum would watch the kids."

"I'm not really sure," Evie said cautiously. "I could let you know."

"Sure," Ginny agreed enthusiastically. "Bye for now."

"Bye," Evie said, and turned away, looking for her father.

Well, that was something. She remembered Ginny from high school. Ginny the bouncy, fun-loving drama club girl, everybody's leading lady, off to study drama in the provincial capital. *Wonder what happened to the career part? Not that it matters. She seemed perfectly happy with, what's his name? Bill? And babies. Pretty babies.*

I just don't get Jase. Why wouldn't he want to be a dad? He likes his dad just fine. Jase's dad, Ernie, had retired from practising law in St. Stephen. He didn't pretend to understand his son's preoccupation with art, but he loved Jase and supported his work and his efforts every way possible. *Even the loft, that's Ernie's building, so our home was thanks to Ernie and Liz, Jase's mom, and they have been nothing but kind to me all these years. I know Liz has been aching for a grandchild. I wonder if she knows how Jase feels about this?*

Well, she wasn't going to have a conversation with Jase's mother about her grandmotherly aspirations. But maybe she would be an ally. Evie pulled out her phone for a moment, and then reconsidered and shoved it back in her pocket. Maybe not now.

Suddenly the farmers market, the crowd, the smells, all seemed like too much. Evie looked around for her father. *I can't do this.*

She finally located James across the way at the firemen's auxiliary table where they were selling chances on cakes. She headed over with purposeful steps, but he was engrossed in conversation.

She tapped at his shoulder, and mouthed, "I'm going for a walk. See you later at home, okay?"

James nodded and returned to his chat, but then turned and tugged at her. "Hey, Jake, this is my girl, Evie. Evie, here's Jake Stevens, remember him?"

Hiding her deep discomfort, she turned back with a smile. "Hello, Jake," she said dutifully, but then recognition bloomed. "Oh, Mr. Stevens! It's nice to see you," and her smile became deep and genuine.

"How you doin', Evelyn?" boomed his familiar bass. "It's been a little while. You still making art everywhere?"

Evie's face warmed under the attention. "Not getting in trouble for it anymore though."

James added, "People even pay for her pictures, Jake. Think about the budding career you almost killed, back then in grade eleven."

Jake chuckled then. "Never wanted to shut down creativity. Just needed redirection, I guess. Nice to see you, Evie. Visiting? Married?"

Evie nodded and then shook her head. "Visiting, yes. Married, no." She felt that now-familiar pang in her chest.

James filled in. "Evie's got a very nice partner in St. Stephen, a boy she met at art college. I'm sure we'll be getting the news soon about them settling down. They're making waves in the art world, right, Evie?"

She squirmed. "I don't know about waves, Dad." She turned to Jake. "It was nice to see you again, Mr. Stevens. I'm headed down the shore for a walk, but I hope I see you again soon." Turning to James, she added, "I'll see you at home, later, okay?"

"Sure thing," he agreed, patting her on the shoulder. She nearly ran off the pier, turning left and heading down along the shore. Married. Not likely. Not now, not ever.

She walked briskly, quickly getting out of breath and having to slow down by the time she reached the liquor store and the branch in the road. Her mind was a mishmash of images. Ginny's babies pictured on her phone, her father's face as he said "...settling down..." And, over it all, Jase's refusal to consider children, refusal to talk about marriage.

She pulled out her phone again as she walked. Nothing from Jase. Nothing at all. She tapped his picture to send him a text, but then thought better of it. Instead, she called her sister Rett.

"Hey, Evie," Rett's musical voice sang out. "Mason, put that down. Right now!" A dog barked and a child cried in the background.

"Hi, Rett," Evie said. "Busy?"

"Ha. It's Saturday morning. What do you think? We're just getting home from swimming lessons and I'm sticking lunch on the table. It'll get quiet here in a minute, once everyone starts eating." Cutlery and crockery noises came from the phone. "Grilled cheese, your favourite. What do you mean, you don't like it?" Her voice was muffled as she spoke to the kids.

"There. They're busy for the moment and I can sit and talk to you. Wait, coffee." A slurp and a sigh later, Rett said, "Okay. Now. Hi, Evie. How are you?"

"Okay. Not as busy as you."

"Oh, well. That's just Saturday. Pretty soon the twins will be down for their fake nap. It's just normal stuff. But why are you calling?"

Evie sighed. "I'm in Stella Mare."

"Oh? Is Dad okay?"

"Yeah, yeah. It's not Dad."

"Well, that's good news. What is it then?"

"I think I need some sisterly advice or something. It's Jase. Or maybe it's me. I don't even know which, at this point."

Rett took another slurp of her coffee. "Tell me. Big sister is on the job. What's up?"

"I think I broke up with Jase."

There was silence.

"You think you did? Or you did?"

Evie dashed away tears as she walked along the beach road. "I don't know really. I think I said I was done, but maybe I was just mad."

A big car roared up behind her and she jumped onto the grassy verge. Rett's voice came through. "Evelyn, where are you? What was that?"

"A car. Don't worry, Rett. I'm just taking a walk. Wait, here's a bench." Evie headed across the grass of a small park and sat. "No cars here, it's okay."

"You were really mad at Jase, and you think you threatened to break up. Is that right?"

Evie nodded miserably. "Yeah. I guess so."

Rett's voice got softer. "What was it about?"

Evie's throat caught. "He, uh, doesn't want to get married now."

She imagined Rett's furrowed brow. "And you do? But why now?"

"Oh, I don't know. Something about being thirty-five, all my friends are on their second kid, well, except the ones that can't figure themselves out or the ones that are still partying like it's 1994 or whatever."

Rett was quiet for a moment. "So, kids. Thirty-five feels a little old, huh?"

Evie swallowed. "Rett, he said no kids. Ever. He doesn't want kids at all." Her voice sounded hollow, even to her.

Rett made a sympathetic sound. "Really? Never?"

"That's what he said."

"Haven't you guys talked about this before? It's been what, nine years or so?"

"More," Evie said shortly. "Twelve years and I didn't know this."

"Well," Rett said, sounding thoughtful. "That says something right there."

Evie looked at the ground. Yes, it did, didn't it? "We were so young and then we've just been, well, busy."

"Jase has been busy showing his work all around, and you've been busy doing what? The background work?"

She didn't know why that got her back up, but she suddenly felt criticized. Or maybe Rett was criticizing Jase? "We work together on that stuff. Those grant applications. Jase's website. He really is brilliant, you know, Rett."

"I don't doubt you, not at all. If you say he's brilliant, then he is. You know you're the family artist. The rest of us have these practical skills and not much taste, probably, but you're different. So if you say so, I believe you."

Silence.

"You believe me, but what?"

"No buts. I believe you that he's a brilliant artist. Do you want to be the backup singer for a brilliant artist?"

Maybe I do. Maybe that's just what I want. But a backup singer with a baby or three. A married backup singer. "I'm tired, Rett. I can't think straight. I don't do this, you know, get mad and storm off. It's not my style. It's exhausting."

"What, Mason? Oh, yeah, you can watch a show. The girls have to take a nap." Rett's voice sounded remote. "Evie, can I call you back? I've got to take care of business here."

"That's okay. This was good. Thanks for the talk. I'll see you tomorrow on family chat, right?"

"Yeah, that's right. See you then."

By the time evening fell, James and Evie were settled into the house, chatting over the burgers James had grilled in the backyard.

"You've been pretty quiet about why you're here," James observed. "I probably shouldn't pry, but maybe you should talk about what's on your mind."

Evie gazed at the old dining table, scarred oak under the placemats Evie herself had woven as a high school art project. "Can you see the scars in this old table, Dad? Look there, beside the bud vase. See that big dent?"

James touched the two-inch scratch. "You changing the subject?"

"Just look at it. This table. I remember crying over my math homework here. Playing Monopoly with my sisters and Dorie always screaming because she hates to lose."

James smiled. "She always lost because she was too little to play really."

"Right. Mum made us include her, but it always ended up with somebody yelling. I think she whacked the table with that big pewter candlestick. That's what made that scar."

"There are a lot of marks on this table. Your mother wouldn't let me refinish it. She said this was the record of the family, that we raised a bunch of kids right here, and let the wood tell the story." He looked up at Evie. "What's this about?"

"I'm so confused, Dad. Dorie's going to make her big engagement announcement at tomorrow's family chat, and I, well, I think I broke up with Jase." She looked away, biting her lip.

James waited.

"But I don't know if that's what I want. I want Jase, for sure, but..." Her voice trailed off.

"But what?"

"He doesn't want to get married, and I do."

James raised his eyebrows. "You do? I thought you were never getting married. Isn't that what you said when you were, oh, thirteen?"

She huffed. "Yes, at thirteen. Not since I got grown up though, I just figured we'd get around to it sooner or later. That's what everyone thought, you and Mum. You even said that to Mr. Stevens today. But Jase doesn't want to marry me."

"Hmm. Are you sure? Maybe its a timing thing. Maybe not right now but later?"

"Maybe. But I want it now. Not later."

"That should count for something, for sure," James said firmly. "Did you tell him that?"

She shrugged. "Maybe. It ended up being more about having kids. I was pretty upset and I'm pretty sure I told him I was done."

James looked at her inquiringly. "Are you?"

She sighed. "I don't want to be waiting for my life to begin. We've been busy living his life, and that was fine, but I figured by now we'd be able to get to what I want too." She lifted her gaze to the kitchen window filled with late evening sunset colour. "I had a talk with Rett too. I don't know. I have a lot to think about."

"It sounds like you do. But maybe you need to be thinking with Jase, not on your own."

"Maybe," she said doubtfully. "But what if he won't even think about this?"

"Don't leave it too long," James advised.

"I've never said anything like that before," Evie admitted. "I was really upset. I don't make empty threats usually." *Or any threats. I just go along. Go along and get along. That works for me.*

"You know I just want my girls happy." James stood and started gathering the dishes.

"Oh, Dad, I'll get those," Evie protested.

He went on, sitting back down. "Thanks. I don't mind handing off the chore. But I hate to see you so upset. It's not like you."

No, it's not. Usually I just find a place to squish it all down, make sure I have a happy face, keep smiling. That works. Maybe I just need to work on my squishing and go talk to Jase.

She turned a smile on her father as she stacked up the plates. "I'm really okay, Dad. But you're probably right about talking some more. I think maybe I'll zip home after the dishes, actually. Thanks for the chat."

Standing again, James took the plates from her hands. "Go now, Evie. I'll do this."

Suddenly infused with energy, she leaned in to kiss his cheek and dashed up the stairs to repack her bag. She just needed to talk to Jase, that was all. They would figure it out.

Chapter 2

She couldn't account for the shift in her energy. The day had been hard, but it was like she finally understood her confusion and realized she just needed to talk to Jase. As she drove to St. Stephen, she realized she was talking to herself. *It'll be okay. We just have to talk. We just have to talk.*

There had been no communication with him since their argument of the day before. She'd flounced out of the loft to Stella Mare in her angry state and she'd not been in touch since then. But neither had he.

But it would be okay. Jase often travelled for work, and lately, he'd been spending more and more time at the St. Stephen farm that was the gallery space for his next show. His works were large and sometimes he needed more space than they had in their combination living and studio space, so he rented a larger area at the barn. Jase was always focused on work, but the intensity with which he came to the final weeks before a big project was due, in this case five large paintings, was like a separate way of being.

No wonder we had a fight. He's been in this intense space of getting work done, I just finished that third grant proposal for his curation project, and we haven't had any down time for ages. Feeling a little bad, she remembered his hurt and angry eyes, so she stopped at the store on the way home to pick up a bottle of sparkling wine and some macarons. *I need to apologize for yelling. We can figure this out. I know we can.*

She pulled into the warehouse parking lot and glanced up at the lit windows of their loft apartment. Good. He was still up. She gathered her purchases along with her courage and headed up the stairs.

Her key scratched in the lock, but when she pushed the door open, the big open space was very quiet. Candles glowed on the low coffee table and she saw the remains of a meal. He'd never go to bed with candles burning. Where is he? Her heart, already pounding, took on a life of its own.

She dropped her packages on the kitchen counter and headed toward the sleeping loft. "Jase?"

She tried again, working to sound light and breezy.

"I'm so sorry, Jase. Can we please talk? I brought some wine."

A scramble of activity came from the loft. "What? Evie? What are you doing here?" Was he angry?

"Who is it?" A distinctly feminine voice. *For crying out loud. I thought my life was cliché before.*

She heard whispered conversation, and then Jase dropped down the ladder, in jeans but barefoot. Landing lightly as he always did, he pulled a T-shirt on over his head.

"I wasn't expecting you."

"Apparently not. What's going on? Who is that?" Evie cocked her chin toward the loft. A young (very young) blonde woman poked her head over the edge.

"Hi," she said weakly. "I'm, uh, I'm just going to go."

Jase looked up, and then back at Evie. "No, Michelle, you stay. I'll take care of this."

Evie's jaw dropped. "What do you mean, take care of this? This?"

"Evie, you left. What do you expect?"

Thunderstruck, she said, "Yesterday. That was yesterday, Jase. And without discussion."

He glared at her and stomped toward the kitchen area. "You left. That's it. You don't get to call the shots like that. If you're gone, then you're gone."

She followed him. "And you've got somebody else in my bed already? What is this?"

"You left, Evelyn. You left me."

Evie glanced back toward the loft to see long, shapely legs descending. Mesmerized, she stared. Who was that?

The woman's long blonde waves contrasted with her tanned bare back. Evie registered a cobalt sundress before she felt sick and turned away. She glanced up to see her with Jase at the door. His hand rested on her bare shoulder as he spoke quietly into her ear, and then he pulled the barn door open for her. She nodded and left, and he turned back to Evie.

"Now, Evie," he began, but a wave of nausea sent her running to the bathroom. Jase followed, knocking on the door. "Evie, you can't hide in there."

Oh, yes, I can. She vomited neatly into the toilet, and then washed her mouth out and looked in the mirror. Was she really going to make herself sick over this? She imagined her mother standing behind her. What would Mum say?

Evie wiped her mouth with a towel and pushed her dark curls into place. The towel had been a housewarming gift from her sister

Helen when she and Jase moved into the loft, she remembered bitterly. Grabbing it, she held it in front of her as she opened the bathroom door.

"Evie." He gazed at her, no longer sounding angry. Instead it sounded a bit like pity.

"Jase." She enunciated carefully. She couldn't think of a thing to say.

"Will you sit down?" He gestured to the kitchen stool next to where he perched.

She considered the question. "No. I'm good right here." At least her legs were holding her. She looked around the kitchen area, demarcated from the rest of the space by the tile floor, tile she'd laid herself. Sourced from a fellow artist who was messing around in mosaics, in fact. Her eyes followed the pattern of light and dark, light and dark, from her toes to Jase's feet, tucked under the rungs of the stool. Slowly, painfully, she raised her gaze to his face.

"I came back to talk," she said, voice shaking.

He looked away. "Talk about what? We did all the talking yesterday. You said your piece and you left. I'm not in the wrong here."

A rush of anger flared in her chest. "Come on, Jase. There was a woman in my bed with you. You can't claim the higher ground."

"Whatever. Yesterday was just the explosion. This has been a long time coming, Evelyn."

"What do you mean? We've been fine. We got the Peninsula Festival grant, you've got that big show coming up, your website has been catching fire lately. Everything has been good. It's all been for you. Everything."

In the silence, her mind echoed what she'd said. *All for you, Jase. All of it. Everything for you.*

"I'm not happy, Evie," Jase said.

"What?"

"No, I'm not. When you said you were leaving, mostly I felt relief."

Her jaw hung open. Relief? *You little jerk, did you just say you felt relief?* She could not form words, but that was okay. Jase filled in the silence.

"Yeah, it was a little shock at first, but then I realized we've been going our own ways for a while now. Better for you to break us up. It's for the best."

"For me to break us up. Me. And it's for the best. Right." She dripped sarcasm. "So you felt free to go collect some, some girl, and bring her home."

"Melissa," Jase supplied helpfully.

"Melissa," Evie snapped. "Where did you find Melissa, ready to come home with you right after meeting you?"

Jase looked down. "It's not like that. Melissa and I, we, uh, well, I've known her for a while now."

"We? You and Melissa are a 'we'?" Evie's jaw was clamped. "How long is a while?"

"Do we have to do this?" Jase pleaded. "You left. You were done. Remember?"

"Yeah, well I didn't know about Melissa," Evie snarled. "It sounds like you were just waiting."

Jase stood up. "Yeah, I didn't realize it, but I guess I was. I don't know what I was waiting for, but you gave me an opening."

"And you took it."

He looked at her. "Yes, I did. It was going to happen, Evie. You made it happen sooner. Easier."

"Easier for you," she growled. "It's easier to pretend you weren't having some on the side if your girlfriend leaves you first. I wonder what your father will think about that?" Feeling her stomach flip again, she turned toward the kitchen sink.

Jase gave a short laugh. "Dad likes Melissa. She works for him."

A painful cramp sent Evie bending over the sink, as Jase went on. "I can stay with Melissa tonight if you want to stay here, but we need to get this sorted right away. You can get your stuff out next week."

Evie poured a glass of water. "Right, Jase. Like I'm going to get in the bed you and Melissa recently vacated. Get real."

"I know you're mad right now." She hated his placating tone. "You'll see this is for the best. For both of us, Evie."

She took a swallow of her water and contemplated tossing the glass at him. But no, it was a nice glass, one of a pair her friend had brought her from Ireland. No reason to waste a nice glass on a jerk.

"I'm going," she said a bit unsteadily.

"Do you want me to walk you to your car?" Jase clearly wanted her to leave, but probably didn't want to have to escort her to the hospital on the way.

"No, I've got it. You've done enough." Bitterness filled her mouth. She started toward the stairs.

"Uh, Evie. Your keys?" Jase held his hand out. Agonizingly slowly, she pulled her keyring out of her pocket and started to untwist the loft keys from her car keys, feeling the twist in her heart. Then she stopped. "No. This place is full of my stuff. No, I'll keep the keys." She pocketed them and turned toward the stairs, head held high.

"Next week," he called after her. "You'll need to get moved out by next week."

She stomped down every step.

Chapter 3

Evie barely remembered her mostly sleepless night in a noisy cheap motel in St. Stephen. Blessed unconsciousness arrived with the dawn. Fortunately, she woke just before check-out time. She drank coffee in her room and took a hot shower, feeling like an automaton going through the motions. Alive, but not really there.

Time to go home. Back to Dad's house. Not her home, Dad's home. Her heart felt like it was tearing open every other moment. *Jase, how can you do this to me?*

In between, she was angry. *Get a grip. He's not worth this.*

Getting into the car to head back to Stella Mare was painful.

This is not what I was hoping my life would be. She rubbed her eyes, pulled on sunglasses, and headed down the peninsula.

What to do? No place to live, no place to work. She decided right then to stop thinking about that. She couldn't do anything about that today anyway. She could feel awful, just for today. For this one day, all she needed to do was survive. Problems would be solved later. For some reason, that decision made her feel a tiny bit better.

She pulled into the gas station and convenience store, taking a moment to text James that she was on her way back. Emerging twenty minutes later from the store, she put her bag in the backseat. She was almost lighthearted as she drove the rest of the way into the village. It was almost time for the family video chat.

Chad's truck was parked in front of the house. Dorie's boyfriend (fiancé, Evie reminded herself) was a documentary filmmaker, at least part of the time, but he was also the family's techno-geek, so he was on hand to make sure that James's video call with his girls went well. Evie thought of Chad fondly; he was a pretty good guy and had blended into their family well.

Entering the kitchen, Evie called out, "I'm back," and dropped her grocery bag onto the table. Dorie flew into the kitchen, laughing at someone behind her, and gave Evie a quick hug.

"I'm super glad you're here in person," Dorie said. "Video is great, but I love being here with you and Dad and Chad."

"And the dogs," Evie added, patting the huge heads that presented themselves to her. "Hey, Custard. Hi, Mallow."

Dorie was unpacking the brown paper bag. "Ooh, ice cream, chocolate sauce, butterscotch sauce, a can of whipped cream, brownies. Toffee bits for on top. And a jar of cherries! Wow, Evie, looks like a breakup binge getting ready to happen." She looked up as Evie's face crumpled.

"Oh, no!" Dorie said, racing around the table to hold Evie. "Oh, no. I'm sorry. I didn't mean..."

Evie clung to her baby sister and cried. Sniffling on her shoulder, she said, "You didn't know. But you're right." With a catch in her throat, "A breakup binge is exactly what I had in mind."

Still hanging onto Dorie, Evie reached across the kitchen table for a paper napkin. "I'm getting your shirt all snotty, Dore." She mopped up and grabbed an additional handful of napkins.

Dorie looked at her, concerned. "This is real, huh?"

Wiping her face, Evie nodded. "Yeah. Real and for good. I'm pretty sure."

"So, like, what happened? You were just there, right?"

Evie was thrust back into that moment of hearing the scuffling in the loft, the feminine laughter. "I don't want to talk about it, not right now. Please, Dorie?"

Dorie agreed. "Sure, okay, Evie. It's about, well, it's almost two. Time to call in the troops, you know."

Evie nodded, and then turned to put the ice cream in the freezer. Dorie shelved the other items and started the kettle. James called from the living room. "You girls about ready? Chad's getting us set up here."

Evie and Dorie looked at each other. Dorie whispered, "Dad won't believe that a video chat is an easy thing. He's gotta have his tech guru with him." She snickered.

Suddenly, James's voice was closer. "What are you two cooking up in here, hey?" he growled, sticking his head around the corner.

"Evie was making fun," Dorie said.

"What! Not me," Evie protested. "That was your baby girl making fun of her old dad." Evie picked up a tray of tea things and headed through the door, kissing James on the cheek as she swept by.

Dorie grumbled, "Don't believe her, Dad. Do you want tea?"

"Is the Pope Catholic?" James joked.

In the living room, Evie set the tea tray on the coffee table. "Hey, Chad. What are you doing?"

Poking around the television set, Chad glanced behind him. "Hi. James asked me to set up a camera so we could all be seen on this call, and we're going to use the TV so we can see everyone. I think it's going to be okay."

Evie sat on the old couch. "Sounds good, but I'm glad you know what you're doing."

Chad stood up and brushed his hands together. "I hope I do. We'll find out. I got my grandmother ready to check in with us too."

"Really? I haven't seen her since last year," Evie mused.

"She's pretty good, even though she had that stroke last fall. She's more comfortable at home, so I set up a laptop for her. I just hope she can remember how to get onto the call."

Dorie came in, carrying the full teapot. "Oh, there's the tray." She set the pot in its cosy on the coffee table. "Showtime?"

"Almost," Chad said, fussing with his laptop and a remote. Soon enough, the screen on the TV opened into an online conference call. Evie saw her sister Rett in one space, Chad's grandmother Alice in another, and Helen, her sister living in Ottawa, in a third. Dorie, James, Chad, and Evie squished onto the couch so they could all be seen by the others.

"Wow, this is cool," Dorie commented. "Hey, there's Mason!"

Evie peered at the TV. Yes, there was her eight-year-old nephew with his mother, Rett. "Hi, Mason!" She waved at him.

"This is very fun," Rett commented. "The girls are here somewhere, and Harry's going to come say hello too." She looked around.

Helen spoke. "Hi, everyone! It's so good to see you all! Hi, Dad!"

James smiled and sighed. "Video meetings. Not as good as having you girls all sitting around the table, but better than nothing, right?"

"Hey, is that Evie there? Hi, Evie!" Helen said. "What are you doing in Stella Mare?"

Evie shrugged. "Oh, you know. Visiting." She could feel the intent look Dorie turned on her. Hopefully nobody else would notice, and Rett wouldn't say anything about her call either.

"That's good. I wish I were close enough for a visit," Helen said, her face dimming. "I miss all of you so much."

"We miss you too," James said heavily. "When will you come home?"

Helen shook her head. "I can't see it, Dad. I keep hoping, but between work and Jake's hockey, it just isn't in the plans."

"Well, you're gonna have to come home for this," Dorie stated with certainty. "Chad and I have an announcement."

"Ooh, an announcement," Rett said delightedly. "Let me get Harry and the kids. They're going to want to hear this too." She stepped away from the screen.

"I hope I like this announcement," Alice said.

"Alice Simmons!" Helen exclaimed. "How are you? I haven't seen you since, well…"

"Not since your mother died, Helen," Alice said. "When you were last home. Chad, here, he's my boy."

Chad reddened. "Didn't you guys meet at our Christmas call?"

Helen and Alice both shook their heads, but before more could be said, Rett returned with her husband Harry, Mason, and the girls, five-year-old twins Callie and Maggie. Greetings were shared, and finally Rett said, "Okay, we're all here and I'm not sure how long we'll have everyone's attention, so let's get on with it. What's the announcement?"

Mason perked up. "A new puppy? Did you get a new puppy, Dorie?" Dorie was known for rescuing dogs.

She grinned at the camera. "Not this time, Mason. Get your mom to bring you out to the sanctuary, though. I have lots of work for you to do. And you'll be the first to know if we get any puppies."

Dorie turned to Chad. "Do you want to say this?"

Evie shrank into her seat on the couch. How can this be happening? *How can my sister, my baby sister, be getting engaged right now? Right now, right when Jase...* She recalled the sight of those long legs coming down the loft ladder and choked. With effort, she focused on Chad as he struggled to find words.

"Well, you know, Dorie and I have been working out at Nan's farm on the dog sanctuary and she's been staying there, too, since last winter. We've been trying to do this with almost no money."

Chad was red-faced and stumbling over his words. Dorie elbowed him. "Just get to the point."

He looked at her. "It's not just a single point. There's a progression. There's a story in there."

He turned back to the camera. "Practically miraculously, we've got a funding source for the sanctuary, and we both have actual gainful employment, and because of that, we're able to make plans for the future." He reached over and picked up Dorie's hand. "For our future. Dorie and I are engaged to be married."

There was a burst of congratulations and applause, and Chad looked relieved as the response was clear. "Hooray for you two!" came from Rett's house, where Harry was clapping and shouting.

"So that's what I'll have to come home for," Helen said with a smile. "A wedding!"

James reached behind the sofa for a bottle of champagne. "We toast a lot with tea here, but today maybe we can have some bubbly." He handed the bottle to Chad, who popped the cork but looked so surprised that Evie grinned in spite of herself.

"Oh, I should have come into town," Alice said. "You didn't tell me there'd be bubbly, Chaddie!"

"We'll bring you some when we come home, Alice," Dorie promised.

Conversation became general then; Helen noted that Jake was at a hockey tournament with his dad for the weekend, and Rett and Harry's kids all disappeared to do whatever kids did when adults were talking. Evie nodded her head a bit, due to champagne and lack of sleep, but she came to full alert when she heard her name. "What? What did you say?"

"I just wondered when we'd be hearing about your engagement," Helen said. "You and Jase have been together forever. I figured it would be soon, since you were thirty-four on your last birthday, right?"

"Not thirty-four. Thirty-five, Helen." Evie felt immense pressure in her chest. "I'm thirty-five. And Jase and I are done." *Oh, I didn't want to do this.* She felt crappy and just wanted it all to be over. She could feel Dorie looking at her again.

Rett was incredulous, despite already having heard a bit when Evie had called. "Done? Just like that? After ten years and building that business and workspace?"

"Yeah," Evie said bitterly. "Twelve years. Apparently he's developed a thing for blondes." Even as she said it, she knew that wasn't fair, this wasn't the whole story, but it didn't matter. She wanted them to hate Jase. She wanted to hate Jase and hating on Michelle was good way to start.

Dorie reached over to pat Evie's knee. James was looking at her face.

"What? What, you guys? I'm okay. You don't have to act like I'm sick or something."

Rett was quick to respond. "All right, Evie. It's a surprise to us, but I bet it was a surprise to you too. I'm so sorry."

"Yeah, me too. I, uh, really don't want to talk about it, you know. Besides, this day belongs to Dorie and Chad." She looked at Dorie and forced a smile. Dorie just looked concerned.

Helen said, "If you need a lawyer..."

"I don't."

James spoke over them. "Let's let Evie be for a while. She's a smart girl. She'll figure this out."

There was general agreement that she probably would, despite what Evie thought privately.

"Maybe it's time to say goodbye," James suggested.

"Wait!" Rett exclaimed. "Dorie, Chad, when's the wedding? And do you need baby bridesmaids? Maggie and Callie would be thrilled."

Dorie laughed and shrugged. "We have no idea about that yet, but we'll be sure to let you know."

Helen said, "Don't forget the Ottawa family. We'll need to know too."

"Sure, sure. We'll keep you all up to date."

Later, after Dorie and Chad took the remains of the champagne back home and James was putting together sandwiches and tea for supper, Evie's phone rang. Rett. She took the call in her bedroom.

"Hey."

Her sister's voice was tight. "Listen, Evie, how's Dad?"

"You just saw him on the video. He's fine. Dad's always fine. Well, mostly."

"Huh. Well, listen to this. It's kind of bad. I ran into Linda Goodwin, remember her? She was a friend of mine from nursing school. I think you met her at our wedding. Anyway, she works for Dr. Swami, you know, the cardiologist."

Evie's stomach lurched again. "Dad has a cardiologist?"

"Well, I didn't know that until Linda opened her mouth to say how sorry she is about Dad's condition and asked how he's doing."

"Condition? What condition?"

"Right. She assumed I knew, and I had to pretend I did because otherwise she'd be breaking confidentiality, and so there's something going on and we have to find out what it is."

"Didn't she break confidentiality anyway?"

"Yeah, but she thought I knew. I know that's not an excuse, but I didn't want to make things a whole lot worse. Can you do some sleuthing? Find out? Otherwise I'm going to have to come down there and squeeze it out of him."

It was late in the evening, but Evie couldn't fall asleep despite her fatigue. She couldn't stop worrying. Either she was fretting about her own situation, or she found herself imagining James in a hospital bed. Or worse.

Finally she tiptoed down the stairs. One of the big dogs lifted a head and moaned a sleepy greeting. "Shh," Evie warned. "Go back to sleep." The big head went back to the floor and Evie headed for the kitchen. Turning on a small lamp, she pulled out a bowl, spoon, and ice cream scoop.

Breakup binging. She'd heard about it on TV but never had an opportunity before. Imagine that. Thirty-five years old and never had a breakup before. *No wonder I don't know how to behave.*

She dipped her spoon into the caramel and chocolate sauce. *I don't think I even like this combination.* She spooned some into her mouth. Ugh, so sweet. She ate another bite. She thought maybe it could grow on her. Like Jase. What had happened?

She pushed aside some whipped cream to find more chocolate sauce. *How could he have brought that girl into our home like that?* She shovelled another spoonful of sweetness into her mouth. He obviously meant it when he said he's been done for a while. *Maybe it didn't seem sudden to him. But it did to me. It still does.*

She absently wiped at the ice cream dripping down her chin. *I thought I was going to marry you and have babies with you, Jase.* What had he been thinking?

But she knew the answer right away. With a sudden chill, she could almost hear his voice saying the words: I want to be successful. I want every gallery in this country to want me, my work. I want to be sought after as a teacher, as an artist, as a leader in the arts world. I want, I want, I want...

Yeah, I know what you want, Jase. All that, plus somebody to do your laundry, maintain your webpage, and write your grant proposals. And great sex.

The thought of the grant proposals warmed her a bit. Right. They might have broken up, but they still had the Peninsula Festival to put together. *When we're working on that, he'll see. He can't do without me, not really.*

She pushed the bowl away from her. The Peninsula Festival. The big project was slated for late September. The funding had been confirmed late, but she'd been busy soliciting artists and venues already. She'd written the grant, but it was assumed that they'd do the work together, like they did most things. Right. She'd have to talk to him about that. Maybe everything wasn't as bad as she thought. At least she would have some income this summer and a big project that he couldn't possibly do without her. There was a bona fide reason to be together. *He'll see what a mistake he's made.*

She suddenly realized the open carton of ice cream was melting on the counter. The spoons, the scoop, and her bowl were covered with oozing sticky stuff. She whisked the ice cream back into the freezer, and then washed the dishes and put them away. Checking again, she wiped the counter and kitchen table clean. *I tidy up. That's what I do.* Tidy up, organize, clean. And run the festival with Jase. Then she went back to bed.

"You got mail," Leonard announced, dropping a thick envelope on Stephen's desk in the cramped office behind the gallery. "Looks important."

Stephen looked at the return address. "Thanks," he said shortly and returned to his laptop.

"That's it?" Leonard inquired. "You're not going to satisfy my curiosity?"

"You're incorrigible," Stephen scowled. "Since when is my personal mail of interest to you?"

Leonard threw himself into his chair. Hands behind his head, he leaned back with a smile. "Oh, pushed a button, did I? What is it, foreclosure? Divorce? Something else juicy?"

Stephen glared. "I'm glad you find my life so amusing. I wouldn't have come here if I'd realized you had so little to occupy your mind."

Leonard laughed. "It is a little dull here in Stella Mare at times, but I'm just teasing. I wish I had interesting mail." He got up and headed for the sink at the back of the room. "Coffee?"

"Always, and thanks," Stephen said absently. He turned the envelope over in his fingers. "It's from my father's lawyers. I'm finally making some progress on my project here, and I don't want to get all caught up in drama from home. Maybe I'll just leave it."

"Leave it?" Leonard sounded outraged. He put a mug of coffee on Stephen's desk and returned to his own. "I'll open it for you."

"No."

"Come on. It'll be interesting."

"Don't you have something to do?"

"My life is full of ease and leisure, now that I have you and Cassie helping in the gallery. I just need to talk to artists and collectors and keep the bank from breathing down my neck while trying to get this business going."

"Yes, I know that part isn't easy," Stephen said, relenting somewhat. "I do appreciate a chance to live right here in town too."

"Ideal location to get the data you're looking for, I think," Leonard said. "So you could at least satisfy my curiosity."

"Knock it off. I already work to pay for my apartment upstairs. Don't be an asshole."

Leonard preened. "It's one of my best things."

They were snorting with laughter when the front doorbell jangled. "Oh, that's me," Stephen said. "Do I look presentable?" He stood and brushed off imaginary lint.

"You're fine. Go sell some art, will you?"

Stephen dropped the envelope into a desk drawer and headed into the gallery space.

"Good morning," he said to the tweedy couple who were looking at the large painting on the far wall.

"Oh, listen to you. Where y'all from, honey?" Her voice was musical and warm.

"Not from here," he said, smiling. "You're not either."

The gentleman leaned on a walking stick. "We like to pretend, but everyone can tell. Just like with you, is that right?"

"With the first word," Stephen admitted. "But I'm trying to learn to speak Maritime. How do you like the Brentwick?" he asked, gesturing to the large piece.

"It's a very nice work," the woman said, turning back to the painting. "Is it an early piece?"

"I'm not sure," Stephen said. "Let me get the catalogue and we can look." The three of them huddled over the document, chatting.

Half an hour later, they were leaving the gallery with a catalogue and a list of upcoming exhibitions. "Now, Stephen, will you be here next Monday? Our daughter is coming from Savannah and I want her to meet you. We can talk more about the Brentwick then."

"I'm here almost every day," he said. "Don't be a stranger."

"We won't. You take care now, hear?" The bell jangled their departure.

"That's why I like having you here," Leonard announced, coming out of the office. "You got more information out of those people than I ever would. They loved you."

"They're lovely people, up from Georgia every summer. He's a retired surgeon and she taught school, but they're art lovers from way back."

"Yeah?"

Stephen nodded. "Yes. They're well past the lighthouse-and-dory kind of work, much more interested in contemporary expressions."

"Hmm."

"They invited me for drinks."

"You are very good at this," Leonard marvelled. "No wonder those fishermen will give you stories and carvings."

Stephen squinted. "I think the stories they give me are largely made up, but thanks. Will you be here next Monday? You probably want to meet this family."

Leonard nodded. "I'll make a point of it. Are you going to drinks?"

Stephen shrugged. "Maybe. It's not like I have a flourishing social life in Stella Mare. But I'm also trying to get a lot of work done."

Leonard looked pensive for a moment. "Thank you, friend, for bringing all that conversational skill here. I know you told me you can't sell anything, and that's fine, but you connect with people in a way that just isn't natural to me."

Stephen shrugged. "I'm glad to help and I appreciate you housing me. But are you on shift now? I've got an interview to code." *And a thick envelope to open.*

Leonard waved him off. "You're no longer on the clock, friend. Besides, Cassie will be here soon."

"Great. See you later."

Once alone in his apartment, he pulled the thick wad of papers from the envelope, a flicker of dread forming in his belly. A packet from his father's lawyer; not always a good thing. He perused the top sheet, full of legalese. *Just get to the point.*

There it was, the point. His father's sister, Margaret, had died, leaving him "a small bequest." Aunt Margaret.

Why would she leave him anything? He barely remembered her, only as a faint, but kind, presence at the occasional Christmas he spent with his father's family of origin. Older than his father, he recalled, but that was about it. And why was this the first time he was hearing about a death in the family?

The postmark date indicated the letter had crept through the postal systems of the US and Canada. It had been mailed more than a month ago.

Impatience made him hasty. As he refolded the papers and shoved them back into the envelope, it tore, leaving an open flap with the lawyer's letterhead showing through.

Not now. He tossed the whole thing onto the table, and then headed to his bedroom, stripping off his shirt. When he came back, he wore shorts and running shoes. *Nothing in that letter that can't wait until I'm in a frame of mind to read it.*

Dark glasses, hat, and a last gulp of water, and Stephen headed down and out into the day.

Chapter 4

On Monday, Evie got a text from Jase. *Check email.* She was torn between looking and not looking; part of her couldn't wait to see what he'd sent. Another part just wanted to hide in her bed. Her sister Dorie's childhood bed, that is, the one she was currently sleeping in.

She retreated to the bedroom to read the note.

He had listed several pieces he thought were hers, including something he called "your old chest of drawers" and "a box of old dishes." Her mind went to the richly polished dresser, made by hand in 1910 by a local cabinetmaker, restored by her with months of effort. The china had been deliberately and thoughtfully selected, piece by piece, from yard and estate sales, thrift stores and the local Buy-Nothing group. Friends appreciated the table she set, and she loved having a crowd to feed from her thrifted china and yard sale furniture.

Friends might appreciate it, but Jase apparently did not. The bile rose in her throat, threatening to overtake her. She looked away from her phone and tried to take deep breaths.

"Evie!" James called from downstairs. "Evelyn, you here?"

She gulped and stood up. Leaning out the doorway, she called to him. "Yes, up here. You need me? I'm coming down."

She stumbled down the stairs. "What?"

"What's the matter? You okay?" James said when he saw her.

She pushed her hands through her tangled curls. "Yes. No. I will be. I'm going for a walk, okay?" She rushed out the door before his kindness undid her completely. Practically running for the first few blocks, finally she slowed her pace. Step after step, soothing and calming. She could almost put Jase out of her mind.

Taking a walk through the village of Stella Mare was like stepping into a time machine. So much was just the way it had been when she was growing up. The high school up on the hill, the massive fancy hotel, the old houses, the little shops in the village. *Has nothing changed?*

Well, yes, there were changes. There was the building where Dorie had her dog spa last year. That building was being renovated, but for what? Evie peered curiously into the big glass windows. Just a bunch of lumber and buckets; not much information there. It was too bad about The Pampered Pooch, but the demise of the shop had led Dorie to her new situation. Running a dog sanctuary and engaged.

Yeah, engaged. My baby sister is engaged and here I am, so much older and nothing to show for it. Really nothing. She continued walking down the main street.

Jase had plenty to show. He had his paintings in galleries in the States and a great website where people can find him. He even had some name recognition. The flicker of pride in his career was extinguished immediately by the memory of his face and his words "this isn't working for me."

Her steps quickened. What on earth did he mean by that? Everything was for him. Evie thought of the hours she spent on his website, the careful way she made him check out his contracts for work, and the weeks she spent preparing grant proposals. The proposal for the Peninsula Festival, the big career-catapulting project that probably will create ongoing work for years. *Well, at least I've still got that going on. No money coming in at the moment, but my joint curator salary will be available starting next month.*

She let out a huge sigh. With an effort, she turned her attention back to the village. Enough time spent thinking about Jase. Instead, she tried to look at Stella Mare as if she was seeing it for the first time.

The familiarity of the Sunshine Diner immediately derailed that process. Memories rose up as she pulled on the heavy oak door and the fragrance of coffee and some lovely baked good greeted her. A rumble from her insides hastened her steps.

The young woman at the counter smiled. "Welcome. What can I get you?"

Evie looked at the menu board over the open window to the kitchen. "It smells so good in here." Squinting at the server's name tag, she asked, "What's freshly baked, Cassandra?"

Cassandra looked back toward the kitchen. "Sonny made muffins this morning, but I always recommend my uncle's cinnamon buns." She gestured toward the glass case.

"Mmm." Evie looked at the pastries laid out on white linen cloths. "Nice presentation," she commented. "But I'll have a muffin, please, and a large latte. To go." She handed over her debit card.

"Sure. It'll just be a minute." While Cassandra was busy with the espresso machine, Evie looked around. Oh, the Sunshine. Where she and her few girlfriends learned to love coffee long before her mother, Agnes, would let her drink it at home.

Cassandra inspected her card while the milk steamed. "Um, are you Evie?"

"Yeah," Evie admitted. "Do we know each other?"

"No, not really. I know Dorie from school and here." She wrapped the muffin in a paper napkin and put it in a bag. "You're the artist, right?"

Evie shrunk back from that. Am I? "Yeah, I guess so," she mumbled. Cassandra went on, undeterred.

"You were kind of one of my heroes growing up. Well, she-roe, actually," Cassandra confided. "I always looked at that mural you painted at the high school and wondered if I had it in me to paint like that."

Now Evie was curious. "Really? Is that thing still there?" She had painted a wall as part of a project in grade 12.

"I think so. I've been out of high school for a while, but my mother still works there. She probably would have told me if someone replaced it."

Curiosity piqued, she asked, "Do I know your mother?"

Cassandra laughed as she handed Evie her coffee. "Probably. Pat McRae, the guidance counsellor. Everyone knows my mother."

"Right, Ms. McRae. Are you an artist, Cassandra?" Evie sipped at her latte. Oh, that was good.

"I'm Sonny's right arm here at the Sunshine," Cassandra said wryly. "But I work at the new gallery too. Fishburne Gallery. Have you been in yet?"

Shaking her head, Evie sipped again.

"It's worth a visit. Leonard is making a point of Maritime artists, and he's wildly creative about what constitutes art. I'm learning tons."

"Hmm. Thanks for the suggestion," Evie said noncommittally. "Thanks for the coffee, too. I'll probably be back."

Cassandra laughed. "Everyone ends up back here sometime. It was nice to see you. Are you visiting?"

"Um, yeah, visiting. Nice to see you too," Evie said, raising her cup in a little salute as she headed out the door.

New gallery. Another time that might have been exciting. Right now, she couldn't care less. With coffee and muffin in hand, she looked for a place to sit undisturbed.

The closer she went to the center of the village, the less likely she'd be recognized, as the place was a magnet for tourists this time of year. The long, long days of June meant people could be kayaking on the Bay of Fundy, hiking the hills on the shore, picnicking on the beach, or browsing the shops. It also meant that a lot of locals avoided the downtown area during the busy times. Just what she wanted, Evie thought with satisfaction, a place to sit and think without anyone bothering her. *I can pretend I'm a tourist.*

She parked herself on a bench near the town pier and opened the muffin bag. Cassandra had tucked a second pastry in the bag: a pair of mini cinnamon buns, wrapped in a napkin with a scribbled message. Evie looked closely.

"Thanks for being my inspiration. These are my treat. Cass."

Unaccountably, Evie's eyes filled. Inspiration indeed. Inspiration to be a server at the local diner? *Guess that's the kind of inspiration I've been.* She dashed the tears away. *Why can't I just appreciate the sentiment?*

She sank her teeth into one little bun. At least she could appreciate good pastry.

Inspiration. She finished her breakfast and sipped at her coffee, looking around the village that had been her home for so many years. So many bad years.

Was it really that bad? This girl, Cassandra, she thought I was inspirational. Well, she was inspired by my mural. She didn't know me at all. She's much younger than I am.

Suddenly Evie felt fifteen again, all rounded hips and shoulders, dark curly hair that would not go straight like her sisters, no matter how much she flat-ironed it. She remembered the girls in her class, tall, long, straight blonde streaks, lean and willowy in their skinny jeans. Her mother fussed at her for dieting, but Evie had been sure if she only could fit into those kinds of jeans, she could be one of the girls. But it wasn't true. No matter how she tried to fit in, she never quite made it.

Her mouth grew dry. *I didn't even make it at home.* Helen and Rett both had that long, straight hair and blue eyes. They used to tease her that she was adopted when she was little. She recalled playing in the living room at home, and her older sisters pretending she wasn't there.

"Oh, that Evie. She was adopted, you know," Helen would say to Rett, and the two of them would giggle and run up to the room they shared. Evie, passionate, screamed at them. "No I'm not! I'm not adopted!" Running up the stairs, she pounded on their bedroom door, but they only laughed evilly and kept her locked out.

"I'm telling!" she shouted at the closed door and stomped down the stairs to the kitchen, where their mother was simultaneously making dinner, braiding Dorie's hair, and singing "Farewell to Nova Scotia" with Dorie trying to sing along.

"Mum! Mum!"

"What is it, Evie?" she asked, hands in Dorie's hair. "Calm down. It can't be that bad."

Tears poured out. "Yes, it can! They said I'm adopted. Am I adopted?"

Agnes laughed and Dorie stuck her tongue out at Evie. Evie glared back.

"Mum!"

"Of course you're not adopted. Believe me, I was there when you were born."

Dorie mouthed "adopted" at Evie. Little brat. She probably didn't even know what it meant.

"But Mum," Evie protested.

"Evelyn, you are not adopted. I know it, you know it, and they know it. If you let them bother you, they'll keep on bothering you. You're just going to have to grow a thicker skin."

Oh, yes, that. Thicker skin. Evie sat on the bench, wondering if she'd ever been able to grow that skin her mother spoke of. Probably not.

Oh, the misery that was high school started in grade 9. Helen graduated the year before at the top of her class. Rett in Grade 11 took advanced science classes. When people at school met Evie, they said, "Oh, you're a Madison? You don't look like one."

They were right, she didn't look like her sisters. And she wasn't like her sisters, not smart and science-y.

Already identified as different, she had layered it on, wearing dark, heavy clothes, piling on heavy eyeliner and mascara. She played with piercings and got deeply absorbed in post-apocalyptic science fiction. Whenever she could get out of class, she was behind the stage in the gymnasium, where drama and art converged. She painted sets for drama productions (Oh, yes, now Ms. MacRae came into clear focus, faculty advisor to the drama club), fooled around with oil paints, drew with charcoal, pastels, and pencils, and learned that what she could see in her mind and feel in her heart could find expression in her art.

She remembered one night right before a production. A couple of other kids took her direction in painting flats she had designed. When the project was nearly complete, they pulled the flats into place while Evie watched from the audience. What a feeling to see your own design taking shape, adding depth and context to the story of the play. She remembered feeling so professional as she and Vince, the lighting guy, collaborated on making things just right. Finally satisfied with the look, the director shut things down for the night. The next night was the dress rehearsal, but Evie's work was essentially over.

The director had called to Evie as they were leaving the gym. "Nice work. You've really got that valley vibe going," she said. "Thanks for all you've done. Why don't you come in tomorrow night when we let the cast see the set for the first time?"

Evie remembered her tentative steps into the gym-turned-theatre that next night, waiting for the curtain to rise and the cast to see the completed set for the first time. Her stomach trembling, she walked through backstage, checking on all the details, and finally sat out in front beside the director, at a distance from the cluster of chattering girls and show-off boys all in costume and getting on their final makeup. The director gave a cue for the curtain to rise before the run-through, so everyone could see the set from the audience's perspective. As the curtain lifted, Evie grew more and more anxious, until she felt like her stomach was in her throat. Then, with the final reveal, her stomach settled. She went into assessment mode. How did it look? Was everything in place? What needed to be different?

She suddenly relaxed. There it was, her design, spread out over the stage. There was nothing to change. The director looked her way and winked. "Pretty nice, huh?" she said. Evie could only nod. Yes, they had done a good job. Now if only the play was up to the standards of the set!

Painting sets, painting murals, drawing landscapes, flowers, people's pets...these activities gave Evie her teenage identity. Her dark clothing hid paint stains. Her life wasn't in the classroom, but in the studio and theatre. It wasn't easy to try to carve out her own place in Stella Mare with two big personalities who came before. Evie was decidedly different from the other Madison girls. She remembered Ms. MacRae, in her guidance counsellor role, saying something like that. They had a meeting to discuss Evie's options after high school.

"Every girl your age has to figure out who she is, who she wants to be." Pat's steel-grey hair was a feature even fifteen years ago, Evie remembered. "When you've got sisters who came before, you can define yourself in their image, or you can define yourself as anyone but them."

Evie looked at her, hopeful. Ms. MacRae smiled. "It's not easy coming after sisters like yours. But I think you'll find the real challenge comes when you leave. When you don't have your sisters' reputation to push against, who will you be? Who are you when you don't have to prove who you are not?"

She remembered herself shrugging. Those words hadn't made much sense to her then, but by the following fall, when she was in Sackville trying to navigate university, they came back to her, and again, now. *Who am I? Who am I now?*

Whenever I'm in this village I return to my old feeling like I don't really belong. But now she felt like she didn't really belong anywhere. Certainly not with Jase.

At least I have the festival to look forward to. She had worked her tail off on that proposal. She flashed on the networking meetings, the late nights poring over documents and writing and rewriting drafts, the exhaustion and excitement of finally submitting the proposal. And the elation of being chosen. Getting funding to launch this huge project, and all of the artists and sites she'd been in touch with, those were big experiences. Jase would come to his senses. *I know he will. When we're working together on this project, he'll see that we are meant to be together.*

She was sure they had both been happy when the funding announcement was made. *What happened to us?* Abruptly her anticipation turned to pain. Hot tears threatened to overflow. She gathered her trash and got up from the bench. *Okay, none of that. This is just a little walk downtown. Get a grip, Evelyn.* She wiped her eyes with the extra napkin and got up to walk again.

Chapter 5

Despite her desire to run home and hide out at her father's house, Evie made herself continue her walk through the village. There was the new gallery Cassandra spoke about. On the water side of the main street in one of the larger storefronts, the old building looked like it has been renovated outside as well as inside.

She looked up to the second and third stories, remembering her father's tales of old Stella Mare. Maybe this building was once a department store, she decided, and wondered if she was right. It had that kind of ornate look but didn't have the ponderous architecture that seemed to be what people once liked in their banks or village office buildings. Who knew for sure?

She gave up speculating and pushed on the front door. She heard a jangle and looked up to see an old-fashioned bell attached to the top of the door. She closed the door firmly behind her and the bell jangled again.

She gazed appreciatively around the welcoming space. Open, clean, well-lit walls. The old wooden floors gleamed. The far wall held a large canvas of an unsurprising seascape. Evie walked slowly about and turned a corner.

"Oh!" The exclamation escaped her lips as her eyes were dazzled by the display of contemporary art. Brilliant colours and abstract designs, dimensional work, and a video installation of someone's performance piece. Well, Stella Mare had leaped into the current century. This was amazing. She stood in the middle of the back room and turned around, taking everything in.

A cough disturbed her reverie, and she startled. "Hello?"

There was the sound of a chair being pushed back against a wooden floor, and a man came through the door at the back. He rubbed his hand over his closely shorn curls and turned sleepy eyes to Evie. "Hey. Welcome. Is this your first visit to Fishburne Gallery?"

"Hi. Yes, it's new to me. I'm amazed, to be honest."

The man looked around the room. "Yes, I think Leonard's outdone himself here. He's willing to take some risks in the off season." He grinned crookedly at her, eyes brightening.

"The off season before the tourist explosion, you mean?" She smiled at him.

"Right now, visitors don't necessarily have expectations. I understand that's different in the summer."

"When everything has to be boats, gulls, and water?"

"Well, to put it bluntly, yes. That's what I've heard is most likely to sell, but it's early yet, and so, we've got much more interesting stuff going on." He extended a hand. "I'm Stephen Culpeper, by the way. Visiting."

Evie's smile deepened. "Evie Madison. I'm visiting too, but I'm originally from here." His hand was warm, just like his smile.

"Evie. Cassie mentioned that you were in town. I'm so happy to meet you. Sounds like you appreciate contemporary art." He looked at her speculatively.

She laughed. "Yes, I guess I do. My, uh, my partner and I have—had—a studio in St. Stephen." She could have kicked herself. Had a studio? Have one? What was her status? "We, uh, we're curating the Peninsula Festival in the fall."

"Is that so? You have diverse professional interests here then." His smile was warm and his accent unfamiliar.

"You're from away," she noted.

"I wonder what gave it away?" His smile deepened. "Can you tell where I'm from?"

"Maybe," she said, trying to place his accent. "Southern US, for sure."

He laughed. "That's right. No such thing as a southern accent, just like there's no Canadian accent. We're both from big areas, with lots of dialects and accents. I'm from North Carolina, currently, but I'm Virginia born and bred. Trying to learn to talk like a Maritimer."

Curious. She was so curious, she forgot herself for a moment. "Why are you here? Of all the tiny little places in the possible world?"

"Oh, Stella Mare is as big a place as anywhere." He gave her an appraising look. "Did you say you grew up here?"

She nodded.

"That explains it. I'm a newcomer, so everything I see or hear, every person I meet, everything means something that I don't understand yet. Y'all are used to the pattern of things, being from here, so it seems tiny." He turned to look out a window at the back of the building. "It's all new and exciting to me." He grinned infectiously. "Have I convinced you?"

Evie shook her head and chuckled. "Stella Mare is new and exciting? Nope. I don't think I'd choose it if I had other options."

He looked like he might ask her about options, so she hurried to turn the conversation back toward him. "What are you doing here?"

"I'm here for a year, actually. On leave from my university to work on my research project. For the moment, Leonard's given me a workspace and a place to live in return for a few hours of work watching the gallery. Can I get you some tea?"

"No, thank you. I just had coffee." Evie felt a sudden need to bolt. She could be all tear-stained for all she knew. Was he looking at her closely? Would he see that her entire world had just crumbled?

"Oh, please stay," he asked clearly. "I'm just going to take a break myself and could use some company. Things are pretty quiet here, as you can see." He gestured around the gallery. "Okay?" He turned to walk back through the door he'd arrived from. "Come on back here. It's messy, but it's home." He chuckled. "Really not home, but the messy part is true."

Evie sighed. Well, what else did she have to do? Why not have a cup of tea? She didn't have to actually drink it. She followed him back into an untidy office space, where he was filling an electric kettle at a small sink.

"I'm learning about what you Maritimers call tea. Have a seat," Stephen said over his shoulder. "Well, if you can find one," he added with a grin. She moved a pile of papers from a chair to the desk and sat down.

"What about tea?"

He smiled. "Tea doesn't mean a hot cuppa where I'm from," he said. "It's served in a glass, with ice, and the big question is whether you have sweet tea or unsweet tea."

Evie laughed out loud. "Unsweet? Really?"

Stephen leaned against the sink, crossing his arms. She noted his hands and strong-looking forearms, sleeves rolled up. Maybe he worked in stone or other heavy materials. He looked comfortable with himself, she thought suddenly.

He continued to look at her, smiling, and she shifted in her seat and looked away. "What kind of research are you doing in this little village?"

"Oh," he said with satisfaction. "Folk art and folk stories. I study wood carvings and the people who make them. I've been collecting data across settings, but this year I'm looking at fishermen's work. I've been collecting stories and pictures of the work of some of the locals and their ancestors."

"Really? I bet some of those old fish houses are full of stuff."

"Yes, and the fishermen are full of something too." He grinned, eyebrows raised. "It's been quite an experience, trying to sort out what they're telling me that's real, and what is made up to fool the strange guy from away." He gave her a rueful grin.

"They're giving you a hard time, huh?" Evie reflected.

He shook his head. "Nah, I shouldn't complain. It's amusing at times. I've been in harder locations. Anyway, turning up stuff and stories has been a little bit of a challenge, but I've only just started. I've been getting more traction now that I'm starting to be a familiar face. What about you? You said you're visiting?"

Evie was suddenly reminded of what she was doing back in Stella Mare. Visiting, yes. Or was she? "My dad lives here, and a sister," she explained. How much of this should she talk about?

Stephen brought two mugs of tea to the table and sat across from her. Suddenly tongue-tied, she stared into the steaming cup. He didn't seem to notice her discomfort, or maybe he just had good manners. "I'm staying upstairs, actually," he said, pointing to the ceiling. "Leonard's a good friend. We met in art school."

Evie looked up. "Oh?" Maybe he would keep talking and she could avoid it.

"Yes. Back in those undergrad days, you know, where you spend all night in the studio trying to find your muse, and then drink coffee to get through classes, then wine to loosen up, and sleep is a distant memory. Did you have those days?" He looked over his mug at her.

Smiling, she nodded. Yes, she and Jase had been like that. Crazy for work in the studio, working harder and longer than needed, getting critique, and working to improve. Barely taking time to sleep during crunch time. Living on coffee, stir-fry, and ramen. And dope, she thought ruefully. That too.

"Funny how hard it was at the time, but now it feels like the good old days," she said.

"Yeah, hard, but you forge relationships. Some of them stick. Like Leonard. We've gone in completely different directions than either of us planned. Neither of us is making art for a living, you know?"

Evie nodded, watching her tea steam. Stephen and Leonard, art school grads, neither of them making art. *Well, me too. Guess I'm not alone in that.* She sighed.

"Do you miss it? Making art, I mean?" She looked up to meet his kind eyes. She watched them widen and glance away as he thought. Then he turned back toward her, his gaze now deeper and somehow softer.

"I don't miss the competitiveness, the pressure, the desperation of feeling like a fraud all the time. Wondering every month if I could make my rent. It took a long time for me to realize that what I loved about the artist's life was being able to throw myself into a project and work on it, letting everything else just go, and work until my mind was so thoroughly full of this project that it was just overflowing with new ideas and completely different conceptualizations, and my body was full of a kind of energy that just had to come out."

"Wow. That's quite a description."

"I have thought about this quite a lot. Creation doesn't always look like making art. I even wrote a paper about it some years ago. The end of the story is that I have found a place where I get to throw myself into my work, whatever the creative project is, just fling my whole self in, and it is very creative work, even though I am not painting or sculpting or doing performance art."

"Didn't you say you're working at a university? Can you work like that there?"

He laughed. "Ah, you're questioning, and rightly so. Yes, I work at the university, but I teach a limited amount and work on these projects for most of my time. During the semester, I'm busy with students and classes but a lot of the time I get to dive into whatever project is next. It works out."

He drank from his mug, and then held it out for Evie to see. "This is a great example. This mug."

"Yeah? It looks like one of Sharon Elsemere's mugs."

He lifted it up to look at the bottom. "SE, it says."

"Sharon's been making pottery here on the peninsula since forever," Evie said. "Or at least since I was a little girl. My mother had a lot of her stuff. Mum loved handmade things. And she knew Sharon."

"See what I mean? This mug holds so much meaning for you because you are embedded in the tapestry of Stella Mare."

"Embedded in the tapestry?" Evie snickered. "Did you just say that?"

Stephen's eyes danced. "Without irony, if you noticed. Think about it. To me, this is a pretty mug. To you, it is a reminder of things your mother liked, a reminder of the artist who made it, and maybe even a reminder of your own childhood. Yet you are so close to it, none of that story feels like a big deal."

"You're right, it feels just like...normal."

He leaned toward her. "You're part of the pattern so you can't see the weave. I'm out here, waving from North Carolina"—he waved his hand—"and I am just starting to find the threads that make up the community."

Evie tried to understand. "I guess it makes sense that you don't know all the details, but why is this town any different from any other? From your town?"

He laughed. "You know the answer to that. My town looks tiny and insignificant to me, just like Stella Mare does to you. I'm of it, so I can't see it."

She nodded. "Yeah, I get it. You picked here because of wood carving though."

"That's the source for the project, but I picked Stella Mare because Leonard had a place for me to live and work. Being here I could spend some time with an old friend."

"Leonard."

He nodded.

"You coming to this village was a little random then."

"No, not random at all. Not in the statistical sense of random. In a way, every step I've taken in my life has led me to being right here at this moment."

Evie looked around the little workroom. "Right here, you mean?" She tried not to laugh.

"Do you think I'm being dramatic?" he asked, eyebrows raised and a smile quirking his mouth. "I'm not willing to get lost in thinking that my life has no meaning. It either does or it doesn't, but I'm going to assume that every little thing matters, and that me being here right now is a culmination of a million little choices." He picked up their empty mugs to take to the sink. Over his shoulder, he added, "And for you too."

This was getting weird. She could start to see him as a college prof, going on and on about abstract things.

"I'll think about that," Evie said politely as she stood. "I'm going to go now, so thanks for the tea."

Stephen walked with her into the gallery. "Don't let my ramblings disturb you," he said with that warm smile. "I'm really not a wacko. Well, not a total wacko." He met her smile. "Y'all come back. Come by when Leonard's here. He'd love to meet another local artist."

I'm no artist. But this wasn't the time to discuss the finer points. "Okay. And thank you."

She headed out the door, but when she glanced behind her, Stephen was leaning out into the June sunshine and watching her walk away. He gave a little wave, and she returned it, then headed back toward her father's house. What an unusual conversation. What an interesting gallery. What did he mean about every single small choice leading you to where you are right now? Evie wasn't so sure she bought that storyline. *Jase's choices have brought me back to Stella Mare. Not mine.* She stomped off toward home, once again holding off tears.

Chapter 6

Stephen leaned on the frame of the gallery door as he watched Evie bolting down the street. A little mysterious, she was. He sighed and then headed to the office and his laptop.

Email notifications floated by. Sabbatical should have meant he didn't have to work on anything but his research project. But that's not how this one was working out.

He skimmed the dozen emails from the university, fielded two from journal editors (one outright rejection, the other a revise-and-resubmit that he put into a file marked "for later"), and one from the colleague who was waiting for Stephen to finish a book chapter. There was infighting in his department: squabbling over office space, complaints about the technology available in one of the buildings, and disagreement about a course change within the history program. With a sigh, he clicked out of email. All the usual and then some. He was glad to be in Stella Mare, out of the fray.

His phone beeped with a message. "Well, apparently I'm not out of the fray," he muttered as he read the text. Wide-eyed, he made a call to his department chair.

"Khalil, it's Stephen."

"I thought I might hear from you."

"Well, of course. This is shocking news. You sounded upset."

"I am upset, Steve. Upset, but coping. I just wanted you to know what's going on here before it hits the news."

"What I saw was pretty confusing. Financial troubles that are worse than anyone knew? That's going to be big news."

"Yes, it is. There's a whole lot about this that we just don't know yet."

"Criminal?"

There was a pause. "I don't know, really. I have heard the word embezzlement. The worst thing is that outcomes won't be clear for a while."

Stephen sighed. "I'm kind of glad I'm here, but I'm sorry I can't really help right now. What do you think will happen?"

Khalil sighed, too. "I expect a lot of people will be affected."

Stephen cleared his throat. "At the risk of sounding selfish, how is this going to affect me? Do you have any idea about that yet?"

"Unclear. We know there are irregularities in the research funding office and the police are investigating. In the meantime, we are probably going to have to freeze some of those grants until we get it sorted. Yours might be one of them."

"I wish you were kidding," he said, "but I know you never joke about money."

"I wish it were a joke too," Khalil agreed. "Unfortunately, we've got a bit of a disaster here and it's going to spill onto a lot of people."

Stephen gritted his teeth. "This is a mess."

"Agreed. A big mess. We don't even know how big yet. I just wanted to give you advance notice."

"I hope your office will also have guidelines on how to handle projects that are in process when the money gets frozen."

"I can try to get someone to do that, but you have no idea what chaos we're in already. Listen, just be prepared for the worst. That's all I wanted to say."

"Thank you, I think," Stephen said. "Good luck."

"I need all I can get. I'm contacting a lot of people today with this news."

He put the phone down and paced to the window. Now he was glad he was not at the university, but he fretted about his colleagues and Khalil. What a mess everyone was dealing with. Sunlight on the bay glinted sharply, catching his attention. *I'm here, not there*, he thought. *The best thing I can do is the work at hand. I can't help them, but I can do something.*

The thought of that letter from his father's lawyer nagged at him.

He returned to his desk and grudgingly opened an email to Henry Culpeper. Dashing off a few lines, he read them over and promptly filed it in his drafts folder. Not yet, he thought. *I'm not ready to take this on yet.*

Fortunately, work, the work he loved, was calling. *I have stories to find and stories to tell*. He was here now and was going to make the most of it.

Deeply engrossed in his work, he had no idea how long it was before the bell on the door jangled.

"It's me!" Cassandra called. "Don't get up."

Her head appeared around the office door. "Hi, Stephen. Working hard?"

"Not excessively," he said with a smile. "But maybe too intensely. I can't believe it's already afternoon. How's life at the Sunshine?"

She shrugged. "Same menu, different stories. You know the drill."

"I don't think I've been here long enough to really know, but I should be figuring some things out. I think Leonard left you a note." He gestured to Leonard's disaster of a desk.

"A list, you mean? Wow, how does he find anything?" She poked around on his desk. "Oh, here it is."

"Cassie, you grew up here. Maybe you know the woman who came in this morning. Evie Madison."

Cassandra's smile grew wide. "Oh, she did stop by. Good. She came in for coffee and I told her about the gallery. I thought she might like it."

"Tell me about her."

Cassandra laughed. "I think she's married or something."

Shaking his head, he said, "Not like that. This is a professional interest. She's an artist, isn't she?"

"Yes. She's older than I am, so I didn't really know her in school. Mostly by reputation. She painted these amazing murals at the high school. Then when I wanted to be an artist, everyone said I could do what Evie Madison did, go to university for fine arts. I thought she'd be a big-name artist by now."

"Is she locally famous?"

"Not even. Famous with high school kids from Stella Mare maybe. I think she lives in St. Stephen. She's mostly associated with Jase Highborn. Do you know him? He's got more name recognition, but I don't especially like his stuff. His painting is aggressive, you know, and he does installations, but the ones I've seen always featured his image in some weird way."

"Hm. Sounds interesting."

"I don't like it. A lot of people love it, but it's not what I'm attracted to. I liked Evie's work. She used to paint a lot. I don't know what she's making now. I'd like to get to know her better."

So would I. "Thanks for sending her this way. You know how I am about talking to local people. Local artists are even better."

Cassandra laughed. "Well, I aim to please. Now I better get started on this list."

"Have fun. I'll be here for another hour. Then you're in charge of the huge crowds thronging the gallery."

"Right. Have you had anyone at all today?"

"Evie. See, it's really a good thing you sent her. But things will start to pick up on the weekends, and in another month it'll be busy all the time, according to Leonard."

"He's right. We have lots of year-round business at the Sunshine, but the gallery will really feel the influx of tourists as things warm up."

Stephen rubbed his arms. "Are you promising that things will warm up? I don't think I've ever been so consistently cold as over the last three months."

"It will get warm, yes, and all the locals will complain about the heat. Just like they complain about the snow and the cold. Complaining about the weather is a local sport, my mother says."

"I think that's everywhere," Stephen admitted, "but I can relate to complaining about the cold. I'm ready for some warm."

"Okay, I'm going to work," Cassandra announced, and headed into the gallery space with her list.

He turned back to his laptop, but his attention to his work had been broken. It felt like enough for now. But Evie. He searched the internet for information.

Not much. A few watercolours, her graduation those years ago, a news item in which she was identified as the partner of Jase Highborn.

She had really stuck with him. Dark curls, deep brown eyes, barely perched on the chair like she could fly away any minute. *What is your story, brown-eyed girl?*

He clicked to search Jase Highborn and was flooded with material. Website, projects he'd been involved in, classes he taught, social media presence. He'd worked on several funded projects, and the website detailed the history of his shows. An interpretation page even talked about the meanings in the work and the changes over time. The critique and analysis were thorough and well constructed. Not the usual thing for a website, though the copy could have been written by a curator for a retrospective. Only this guy, Jase, was just thirty-five or so. Pretty young for a retrospective.

Wait, why am I feeling so critical of this man I've never heard of before? As if in answer, he again saw Evie's curls, her drawn face, the depths of those eyes. What was it about her that drew him? In the entire world of possibilities, how did it happen that she arrived in the gallery right now, right when he was there?

If it's true that everything matters, then it matters that I met Evie Madison today. He didn't know how or why, but it mattered.

Chapter 7

Back at home, Evie bypassed conversation with James to drag her exhausted body up the stairs. *I don't want to be here. I don't really want to be anywhere. I miss Jase.* She threw herself on the bed, arms over her head. No home, no boyfriend, no job, no future. She wondered if it was possible to feel worse.

Turning onto her side, she curled into a ball and pulled the extra blanket over her. Her eyes closed and she dropped into a deep, dreamless slumber.

She woke, immobilized, realizing that she had been deeply asleep. She remembered her last thought: was it possible to feel any worse than she did? Her eyes opened to see the dresser with the framed photos of the family—well, the girls and Agnes. Gazing at her mother's picture, she slowly realized that she knew what worse felt like. She didn't have any experience of breaking up, but she knew about losing somebody. She knew about grief. Yes, it was possible to feel much, much worse.

With a sigh, she threw off the blanket and her feet reluctantly hit the floor. Her phone pinged with an incoming text. *Jase!* Her spirits took flight and she tapped to see his message. It was terse; just telling her to check email. *Again! Oh, maybe he's come to his senses.* She clicked through to his email, heart in her throat.

But no, apparently not. Instead, he'd upped the ante on his demands to get her stuff. Attached to the email was an inventory of the contents of their studio and loft, organized into columns labeled with their names. *How did he do this? He has no idea how to use a spreadsheet. I bet that Melissa had something to do with this.* Now gritting her teeth, she looked at his accompanying message. "Arrgh!"

Instead of throwing her phone, she stomped down the stairs to find her father.

"Dad!"

James sat in the living room reading, cup of tea at his elbow and a big silky dog head on his knee. He and Custard both looked up placidly. "Evie."

She perched on the edge of the sofa across from his recliner.

James took off his reading glasses. "You seem a dite upset."

She sniffled. "More than a dite, I think. Can I talk to you?"

"That's what I'm here for."

She giggled a little. "Okay, I know better than that. But I'm just so frustrated! Jase wants me to get my stuff out of the loft this week."

James raised his eyebrows. "Not wasting any time, is he?"

She shook her head miserably. "I think he's rushing things. We have a lot of history, you know?"

James nodded. "You do. Including what happened when you went back there last weekend."

Oh, yes. That. Her stomach contracted.

"Yeah, that's pretty awful. But we have this big festival project that we have to do together, and I just know he's going to realize that breaking up was a mistake. He'll see that he really needs me. I don't want to do all that work of getting my stuff just to move it back in a few weeks."

James gazed at her.

"What? What are you thinking, Dad?"

"I'm thinking a lot of things. Unlike your sisters, I don't have to say everything I'm thinking. What can I do for you? What would help you?"

Evie shrugged. "Well, can I stay here for a few weeks? Until we get the project started and we get back together?"

"Of course. A few weeks is fine. I will require compensation though." He looked at her meaningfully.

"Compensation? You mean rent? I don't have much coming in until the grant funds start flowing at the end of the month."

"No, not rent," he said with a snicker. "But to stay here, you'll need to tolerate your old dad giving advice. I think that's the main reason Dorie moved out. She'd had enough of the fatherly advice."

"Oh, Daddy!" Evie moved across the room to hug him. "Yes, give me all the advice. I can listen. I don't promise to take it though."

"I won't get upset when you don't. I've raised four young women, you know. I understand exactly how valuable my advice is."

"Advise away!" Evie chuckled. "Thank you."

"There is something else though," James added thoughtfully. "It sounds like you're going to have some free time until that grant money is available."

"Well, there is work to do on the project before the funding comes, but generally, you're right."

"Maybe you can help me with a project," he confided. "This place is getting a little big for me. I'm going to sell it and move into a new senior's development out toward the golf course."

Evie caught her breath. "Really?"

He nodded. "They won't be ready until fall, but I think it's going to take a while to clear this place out. After all, there's about a hundred-fifty-years worth of stuff here."

Evie was struck silent. Her father selling the family home. Moving out to live with a bunch of seniors. "Are you okay? I know you were having tests and stuff at the hospital."

"I'm as right as rain. You don't need to worry about me."

"Really? If it isn't your health, then why?"

He shrugged. "There's a lot of upkeep to an old house. Plus there's company there. Other people. This place feels too big for one."

She tried to imagine it: Dad, playing bridge, or worse, golf. Hanging out with the blue-haired ladies. Sitting around with a bunch of old people. What about his dogs? His truck? His fishing? What about their hours-long family dinners around the big kitchen table? "Are you sure about this?"

He gave her an appraising look. "Well, no, not entirely. If I do decide for sure, it will help to have the house cleared out. You can help with that. You can ask Dorie and Corinne to help, too."

"Our family really has been in this house for a hundred fifty years, huh? That's a long time."

"You'll be sure of it when you start going through the stuff in the attic and the shed. Some of those closets upstairs have stuff from your grandmother still in them. Great-grandmother, too."

"Your family, right?"

"Not only my family. Even I'm amazed at the piles of cultch we've got everywhere. Anytime one of the old folks died, we got their stuff, and we kept every bit of it. We've got as much of your mother's family stuff as mine, even though this house was in the Madison family all these years."

"And Mum was from Stella Mare too."

"Right. Only her sisters sold their family home and moved away. When we got married, Aggie moved in here with me and my mum. When your Grandma Sarah moved in here a few years later, she brought all her family's treasures. Anything we thought we might be able to use." James stood up heavily. "There's more than a few weeks' worth of work in clearing this place out. Better for you girls to do it than me, and your mother would never have been able to let go of anything. Everything had meaning, you know? All of it meant something, was connected to family."

"Why do you think we'll do better?"

"Oh, you're youngsters. You're all about this minimalism and all that. Old stuff is just clutter."

Scoffing, Evie said, "I don't know who you're talking about. When was the last time you visited my place in St. Stephen?"

"Tidy and spare, that's what I remember." His eyes twinkled as he picked up his cup and headed for the kitchen. "You can stay, of course. But I get to give you advice that you can ignore, and you get to help me with the house-clearing project."

She nodded. "Good deal. Have you talked to the sisters about this senior housing idea?"

He glanced back at her. "No. But now I won't have to. You will."

"Dad!" But he was right. She'd have to tell the sisters right away.

Evie was grateful that she had something else to think about besides Jase, even though the magnitude of the house-clearing task was daunting. Wandering through the house making a list pushed away the image of Michelle's long legs descending the loft ladder.

The house wasn't all that big. It felt small enough when they were all kids, with dogs and cats and the neighbourhood children roaming through all the time. Maybe it felt larger now with just Dad, but still. How hard could this be?

She took her notebook into the kitchen. The pantry under the stairs was uncharted territory. She cracked open the old door and pulled the light string. Near the door were canned goods, a couple of bottles of wine, a crock that once held flour but now held dust, and a big bin of dog kibble. Pushing deeper into the space, Evie had to turn on the light from her phone to see into the crevices. Old pots, cardboard boxes, a layer of dust and, oh, spiders. She spluttered and tried to wipe the web off her face but dropped her notebook. Bending over to get it, she noted the ancient linoleum on the floor, different from the vinyl tiles near the front of the pantry. She sneezed and backed out.

Whew! She scribbled some notes. That would take time and a great big light. Backing toward the sink, she set the electric kettle to boil. Then she pushed open the screened door to the backyard.

Crossing the overgrown lawn, she pushed on the shed door to find it locked. Feeling around the doorframe, she found the key (predictable, she thought, like every old house in town) and unlocked the old door. Shouldering aside the creaky panels, she stepped into a space dimly lit by the dusty window onto the backyard. Near the door were the snow shovel and scoop, and a couple of old snow brushes from the car. Walking in, she saw ancient bikes from her childhood, garden tools in disarray. Piles of plastic and clay plant pots sat on a potting bench covered with mouse droppings. She grimaced in distaste. The whole place was full of dusty, dirty, ancient stuff. Like the pantry, the things James used on a regular basis were near to hand, but the rest of the place had been turned over to time.

Well, except for the rocking chair. Floating on filtered sunlight, it invited her to sit. She perched gingerly at first, but then slid back onto the wide seat and pushed with her feet. Settling into a gentle back-and-forth, Evie considered her project.

The mouse droppings were kind of gross, but the rest of this shed was charming. Well, it had potential to be charming. It could be a great studio. *But I'd have to steal it from Dad.*

But of course, he was planning to sell. The morning light intensified, and the view of the woods behind the yard was backlit. She wondered how Dad was able to overlook the generations of mice that called the shed home.

Nice space, she thought, but too much stuff. Most of it junk. Satisfied with her assessment, she stood up and brushed herself off. She locked the shed and made sure the key was in the expected spot, and then she went back to the house.

She brewed tea in her mother's old Brown Betty teapot and sat at the kitchen table with her notebook. Jotting notes, she realized she was glad to be occupied, and that there was plenty to do. She could keep her thoughts under control.

The downstairs rooms and bedrooms all had closets. Without looking, Evie was sure they were all full to overflowing. The little den off the kitchen was the same way. The basement was empty only because of annual flooding, but there was also the attic.

Evie sighed gustily. Yes, the attic. She might as well have a look up there. Carrying her notebook, she pulled down the ladderlike staircase to the far upper reaches of the house.

It was hot. Blisteringly hot air pulsed down the stairs. *Maybe I'll just have a quick look.* She dropped her notebook and pen on the hall floor.

Curiosity competing with resistance, she climbed up gingerly. Getting things down would be a massive job. She wondered who could help, but as her head cleared the attic floor, thoughts of movers and trucks left as she was transported back to childhood.

We played dolls up here, and dress-up. I wonder if the costume box is still here? Mum had called it a Tickle Trunk from that old TV show. She reached the top and stepped gingerly onto the attic floorboards. It seemed sturdy enough. *Look at all the crap this floor is holding.*

She walked toward the front of the house, picking her way through blanket-covered furniture, towers of cardboard boxes, standing lamps, a rolltop desk that looked like a downtrodden twin to the desk in the downstairs den. *My family keeps everything*, she marvelled, recalling the spare décor of the loft she shared with Jase. *Who are these people? Can I really be a Madison?*

From far away, she heard a phone ring. She hurried down the stairs, brushing at the cobwebs that trailed her, and grabbed the phone in her father's bedroom. James was out, maybe having coffee downtown with a couple of buddies. A businesslike voice asked for James and then left a message. James had a medical appointment with Dr. Swami next week. She promised to deliver it and hung up slowly, and then she headed to the kitchen.

Oh, Dad, you little liar, she thought grimly. *Now at least I have an excuse to ask him about this. As right as rain. We'll just see about that. When Dorie and Corinne come over, we'll have a talk with Dad.*

She looked up Dr. Swami on her phone. Cardiology.

Right. Rett had said that. Suddenly, everything came crashing down on Evie. Dad with a cardiologist, looking to move out of the house. Her own situation suddenly felt precarious. *I have to solve this problem*, she thought. *My home here is temporary. Jase has to shape up. He's got to figure out that he needs me.*

Almost against her will, she looked again at the email accompanying his inventory list. "I need you to get your stuff out of the loft and studio. Since our relationship has ended, we no longer cohabit. Your goods are an impediment."

Impediment? Whose word was that? Since when did Jase talk about impediments? It would be foolish to move my stuff out when I'm sure I'll be moving it back in. As soon as he realizes...

Her eyes were glued to his words. "Since our relationship has ended..."

What does he mean, our relationship has ended? It sounds like he had an end date in mind. It ended on this date.

Well, Jase might think their relationship had ended, but Evie knew the Peninsula Festival would change all of that. It had to.

Stephen pulled into the little parking lot at the side of the gallery. The afternoon sun was still warm, but cool breezes blew off the harbour. The back door opened into the office, and he walked through to stick his head into the gallery proper.

Cassandra was seated at the small table, pondering something on her laptop. She looked up at his greeting.

"Oh, you're back. How was your meeting?" she asked.

"Good, good enough," he said.

She snickered. "You've been here too long. That's how everyone answers everything here. Really, how was your meeting?"

He came closer, pulling up a chair at the little table they shared while working in the gallery. "It was very nice to see my colleague," he admitted, "and the food was pretty good."

She looked at him curiously. "But?"

"Nothing, really. It was fine. I hadn't seen Marta for about five years, so we had a lot to catch up on." *But not what I was hoping for.* His jaw tightened.

"It's nice to see old friends."

"What?" he said, startled out of his dark thoughts. "Right, it is nice."

"She's in Fine Arts, right, at the university in Sackville?"

"Right." He nodded. "Did you apply there?"

"I was hoping for Nova Scotia. But now I'm not sure about anything. I really like the work here, especially when Leonard gives me things to do with the artwork."

"You do seem to have an affinity for displaying work so it makes sense to the viewer."

She nodded happily. "Thank you. I had no idea that was even a thing. But I love it, love thinking about it."

"Leonard's lucky to have you," he said and got up. "I'm going to wash up a bit and then I can relieve you if you like."

"No, thanks. I'm happy to stay until we close tonight. It's quiet."

"Okay then. You take care. I'll probably see you tomorrow."

He headed through the office and up the stairs to his apartment. His reasons for his lunch date went beyond catching up with old friends, though that was a reasonable assumption. He'd been fishing for information, and Marta called him on it.

"Why are you so interested in Evelyn Madison?"

He shrugged. "I just met her. She's an artist and right in the village. That's all."

With a sideways smile, she said, "Forgive me, but I don't believe you. Anyway, if she graduated twelve or thirteen years ago, I would have missed her. I've only been there for ten. I have heard of Jase Highborn, though. His name shows up all over the place. I don't know if I've seen his work, but I do recognize the name."

"Right. Well, I wondered. That was what it looked like when I did an internet search, too."

"Stephen! Isn't that kind of like internet stalking?"

"Well, I hope not. How are you supposed to find out about somebody's work?"

She snickered. "It depends on whether it's really their work you're interested in."

"I can't believe you want to give me a hard time about this, Marta," he said, aggrieved. "We haven't seen each other in years and you're already giving me the big sister treatment."

She laughed and patted his hand on the table. "You've missed me, haven't you?"

"I really have." He sipped his drink. "How would I ever have navigated social life in Baltimore without your guidance?"

"Look how well that turned out," she said darkly. "How long have you been divorced?"

"Oh, well, we don't have to talk about that," he said. "Eleanor and I parted as amicably as possible, you know. It wasn't nearly as bad as some."

She looked sad. "I wish I hadn't been the one to introduce you. I felt responsible."

"Nonsense. No, it was a life experience, all of it."

"You're all about learning from your life experiences, aren't you?"

He shrugged. "What else? If you don't learn, then what good are they?"

"Fair enough," she agreed. "By the way, did you know I'm now the editor for the *Women's Voices in Art* journal?"

"Tell me. You mean like interviewing women artists?"

"Not really, although there is an affiliated podcast that does that. No, this is more like your stuff around stories. Women's stories in art. Just in case you see anything like that coming your way."

"I'll keep that in mind. And, by the way, if you see any jobs coming your way, would you let me know?"

"Oh, no, Stephen. I thought you had tenure?"

He did. He'd worked hard to get to the point where his job was not endangered, but there were exceptions. "The university is in big financial trouble, Marta, and anything could happen. Even with tenure. I'm just trying to be proactive here."

"Well, of course. I just hope it doesn't come to that."

"So do I."

Upstairs with his thoughts, he pulled on his running clothes. Nagged by unfinished business, he opened his laptop to scroll the *Chronicle of Higher Education* classifieds. Looking for work when you had a job was smart. The listings were depressing, though he knew that June was likely to be a slack month for academic postings. He bookmarked a couple to look at later.

His email program pinged with a notification. He looked long enough to delete it without opening, but his draft to his father sat there, quietly mocking him.

Why can't I address this? It's not like a big deal.

He opened it and looked over his words. They were fine; respectful and kindly inquiring after his father's well-being in light of the death of his sister. That wasn't the problem.

The problem is that I should have called him right away.

No, the problem is that he should have called me.

No. The real problem is that we have such a bad relationship that neither of us is willing to reach out to the other, even when bad things happen. He sighed.

More than ever, he needed his run.

Chapter 8

The morning after taking the phone message for her father, Evie was up early. Sleep was a valuable and rare commodity since this nonsense with Jase. Her nights were accompanied by demons, she thought with grim humour. Little nasty guys with pointy tails and pitchforks poking holes in her confidence. The "where will I live?" demon, the "what will I do?" demon, and the "will Jase come to his senses?" demon all danced around her consciousness keeping sleep away. In daylight, she could push those thoughts away by reminding herself about the festival and having faith things will work out the way she wanted. At night, though, it was another matter.

Now there was a new demon, a meaner one, who kept asking her about her father. She didn't want to even hear the question, but she knew what it was. *What if Dad dies? What if we lose him too?* Because the very idea sucked the breath out of her, she got up and made coffee.

Seated at the table with her notebook, she tried to focus on her task of making a plan to clear the house. Instead, she found herself sketching. Well, it was really more like doodling. First she drew the demons she imagined stealing her sleep. Scratching them out, she drew Dad's hand on Custard's big silky head, the dog looking blissful and soaking in the attention. The coffee bubbled in the background as she sketched her mother's face from memory; from the memories of her own frantic sketches that she had made obsessively when they found out Mum was dying. Was this her mother's face, or was it the face of Evie's own anticipatory grief? No, it was Agnes, Evie thought, settling in to add details. *Hi, Mum.* She smiled at the drawing and got up to pour her coffee.

The dogs scratched at the outside door. When they returned from the yard, they had expectations. She handed each a treat and then returned to her spot as they lumbered into the sun porch and then thumped onto their respective dog beds. The rhythm of life in this house hadn't changed even with Agnes gone. Coffee in the morning, dogs out, dogs in, treats, naps.

Maybe Evie needed a new routine. The old one was gone for sure. She needed to figure out how to work on the festival while helping her father. It seemed like he really did need help. Absently she wrote Jase's name on her pad. Then she struck it out. *I guess I have to talk to him. Get things underway.*

She imagined having lunch in their favourite café in St. Stephen. She would be sweet and efficient and he would see, would have to see, how much he needed her. They had to get this festival off the ground, make it a success, both for local artists but also for local businesses, and there was a lot of work to do on it. He couldn't fail to see what she had done for him, for them both. By now, a few days into this so-called separation, Jase would be feeling her absence. Who was handling his mail orders? His calendar? Who was scoping out new grant possibilities? For sure, he wasn't doing it. He didn't know how to manage his business. He just made art and talked to people. Increasingly confident and fuelled by caffeine and her own fantasy, Evie sent a text inviting him to a lunch meeting next week.

Satisfied with her progress on that front, she turned back to the house project. Dad had assumed she would let the sisters know his plans. She put together a message for all four of them: the sisters, plus Corinne. Dad wasn't the only one who needed help. The house was an overwhelming project. How could she remove things from the house if all the sisters weren't there to see what each of them wanted to keep? Corinne and Dorie were local, at least, and technology would help with the rest. Keeping everyone happy while still clearing more than a century of accumulation was not going to be simple.

Dad wants the house cleared of stuff in case he decides to move into senior housing. We need to get everything cleared out. I need you all to help with the decision making. Also he has an appointment with a cardiologist next week. I don't know why. I'm just doing my sisterly duty to keep you in the loop. FYI.

Okay. That was a good morning's work for only seven a.m.

She took her cup and went to the back door again. The big dogs were snoring in the sun porch at the front of the house, but when she clicked the backdoor open, Mallow lumbered into the kitchen. "Okay, you can come," she agreed, and they headed into the morning sunshine.

Evie was sitting in the living room, pondering her list of tasks, when Dorie arrived in the early evening. James was tapping at his laptop at the kitchen table.

"Hi, Dad," Dorie said. "Whatcha doin'?"

"Not too much," he said. "Cup of tea?"

"I can make it. Evie here?" Water splashed in the sink.

"I'm here," Evie said, entering the kitchen. "Make enough for me, too, please."

Dorie glanced over. "Sure." She set the kettle back on the electric base and flicked it on.

"Well, I'm glad you girls are here," James said. "I've been thinking about my will."

"What?" Dorie sounded surprised. "What about your will?"

"Well, I been thinking. You might not think we have much, but me and your mother, we saved pretty good, even for having four little girls."

"Yeah, that's for you, Dad. To take care of you." Evie was certain.

"A father likes to know his girls are taken care of even when he's gone, Evie," James said seriously. "I've been thinking about how to do that. I was a little worried about leaving Dorie here, if I died, but now she's got Chad, and I figured you girls were all set. But now I am a little worried about you." He looked at Evie over his reading glasses.

"Me? Why?"

"Well, it's comforting to see your girls all married and settled, and I figured you and Jase would pull the trigger on that pretty soon. Then I guess it would just be a four-way split for the four of you now that Dorie and Chad are gonna tie the knot."

Evie was getting irritated. "Dad, you pull out the worst clichés when you're trying to make a point. Are you saying you don't trust your daughters to take care of themselves? We have to be married?"

James raised his eyebrows and pulled off his glasses. "Well, maybe. Am I being old-fashioned, Evelyn?"

Dorie was laughing. "No, Dad, I can't buy that. Once your girls are married off, they become their husbands' responsibility? Is that it?"

"What's wrong with that? Is that sexist?" James sounded affronted.

"What do you think? Yes, it's sexist. Come on, Dad. That's like thinking I can cook because I'm a girl." Dorie giggled.

James leaned back in his chair. "Well, maybe I am a sexist then. I do know that I'll feel easier in my mind if I know that you girls have your families, have someone to be your partner, your helpmeet, your support. Not just financial support."

Evie was stung. She had been okay in Dad's mind, but now she wasn't. Not okay. Jase being a jerk made her not okay. Oh, this felt bad.

Dorie was persistent. "So now that I've got Chad, you aren't worried about me?"

He shrugged. "You seem to have your feet on the ground a little more. That's all."

Evie's face heated and her voice was tiny. "But I'm not okay. You don't think I'm okay."

James turned to face her. "Do you think you're okay?"

Her stomach turned again. "Oh, I don't know. Sometimes. I'm going to be okay, just right now things are kind of a mess. I wish I hadn't told everybody what was going on." A tear slid down her cheek.

"Listen, I know that your situation is temporary. Everyone's situation is temporary. My job is to make sure you girls are okay. When Aggie left us, that's what she asked for, and I promised."

"Dad," Dorie started.

"No, you hear me out. I know I can't control if you're okay. I can make sure you have all the help I can give. That includes having some money after I die."

"Die! Dad, why are we talking about this?" Dorie looked incensed.

Evie said grimly, "You know why. He's seeing a cardiologist."

"But he said he's fine. Right, Dad? You said you're fine."

James suddenly looked tired. "Yes, I'm fine. Talking to the doc, sometimes feeling my age. These things make me realize that I can be fine one minute, but that doesn't mean fine in the next one. I'm just being prudent, girls."

Evie sniffled. "You don't mind if I withhold my judgment about that, do you?"

"Me, too," Dorie concurred. "Can we talk to the cardiologist? Can I go with you to your next appointment?"

"No!" James was emphatic. "This isn't your problem. Or it isn't a problem at all, and I don't want you girls to worry. The subject is closed."

"But I want—" Dorie spluttered.

"No. Final no." James was firm. "Conversation over." He stood, pushing up with his hands. After a moment, he headed for the kitchen door, lifting the leashes from the hook on the wall. With a jangle of hardware and clicking nails, the big dogs jostled across the kitchen to James. "We're going for a walk," he said unnecessarily.

Evie noted he had his customary quiet tone back. How did he do that? She couldn't calm herself as quickly and completely as her father.

When the door closed behind them, Dorie caught Evie's eye. "Well, that was something."

"Yeah. Dad hardly ever raises his voice." She grabbed a fistful of tissues and blew her nose. "He's worried."

"But I don't think he's worried about you, Evie. I know he says the words, but I bet it's more about himself. Only he can't let himself think that way."

"Really? Oh, yeah, I know what that is." Evie pondered. "Projection. He's worried about himself, but he makes it about me. Do you really think that?" She turned to Dorie for reassurance. "I don't want to be the one causing worry."

"That's our problem in this family," Dorie proclaimed. "None of us wants to be a worry to anybody else. We just keep on doing what we do without asking for help. I think you did the right thing to come home. If you need help, ask."

"Well, I need help on this house job Dad's assigned to me."

"Right, and Corinne and I are coming. But I mean the other kind, big help. Somebody to hold you up."

"Hmm."

"Okay, I know I haven't always been the best at that. But I am trying to learn."

"I'm going to be fine, thanks. Next week. I have a meeting with Jase about the Peninsula Festival. We'll be working on it together, and he'll realize he needs me in his life."

Dorie looked at her curiously. "Is that what it is? Do you need to be needed?"

Evie was confused. "Well, yeah. What's the point otherwise?"

Dorie looked at the table. "Well, I'm new to this relationship stuff, but I don't think Chad needs me. He lived by himself for years, knows how to take care of himself just fine. But he wants me. That's a different thing." She looked up at Evie. "Does Jase want you?"

Her stomach gave a familiar flip. That was a different question, wasn't it? "Well, I'm meeting him to discuss the festival. Maybe I'll find out."

The entire week before her meeting with Jase felt surreal. Unmoored, untethered, Evie felt like her whole being floated in a sea of uncertainty. The only thing perfectly clear was the need to get stuff out of the house. She tackled the attic again on Wednesday morning.

Armed with a big trash bag, her notebook, and her phone for documentation, she headed up the stairs. She'd tied her mass of curls into a knot at the top of her head and wrapped a kerchief around them. I look like that Rosie the Riveter, she thought absently. Rosie the Riveter with a cell phone. She giggled at that.

The attic hadn't changed from her last look. Sunlit and full of dust, it exuded a sense of age both comforting and foreign. As she explored, she began to understand there were layers. Each layer represented a different stage of the family. Nearest to the stairs were boxes of old toys, school papers, and even some baby clothes her mother had no doubt saved. Each of the girls had a box. Evie opened hers to find her school report cards, an old ballet costume, her Girl Guide badges, and a folder full of drawings from elementary school.

Wow. I didn't know she had this. Her eyes filled again as she thought of her mother carefully archiving her artwork. She pulled out a certificate of achievement in art from high school. It was her only high school achievement besides almost getting kicked out for graffiti. After that was when Mr. Stevens had asked her to paint the hallway mural.

She piled everything back in the box, sliding it toward the stairs along with the boxes labelled Helen, Loretta, and Doris. She wouldn't pry into her sisters' boxes, but her own was a welcome surprise. *Mum loved me. That's a solid fact.*

Energized, Evie dug farther into the attic. She pushed past old furniture that she recognized into foreign territory populated with ancient items that she couldn't recall. Hiding behind Grandma Sarah's bed were a trunk, a dresser, and another table. Was this treasure or just clutter?

They had to go, regardless. She pulled out her phone to take quick shots of the larger pieces of furniture. Even the distant sisters, Helen and Rett, would have to help determine the fate of various things. *This is way too much for me, even with Dorie and Corinne helping.*

She scrolled through the pictures before sending; dresser with mirror, mahogany-looking table and three intact chairs, plus one more that was broken, and the trunk. Is that our Tickle Trunk, she wondered, where they had kept a childhood dress-up collection?

Curious, she ignored being hot, sweaty, and ready for a break. Instead, it was like the trunk exerted its own traction. She really wanted to look inside.

It wasn't really a trunk, more like a big wooden box. On closer inspection, she noted the care and craftsmanship that persisted despite its age. Pegs covered the screws and the panels on the top were dovetailed. What kind of wood was it? Who made this box? Whose hands carved out that lid? Shaped the sides? She wondered briefly what Stephen might think of the workmanship on it. Somebody spent a lot of time and energy making this thing. She fiddled with the latch and finally flipped it. Then she lifted the lid.

It creaked, but it opened. If this were a kids' story, gold and a golden light would be spilling out, she thought nervously. The cover fell back to reveal a mound of yellowed tissue paper. Evie plopped on the attic floor and settled in. Maybe there was treasure.

Pulling out the covering tissue, she laid it on the floor beside her. Somebody thought enough of the contents to try to protect them. The top item was a cracked leather-bound book. She lifted it gingerly, opening it gently to flip through the pages. Though full of faded hen scratching, when she squinted, she could make out some of the words. "Hannah's Journal, June, 1927," she read. She recalled Corinne talking about Aunt Hannah, so maybe her great-aunt. None of it was clear.

She carefully set the book onto the tissue and pulled out a big wad of heavy fabric; a cotton cover protected a big roll of burlap. Heavy burlap. A lot heavier than she would have expected. With rising excitement, she unrolled it. Even in the dim light of the attic, the colours were unexpectedly brilliant. Boats—two boats—on the sea, and a house on the shore. Turning it over, she tried to separate the burlap backing from the base of the weaving. She wiggled her finger into a gap and peered at the construction. No, not weaving. Hooking. A rug, she thought triumphantly. Look at this, a rug, probably made out of scraps. She stood up and shook out the piece, laying it over the edge of the open box.

It really was a treasure box. Somebody had treasured these items, for sure. The rug carried some wear. Beautiful, but practical too. Excited, Evie dug deeper into the box.

She found several more rugs, though none as bright as the first. The next one she pulled out had a lot of wear, so much that the colours were greyed and the shapes indistinguishable.

Beneath the rugs she found an old cardboard box containing an extremely fragile-looking christening dress for an infant, some hand-knit mittens and a hat, and some lacy-looking stuff made of cotton thread. Reaching toward the bottom of the box, her hands touched something hard, and she pulled out two framed photographs. Ancient black-and-white, maybe even antique, photos. She glanced at them briefly but couldn't identify any of the people in them, so she piled them back in the box. She put the clothing, most of the rugs, and the journal back in the box, covering it with the tissue. She closed the lid of the box and gave it a pat.

With a little shiver of excitement, Evie rolled the large rug back into its well-worn creases and carefully wrapped it up again.

Hugging her bundle to her chest, she looked down at the box. *I will be back for more treasure*, she thought with a giggle. But it wasn't silly. Whoever put those things away had surely meant for others to treasure them too. Whoever it was, she would care for their treasures. She headed down the stairs.

At the kitchen table, Evie pushed aside the morning paper, James's coffee mug, and the doily and vase to make space. Laying out her find, she marvelled again at the bright colours. She snapped pictures of the piece from all angles, turning it over and, again, she noted the burlap backing.

"Hey, Daughter," said James, coming in with the dogs. "What do you have there?"

She looked up. "I really don't know. It's from the attic. Boy, there's a lot of stuff up there."

James handed out dog treats, hung leashes, and then he sat beside her. He fingered the artwork. "This is a rug, you know. A hooked rug."

"That's what I thought too. Or a tapestry. Nobody ever walked on this."

"Why would you make a rug and never use it? Seems a little wasteful to me."

"Look at it, Dad. It's art."

"Mostly that old stuff's seen a lot of use. This must have been a special one. Maybe it's a real place." James looked over his glasses. "Could be Newfoundland, with all those cliffs. Or Cape Breton."

"What's it doing in our attic?"

He shrugged. "Your guess is as good as mine. Your mum's people, some of them, came from away, you know."

"And their stuff is here?"

He laughed. "Everybody's stuff landed here. We've got stuff, and because we had an attic, we got more stuff. I'm going to try to make some headway in the shed today. What about you?"

"I'm not sure," she said, still gazing at the rug. "This has caught my interest. Maybe I'll do a little research."

"Don't forget your job here," he warned. "I know how you can get caught up in something."

She looked up with a sheepish grin. "Yeah, you're right. Nose to the grindstone. That's me."

Chapter 9

The week passed somehow. Evie noticed the sun rose and the night fell. Otherwise, she continued planning the house-clearing. Really, though, she was thinking about Friday. The day she would meet with Jase.

When Friday finally arrived, she dressed carefully for her lunch date. Technically it was a meeting, a business meeting, but she considered it a date. Why not? She pulled on a silk tank and a long skirt, but then she pulled them off in favour of a slightly fitted dress that accentuated her dark eyes and skin. Brushing on mascara and lip gloss, she looked at her reflection and smiled. "Hi, Jase," she tried out. Then she took a deep breath to try to calm her butterflies. She still had a forty-minute drive to get to the café. Plenty of time.

She arrived a few minutes early, as planned. She ordered for them both. Jase would be pleased she was being efficient with his time. He would appreciate that she got his favourite sandwich. She settled in, looking around with some pleasure. The handwoven tablecloths and napkins were all different from each other. The food was served on unmatched pieces of pottery from local potters. The fresh vegetables came from the café gardens during the summer months. Even the tile floor had been beautifully designed and installed by a fellow artist. It was a nice place to wait, but Evie's stomach was tight despite herself.

When Jase came through the door and looked around the café, she caught her breath. *Oh, he is handsome. This has to work. I can't be without him.* She rose slightly and waved at him.

"Hi," he said shortly and sat.

She smiled at him. "Hi, Jase. It's good to see you."

He frowned and shook his head slightly. "You too." He looked around for a server.

"Oh, I already ordered," Evie said. "Coffee's coming."

"Good. Let's get to it," Jase said. "When are you getting your stuff?"

"That's not what I wanted to talk about," she said.

He huffed. "Evelyn, that's what I want to talk about. It's the only reason I'm here. Getting the loft cleared out is my priority."

She leaned forward. "But Jase, that's just stuff. We need to talk about everything. About the Peninsula Festival. About, well, about us." She reached for his arm, but he pulled back into his chair, stony-faced. The server came by and put two steaming lattes on the table.

"Extra whip, just like you like it," Evie said.

Jase grunted and sipped his drink and then leaned back again. "You want to talk? So go ahead then. Talk." He lifted his chin.

Evie hated it when he did that. He'd shut off his ears and was pretending to listen. She started to crumble, but she had to take the opportunity.

"Jase, think about it. How are you going to get on without me?" She leaned on the table again. "Seriously. You don't even know how to log into your website, do you? Do you know where we order supplies? Do you know how to wrap and ship your work?"

Jase picked up his cup but didn't look at her. He continued to lean away.

"Jase, listen to me." Evie felt increasing panic.

He looked up and his eyes were hard. "I am listening, Evie. I'm listening to you tell me all the ways I'm incapable. Is that what you intended?" He finally looked at her, but his eyes were cold and distant.

The server arrived with their sandwiches. "Here we go: chicken salad on a croissant, light mayo, and for you, turkey and avocado on sourdough with arugula."

Jase shook his head. "No, thanks. I don't want anything."

The server's face held a question.

"No, really, just take it back. I didn't order it." As the server picked up the plate to leave, Evie hissed, "Jase! It's your favourite. I just ordered your regular lunch."

He looked at the server. "No, take it, please," he reiterated and waved it away.

Evie's face flamed, and she gazed at her sandwich, feeling sick. Despite her best efforts, hot tears pooled in her eyes. Jase had never embarrassed her in public like that.

"Evie, we're done. You said it first, but I realized you are right."

"But Jase, I was wrong. You need me."

He shook his head slowly. "No, Evie, I don't need you. You've done lots for me. I know what you've done for me, and it's probably my fault for letting it go on so long. But we can't stay together because you're good at managing my life for me. It's not good for me. It's probably not good for you either."

"What do you mean, not good for you? I've done everything. You know I have."

"I do know it. Some of the time I've even appreciated it, but right now I'm thirty-six years old, and I don't even manage my own life. I don't even get to order my own lunch, Evie. Even if you hadn't started this, I would have to leave you."

Unable to speak, she grabbed a napkin to dab at her eyes.

After a moment, Jase continued. "I'm sorry about the other night. I wish that hadn't happened."

Evie felt a flash of anger and humiliation. "Yeah. That was awful." Then she went on. "But a one-time thing, we can get over it, work it out, maybe." She thought about those long legs descending the loft ladder and her stomach clenched. "Maybe," she repeated doubtfully.

Jase just shook his head. "No."

"No to what? Work it out? Or one-time thing?"

Jase sighed loudly. "It doesn't matter, Evie. Don't you understand? We are no longer a couple."

"I won't argue about that, Jase. I really don't understand, but I'm not going to fight about it. After all, we still have the festival. We've already done so much, and the funding hasn't started yet, but there is a ton of work to do. We're going to be working together on that."

He started shaking his head before she finished. "No, Evie. You're off the festival. That's part of this."

"What? You don't get to decide this. I wrote that proposal. That was my work!"

"Evie, come on. Whose name is on that proposal? Whose reputation got us that grant?"

"That's not fair and you know it."

He shook his head. "The proposal is in my name. It's based on my history of managing shows, and my network of contacts in the art world."

"You have no history of managing shows. I've always done the managing."

"Nobody knows that but us. As far as anyone knows, I've done it all."

"But we always worked that way." Desperation crept into her voice. "We were partners. Real partners."

He just looked at her.

A bitter taste filled her mouth that had nothing to do with coffee. "I always gave you the credit and you always took it. I did the grant writing, the legwork, the research."

Jase nodded. "You did. I'm not proud of the way I let that happen. It was easy. You made it easy. You just jumped in and did whatever needed to be done, and I just had to show up."

"Just show up and let people assume you'd carried the whole load." The bitterness was in her eyes now too. "You did that well," she snarled.

"Yeah, well. As I said, I'm not proud of it, and things are changing. You won't be working on the festival, Evie." She could hardly stand his gaze. What was that? Pity?

"I invented the festival." She hated that her voice was getting louder. "My files, my contacts, my grant proposal. Of course I'm working on it."

"Michelle..." he started.

"Michelle! What about Michelle?"

He sighed again. "Michelle is going to pitch in and help me out. She's been doing a lot for me already."

"Yeah, I just bet. Come on, Jase. You try to sound so big-minded, like you don't want to take advantage of me anymore, but you've already dropped Michelle into every slot I used to fill. Where's the big personal growth in replacing one woman with another one?" She pushed away from the table and stood up. "Letting a different woman take care of you isn't really different, is it?"

He sighed tiredly.

"So sorry for wearing you out." She stuck out her chin. "It would be nice if you had a single clue what this situation means for me. I know you don't care, but you've single-handedly dismantled my professional and personal lives. I've lost my work, my home, my partner."

"I do know, and I'm sorry for my part in all of that. Neither of us should have let it go so far."

"You really don't get it. You don't see any consequences to you in this situation. I'm the one who has to deal with all the changes. You just go on, making art, talking to people, letting Michelle do the heavy lifting."

"Evie." He stood up across the table. "Evie, it's not that bad."

"How do you know what anything is like for me? You've never gotten your head into the daylight to see. Everything that's happened lately is bad enough, but stealing the Peninsula Festival, well, you've dropped to a new low, Jase. I hope you fall flat on your handsome face. You and Michelle."

She took a deep breath. "You know, Jase, you can really just go to hell." She left him to pay the cheque.

Chapter 10

"Evie Madison stopped by," Stephen said to Leonard. "Cassie knows her. She grew up locally but has been working, I guess, in St. Stephen."

Leonard looked up. "And?"

"She's an artist, Cassie says. Works in watercolour."

"Come on, man, say what you mean," Leonard said. "What's that got to do with me?"

Stephen shrugged elaborately. "Oh, nothing, I guess. Except maybe you'd be interested in featuring new work from a local woman who is back in the village. Maybe something like that."

Squinting, he asked, "What's your angle, Steve? What's in it for you?"

"Leonard, Leonard," Stephen said, widening his smile. "Everyone doesn't have an angle. Maybe I'm just interested in seeing local artists get some space."

"Ha. Maybe you're interested in said local artist. I bet she's not too old and ugly either."

"That's irrelevant, friend. I'm just suggesting a possible business opportunity for you. A chance to make a statement that will make the villagers wrap you in a warm embrace, taking you in as one of their own."

"You're piling it on pretty thick, Steve," Leonard warned. "Don't think I'm unaware that you have an agenda here. Besides, who knows anything about her work? It could be terrible."

"That seems unlikely, but maybe you could ask. She probably has a portfolio," he said. But not a website, none of her own work showing up anywhere. No need to say that out loud, though.

"Well, as a favour to an old friend, I'll see if she wants to leave some paintings here on consignment. That might be a good beginning."

"I'll send her a message," Stephen said. It might get Evie back into the gallery and give him a reason to get to know her better. That's all he was looking for.

Driving while I feel like this is hazardous. The wave of anger that prompted her outburst had propelled Evie to the car and out of the parking lot, but before she had gone four blocks, she had to pull over because she couldn't see through the torrents of tears. Rummaging in the car for tissues, she tried to hold onto her anger.

What a jerk. How could he just take everything away like that? *He's right, he needs to grow up. But why does that mean he has to leave me?* A fresh torrent of grief overtook her. She gave in to deep, wracking sobs, sitting in her car in an empty parking lot. *He's going to be sorry. He'll regret his decision.*

A buzz on her phone brought her back into the present. A text. Had it happened already? Her heart leaped at the idea of a contrite Jase sending a text.

No, from Stephen Culpeper, that guy with the accent from the gallery. Asking her to drop by to meet with him and Leonard. She dropped the phone in her lap. This was not the time. Later. She could answer that later.

All she wanted to do was get back to her father's house and hide under the covers. Damn, her turncoat body was betraying her again, this time with hunger. *I was hoping I might fade away from heartbreak. That would show him.* But no, she still wanted to eat. Maybe she wasn't a total wreck if she could still joke with herself.

She wouldn't starve to death on the way to Stella Mare, but what a waste of a perfectly good sandwich. *At least I stuck him with the cheque.* She liked the nasty satisfaction she felt with that thought.

Driving down the peninsula felt strange. This time, she wasn't just going for a visit. She truly had no home to return to in St. Stephen. She remembered her sister's dog Chester after he'd gotten into a fight with a coyote. *I'm just like Chester, going home to lick my wounds.* But for the third time in just a few days. *Man.*

Parking in her father's driveway, she tiptoed in through the perpetually unlocked kitchen door. A white poodle greeted her as she entered.

"Hey, Frou-Frou," Evie said. "Who's here with you?"

Dorie walked into the kitchen. "Just me." She caught a glimpse of Evie's face. "What happened? Oh, my gosh, Evie, are you okay?" She took Evie's shoulders in her hands.

"Do I look that bad?" Evie asked, palms to cheeks. "It's been a, um, difficult day so far."

"It looks like it," Dorie said sympathetically, pouring a glass of water. "Need a drink?"

Evie gratefully sipped. She needed to replenish what she'd cried out. Aware of Dorie's expectant look, she mumbled, "Bad meeting with Jase. I don't think I want to talk about it."

Patting her on the back, Dorie said, "Okay, I'll try not to ask too much. Do you have stuff in the car?"

Evie shook her head. "No, no stuff. I'm not, uh. No stuff. Yet."

"Okay. I was just talking to Dad." Dorie led the way into the living room where James sat with a huge dog at his side. Frou-Frou followed Dorie and neatly leaped into James's lap.

Evie curled into a corner of the couch. Dorie tossed her a fleecy blanket, and she snuggled down into it. Dorie and her father were talking about paint or stain, and about renovations at the dog sanctuary. The conversation washed easily over her, and she leaned her head back against the couch and closed her eyes. The moment her eyes shut, her mind went into high gear. *What am I going to do? No income, no place to live, no place to make art, nobody to take care of.* And then her anger snapped back...*how could he? How could he just take over the festival as if he knew how to pull off a big project like that one? How could you, Jase? How could you?*

Hot tears slipped out of her closed eyes. Wiping surreptitiously, she tightened her jaw. *You can't lose it. Not now. Not ever, really.* She sniffled. Without stopping the flow of conversation, Dorie tossed her a box of tissues.

With a mighty groan, Mallow hoisted himself from the dog bed in the sun porch and lumbered into the living room. He headed unerringly for Evie and laid his big silky head in her lap. Evie stroked the big dog and scratched behind his ears. His blissful moan made her giggle in spite of herself. "Mallow, you goof," she said. "I needed a dose of dog right now."

He pushed his head closer, butting her chest. She tipped her face down onto his big head and sighed. Dog love. It was the best kind. Way better than boyfriend love.

Her hunger reasserted itself. Giving Mallow a gentle shove, she got up to head to the kitchen. "Tea? I ended up missing lunch, so I'm going to make a sandwich. Anybody else want one?"

James and Dorie shook their heads and continued their conversation. Mallow accompanied Evie to the kitchen. "What are you now, my bodyguard?" she asked, speaking gently. It felt good to have the big dog to hang out with, even if he was hoping for treats. Setting the kettle to boil, she made a sandwich. "Peanut butter isn't chicken salad on a croissant, is it, Mallow?" He seemed to agree. "But the company is much better."

She sat at the table to eat and sipped her tea, absently looking at her phone. Mallow settled on her feet. Funny, she and Jase had been living without pets for twelve years, and now Evie wondered why. She loved having dogs around, had grown up with multiple pets in the house, and yet had not had a dog of her own. She bit thoughtfully into her sandwich.

Stephen Culpeper's text was still visible on her phone. She thought about walking downtown and into the gallery but rejected that idea immediately. Today was not the day. Today was a good day to, oh, watch shows. Eat ice cream.

While Evie was investigating the freezer, Dorie and James came into the kitchen.

"Okay, Dad, thanks for the advice," Dorie said. "Hey, Evie, are you going to be here for a while?"

Just like that, she lost the grip on her feelings. Evie gasped like she'd been punched, bent over at the waist. Her situation crashed in on her, and tears flowed hot and humiliating. Wracked by sobs, she covered her face with her hands. In a moment, she felt James's big hand on her back, heard Dorie's gentle words of comfort, and felt Mallow leaning against her. When she could stand upright, she choked out, "Um, yeah. I guess so."

Dorie's brow furrowed. "Oh, Evie. Come sit down." She helped her to the kitchen chair.

"What were you after in here?" James asked, closing the freezer. "Wait. I know. Ice cream."

"Not a cure, but it can't hurt," Dorie said.

Evie took a breath. "I went to see Jase. I thought I could talk sense into him, thought he'd see reason. But he's done."

Dorie looked surprised. "Is this different than before? I thought that happened already."

Evie sighed. "Yeah, well. I thought we'd get back together over the Peninsula Festival. I've been working on that for about eight months, not including writing the grant proposal."

James nodded. "That's a majority of your income for the year, isn't it?"

"That was the plan. Now he's dumped me off the project, even though we haven't yet received funds to cover the work I've already done and put someone else on it."

"Evelyn, how can he do that? You wrote the proposal. That's your work." Dorie's face was reddening.

"Yeah, well," she sighed again and looked at her father. "I wrote it, and I did it, but I put it all in Jase's name. On paper, he's the one organizing and curating the project, and getting the funding. So I guess he can decide to throw me out."

"Oh, my dear," James said, comprehension dawning. "It's been all about Jase."

She nodded. "Yes, pretty much everything. I've been running his business, writing his proposals, living in his loft, painting in his studio. Daddy, I don't have anything." Tears flowed again, and James reached across to hold her hands.

Dorie was incensed. "I don't think it works like that. You've been cohabiting. You must have rights to some of the proceeds or property, or something. That's unfair!"

James stood up, pulling Evie up and into a hug. "Not now, Dorie. You might be right, but that's for another time."

Evie sank into her father's embrace. "I don't know what I'm going to do," she wailed. James patted her back while she cried. Soon her sobs subsided to sniffles, and Dorie handed her a fistful of tissues. Pushing back from James, she sat. "Thanks," she said with a hiccup. "I've got to stop crying about this."

James sat and leaned back in his chair. "You will. Maybe not right away."

"I know you're planning to move out, so I can't stay here." She gazed at the kitchen table.

"Well, that's true. But it's not like I have any plans, yet. Only vague ideas. So maybe you and me, we can both be working on figuring things out. You can be here until then, Evie. You know that, right?" Her father's voice was as calm and mellow as always. She felt comforted by his tone.

"You can come hang out with us, Evie," Dorie offered.

Evie frowned. "You just want some volunteer labour at the dog sanctuary."

"Well, yes, but that's good honest work, right? Doing good? Anyway, if you have nothing to do, we can always find something." She grinned and stood back up. "Speaking of which, I need to get back. Evie, this just stinks, for sure. But your family is here." She gave Evie's shoulder a quick squeeze, called for Frou-Frou, and the pair—girl and dog—headed out the door.

"I see you had lunch," James noted approvingly. "That's good. I'm going to work on the shed this afternoon, but maybe you want a nap or something?"

At his words, Evie couldn't believe how exhausted she felt. "I haven't done anything today, but I could sleep for a week," she admitted. "I guess you're right. Call me if you want help with the shed."

James shook his head. "I have dogs to help," he said. "No worries."

When she woke up, the rosy glow of sunset suffused the room. She felt like she'd been deep underwater, but as she swung her feet to the floor, the day's events surfaced in her mind. *What am I going to do?*

Her eyes fell on the photo on the dresser. Mum and her girls. She knew what her mother would tell her.

One foot in front of the other. That's what Mum would say. Just take the next step, whatever it is. You can't figure everything out all at once. Besides, we never know what kind of treasures life has in store. You wouldn't want everything to go the way you planned, because then you'd miss out. Of course, Mum always had looked adoringly at Dorie when she said stuff like that, but it still might be useful advice.

Evie couldn't imagine life had something in store better than curating the Peninsula Festival with Jase, getting married to Jase, and having babies with Jase. But just because she couldn't imagine it didn't mean it might not happen. At least her mother would have said so.

Evie got to her feet and headed downstairs. One foot in front of the other.

James looked up from the table when she came into the kitchen. "Hi."

"Hi." She checked the kettle for water and turned it on. "You ever think of what the world looks like from the kettle's point of view?" she asked, turning to look at James. "When it's empty, we fill it. When it squeals, we jump up to attend to it. We think it belongs to us, but maybe we belong to it. Ya know?"

James nodded solemnly. "Like the dogs. Clearly, they're the princes of the house. Their food is delivered to them, their needs are anticipated, and I even pick up their poop in special little bags. This idea that we own dogs, that's a farce."

"It's probably a good thing we don't have a cat." She chuckled. "Then we'd really be put in our proper places." She took her mug to the table.

Settling in a chair, she asked, "How did it go in the shed?"

James grimaced. "Oh, you know. I keep picking things up and putting them down. Everything is full of memories."

"Like what?" she asked with interest. As far as she knew, the shed was full of tools and gardening equipment. And mouse droppings.

James gazed at the far wall. "Well, old tile from when I attempted to renovate the bathroom."

"Attempted? You did renovate it."

He gave her a look. "No, I started to. But it was such a disaster I had to get someone in to fix my mess, and it ended up costing twice as much as I budgeted. Oh, your mother took me to task for that." He chuckled.

After he was silent for a while, she prompted him. "And what else?"

"Silly stuff. Like old plastic sand buckets you girls played with. Your mum's gardening apron, you know, the one with all the pockets." His eyes grew misty. "A bunch of planters I haven't used since she died. Ones she always filled up with those purple-y flowers, you know the ones."

"Clearing out is going to be a big job, isn't it?" Evie said gently.

He nodded. "Bigger than I expected. Well, not bigger. Just harder."

"Dad, are you sure you want to leave the house? I know you've been thinking about it for a while, but still…" She trailed off. "Are you certain?"

She could see him considering his words. "When I was a kid, I couldn't wait to grow up so I could do whatever I wanted. I figured I'd eat candy for supper, stay up late, play all day, never do chores. I couldn't understand why adults didn't take advantage of their opportunities."

Evie smiled at him. "For me, it was cake for dinner. And watching all the TV I wanted."

He chuckled. "What happened when you got to be a grown up?"

"Yeah. Cake for dinner isn't very nutritious."

"And none of us can just go on, doing whatever we want, without thinking about the other people our decisions affect."

Evie tasted bitterness. "Jase can, apparently."

James shrugged. "Maybe. We don't know what's in another person's heart, even the ones we're closest to. We only know what they're willing to share."

She thought about that. "It sounds like you don't want to leave the house."

"Whether I want to or not isn't the question."

"But why not? If you don't want to leave, stay. It's your house. It's been our family home for, what? A million years. Why go?"

"Repairs. Snow removal. Ancient plumbing. Uneven floors. Yard work. I don't think I have it in me."

"You've had it in you this long. What's different?"

James looked at the table.

"Dad. Why are you seeing a cardiologist?"

His hand slammed down on the table with shocking force. "Evie, that's none of your business." His lips pressed tight, he pushed himself up from the table.

"Wait, wait!" Evie blurted. "I'm sorry. I just thought..." She scooted around the table and put her arms around her father. "Dad, I'm sorry."

He held himself stiffly, at first, but gradually he softened into her familiar father. He patted her back. "I'm sorry too, Evie. I didn't need to make such a fuss." They pulled apart but he kept his hands on her shoulders. "I think this process was harder on me than I realized. Maybe you girls won't get as caught up in the memories as this old man."

"You're not old," she protested, but her words felt weak. James wasn't old, but it did seem like he'd aged a lot in the last year.

"Seventy on my next birthday," he said briskly. "Now I'm going to go do an old man's activity and watch TV. Coming?"

"No, you go ahead. I might go for a walk. Have the dogs been out?"

"Yes, but they're always happy for another chance."

Lifting the leashes from their hook by the back door, she saw, as if for the first time, a small, framed print on the wall. It was a watercolour painting of an almond tree in bloom, with some Chinese characters and a quote from Lao Tzu in English: A journey of a million miles begins with a single step.

It's all very well to keep telling me to take the next step, Evie thought irritably, but how am I supposed to know what it is? Annoyed, she clicked leashes to collars and they tumbled out the back door.

Her phone pinged as she wandered the sidewalks with the dogs. The text was from Jase. Her stomach hurt when she saw it, but she opened the message anyway.

It was pictures: boxes and boxes, piled in the warehouse part of their building. The dresser from the kitchen. Oh, and her little desk, the lady's desk her mother refinished for her when she went to high school. Her heart hurt to see it dumped on its side by the boxes. And a message: "Pick up by Tuesday or everything goes to the dump."

Quick, hot tears threatened to overflow. *Such a jerk!* she murmured, surprising herself with her vehemence. *Scum. Grr.* She shoved her phone back in her pocket. Angry and sad, she felt the worried feelings wash over her again. *What will I do?*

When Evie returned to the house, James was dozing on the couch, the television on low a few feet away. Deciding not to disturb him and still restless, she climbed two flights to the attic. Late sunset meant the attic wasn't completely dark, but she was happy to see the dim lightbulb flare when she pulled the string.

The stuff had to go somewhere. The first step was down the stairs. Break it down further, and the first step was getting closer to the stairs. Evie threaded her way through boxes, stacking them to the side. Finally she tugged on the big dresser.

It went exactly nowhere, so she got behind it and shoved with her shoulder. There! Movement. Not a lot of movement, but some. She gritted her teeth and pushed some more. Shoving heavy furniture around felt good.

After the dresser was the dining table. That was almost easy, and she carried each of the chairs closer to the stairs. Sweating, she went to the dormer window and pushed. "Open up, dammit!" she growled. She planted her feet and pushed harder and harder. "Open up! Open, open, open! Oh, you make me so mad!"

A final shove sent her onto her butt on the floor, trying to catch her breath. *This is my life, isn't it? Pushing as hard as I can and getting nowhere. I'm so hot. Frig.*

The window was stuck, but at least some of the furniture was ready to move out. That was something. From the fatigue in her muscles, she thought sleep might be possible.

Getting to her feet, she almost tripped over the wooden box. *Oh, the treasure box. I wonder...* She flipped the lid open. In the semidarkness, it was hard to see inside, so she used her hands to locate another fabric bundle. She tucked it under her arm and headed back down the stairs.

Her phone pinged with a text message. Sighing, she paused in the upstairs hallway and pulled it out of her back pocket.

Evie. So sorry to hear you're not handling the festival. I withdrew my application when I heard this. No offence, but I don't want to work with anyone but you. I hope you're well. Ellen.

Jase clearly hadn't wasted any time in making some big announcement. Ellen was a member of a cluster of women performance artists, several of whom Evie had recruited to the festival. Deep in her belly, Evie felt a little shimmer of satisfaction.

Chapter 11

When Evie got up the next morning, fatigue dogged her from another sleepless night, and she felt groundless not knowing what to do next. Beyond that, her shoulders and upper back ached from pushing around old furniture. She sat alone at the kitchen table, a cup of tea steaming in the sunshine. Morning light slanted in through the window, marking the old oak table. *We used to be able to tell time by where the sun fell on this table. I always knew if I was running late for school, at least in the spring. In winter, there was no sun on the table for breakfast.*

Were those the good old days? At thirty-five, she didn't think she should be pining for the good old days. But she felt the absence of her mother acutely. Maybe she even missed being a kid. She's always felt like the odd kid, but at least when you're a kid, somebody tells you what you're supposed to do next.

Maybe the next thing was to look at the new rug she'd liberated from the attic last night. She found both bundles where she'd left them, stashed on top of some boxes in her father's little den. She opened the new bundle first.

Carefully unwrapping the cotton cover, she unrolled a smaller piece, maybe a foot by two feet. This one was a garden, full of unrecognizable flowers. Dirty, too, and worn in places, it looked like something a family had used. The details were delicate, though, and the colours, though faded, must have been something to see at one time. Evie turned it over to see the back side of the stitching, noting the care and precision taken by its maker.

Nice, she thought. But not as nice as this one. Opening the larger bundle, she spread the rug out into the pool of sunshine on the table. Sunlight touched the cobalt sea, scarlet dories, the green foreground. *Somebody took very good care of this. Protected it from too much sun. Wrapped it carefully in a sheet before storing it in that trunk. Nobody's dirty feet ever touched this rug.*

Turning up the lower right corner, she looked again for a signature. Nothing. She wiggled her finger into the gap where the backing was sewn to the front. Gently she pulled, exposing the back side of the design.

All those tiny little bits of fabric, tucked neatly into the folds of burlap. Each one so small, so precise, so perfect. Who did this? She looked again for a signature, anything to tell her who the artist had been.

Fine. Keep your secrets. She turned the rug over again. *I'm over secrets now anyway.* Pushing the rug aside, she picked up her cup. She kept stealing glances at the rug though, and finally she rewrapped them both, parking them on a chair. *Later. I'll look at you later. Maybe.*

She sagged at the table, resting her head on one hand. Absently she pushed the doily in the center of the table back and forth with her finger, rattling the lobster-shaped salt and pepper shakers in the middle. She gazed at the dust motes floating in the column of sunlight in the room.

Her reverie was interrupted by footsteps and the kitchen door opening. A burst of cool air came in, followed by James, who was closely followed by Mallow and Custard.

"Morning, Evie," he said, hanging up jangling leashes amid a swirl of canine energy. Both dogs offered their greetings too, in the form of sniffs and licks of her hands. Then they returned to stand watch over James as he shucked his boots and headed for the dog bowls.

"Single-minded, aren't they?" she observed.

"What? Oh, these two." James smiled. "Well, they have a routine, you know. Walk, eat, nap. Keeps things organized."

Feeling flat and lifeless, Evie watched her father measure out kibble, refresh water bowls. Finally he poured himself a cup of tea. He sat across from her at the table and she gazed mutely at him.

"It's not a bad thing to have a schedule," James said mildly. "Helps you get through that period of disorganization."

She wrinkled her brow. "Disorganization?"

He nodded. "When things change suddenly. Like after your mother died. We'd organized ourselves around her treatment for so long, when she was gone, there was just nothing. Nothing to do. No appointments, no phone calls, no nothing."

"Mmm. I remember."

"You girls went home to your lives, but me, well, there was nothing."

Evie objected. "But Dorie was here."

"Yes. She was in her own nothing. She'd been helping out for so long by then that both of us landed in a place of nothing. She handled it better."

"Really? I thought you handled things fine." Evie was puzzled. "I mean, grief, but that's expected."

"Grief, depression, nights that lasted months. The dogs helped, because they require certain things. You have to walk them, feed them, hang out with them. These big lugs gave me the start of a schedule. Even though I didn't want to do anything, I had to follow the schedule. It gave me a reason to get up."

"Hmmm." Evie sipped her tea. She wasn't sure she wanted to know this much about her father's suffering. Besides, it reminded her of how she felt when Mum died. That was like losing part of your body, kind of. She remembered that black hole of devastation. Except back then she got to go home to Jase, curl herself around him in the loft bedroom, just let the reality of her loss float away. In the daytime, she could work. That was when she first started finding grants for Jase's projects. With a start, she realized her mother's death had fuelled her ex-boyfriend's career. At least to the degree that she, Evie, had promoted it. *So weird. I never realized that before. I escaped my grief by throwing myself into building his business. That's just messed up.*

"I have absolutely no idea what to do next," she said.

"I know," he said comfortingly. "But you will. Time, Evie. It makes a difference."

"No doubt," she said heavily. "I will help with the house. I've started, up in the attic, but it's like my brain isn't working. I can't imagine how to move ahead in my life."

"You could think about a schedule," James said. "Simple. Basic. Like the dogs. Eat, sleep, walk, play."

She groaned but then softened into a little smile. "Will you give me treats?"

At the word, Custard scrabbled to his feet. Evie glared at him. "No, not you. Me!" The dog lay back down on the tile.

"I think you can figure out what the next small thing is, can't you?" James encouraged. "Just do the next right thing, and let the future take care of itself."

"Like Mum always said? One foot in front of the other?"

"It works. Just pick the right step."

"The next right step is, like, washing my cup?"

He shrugged. "If that's what looks next, do it. That's how I'm trying to figure stuff out too, you know." He got up, patted her shoulder, and left the kitchen. Mallow and Custard rose heavily behind him and clicked out as well.

Alone in the kitchen, Evie looked at the sunlight tracing a path on the table. It felt like time to do something. Too bad the sunlight didn't suggest what. She glanced over at the bundled rugs and sighed. *You're not going to tell me, either. I'm going to have to figure this out for myself.*

While Evie rinsed her cup at the sink, she noticed the layer of greasy dust on the backsplash. The next right thing, she thought, and found rags, vinegar, and dish soap. Filling the sink, she started scrubbing the wall and the old countertop. That done, she washed the cabinet doors. Opening the cabinet, she unloaded the contents onto the old oak table, wincing as her sore shoulders reached and lifted. Once she'd emptied the cupboard, she cleaned the inside.

The shelves were lined with paper. Probably put here by Mum. A mixture of longing and distaste hit her. How long has it been since anyone had actually cleaned here? Probably before Mum got sick. Dorie probably never considered cleaning out a cabinet.

The attic would wait. She needed some additional muscle up there anyway. She had plenty to do elsewhere in the house.

She eyed the clean cupboards and piles of dishes on the table with some satisfaction. She could box up some of those items, but her body was calling for fuel. Break time.

Wiping her hands on her jeans, she emptied the sink of wash water. She set the kettle to boil and looked for ground coffee and a filter, poured milk into a small pot, and dropped bread in the toaster. Seeing the living room empty of father and dogs, she put on one of her mother's old favorite albums. A CD, though Agnes had often told of listening for hours to the original vinyl. The familiar music mixed with the fragrance of toast and coffee, and Evie felt strangely energized.

With the table full of dishes and no place to sit, Evie took her toast and coffee to the back porch. Shrugging uncomfortably, she returned to the kitchen for an ice pack for her shoulders. It was still morning according to the sun, and the porch was in full light. The sounds of Santana's sultry guitar came through the open window as Evie settled onto the old willow chair.

A few late daffodils bloomed near the porch step. She wondered if her mother had planted them but knew it could have been any of the ancestors. *Mum came to this house as an adult, but Dad grew up here. How did Mum live with her mother-in-law?* Then, later, Agnes had brought her own mother to live here, after Nana died. *Always family, family everywhere. Everywhere you looked in this house too. Mum had a story, and it wasn't even her family home. Women are the story-keepers.*

Drinking the last of her coffee, Evie pulled her phone from her pocket. Silence from Jase. She narrowed her eyes. *I'm not going there.* She looked through earlier messages. *Oh, right, that Stephen guy. I don't have the juice to talk to anyone right now. But I think I can text.* She tapped for a moment.

Before she had a chance to gather her dishes and get up, there was a reply.

Stephen: Leonard wants to offer some of your paintings on consignment. Can you come into the gallery to discuss?

Paintings? What paintings? She had no recent work. Maybe ten years ago, she would have had paintings. But now... She could hardly remember the last time she picked up a brush. *Has it really been that long? What else did I give up to be with Jase?* She gulped hard and shoved her phone into her back pocket. That conversation could wait too.

Jaw held firmly, Evie took her dishes to the kitchen. Then she found some boxes in the shed. The next right step, she decided, was putting crockery into cardboard. Back in the kitchen, she picked up an ancient china soup tureen and looked at it helplessly.

That soup tureen.

She could hear her grandmother Sarah talking about cream of fiddlehead soup, served in this very tureen. It was like watching a video in her head. "You should go out there and pick some right now, Aggie," she said. "Soon it's going to be too warm, and you'll miss the season."

Evie's mum protested. "Mama, you don't even like the things. You always said they were nasty."

"Well, they are. But we've got Auntie Agatha's tureen. She always made cream of fiddlehead soup."

Oh, my goodness. No wonder Dad couldn't get through the shed if he had to deal with this kind of thing. Maybe she could just shake it off—every item didn't need to be a whole drama. With a deep breath, she settled the soup tureen into the cardboard box.

It might be easier to decide what could stay rather than what had to go. She picked out plates, bowls, cups, everyday dishes that she knew were in regular rotation, and slid them back in their places in the clean cabinets. *Best not to move anything from the usual place, or Dad will have my head.* Well, not really. But why make it difficult?

Once she put away the essentials, the nonessential nature of other things became clearer. She piled them in the boxes, closed them up, and set them on the back porch. The sisters would have to look before any final decisions were made. Dad too, of course, though Evie was uncertain he'd be able to let anything leave the house.

Returning to the kitchen, she opened the tidy cabinets to admire her work. Not too bad. She flicked the doors shut and refilled her coffee. Idly, she pulled open doors to the lower cabinets at the far end of the kitchen and recoiled. *What a disaster!*

She sat on the floor, coffee at her side, and looked into the deep corner cabinet farthest from the sink. This was where everything that didn't have a place went to die, she thought with some bitterness. *I bet Dorie just shoved things in here instead of trying to find them a place.*

Plastic containers, old grocery bags, battered cake tins, and a peculiarly peeling nonstick Bundt pan were visible. *Yeah, I'm not touching that.* At least not today. When she leaned in to shut the door, something deep inside caught her eye. She shoved aside old yogurt containers and...was that a roll of Christmas wrap? *I think I'll regret this.* Reaching, she touched something else that was paper and pulled it out.

Her mother's cookbook. Who tossed that in like it didn't matter? Affronted, she shoved everything else back in and slammed the door on the tumbling Tupperware. She only had eyes for the tattered book in her hands. Taking it to the now cleared table, she brushed off the dust and opened the front cover.

The book had seen some use. Splatters and pencilled notes covered many pages, and stray papers had been shoved in without apparent plan. Paging through, she recognized her mother's handwriting, but she saw notes in other hands, as well. Maybe this book had been her grandmother's, too, or even Aunt Agatha's. A scrap of paper fell to the floor.

Evie retrieved it. Predictably, it was a recipe, handwritten, but including a variety of notes, with dates and commentary. Mum's toffee pudding. Really?

Toffee pudding. Now that could soothe a broken heart. Evie looked more closely. What's the next right thing to do? Well, when a vintage recipe of your mother's practically drops into your lap, you should probably take note. She scrutinized the ingredients. Maybe a trip to the grocery store was the next right step.

Cradling the ancient cookbook in both hands, she set it reverently on the sideboard. *Mum's cookbook. There's a lot of family history in there. Other people might have family Bibles but, in this house, the cookbook holds the memories. Including toffee pudding. Yum.*

She scribbled ingredients on a scrap of paper and then checked the refrigerator. The house was not well stocked for a man alone, less so for two people. Her list lengthened, and she realized she'd be taking the car to the market, so she wandered the house to check on dog food and cleaning supplies too.

She'd never seen supplies get this low. Maybe Dad really wasn't keeping up. At least she could help her father.

Driving down Water Street past the new gallery, she saw Stephen sitting on a bench outside in the sun. She pulled over and parked.

"Hey," she greeted, pushing her sunglasses to her head.

"Hey yourself," came from behind dark glasses. He was slouched back on the bench, face full in the sun. "Have a seat," he invited without moving.

Evie thought of her mission. "No, I'm on my way somewhere. But you wanted me to drop by."

He barely nodded. "That's right. I did and I do. Have a seat."

Something about his entirely relaxed body was inviting. Were his eyes closed under those glasses? She couldn't tell. But she sat down anyway.

The bench was warm under her. After a moment, she slid down so that she, too, faced the sun, glasses back in place. She let out a deep sigh.

"Pretty nice, huh?" His voice was as warm as the sun.

"Mmm hmm."

They sat companionably soaking in the rays.

"Is this why you wanted me to stop by?" Evie's voice was slow.

"Well, no, but this is pretty good, isn't it?"

"Mmm, very nice. I love the sun on my face."

"This southern guy needs to grab the heat whenever it's available," Stephen murmured. "I think I've been cold for months."

"This is pretty darn warm for early June," Evie agreed. "It won't last. We've had blizzards this time of year."

"Ouch! Don't even say that." He groaned. "Let me just enjoy this moment, the way the world is supposed to be for humans."

Evie snickered. "You must have really needed this sunshine if spring in New Brunswick is that hard on you."

He stretched and sat up. "Well, yeah, I really needed it. I got here in March, so I know about spring snow and all that. I don't whine a lot when it's cold. But I refuse to waste a warm day in front of the computer." Turning to her, he slipped off his glasses. "Hello, Evie."

"Hi, Stephen," she said without moving. "You've convinced me. It's really nice to just sit right here." Poor sleep, an emotional rollercoaster, and a night and morning of exertion combined to make the rest and warmth feel extra good. Or maybe that was the company? From her somnolent pose, she murmured, "You sent me a text. About something."

"I did. I want you to come in and meet Leonard. When I told him I met you, he had some brilliant thoughts to share."

"You mentioned paintings."

"Right. He's interested in taking some of yours on consignment."

"Yeah, about that. I don't have anything." Her shoulders tensed up, but then she allowed the warmth of the sun to soften them.

"But you could, right?"

She paused. "I guess so. I haven't been doing a lot of painting." Any painting would be more precise. "Right now, I'm helping my father clear out the house."

"Well, maybe it's not a good time for you then," Stephen said. "I just thought you might like to get in on his idea of featuring local artists."

Despite herself, her mind started flowing. "He wants to feature local artists? Well, maybe I could paint." It might fill up the time she wasn't sleeping, because even she couldn't move furniture all night long.

"I realize I might be overstepping here. I just assumed, and maybe that was wrong."

"No, no, that's okay. I'm always interested in a little extra work." Evie sat up. "Turns out, I could use some more work." Any work, apparently, but painting hadn't been on the list of possibilities.

Stephen smiled. "Come on in then. He's in the office."

Evie gave a momentary thought to her appearance. She probably had cobwebs in her hair. It was one thing talking to Stephen, who was just a regular colleague, but a potential employer might care how she looked. It can't be helped. *What you see is what you get, at least right now.* She followed Stephen through the gallery.

"Leonard, here's Evelyn. Evie."

Leonard was short, dark, bearded, and wore black-framed glasses. He came around the side of the desk with his hand outstretched. "Evie."

She reached back. "Hi. Evelyn Madison." His grip was quick, assured.

"Hi, Evelyn Madison," he said. "Leonard Fishburne. Steve told me you're curating the Peninsula Festival."

Gut-punched, Evie tried to respond. "Oh, uh..."

Leonard kept on talking. "You're probably too busy to help me out then, but I figured I'd ask."

"Please, ask," Evie said. "What do you have in mind?"

Leonard smiled. "Well, I'm trying to get a business going here. Seems like in Stella Mare it's important to be a known quantity."

"I guess so. It's not like a big city where everyone is from elsewhere."

"I notice that everyone wants to know who your people are." Leonard's smile looked a little strained.

"I guess that's true," Evie admitted. "I never thought about it being hard to find a place here, though."

Stephen chuckled. "That's because..."

"I know, you told me." Evie smiled at him. "Because I'm embedded in the place, so I can't see the patterns clearly. But you do."

"Well, not yet."

Leonard cleared his throat and Evie returned her gaze to him. "I'm here for the duration, but everyone expects me to disappear as soon as we have a big winter or a bad tourist season. It's important for the village to see the gallery as a permanent fixture, a place that celebrates local talent. You can help with that."

"It makes sense, but I don't see what I have to do with it." Or why I should help you, she thought uncharitably.

"You're a local celebrity, right, so I thought maybe you'd be interested in doing some teaching for us? We're trying to offer programming to bring the residents in, so the gallery isn't completely reliant on the summer folk. Not a big thing, but maybe painting classes or a workshop on whatever your art interests are? Steve here is going to do a couple of talks about carving and carvers. What do you think? Want to help us out?"

Evie squinted. "Watercolour classes?"

Leonard looked abashed. "Well, sure. I don't even know if you still paint. Cassie told me you're quite an artist."

"Cassie? Oh, Cassandra. The girl at the Sunshine."

"Leonard likes nicknames," Stephen offered.

She nodded. "Well, I used to paint watercolours."

"Do you have a portfolio? Maybe we could take some on consignment." Leonard's eyes glinted. Stephen gave her an encouraging nod.

"I've never really sold any of my work," Evie admitted. "Well, except I sold small ones at a kiosk run by my mother's friend back when I was in high school. Boats, gulls, that sort of thing."

"Those sound marketable," Leonard said agreeably.

"And boring," Stephen put in.

Leonard glared. "Are you trying to help here?"

Stephen kept his gaze on Evie. "What would you love to paint? If you had time and space and freedom?"

Evie wasn't sure. "I haven't thought about that." *At least not in the last twelve years*. She looked back at Leonard. "I can probably make you some paintings, but I never taught anyone anything."

He shrugged. "It would be great if you could consider it. Steve said you were just visiting, but you're originally local, so I hoped we could connect."

"Yeah, we probably can," she agreed slowly. "A lot of things are changing for me. I'm not really sure of anything right now."

"I don't want to pressure you," Leonard said, "but I'm trying to put together a calendar of activities for June and July. How soon can you let me know?"

Work is work, she thought suddenly. *What am I waiting for? Nothing is going to change unless I change it.* Her fingers suddenly tingled as she thought about painting.

"Let me mess around with some paint and get back to you. I haven't painted in a long time, and you have no idea what I can do."

"That's fair. Are you sure you don't even have digital images of your work?"

She shook her head. "I was prolific at one time," she said wryly. "I'm out of practice."

Stephen was watching her face. She looked away then, at Leonard. "I don't expect you to take my paintings without seeing something first. But as far as teaching goes, if you don't have any other requirement than being local, well, maybe I could teach a class."

Leonard clapped his hands. "Oh, that's wonderful!"

"A one-time thing. A very small class. Of children."

The men both gazed at her, Leonard grinning. Stephen's forehead was wrinkled.

"Is that okay?"

"Better than okay," Leonard responded. "Do you know any other artists who might like to be part of a collaborative program?"

She shook her head. "I only grew up here. I've been away for my whole adult life." Sudden exhaustion propelled her to the door. "It was nice to meet you, but I've got to get going."

"I'll walk you out," Stephen offered.

He opened the gallery door for her. As she stepped outside, she took a big breath. He followed.

"Are you okay?" he asked.

"What? Oh, yes," she said absently.

"Leonard can be intense when he wants something."

"No, he was okay," she said. "I'm tired, but I'm also a little excited about painting, actually."

He finally smiled. "Good."

The sun still shone warmly on the street, and Evie looked longingly at the bench where she'd been so relaxed. Maybe she could come back another day.

"My errands are calling me," she told Stephen. "Thanks for suggesting this to Leonard. I, uh, I'm going to be spending more time in Stella Mare than I thought, so this could work out."

He raised his eyebrows. "I'm glad you'll be around. My mama wouldn't approve of me asking personal questions of a lady, so just let me say that."

A wave of gratitude washed over Evie. No explanation was required. "Thanks."

"Maybe you'll indulge me sometime with a visit. I'm interested in hearing all the old stories."

"Well, you probably don't want me for that. My father, now, he'd have some stories. Or my sister's boyfriend's grandmother."

She could see him puzzling that one out. "Never mind. I just mean the older folks who've been here their whole lives, and whose families are from here. That's where you find the stories."

"Maybe you could introduce me."

"Maybe I could. But right now, I have to go."

"Thank you, Evie. Enjoy your afternoon."

She gave Stephen a quick wave, then she headed for the car. Well, that was a good visit. She left with a job, even if it is a little bitty one, and a good reason to paint. The next right step had appeared again.

And Stephen is glad I'm here. He might be the only one, but at least he's one.

"That was great," Leonard said when Stephen returned to the office. "She's lovely, and maybe she'll improve my local credibility."

Stephen shook his head. "Incorrigible. Are you always looking out for Leonard? Maybe you're doing her some good too, you know."

"Well, of course," Leonard agreed. "It only works if it works for both of us. In this case, maybe for all of us."

"Are you talking about me?" he asked.

"You're the one who's interested in the young lady," Leonard said, clipping his words. "She's not my type."

"I'd claim that my interest is only professional, but you'd give me grief anyway. You know, you are a pain in the neck sometimes," Stephen said.

His friend grinned. "Yeah, but you love me anyway. Besides, this way she'll be around. You get to spend time without looking like an old fool chasing a local woman, and everyone benefits."

"You're probably unredeemable."

"Probably," Leonard said with a satisfied smile.

Stephen took his laptop into the main gallery space, partly because it was his time in the gallery and partly to escape that smirk.

A flurry of emails had arrived from the university. Scrolling from the latest, he scanned the entire thread. It went from bad news to worse.

He sent a text message to Khalil Salah, his department chair, and his phone rang immediately. Looking around the blessedly empty gallery, he popped in earbuds to take the call.

"I hope you're enjoying your time away," Khalil said, voice tight. "Up there with the moose and polar bears."

Stephen chuckled. "And blizzards every day. Canadian stereotypes aside, it has been a good trip already. I've been trying to avoid all the drama back home, but what I read this morning sounds serious."

"It is serious," Khalil said. "I'm glad you called. Can we talk off the record?"

"Wait, what do you mean?"

"I mean like friends, not like I'm your department chair."

"Oh." Stephen leaned back in his chair. "It's like that."

There was silence.

"So yes, off the record. Unofficially. What do I need to know?"

On the other end of the line, Stephen heard a door closing. "Just keeping things between us," Khalil said. "Big ears everywhere. Everyone's running a little bit scared."

"Scared of what? The university boogeyman?"

"In a way. Every university's boogeyman. Financial disaster. I know you're aware of the current financial crisis."

"Yes, everyone knows. We all agreed to a pay cut last year."

"It's worse than anyone thought. As I told you, the police were investigating."

"That's what I heard."

Khalil sighed. "We don't know for sure if the university will survive, but the first line of defense is the restructuring. No announcements have been made, but I know some of what's likely coming."

"Yes?"

"Restructuring as in collapsing programs with low enrolment into other programs, and outright cutting the smallest ones."

"You mean like mine."

Khalil sighed heavily. "It's certainly on the table, Stephen. I'm advocating as hard as I can to take another route, but I am not the decision-maker here."

"So what would happen then? The Art and Folklore program closes and Jessica and I go to Art? Or anthro? Or history?"

Silence again. Stephen's stomach twisted. Then Khalil said, "Faculty positions will be cut along with their programs."

"You're cutting my program and my job?"

"No, Stephen. I'm not doing any of this. Please remember that it is rumour at this point."

His head was spinning. "Off the record."

"Off the record. It might not happen."

"But it might."

"Yes. That's true."

Stephen sighed. "When will we know?"

"That's another problem. Nobody seems to have a good idea. The place is full of rumours and anxiety. It's not nice here right now. You're way better off with blizzards and polar bears."

Stephen was unamused. "I'm here and I'm funded through next spring. That doesn't change, right?"

"That doesn't change. You're on sabbatical. We just don't know what you'll come back to."

"Who else knows? Have you talked to Jessica?"

"Only like this. On the QT. It's probably better for me if you two don't discuss this elsewhere."

"Yeah, yeah, I understand that. I think I appreciate having a heads-up, but right now it's hard to know what to think."

"I'm sorry about all of this, Stephen. It would never happen if I had anything to do with it."

"Well, will you keep me looped in where I need to be?" Stephen hoped his emotion wasn't audible.

"I will. Do some good work up there, hear?"

Stephen's chest remained tight as he clicked off the phone. No program to work in, no job to support his work. No students. No office in a big brick building under old sweetgum trees. No colleagues to share coffee and criticism of each other's work.

It was too much to think about. The jangle of the bell on the gallery door brought him back to the present. Gratefully he got up to greet visitors.

Chapter 12

Evie woke up at a ridiculous hour, with the sun just creeping over the horizon. Melatonin worked for getting to sleep. It was less helpful for staying asleep. She glared at her clock. Before she let the worries creep in, she tossed on her clothes and headed quietly for the kitchen.

Custard and Mallow barely reacted when she walked past their sun porch. It's even too early for the dogs, she thought bitterly. *How my internal clock has failed me.*

She set the kettle to boil and then turned on the oven to preheat, proofed yeast, and tossed ingredients in a bowl. *If I have to be awake, I can be productive.*

By the time James came down at seven a.m., bread was rising in the pan and blueberry muffins sat warm and inviting on a plate. There was a bowl of cut-up fruit and a little vase of dandelions she'd picked from the yard. The dogs had been walked, fed, and were having their morning nap. *Earning my keep.*

"Good morning," she chirped brightly.

"What's going on?" James asked, looking around the kitchen. "Pretty industrious for so early."

"I guess so," she agreed. "Better than feeling sorry for myself."

"Well, almost anything is better than that. Mmm, good muffins."

"Thanks. Mum's recipe. I found her old book, stuffed with loose papers. Down there in the cupboard from hell." She pointed.

"Oh, that one. I always wondered where Dorie put stuff. Maybe that was her secret place to stuff things."

"It's pretty bad. I didn't have the energy to really tackle it yesterday, but I'll clear it out today."

James gave her a look. "You don't have to do it all, Evie. You have sisters. Your aunt Corinne said she'd help."

"I'm not doing it all. I'm supposed to be helping you do it."

"Yeah, but as we established, I'm not very effective." James looked a bit misty. "Every darn thing has a story."

"About that," Evie started. "I met someone who wants to learn more about Stella Mare. He's an art historian from North Carolina."

"North Carolina. Really. Coming up here?"

"I know, right? Sounds peculiar to me too. He's really nice and he wants to talk to some people about the village. Old stories. Plus he's looking for fishermen who make wood carvings."

"He won't have any trouble. Most folks here like to talk."

"I've noticed," Evie agreed. In the quiet, a big dog padded to the kitchen to slurp at his water bowl. Then Evie continued. "His friend owns that new gallery. Leonard Fishburne. He offered me, well, I guess some work. To teach classes or give workshops, or something. He's trying to get connected in town."

"Oh, yeah? Work is already coming your way. That's not bad."

She sighed. "I don't know how to teach anything."

"Nobody knows how to do anything until they try it," James said a little sharply. "Don't write it off without some thought."

"Okay. He also might take some paintings on consignment. I think he wants tourist stuff, but it's kind of a neat idea to think about painting again."

"Good for you," James said. "Been a while, hasn't it?"

Evie looked down. "It's kind of embarrassing. I don't think I realized that I was letting go of things that were important to me."

James gestured to the framed painting over the sideboard. "That's been there for a long time. So long you probably don't even notice it. But I notice it, every single day. I look up at those cliffs and I remember you painted them for our anniversary."

Evie looked at the painting in question. "You know, you're right about never even seeing it. I was trying to think about where I might have some old pieces to show Leonard and that one didn't even occur to me." Her gaze sharpened. "It's not too bad, really."

"It's great and you know it," James said.

"Dad, you're my father. It's not great, but it's pretty good and I know more now."

"Are you planning to make some things for the gallery then?"

"Yeah, seems like it would be foolish not to. It just reminds me of when I was a kid, and Gillian sold my little boats and lighthouses at her kiosk for pocket money." She sighed.

"Not where you wanted to be, huh?" Her father looked sympathetic. "Good for you to take initiative though."

"I guess. It won't hurt to have a few bucks coming in, and it doesn't tie me down here permanently." She caught a flash of something in his eyes. "Sorry, Dad. Not like this isn't great, but I want to keep my options..."

"I know. Keep your options open."

She nodded. That sounded good. She knew, though, what she meant was in case Jase realized he was wrong, but she knew better than to say it out loud. Her stomach suddenly upset, she pushed her muffin away.

"Okay, time for my next right step," she said brightly, looking around the kitchen. "What do you think that should be?"

He shook his head. "You're going to wear me out. I'm heading out for my morning walk. See you in an hour."

"Okay. Have a good one." She bid him farewell, popped the bread into the oven, and opened up the cabinet from hell.

By early afternoon, the day already felt very long. Tired as she was from her early morning, baking bread, and clearing clutter, she knew she couldn't stop yet.

In order to paint, she needed supplies. Getting art supplies was the next right step, but the closest art supply store was in St. Stephen, and she was afraid of running into Jase. Irrationally afraid, but scared nevertheless.

Her stuff was there in St. Stephen too, waiting for her. She thought of the pictures of her stuff dumped on the warehouse floor. It was there and she was here.

It seemed an unsolvable dilemma until Chad called to see if she needed anything moved. Maybe he was prompted by Dorie, but it didn't matter. He offered himself and his truck.

"You have no idea how helpful this is," she said. "I've got a couple of pieces of antique furniture ready to go to St. Stephen, and, actually, I need to get my stuff from there too." Her throat felt thick. Face hot with humiliation, she waited for Chad's response.

"No problem. I've got the day, and my friend is here to help out. At least get those pieces from the attic." Chad's calm, uncomplicated voice brought her comfort. At least he wasn't going to focus on her humiliating circumstances.

He backed in his big truck, and he and the friend he introduced her to, Declan Kelly, carried the two heavy pieces of furniture down from the attic and piled them in the back while Evie watched, tense.

"That wasn't too bad," Declan said, wiping his hands on his shorts. "Hey, Evie, this is some fine furniture."

She brightened. "You want it? You could save us a trip to St. Stephen."

He grinned. "Can't take it on my bike. Next time maybe." He high-fived Chad, waved to Evie, then pedalled away.

"He's a nice guy," Evie observed.

Chad, tying furniture into the truck, grunted assent. He jumped down. "Yep. I met him mountain biking. He's a teacher. Girlfriend's got a nice dog."

"Teacher? Why was he free today?"

"Exams, I guess. Almost summer."

"I guess so." She was gazing off into the distance.

"Evie? Ready?"

She shrugged. "Probably not, but I have to do it. Let's go."

Evie looked out the truck window along the way. Chad was easy to be with. He didn't talk too much, and he didn't expect her to entertain him. He always said what he meant. Evie wasn't even uncomfortable telling him she didn't want to go to St. Stephen alone. Chad didn't judge.

"It's really nice that you don't mind us taking advantage of you," she said diffidently.

He smiled at her and then turned back to his driving. "A truck and a strong back come in handy. I like helping family."

"I appreciate this a lot. I just don't want to run into, well, anyone."

"Get in, get out. Understood."

"I need to get some art supplies too. Maybe we can hit that store before we get my stuff at the warehouse."

"You're the boss."

She sighed. *Maybe I can make him some cookies. Heaven knows Dorie doesn't bake. Now to get this over with.*

Furniture dropped at the antiques mall, art supplies onboard, they headed to the warehouse where Evie and Jase had lived for years in a loft.

She was grateful it was a quiet afternoon, nobody was around the warehouse, and Jase's car was not visible anywhere. Maybe they could just get the stuff, get out, and get back to Stella Mare where she could settle into invisibility. Chad backed the truck up while Evie rapped on the door and then let herself in. Looking around, she located her boxes immediately: they were close to the truck bay doors. With both hands, she gave the door a mighty shove. Daylight flooded the space as the door rose.

Chad came in. "Is this it?"

Nodding, she said, "Yeah. These boxes and that little table over there. The dresser. And my desk. It's not a lot, is it?" Not a lot to show for a twelve-year investment, she thought bitterly. She picked up a box and headed for the truck.

They worked together to move the furniture. Chad used a big moving blanket to cover them, and he did some things with bungee cords. "Should be secure," he noted. "Let's get the rest of the boxes in."

"Yeah." As they finished up clearing the downstairs, she pulled her key out of her pocket. "Guess I need to leave this upstairs," she said slowly.

"Whatever you think," Chad said. "I'll get things secured in the truck, and you do what you need to do."

"Okay."

Jase appeared to be out and everything seemed quiet on this slow afternoon, but Evie's heart still pounded while she climbed the stairs to their living space and unlocked the big security door. Pushing aside the barn door, she peered in. Then she stepped quietly across the threshold.

The apartment was quiet and felt empty. A lot was missing, bare walls where paintings had hung, the empty space for her little desk, and the kitchen seemed particularly bare. She dropped her key ring on the kitchen counter, took a picture of it, and sent it to Jase. Pausing a moment, she deleted him from her contacts. Then she headed back down the stairs.

Over.

Done.

Chad had closed the big garage door, so she slipped through the regular door, clicking the lock in the doorknob, and pulled it tight behind her. She gave the building a last look and walked a little unsteadily toward the truck. Clambering into the cab, she sank into the seat. Last time here, she thought. Last time.

Chad climbed in. "All okay?"

"Yeah, I guess. Good enough."

"Ice cream?"

"What? Did you say ice cream?" She looked at him curiously.

"Sure. Ice cream always makes me feel better. This is kind of crap, you know. Maybe ice cream would help."

She smiled. "It absolutely is crap. And ice cream sounds like a good idea."

"I think they have moose tracks at the Creamery."

"Moose tracks?"

"Oh, yeah, the very best for a crap day. My treat."

She had to smile. "Thanks. You're a great almost brother-in-law. You fit in the family just right."

He reddened. "It's all new to me, but I'm trying."

"You're doing fine. Thanks for all the help and the moral support."

"You're welcome. Now let's find those moose tracks."

By late afternoon, Evie was settled at the kitchen table waiting for her muse to strike. "Action in the absence of inspiration," she murmured to herself, starting to play with colour and water on the page. Soon she was absorbed in her process, aware only of the clock ticking on the sideboard.

She had no idea how much time had passed when she finally put down her brushes and stretched. Wandering to the back door, she looked into the long daylight of the evening in the backyard. Her hand hit the latch and immediately heard the scrabble of dog claws in the living room.

"Yeah, come on, guys. You need a break too," she called. The big dogs stumbled sleepily into the kitchen and then perked up as she opened the door. The three of them, dogs and woman, went outside into the June day. She wandered around the perimeter of the lawn, pulled an occasional weed, and sniffed at the remaining tulips.

The sun, still warm, made Evie sleepy. It had been a short night after all, but part of her was excited to get back to painting. She needed to have something to show Leonard sooner rather than later. Leaving the dogs in the yard, she headed back to the kitchen.

By the time James got home, she had a couple of attempts that she didn't hate.

"Want to see what I've been doing?" she asked him.

"Yes, just a minute," he replied. "Let me get my glasses and I'll take a look." His voice sounded funny, and she gave him a sharp look.

"You okay, Dad?"

"Oh, yeah, yeah," he muttered. "Just need to sit down for a bit."

"Go ahead. I'll put the kettle on and bring them into the living room."

"Okay." He sounded tired. She heard him sit in his big chair, and some dog's toenails clicking across the floor to greet him. Without even looking, Evie knew a dog's head rested on her father's knee, and his hand scratched silky ears. Then she heard James sigh.

Wincing at the sound, she took her time to tidy her equipment and gather what she'd been working on. The kettle boiled and she made tea. Then she carried it in along with her paintings.

"Rough day?" she asked, sitting on the couch.

He sipped at the tea. "No, not really. Just kind of long. This old guy gets tired out easy now."

"You're home now," she said.

He raised his eyebrows. "I had noticed that."

She giggled. "That's me trying to be supportive. Stating the obvious."

"You are supportive," he said. "I didn't think about these dogs all day because I knew you were here for them. That's support. Show me what you've been making."

Evie suddenly felt shy. "Now I remember being six years old and wanting you to like my drawings."

"I'm sure I'll like your drawings," James said stoutly. "You can hand 'em over."

"There's something nice about knowing that somebody will always like your work, no matter how amateur it looks," Evie noted. "But I don't count on you for critical advice."

"And so you shouldn't. I'm your dad and I have a built-in bias."

"I appreciate that." Still, she hesitated to hand the sheets to him. "You know I haven't painted anything at all for about ten years. Maybe more."

"Is it like riding a bicycle?"

"Well, that's not how it seems right now. I feel like I'm starting from scratch."

"Okay. Are you going to let me see or are we going to spend the whole evening talking about it?" He stuck his hand out.

"Yeah, okay." She handed them over, still feeling reluctant.

She watched him take in each of the pages she'd handed over, watched his face as he looked at the images, saw his little smile. When he looked up at her, she held her breath.

"I can see changes across these pages," he noted, "like your skills were waking up. I bet I could put them in chronological order just from this afternoon."

"Really? I know it felt smoother, but I didn't think it was visible. Show me."

"Yes. Look here, and here. See how your brushstrokes were more confident and more precise. I bet this was your last effort, right?" He held up one of the pages.

"Right. It's just a study though, like all of them. Practice."

He looked intently at the page he held. "I've seen this before, haven't I? It's familiar. Something I saw recently." He looked at her. "Well?"

She nodded. "It's that rug I found in the attic. I was trying to recreate the design from memory."

"It's a nice subject. Layered, right? You use the design to make a painting, the rug maker invented the design from real life. Maybe real life."

"That's right. We don't know if the design came from another artist or was original. I don't even know who made that rug actually."

James handed her stack of papers back. "Probably some ancestor. On your mother's side, I guess, because I hadn't seen it before. You could probably find out."

Dubious, Evie said, "I don't know how."

James raised his eyebrows. "You can start by digging through the rest of the attic."

"Right. Oh, by the way, Chad helped me take some furniture into St. Stephen to the antiques center. Small progress but progress." She didn't mention the items she'd brought back with her. Chad had taken them to the barn that housed the dog sanctuary. At least they weren't cluttering up this house.

"The next right thing," he said with a weary smile.

She got up and kissed his cheek. "I'll cook. Dinner in an hour. You look like a nap might be in order."

"Maybe," he said, but his eyes were already closed. She drew the afghan over his lap and went to the kitchen, paintings in hand.

Chapter 13

"Ahoy, the house," sang out Corinne, coming through the kitchen door. Evie was busy at the sink early Sunday.

"Hi, Corinne. Coffee's on," she said, nodding toward the pot.

"Oh, you're bribing us with cinnamon rolls, I see," Corinne said, pouring a cup.

"Whatever it takes," Evie said, pulling a second tray out of the oven.

The door opened again to let in Dorie and the white poodle. A deep woof came from the inner rooms of the house. Dorie called out to Evie and Corinne, and the big dogs converged on the kitchen to greet the newcomers, human and canine.

When the kerfuffle subsided, the women moved to the table with pastries and coffee. "Mm, Evie, you've taken up baking. I'm impressed." Dorie's mouth was full.

"I found Mum's old recipes," Evie said. "In that cupboard where you apparently pitched everything without a home for three years." She nodded toward the now-tidy cabinet.

"Probably more like five years," Dorie said comfortably. "Good for us though. You're the right one to have the recipes. Nobody else in the family cares much about cooking."

"Right now it's keeping my mind occupied," she admitted. "I don't know if Dad told you, Corinne, but right now I'm mostly without a job or a home."

"What?" Corinne said, "I thought you had this grant thing figure out."

"Yeah," she said slowly, "I have learned to write a decent proposal apparently. A funding-worthy proposal. Unfortunately, nobody reminded me to put my own name on my work."

"Yeah, Corinne, listen to this," Dorie said. "That miserable jerk stole Evie's grant."

"He's not a..." Evie started automatically and then stopped. Well, maybe he was. "He didn't have to steal it. It's my fault. That big grant, all the grants, they all look like Jase wrote the proposals. Jase got the funding, Jase did the follow-up reporting, Jase did it all. Everything is in Jase's name."

"Oh, Evie, no," Corinne protested.

"Oh, yes," Evie said bitterly. "I thought I was supporting my partner. Mostly I was shooting myself in the foot. The only evidence that I did anything at all comes from a small stipend I took as Jase's assistant on a summer grant a couple of years ago. Everything else we just ran through his business, under his name."

"This sounds like a cautionary tale from the 1970s," Corinne said. "Women used to be required to take their husband's names. Married women couldn't sign contracts or hold property without their husbands."

"This isn't the 1970s," Dorie objected. "Can this really happen today?"

Evie shrugged. "It happened. It was my mistake, and you can believe I'll never make one like that again. He is completely within his rights to cut me out of the Peninsula Festival. But he's going to have a hard time making that project happen."

"Good," Dorie said, "I hope he's a big public failure." She tucked into a second cinnamon roll.

"It's been kind of gratifying that some artists are already pulling out," Evie said. "I know that's mean-spirited."

Dorie's eyes lit up. "You mean they're telling you that they're pulling out? That's a big deal."

Evie grimaced. "I should feel sorry for Jase, but mostly I think he deserves it. Then I feel petty even thinking that. I'm not a very nice person."

"Maybe Jase isn't the great guy we always thought." Corinne was frowning. "He knows you were counting on that income. That's pretty small-minded of him."

"Listen, I don't want to spend my morning bashing Jase. It doesn't help and just reminds me of how crappy I feel. Can we figure out how to tackle the attic? Dad wants to get this stuff cleared out as soon as possible."

As she hoped, they switched gears. "What's the rush? This is a big project," Corinne said.

"Is he really sure about moving?" Dorie asked. "I'm not convinced he wants to go."

"He doesn't want to," she agreed. "But he thinks he has to. And I think he could be right."

A sudden loud beeping and clanging sent them out onto the porch. A huge truck carrying a dumpster was backing into the yard.

"Where do I put it?" a man in a baseball cap shouted to the women. Before Evie could reply, James and the big dogs strode into the yard. He went to the open truck window and began waving his arms.

"Guess Dad's got that under control," Evie said and turned back to the kitchen. When the three returned to the table, she said, "Well, I guess we know what to do with the items that are trash. Are you guys ready? We'll need to figure out what to save and where to put it."

Dorie took a breath. "Sure. Just let me wash these sticky fingers."

"Oh, and by the way, those boxes on the porch? That's kitchen stuff for you to go through."

"Us?" Corinne asked.

"This is a lot of work for us," Dorie commented. "Why do I have to go through boxes you already packed?"

"In case there's anything in there you want," Evie explained patiently. "I'm not thinking for you. I only left the essentials in the cabinets I've cleaned out so far."

"What did you do with your mother's china?" Corinne asked. She started opening cabinet doors. "That china meant a lot to Aggie."

Evie sighed. "Here we go."

Corinne smiled at her. "Really, Evie. It did mean a lot. It was a wedding gift and used even then. Our great-grandmother saved it for her."

"This is how we get so bogged down. Every darn piece of stuff has memories attached. I honestly don't know how we're going to be able to let go of anything." She held her head with both hands. "I might love hearing about Mum's china, but I don't want to take it home with me. Especially now that I don't even have a place to live. Ugh!"

"I don't think we should just impulsively pitch everything though," Dorie objected. "I might like Mum's china someday. Like when Chad and I get married, you know."

Evie shook her head. "The problem is we have to get it out of the house now. Are you prepared to add to whatever Alice has in her house? Then yeah, you take it home with you. Dad can't have it here; it's got to go."

Corinne said, "It's sad to see this happening in our family. I've helped a lot of clients do this: pare down and move out. I never thought we'd have to do it in our family. I guess I figured one of you girls would be in the house."

"You're kidding, right?" Dorie was appalled. "Mum and Dad never thought like that. At least, not that I knew of. They were always telling me to stretch my wings."

"Irritated you to no end as I recall," Evie said with an evil grin.

"Yes, it did," Dorie admitted with a laugh.

"Attic," Evie reminded. "First, I want to show you what I found up there." She unwrapped the burlap bundles and spread the rugs out on the kitchen table.

"Oh, wow," Dorie breathed. "Look at that!"

Corinne shook her head in wonder. "Unbelievable. I wonder how old those are?"

"No idea, at least not yet. There's some papers and stuff in the box where I found them, but I haven't spent a lot of time looking. I just really loved these colours and the way they are made."

"Rag rugs, I think, where women took old scraps of fabric and hooked them through burlap. Every little thing had to be used until it was used up." Corinne fingered the corner of the large rug. "I wonder who made these?"

"You can see this one was used as a rug," Evie pointed out the wear, "But this other one looks like it was preserved like artwork."

"It is art, isn't it?" Dorie asked.

Evie shrugged. "It's art to me. It sure took an artistic eye to see the world like this."

"What are you going to do with them?" Dorie asked. "Thrift store?"

"No way!" Evie surprised herself. "These are not going anywhere."

"Yeah, that's our problem," Dorie said. "Everything has a good reason to stay. But let's get going. What's on the agenda?"

"You're right. Let's head up. You can see what we've got to work with. I've gotten some stuff out, Chad and I delivered some furniture to a consigner, but there is still an unbelievable collection."

They gathered in the upstairs hallway at the bottom of the attic stairs. "I brought up some trash bags and boxes, but honestly, I don't even know how we're going to deal with this."

Corinne said, "I haven't been up here since Dorie was a baby."

"No kidding!" Dorie said. "That's been a little while."

"Until last week, my last time was before high school," Evie admitted, "playing hide and seek and breaking all of the rules by going upstairs."

"Yeah, Mum didn't think it was too safe up here," Dorie agreed. "Are we just delaying, here?" She turned and tromped up the steep steps, sneezing twice. "Dusty," she called back down the stairs.

Evie and Corinne looked at each other, and then started up.

As Dorie noted, except where Evie and Chad had disturbed it, a thick layer of dust coated every surface. Sunshine streamed weakly through the window in the eastern dormer, pushing through layers of grime to illuminate the old wooden floorboards, beams, and thick, rough-hewn uprights. Dorie put a hand on one of the posts.

"This place was built," she said. "Look at this wood: this must be sixteen inches to a side, cut from a single log."

"Hand hewn, looks like," Evie added.

Corinne nodded. "My grandmother used to talk about the history of this house. The man who built it worked as a boatbuilder, back in the day, and back when logs that size were common."

"Wow, what a lot of physical labour," Evie mused, reaching toward a timber. "Hand cut, hand hewn, and I bet they peeled the bark off the tree the same way. Look, there's even some bark still on it."

"Yeah, it's great," Dorie said, "but we're supposed to be looking at the stuff. Did you bring a flashlight?" She was poking around in a dark corner. "Is there a light anywhere?" She found a string hanging from a rafter. "Look, light!"

"Dorie, there's a box here with your name on it," Evie said. "Mum saved stuff. You'll probably want to keep that."

"Oh, you bet," Dorie said. "What's in it?"

Evie shrugged. "I only looked in mine. Old school papers and stuff."

"Hmm. Well, that's going to be more fun than the rest of this stuff. Let's see what else we can move out." Dorie moved toward a corner. Away from the center of the big room, the periphery was dark and full of objects.

With Dorie and Corinne there, Evie was willing to dig deeper than she had been by herself. "Look at all this," Evie said. "Furniture. Look at it all." She pushed into a corner of the attic, drawn by reflected light. A mirror, dark and stained, sat atop a dresser. She tripped over what turned out to be an empty chamber pot and caught herself from falling on the edge of a small wooden table. Chairs were upended under the table, and a small bookcase sported a broken shelf. Everywhere were boxes, boxes, and more boxes. Some had labels but many more were just marked with their original use.

"Lots of oranges up here," Corinne noted.

"Oranges?"

"A joke. Orange boxes. Lots of them. Shall we open these boxes up? How are we going to do this?" Corinne's voice sounded squeezed.

"It's a lot, isn't it?" Evie said.

"A lot. I know you already got some of it out, but honestly, I can't see any extra space," Corinne noted.

"I know," Evie said, looking around. "It's like the stuff expanded to fill in the space we made."

Dorie sighed. The three gathered again in the middle of the attic.

"It is sweltering up here," Dorie said. She went to the dormer and pushed on the window. "I don't even know if it opens."

"Watch out. I landed on my butt trying to open that." Evie looked around. "Oh, here's this." She scrounged a big box fan from the other end of the attic and found an extension cord. "At least we can move some air."

With an expletive, Dorie finally got the window to budge. A small breeze entered the stifling space.

"Between the window and the fan, we won't melt right away," Evie said. "But cleaning out here is a morning job…it's gonna be too hot by afternoon."

"I have no idea how to start," Corinne admitted. The three looked around the attic again.

"One step at a time," Evie said. "Maybe we can each take a corner to start with. Bring things out to the middle and decide what to do with them there."

"Sounds like moving the mess around," Dorie objected. "But I don't have a better idea. So okay."

They picked corners, leaving the one that was most jam-packed for later. Evie felt like an explorer, stepping with her garbage bag into her assigned corner, poking into boxes, and identifying and tossing trash. She was deep into the thicket when Corinne called for assistance.

She and Dorie were trying to haul a wooden box from Corinne's corner into the light.

"Oh, yeah, this," Evie said. "I've already been into this one. But I didn't try to move it."

With a mighty heave, they slid the box along the floorboards to the middle of the room.

"What's this, a treasure chest?" Dorie asked. "Pirate gold?"

"Wouldn't that be great." Evie giggled. "I found those hooked rugs in it. No doubloons."

"I think it's your great-grandmother's trunk," Corinne said seriously. "The one she brought from Cape Breton when she came here after the war."

"Which war?" Evie wondered.

"The First World War. In my mother's family, not the Madisons. You remember your grandmother Sarah, my mother, came to live here with Aggie and James after his mother died."

"Yeah. It was like one grandma left and the other one came to fill in," Dorie said. Evie gave her a sharp look. Defensive, she amended, "I was little, Evie. That's just how it looked to me."

"You weren't wrong about it, even though it was a bigger deal to the grownups than to the kids. When my mother came, she brought stuff, of course, and part of what's in this attic is all of that history too."

"Wait," Evie said. "So we not only have a hundred years of Madison history here, but a hundred years of, what, O'Neill history too?"

"Not only. Kellys, and when you get back to the original owner of this trunk, you're into LeBlanc territory."

"Really? We have a French ancestor?"

"Not French from France but Acadian, from Cape Breton. Didn't you know that?"

"Yeah, I knew. I never thought much about it though. This stuff belongs to them?"

Corinne looked uncertain. "Maybe. My grandmother, Leonie. She and Charles had like seven kids. That's where Aunt Agatha came from. And Aunt Hannah, and your grandmother, of course. I think some of this came from Leonie's family, but who really knows? Nobody took pictures or kept records."

"Listen, you guys, let's just continue with Evie's idea, big stuff first," Dorie said. " There's a lot of junk furniture here."

"Antique," Corinne and Evie said as one. Then they grinned at each other.

"Okay, whatever," Dorie agreed. "Somebody might want that stuff. Let's haul out the furniture, and then we can see what's left."

"Sure," Corinne agreed. Evie shrugged. At least it was a plan.

Together they wrestled more dressers, tables, and a velvet Chesterfield out of the shadows and into the center of the attic. Sweaty, tired, and in need of a break, Evie called it.

"That's a good morning of work, you guys. Let's let this go for now. We've gotten a start."

"Yeah. Chad can come help us get this stuff out of the house," Dorie volunteered. "Getting this furniture down the stairs is going to be a big job."

"He and Declan moved a couple of huge pieces yesterday. That was so helpful," Evie said. "I hope I haven't worn out his willingness."

"Does your boyfriend know you're volunteering him for the heavy lifting?" Corinne asked Dorie.

"No worries there," Dorie assured them. "Chad is great at saying no when he doesn't want to do something."

They trooped downstairs, laughing and talking, to wash off the dust and cobwebs, grab a final pastry, and head out the door. The energy and laughter left with Dorie and Corinne, and Evie slumped at the kitchen table.

What a pile of work they had in front of them. She absently picked up her phone. What was new since they tackled the attic?

The little red flag showed messages. Stomach tight, she clicked to open. Another artist telling her she was missed. She and two colleagues were withdrawing from the festival. The next message was essentially the same.

She sat back in her chair. What could this mean? Jase was going to fall flat on his face, she thought with some satisfaction. He had no friends among these artists apparently. Worse, they didn't trust him professionally.

She tapped return messages to both artists, carefully professional. Then she noted her new location and invited them for a visit.

The next day, Evie's phone blew up with text messages, but they weren't from artists.

Who are these people? She read through four messages, increasingly bemused. Finally she called Dorie.

"Hey."

"Have you been giving out my number?"

"No," Dorie said slowly. "I don't think...oh, wait, is it about hooked rugs?"

"Yeah."

"I was talking to a lady about a dog."

"Imagine."

Dorie snickered. "Yeah. But anyway, somehow, we got talking about the rugs from the attic, and she said her grandmother had some and so I gave her your number. Is that okay?"

"Well, I guess so. I've got messages from four people in town about rugs. All different people."

"I think Corinne knew somebody too. And I told Alice. Maybe you can blame Alice, not just me."

Evie was silent.

"Evie? Maybe it's a good thing. It's not just our family, but others. There's probably a story there, Chad would say."

"There's probably a lot of stories there," she finally agreed. "Okay, mystery explained. Thanks."

"Bye."

She looked more carefully at the messages. Two had pictures attached and the people wanted her to come look at their rugs or take them. She was trying to clear out the house and people wanted her to bring rugs home. Not possible.

But when she looked at them, she softened. Some were lovely, ancient works made by some woman's careworn hands. Oh, fuzzy sheep on a hillside. She swiped for another picture, wondering about technique.

But...what do I care about this? There's no job or home in looking at people's rugs.

True, true. But Evie did care, though she didn't know why. *Maybe why doesn't matter right now. Okay, I'm done for. I've got to see these rugs.* She tapped away at her phone.

Over the next week, Evie collected pictures of rugs and actual rugs from all around Stella Mare. Some people were happy to hand them over, while others wanted to keep their family heirlooms but had also wanted Evie to see them. The den was filling up with various fabric creations.

James knocked on the doorframe one evening when she was taking pictures and adding to her database.

"Quite a collection you've got going," he noted.

"Yeah, I know. Look at this one. Little sheep in the field, the deep green forest, a red barn."

"Any idea where you're going with this?" he asked. "We are trying to clear out the house."

She grimaced. "That has occurred to me. But look at these. They're art, real art."

"Art might belong in a gallery or a museum or something."

"I know. I'll see if I can find some other place to store them. They're just so, so full of..."

"Moths?" he joked. She glared.

"Sorry, Evie," he said. "I know they mean a lot to you. Didn't mean to make fun."

"Yes, you did," she said with a little smile. "No moths. They're just full of history, like they have secrets. You know. Like any antique."

"Even me?" He gave her an arch look.

"Yeah, Dad, even an antique like you. Don't worry, I'll take care of them."

Her phone pinged again, this time with a message from Stephen. He had attached a selfie from the sunny bench in front of the gallery.

I'm sitting in the sun and saving your place. Y'all come over soon, eh? See what I did there? Got my Canadian on.

Smiling, she slipped her phone back in her pocket.

Chapter 14

Evie's spreadsheet where she catalogued house stuff was growing. James looked over her shoulder as she worked on her laptop.

"What's all this?"

"I'm trying to keep track of the stuff we've uncovered. See, I have a list here, plus where we found it, and anything important about it, and a link to a picture file."

"That's a lot of information. What's that last column there? The mostly empty one?"

"That's where each item is going."

"No answers so far, huh?"

"Well, I'm sharing this with the sisters and Corinne as I work on it. I just want to be sure I'm not giving stuff away that somebody wants."

"You've been doing a lot of work."

"I'm not tracking every rag or dish. Just the big stuff."

"Do you think those girls are looking at it? I'd be some surprised."

Evie shrugged. "That's not my problem. I'm sharing the information. Besides, doing a spreadsheet is less work than having everybody mad at me because they don't like what I did."

He laughed. "Good luck with that. Somebody's going to be mad, no matter what you do."

"Yeah, I know. Sisters. But everyone is getting a chance to say yes or no on the big items."

"Helen too?"

"Yeah, but I told her she has to get them moved into storage or something if she wants anything."

He chuckled. "That'll put her off. More coffee?"

She looked up. "Sure. Thanks. Maybe bring those scones back to the table too. It must be snack time."

A truck roared in the driveway. The screen door banged behind Chad and Dorie, and the big dogs galumphed into the kitchen.

"Hey, you guys!" Dorie sang out, scratching big heads. "Coffee for us?"

"Sure," Evie agreed, getting up to pour two more cups.

"What's the occasion?" James asked, leaning back in his chair.

"I'm going to help you with the shed, Dad," Dorie announced. "Or whatever project you're working on here today."

James shrugged. "The shed's a good one. Did you see Evie's spreadsheet? I see you got started in the attic."

"Yes, that's why Chad came. He's going to haul stuff down." Dorie glanced at Evie's screen. "Yes, that's a spreadsheet. Obsess much, Evie?"

Evie glared at Dorie, even as her sister grinned and grabbed a scone from the table.

"Yep, I'm here to move stuff," Chad agreed. "After that, we can help you in the shed, James."

"What did you find up there? Anything besides those pieces?" James asked, gesturing to her files.

"These already found new homes, but the attic, well, it's hard to describe," Evie said. "There's a bunch of stuff, some broken, mostly a mess, but maybe somebody would like to have it. We won't know until we get it into daylight."

"Well, the weather's supposed to be good enough today, so let's do it," James said agreeably.

"Then I'll take pictures, add them to the spreadsheet, and get everyone to claim their treasure."

"Or not," Dorie said darkly.

"Right. We have to find homes for the rest. We did the St. Stephen run once, but we can donate locally too."

"Sounds like progress," James said. "I'm going to get out of your way." He poured more coffee and then headed out the door.

"I think this is a little hard on Dad," Dorie observed.

"Yeah. He wants it done, but it's hard. I don't know how to make it any easier."

Chad stood up. "It probably can't be easier, but we can help by not dragging it out. Ready?"

"Slave driver," Dorie chided, but they headed up to the attic.

Amid a lot of banging and laughing, the three brought out four dressers, two bedsteads, a small desk, a three-legged table, and a bookcase, carrying them down the ladderlike stairs, along the hallway, down the other stairs, through the kitchen, and out into the backyard. Custard and Mallow sniffed each piece as it emerged and then went to flop on the grass under an oak tree.

"Okay, that's probably more than enough for one day," Dorie said. "We're going to have to do something with all of these, so let's stop here."

"That's right," Evie agreed, appraising the furniture. "I'm not sure I recognize any of these. I wonder if Corinne knows anything about them?"

"Corinne doesn't want this mess either."

"You're probably right. I'm checking with everyone, though, so get your bid in now if you want something."

Dorie surveyed the yard. "Looks like a junk pile here. Nothing I want. Except the box with my name on it."

"Well, that's a given. But otherwise, we need to re-home this mess."

Dorie looked over the piles on the lawn. "If I can sell some of this stuff, is that okay with you? Do you think you want any of these?" She gestured to the pile of furniture.

"Are you kidding? If you find someone to buy them, go for it. Whatever is left over, we'll donate."

"Maybe a sale to benefit the dog sanctuary?"

"Whatever you like. But it all has to go somewhere today. There's no rain in the forecast, but can you imagine what Mum would say if she saw this?"

Dorie giggled. "That's not a happy thought. Okay, I'm on it."

Helen and Rett signed off on everything in the yard except the two metal bedsteads. Rett wanted to keep them for the twins, and convinced Dorie to store them at the dog barn until she could get there. Helen said she was relieved that Evie and Dorie were doing all the work.

"Sounds like Helen," Dorie said. "What about Corinne?"

"She says it's hard to let things go, but she knows it's time. She's going to stay away today, but she gave me carte blanche to let it all go." Evie looked up from her phone. "That's probably good, given how she reacted about Mum's china yesterday."

"I wondered if she was going to have trouble," Dorie said. "Okay, sell, donate, trash...let's see what goes in that big dumpster and what we can turn into cash."

It hadn't seemed possible at midday, but by suppertime the yard was cleared. The attic wasn't, of course, but there was a swath of open space up there that hadn't existed yesterday.

Evie fell into bed that night so tired she expected to drop right off. Instead, it was like a video started to play on the inside of her head: Jase and that girl, Jase dumping her stuff down in the warehouse, Jase pushing away the sandwich, all Jase, Jase, Jase.

She pushed aside the duvet and swung her legs to the side. *If I'm not going to sleep, I might as well get up.* She padded down the stairs, stopping by the sun porch to pat Mallow on the head so he wouldn't get up, and then she went to the kitchen. Moonlight played on the old table, barely illuminating the doily and dusty flower vase. The house settled around her.

Somewhere in the night, she heard an owl hoot. She thought of the yard beyond the back door; grass and her mother's flower garden, now overgrown. She imagined walking down the driveway, onto the road and down toward the shore, following the moonlight to where the gulls slept, and the sea shone with phosphorescence. Her eyes closed as she imagined the waves gently touching the shore, over and over. And then Jase. The feeling of his face against her hands. Being wrapped up in his arms, his breath as a metronome to quiet her at night. The image morphed into his angry face, and suddenly, Michelle's long, bare legs were again coming down from the loft.

Evie startled, heart pounding. She was fully awake again. *What am I going to do?* The moonlight on the table faded, and the room went dark, the wind picking up outside. What to do? What on earth would Mum say, Evie thought with desperation. *I wish she were here. I want her. I want Jase. I just don't want to feel this terrible.*

Her body was wracked with sobs. *I sure don't want to wake Dad up with my crying. And Dad. Please be okay, Dad.* Her sobs intensified, but she choked them down. Mopping her face with her sleeve, she drank some water. Still unable to consider returning to her bed, she pulled on her jacket and crocs and headed into the breezy darkness.

This time, instead of imagining a walk, she let her feet take her down the driveway, across the road and down toward the beach side of town. Walking soothed her, kept her from thinking, and when she got to the beach, she walked until she was so tired, she had to sit. She found a driftwood log and perched there. Watching the waves kept thinking at bay too. After a while, the moon returned, pouring light on the bay like a long highway. *I'd like to walk that highway. Where would it take me?* Somewhere other than here. Somewhere else.

She sat until the moon set and the sky lightened ever so little in the east. She could imagine the fishing folk tossing back coffee at the Sunshine Diner and then heading for their boats. It's probably four thirty, she thought. Morning for some. *Maybe I can sleep now.*

She crept into the house and up the stairs without disturbing the dogs. Her bed looked welcoming, at least, so she crawled in and finally slept.

Chapter 15

She heard movement downstairs, rattling and clanging of leashes, a door slam, and then quiet. She stirred, but then sank into the depths again.

Some time later, she heard conversation.

"She's sleeping, Corinne. She's been sleeping all day. But I think she was up all night."

Evie sat up, affronted. *They're talking about me.*

Corinne's response was unintelligible, but James went on. "It's gotta be hard on her. She's lost a lot more than we realized. My little girl hasn't even been making her art."

Evie's eyes pricked.

More unintelligible conversation floated up the stairs, then suddenly she caught the fragrance of frying onions and garlic. Her stomach grumbled. *My traitor stomach! Can't I just be a lost, lonely, brokenhearted person without my stomach telling me I need to eat?*

"Hey," she said, coming down the stairs into the kitchen. James looked over his shoulder from the stove, where he wielded a wooden spoon, and Corinne got up to give Evie a hug.

"Hey, yourself," Corinne said, holding Evie by the shoulders. "How you doing?"

"You know," she said. "Good enough."

"That's my girl," James said. "Good enough for dinner?"

"Yeah, thanks." She and Corinne sat, and James put plates in front of them. "Yum, taco Tuesday," she mustered.

"Yep," James agreed. "Good any day of the week. Simple, easy, and scalable."

Corinne laughed. "Scalable?"

"My new word for the day," James said. "Means I can add more folks to the dinner table easily by just shifting the proportion of beans to meat. Pretty up-to-date for an old guy, eh?"

"Well, I appreciate it," Corinne said.

"Yeah, me too," Evie said. "I'm sorry you have to feed me, Dad." She teared up.

"Oh, you go on," James said, lifting his chin. "Corinne shows up for dinner and she isn't sorry, not a bit, are you?"

Corinne shook her head. "Not a bit. I've been showing up here at dinnertime since I was about seventeen."

"That's different," Evie objected. "I'm supposed to be able to take care of myself."

"You take care of yourself," James pointed out. "Corinne does too. But the point of being a family is that you have a place to come home to. Where you can let someone else take care for a while."

Yeah, you with your cardiologist appointment. She said, "Well, thanks, Dad. I promise to not make too much work for you, really."

"Will you quit with that? You're doing work here too, Evelyn. Lots of it. Just eat your tacos."

She giggled a little. "Well, my back tells me I've been doing work. Hauling that furniture out of the attic used some muscles."

"What happened to it?" Corinne asked. As James filled her in, Evie's attention drifted. She stood abruptly and gathered their plates. "I'll clean up. Thanks for supper, Dad."

Later, Corinne and James returned from a tour of the shed and a brief dog walk.

"You been sitting here all this time?" James asked curiously, turning on a lamp in the kitchen.

Evie startled. "Yeah, I guess so," she said, rubbing her eyes.

"We're going to watch a movie. Corinne is indulging my preference for old cowboy flicks. Want to watch with us?"

Corinne parked herself at the table with Evie. "James, you go ahead," Corinne gestured to the living room. "I'll be right in."

Evie tented her hands over her eyes and peered up at her aunt. Corinne was a young aunt; Dad's generation but barely. At forty-nine, she looked more like one of the Madison girls, even though she wasn't a Madison. She had the blue eyes of Evie's three sisters, the straight hair, the long, willowy frame.

"What?" Evie asked ungraciously. If Corinne looks at me too hard, I'm going to cry, and I'm so sick of crying I can't stand it.

"Good job on getting that stuff out of the attic," Corinne said mildly.

Startled, Evie said an automatic, "Thanks."

"And I noticed the kitchen looks a lot different too."

"Yeah."

"I'm not going to pry."

Evie raised her eyebrows.

"Really. I'm the soul of discretion. I just wanted to tell you that what you're doing here, doing for James, means a lot more than you probably can see. Don't discount yourself. Okay?"

"Um, sure?" Evie was uncertain.

"You know your mother's memorial is next weekend. I'm glad you're here this week."

Evie felt a punch in her gut. Yes, her mother's memorial. "This is number four. Do you think it will ever get any easier?"

"Will it ever get easy? No, of course not. But it is already easier, isn't it? Compared to the first year?"

"Different, that's true. Easier? I'm not sure."

"You being here for this week is a help. Even if you don't feel that way." Corinne patted her shoulder. "I'm sorry about what's happened, but I am glad you're here, if that makes sense."

Evie half-smiled. "I guess so. Two sides to everything, right? Mum used to say that."

Stephen ran into Evie in front of St. James Church. She had her arms wrapped around a cardboard box. With her sunhat and dark glasses, he almost didn't recognize her.

"Evie! It is you," he said, wondering if his delight was visible on his face. "What have you got there?"

"Old dishes and cookware. There's a rummage sale next weekend, and I'm dropping stuff off." She seemed to be in a hurry.

"Can I help?" He reached for the box in her arms.

"Well, actually, yes. I've got this one, but maybe you could grab some stuff from the car?" She jerked her head toward the parking lot.

"Sure. I'm happy to help," he said. As she headed into the fellowship hall, he went toward the car. The open trunk had boxes and bags of stuff. He grabbed what he could carry and followed her inside.

She stood at a long table on the far side of the hall talking to a woman there. He went in her direction, but another gray-haired lady waylaid him, pointing him toward a different table. By the time he dropped off his box, Evie was outside again, getting another armful. He followed along behind, always a step away from getting to talk to her. After half a dozen trips, the car was emptied. As she was getting behind the wheel, he caught up to her.

"Oh, Stephen, thanks for your help," she said hurriedly.

"You're in a rush today," he noted.

"Kind of," she said, but then apparently she relented and got back out of the car. She slammed the door and leaned against her car.

"We're cleaning out the house. I think I told you my father wants to sell it."

He nodded. "Not easy, I suspect."

She shook her head. "So much harder than I ever thought. You know that thing you said about objects being connected to memories and stories? That's the problem. It really isn't the things themselves. If we can separate the thing from the story, then we can find it a new home."

"Like via a rummage sale."

"Or selling it or donating it in some other place. It's the stories that keep objects sticky."

He folded his arms. "Not a bad thing, in my line of work. If people didn't hold onto their family carvings, I'd have nothing to study."

"Well, except the stories. I agree, the stories mean more when you have the object, and vice versa." She sighed. "I can see both sides."

"Have you unearthed any wood carvings in your house clearing? Don't forget me," he said with a smile.

She gave him a warm smile in return. "No wood carvings. No, but I have found some remarkable hooked rugs. Look, let me show you." She pulled out her phone and showed him pictures.

"Look at those colours!"

"That's what I thought too. They're old. Probably close to one hundred years old, maybe a little less. I'm not yet sure who made them, but I'm working on that."

"This is a beautiful image."

"It's also amazing craftsmanship. The stitches are so precise, but on burlap, of all things. Probably with rags, or at least cloth that had other uses before becoming art."

"This gets you excited," he said, gazing at her face. "Your face lights up."

"It is a little exciting," she agreed. "Listen, I've got to go. I'm working on a painting for Leonard though, will you tell him?"

"Sure. When will I see you again?"

Her eyes drifted off.

"I mean, when will you be coming by the gallery again?"

"I was just thinking about how nice it was to sit in the sun on that bench."

He laughed. "Did you like my selfie? Benchie?"

"I did. I want to hang out there again."

"Soon?"

"I'm hoping tomorrow or the next day. As soon as I have something to leave with Leonard."

"Well, don't be a stranger, okay?"

"What?" She looked startled. Then her expression settled into understanding. "Right. Bye."

He watched her drive off. She was an enigma. Who is Evie Madison, after all?

Corinne might have thought I'd be helpful this week, Evie thought on Thursday, but I'm barely holding on by my fingernails. If I don't get some sleep, real sleep, like at night, I don't know what will happen. She couldn't bear to see her reflection in the wavy glass of the dresser in her room. Raccoon eyes stared back at her. She pulled on a sweater to head downtown on foot.

Cold, she wrapped her arms around herself as she walked. Covered with her sunglasses and hat, she hoped to be incognito.

She slipped into the drugstore to check out the sleep aids. Squinting at the labels, she finally grabbed a handful to take to the register. She pushed her shades up long enough to pay, then slid them down once again to head out.

The Fishburne Gallery door was open across the street, and despite herself, Evie crossed against traffic to stick her face in the door. She didn't want to see anyone, but the gallery itself was a draw. She drew a big breath. It smelled wonderful, like home and creativity and life.

"Hello?" A voice came from the back room.

Caught! She slipped in, letting the door close behind her.

"Oh, hi, Leonard," she said. "It's me. Evie."

Leonard emerged, glasses in hand. "Evelyn! How nice to see you." He looked at her face: Evie nearly cringed. She really didn't want to see anyone, but she had put herself in this position.

"Are you here to talk about your class?"

"No, not really," she demurred. "I was just walking by."

"Have you given any thought to my proposal?"

"Yes, I'm painting. I've got something I'm working on for you," she said faintly.

"Wonderful! I'm looking forward to seeing what you've got. Since you're here though, let's get that class scheduled."

"I really don't know how to teach."

"You could do something, I'm sure. Maybe a 'paint the boat' class, you know."

He was bubbly; like a puppy, Evie thought. Like a dumb, irritating puppy.

"Paint the boat? Are you serious?" Evie couldn't believe that he wanted her to do one of those step-by-step copy the artist painting workshops. "You mean like the ones where people drink wine and paint?" With effort she kept her voice even. "I thought you were a purveyor of fine art?"

"I am, I am. I'm also trying to run a business. But you're right, that's not a good idea. You can do a class to teach the craft, colour theory, and how to put paint on paper."

"For children."

"Well, I was thinking for everyone."

He was not making it easy. "Leonard, I don't have the skills to teach adults anything. I can probably help kids explore painting though. A one-time thing."

He brightened immediately. "That's wonderful!"

She suppressed a sigh. "Yes, and apparently I need the work."

A wave of sadness crossed his face. "I'm sorry things are not going well for you." He brightened considerably. "That seems to be my gain. It will be wonderful to have you offering classes this summer."

"One class."

He was undeterred. "I understand that you're a well-known artist in Stella Mare. People will line up to study with you."

Evie shook her head, backing up a step. "I don't know where you get your information, but no. I'm not and they won't."

He looked puzzled. "That's not what I heard. But okay, the risk is mine. Can we talk about this now? Or are you busy?"

"Now, I guess," she said.

"Great. Come on back and we'll get the details sorted."

"One class," she said firmly.

"Let's talk," he said winningly. "We can talk about your consignment contract when you bring in your painting too."

They were discussing a teaching schedule when Stephen clattered down the stairs from his apartment. "Good morning, Evie, Leonard," he said, smiling.

Evie's stomach gave a little leap of joy.

Could she stay hidden behind her dark glasses? She didn't want to expose him to her raccoon eyes. Not today. She realized she didn't care that much what Leonard thought, but somehow Stephen, well, Stephen was different. Funny, last week she'd thought the opposite.

She peered at his smile and finally slid off her glasses. He was so solid, so there. So focused on her.

"Hi, Stephen," she murmured.

"We're just firming up her schedule, Steve," Leonard said happily. "She's going to be here once a week!" His glee would have been infectious if she hadn't been so incredibly self-conscious.

"Once. Not once a week. I said a one-time workshop."

Smiling even wider, Stephen said, "That's wonderful news! Maybe I'll take your class." His eyes twinkled and Evie warmed; he'd picked up on her discomfort, despite Leonard's obliviousness.

"It's for children."

He moved closer. Oh, he smelled good. "Well, that won't work. I haven't been in that category for a while."

"See, Evie, we need an adult class," Leonard insisted. They ignored him.

"I'm glad you're here," Stephen said, looking at her. "I needed to see you."

"You did?" His eyes are hazel, she thought, distracted from the conversation.

"I have lots of questions about Stella Mare."

"You do?" Is that why you needed to see me? she wondered. *I might have a few questions for you too.* She surprised herself. The fog of fatigue, anger, desperation, and sadness lifted ever so slightly. She inhaled again. Pine, clean cotton fabric, a little spicy...

"Can I walk you out?" he asked.

"Fine," Leonard said. "A child's class. One. To start with."

"Bye, Leonard," she said. "I'll send you a course description and bring a painting. Soon."

"Great. I'll start getting the word out. I'm sure we'll have a full class in no time."

"If you say so." She waved airily. Stephen accompanied her through the gallery to the street.

"He's persistent," she noted.

"He can be," he agreed. "He'd say that's how to run a business. Do you have time for a coffee?" he asked.

"Oh, no," she said with real regret. "I'm not, uh, not really presentable." She dropped her sunglasses over her face again. "I've got to get home. We've got a lot going on there."

His face fell and she couldn't stand his disappointment.

"But maybe you'd like to come to the bonfire this weekend? We're having a picnic on the beach."

Lighting up again, he said, "Well, thank you very much. Your family? I'd love to come."

"Yes, mostly my family, but friends too. It's an annual event. You might like to meet some of the people."

"That sounds lovely. I appreciate that, Evie."

She considered. "You should probably know that it got started because my mother always loved beach bonfire picnics. We do this every year to remember her."

"Your mother is gone?"

"Died. Yes. Three years. Four, now. It's fun. Sad, of course, too, but mostly fun."

Stephen looked serious as he said, "Well, I thank you very much for inviting me to join you for such an important event."

She nodded, tightly. "I have to go now." Turning quickly, she walked down the sidewalk toward home.

Chapter 16

The days before her mother's picnic passed in a fog of fatigue and physical labour. Evie worked, but only in short bursts of activity. Sleep was elusive, but the need struck her at odd times of day. Then she crept into her bed and welcomed brief oblivion.

Asleep in bed really was the only place she wanted to be. She got up at night, after the house was quiet, James and the dogs sleeping, and wandered, ghostlike, into the kitchen. She picked at food, sat in the living room, got up and went out to the porch and gazed at the moonlight. Then she wandered back inside. Sometimes she baked recipes from her mother's cookbook. Then she'd tidy the kitchen and go back to bed.

But she couldn't just stay in bed. The house wouldn't declutter itself. Each day she pushed herself to do one thing, if only so she could update her spreadsheet. The physical work sometimes felt good, but other times, it was just too much, and she retreated upstairs. Beyond decluttering, she had to paint, and those darn recipes were calling her. She craved the comfort of her mother's family recipes.

Then there were the rugs. Those rugs showed up in her mind and in her dreams. When she was able to stop worrying about her life, she thought about the rugs. What else was up in that attic, anyway?

One morning she pulled on sweats and sneakers and headed up late in the morning, after she'd heard James leave for the day. With odd determination, she found the diary and the associated papers in the treasure box and headed back down. On a second thought, she turned back and grabbed another rug from the middle of the box. Taking her treasures, the books and the hooked rug, she headed to her room. She spread out the rag rug on the floor. This one had fish, oversized and oddly coloured, and fishermen with poles, not like real fishermen with boats. Maybe they were children? A red barn and cottage sat on the shore. Was that a clothesline strung from the house to the barn? Yes, complete with sheets or something. Evie squinted at the design. Too pretty for the floor, she decided, and draped it over a chairback. She peeled off her sneakers and crawled back into bed with the diary in hand.

What was it about this dusty little book? She ran her fingers over the spidery handwriting on the first page of text. May 22, 1945, had been written at the top of the page. She flipped back to the inside cover. Nineteen twenty-seven? None of the dates matched. What was going on? When no answer arrived, she turned back to the first page of handwriting.

"My mother came to Stella Mare on May 22, 1919, from her family home in Cheticamp, Cape Breton. She had no idea what it would be like to be the only French woman in a town full of English settlers and Irish immigrants. She would find out. These are her stories, as told to me. H.O."

H.O. meant Hannah O'Neill, as it said in the front. Was this her great-aunt Hannah? Evie turned the book over, looking for clues to spark her memories. Who were the children of Leonie and George? Hannah O'Neill. And Grandma Sarah, Sarah O'Neill Smyth. Mum's mother, Evie thought, with the sudden recollection of Sunday dinners at Sarah's house and later, Sarah moving into the Madison family home, after Grandma Madison had passed away. That was a long time ago though. *I was only little, and she died soon after that.*

This is too confusing. Hannah, Sarah, Leonie...what do those old ladies have to do with me? She dropped the journal on the floor and slid back under the covers. Daylight was irrelevant. She slept whenever her mind would let her.

She woke again in the middle of the night. The journal was there, lying in a puddle of light from her bedside lamp. Papers spilled out of it, and Evie felt faintly guilty for letting a family artifact sit on the floor that way. She rolled out of bed and gathered up the loose sheets, stuffing them back into the book. Carrying it, she creaked open her door and tiptoed down the stairs. Yes, after midnight. The big dogs groaned in their sleep but otherwise took no notice of her perambulating.

She turned on the little lamp on the sideboard, boiled the kettle, and settled down to decipher Hannah O'Neill's diary.

Mum came when she was only twenty-two, had almost no english and Dad barely any french. But he told the story about how they met and I knew it from my earliest days. Daddy was a sailor, like a lot of fellers in the Maritimes, and when the War happened, he wanted to help. So he joined the Merchant Marines out of Halifax and after his time was over (he never said a lot about that time, that war time) he went with his friend Samuel LeBlanc to Sydney, Cape Breton. They were dropped off the ship in Sydney, and Samuel took Daddy home with him to Cheticamp. They were just boys, really, Daddy would say, but when he and Samuel got to Samuel's family home, the first person Daddy laid eyes on was his little sister Leonie.

Oh, that Leonie! Daddy's eyes would gleam when he talked about Mum like that. Now she was the prettiest thing I'd ever seen. Mum would laugh and remind him that he'd been at sea and at war, and he hadn't been seeing a lot of girls, but he stuck to his story. She was the prettiest girl in the world, and I couldn't take my eyes off her. But her father, he wasn't having his daughter to do anything with any english, and so there we were.

But Samuel was my friend, and we'd been through a lot together. So we boys bedded down in the barn, and your grandfather, Marcel, he could always use some strong arms, so I set about to make myself into another son for him. I worked the fields, and when it was fishing time, Samuel and I worked on the boat, and I kept my eye on that pretty Leonie. Marcel, him, he wasn't easily impressed, especially if you were english, but I kept at it. I had decided that I wasn't going home unless Leonie was going with me, and I knew her father was the obstacle.

Mum would say something here like, what about me? You sure thought a lot of yourself, mister. And Daddy would laugh. Oh, I saw how you looked at me, Leonie LeBlanc. I saw you looking when you didn't know I was watching. When you brought us our dinner out in the fields, I noticed how you held my gaze.

Ha, Mum would say. That's because you couldn't stop staring at me.

Well, and that's the truth, isn't it? Daddy would laugh. So finally Marcel decided I was okay, maybe almost as good as Samuel, and he let me start courting Leonie. Before long, we got married, she learned a little english and I learned a lot of french, and we had a little cabin behind Marcel's house. Still working the farm and fishing, and then a baby boy came, Michael. But he came too soon, and he died. And about the time I thought Leonie and I might die of grief, I got a letter from my sister telling me my father was dying. It was time to go home to New Brunswick.

So we packed up our things, what we'd built or gathered, and we headed from Cheticamp to Stella Mare. And that's the story of how I got the prettiest girl in the world to be my wife. Daddy would beam at Mum, and all the kids would giggle and Mum would usually throw something, a dishtowel or a rag, at Daddy, but she liked hearing the story too.

Evie looked out the kitchen window. Had she ever heard this before? Leonie LeBlanc and Charles O'Neill, her ancestors. There weren't many Acadian women in Stella Mare back then. Maybe none. She imagined the family sitting around the living room listening to Papa telling his story, and about Great-Aunt Hannah soaking it up to write it later, as an adult.

Leonie having only French and coming from Acadian people, living in Stella Mare among the English and Irish ancestry. It was probably hard. Evie flipped through more pages of the diary. Oh, that looked like a recipe.

Mama's Galette Blanche, Mama's Ployes, Mama's Rhubarb-Blackberry compote. All written out like telling a story...first you put the yeast in the water and swish it around with your fingers. Evie rolled her eyes. *How is a person supposed to follow this?* But oh, Grandmother's galette blanche—those words evoked a memory of some sort of soft, warm, buttery bread rolls. She headed for the pantry and let her fingers do the thinking. Like painting, she thought dreamily. But you get to eat at the end.

It didn't seem like a long time passed, but daylight was touching the windows when James tiptoed down the stairs, hushing the big dogs. "Quiet, Mallow. Evie's sleeping."

"Hi, Dad." Evie was lying on the couch. "It's okay. I'm awake." She got to her feet. "There's warm bread for breakfast. I'm going to bed." She passed her father at the foot of the stairs.

"Good morning to you then," James said. "Have a good nap."

"Mmm."

Leonie turned, looking at Evie. "I know you," she said. "You're Aggie's girl, the dark one."

Evie walked around to face her as she sat in the big chair. She tried to answer but no words would come. "The painter girl." Leonie's face darkened. "The one who knows."

Knows? Evie thought, but her voice would still not work.

Leonie went on. "You know what it's like to be different. To be outré, not like the others. I know what it is like to never see anyone who looks like you, talks like you, knows the same songs, the recipes, the stories." The old woman looked at the pile of fabric in her lap. "All I could do was make the pictures. Make the food, tell the children the stories, make the rugs."

Her lap was full of burlap, and there was a basket of rags beside her chair. She picked up a rag, twisted it, and used a tool to pull it through the burlap. "Ma chère, you have to make your own place."

Evie studied the gnarled hands twisting fabric, watching a design take shape in front of her eyes. From a plain length of burlap, Leonie shaped a boat on the water, a house on the shore, gardens, a cow, and clouds in the sky. It was like magic.

Music started from another room; a fiddle, playing a jig, and the sounds of children laughing came through it. Evie went to the door and looked in. Where was she? Some small house she'd never seen before, but there were five children and a man with a fiddle, and a much-younger Leonie tending the fire. Laughing, she swatted away one of the big kids and opened her arms to a little one. The fiddle got faster and faster, and the children danced in the room, and Leonie called out, but this time in French. Evie only caught part of it.

"Hannah!"

A girl of twelve looked up from a book. "Are you writing this all down, chère? Papa, look at our big girl, writing her stories."

The man dropped the fiddle into his lap and smiled toward Hannah. "You'll be our teacher, won't you? Oh, Mama, we are so lucky to have these children."

"Even me?" A little one, dark-haired like Evie, perked up from beside the chair.

Leonie stroked the tousled curls. "Of course you, Sarah," she said fondly.

"Enough music for tonight," Papa said. "Time for bed. Morning comes early for fishermen. You'll come, Gerard."

"Me too, Papa?" a small boy asked eagerly. "I'm old enough."

Papa shook his head. "Not yet, Samuel. You have to get more schooling and maybe get a little bigger. We don't want to be feeding you to the fish, do we?"

The room started to fade, and Evie opened her eyes to a bright early afternoon.

A dream? Had to be, but it had been so peculiar. How could she know it was Leonie? How could she understand the language? *My French had barely been passable in high school and hasn't improved.* Was there a message there? She picked up her little notebook and scribbled what she recalled.

Message or not, real life was calling. She shook off the dream and got up.

Chapter 17

Thursday night Evie stood in the bathroom with a handful of sleeping pills in her hand. One of these, one of these, and two of those, she thought. All within recommended dosage, right? All okay. *I'm going to sleep tonight. I have to sleep tonight.* Washing them down, she glared at the mirror. Don't look like that, she warned. You are going to sleep. No discussion. Her sleepy reflection did not respond.

The clock in the living room dinged the hour; it was only ten p.m., but Evie's days and nights had been running into each other. Her bed looked inviting, if messy. She climbed in and clicked off the lamp.

Okay, do your worst, she invited Jase in her head. *I'm ready for you. I've got meds.* Oddly, the usual images of Jase laughing, Jase angry, Jase and Michelle didn't appear. Instead, it was Leonard and his untidy office, telling her how happy he was that she'd be working with him. Stephen's kind eyes behind his glasses. Corinne patting her on the shoulder, telling her that being around for Dad was worthwhile. She drifted off to sleep feeling settled and comforted.

Evie? Evie, wake up. This is important. As she opened her eyes, Leonie's brown ones were intent on her face.

Oh! What's going on?

Evie, I have a message for you. You must listen.

I'm listening. Groggily, she tried to tune in, but Leonie's face grew dim.

Waking late once again, she struggled to come to awareness. Stupid sleeping pills were supposed to make things better. *Ugh. I feel like I've been hit by a truck, like I had no sleep at all.* Maybe it would take a few nights to catch up.

She headed toward the fragrance of coffee. Thank goodness Dad was a coffee drinker too, she thought, pouring a mug. Oh, who made this? Bread pudding? She sniffed at the casserole dish. Umm, rum sauce? She spooned a little into a dish.

Sitting with her coffee and bread pudding, she started to feel a little more awake. The sunshine was beautiful, even though she felt dark and grim inside. What's today? Oh, Friday, right. This weekend is Mum's picnic. The weight of that couldn't be lifted by sunshine. Mum was gone. Jase was gone. Evie's life had no direction or shape, and things just sucked.

A part of her was irrepressible though, annoying as it was. Part of her remembered the upcoming watercolour class, Leonard's assertion that she was a well-known local artist (she scoffed in her head), and the warm feeling Stephen gave her. Maybe everything wasn't totally awful. She took an exploratory bite of the bread pudding. Umm, good. Like Mum's, only not quite.

Her phone buzzed.

Dorie: How you doing? Good for tomorrow? Chad's got firewood in the truck, and I'm bringing the vodka watermelon and the chips. You?

Evie frowned.

Evie: Those are easy picnic items. Cheater.

Dorie: I called it. You could have but you didn't. Rett's bringing sandwiches for everyone. Harry's doing his signature salted caramel chip cookies.

Evie: What's left?

Dorie: You can make Mum's potato salad. Or macaroni salad.

Evie: Ugh. I hate macaroni salad. Maybe I'll check with Dad.

Dorie: Okay. Keep me posted.

Stephen asked for Cassandra's advice. "Evie invited me to a family picnic, so I can meet some locals."

Cassandra blinked. "Of course, so you can meet some locals."

"I'm going to ignore your innuendo, Cass. You're starting to sound like Leonard. But I do need your help."

"Sure. Ask away."

"I think people do potluck everything here. What would be an appropriate contribution to the family picnic? I don't know if these people drink, so I don't want to bring wine. I don't know anything about them. Help!"

Cassandra laughed. "You're right about potluck everything. But you're from the South. Isn't it the same there?"

"Of course it is. But I'm not bringing hush puppies or grits to a beach picnic, especially in New Brunswick."

"Oh, hush puppies," Cassandra breathed with longing. "Oh, my goodness, that brings back a memory…"

"Cass."

"Right. You can take a bag of chips, honestly. Cookies. Those fancy macaron things they make at the bakery. Pretty much anything will do, but you are correct; it's the usual thing to arrive with a contribution."

"Flowers? The picnic is a memorial event for her mother."

Cassandra looked doubtful. "You can't eat flowers. It's a beach thing, right? Nah, stick with food."

"Okay, thanks."

"Unless it's Evie you want to give the flowers to," Cassandra added and then went off into a gale of laughter.

"I swear, Cass, sometimes it's like having a teenage kid around here."

Leonard called. "Your first class has filled up, and I have a waiting list for the next one," he said with some glee.

"Great," Evie managed. "End of the month. There is no next one, remember?"

"End of July is correct, and can we put another one on the calendar?"

"Oh, I don't think so. Not yet. Can we just see how this class goes?" The idea of it made her tired.

"I'd love to be able to put these wait-list people somewhere," he wheedled. "Please?"

She walked into the den from the kitchen, still listening. Rugs were piled everywhere. "Do you have any storage space at the gallery?" she asked abruptly.

"Maybe," he said. "What do you need?"

When she described the rugs, he said, "How about a deal? You agree to teach a second class and I'll house your collection for the summer. I do have a closet off the back office that I could clear out."

A closet? Not ideal, but probably no worse than the attics most of the rugs were coming from. "You're pressing your advantage, Leonard."

He giggled. "Yes, I am. I really want you to teach."

"I really want to see how it goes. I might be terrible at this, you know."

"A compromise? You can have the closet as long as you are teaching here."

"Not great, Leonard. But I think I have to take it. I'll be down later today."

She could hear his smile. "Okay then. I'll have a key for you. And I'll let Stephen know you're coming."

"Stephen? Why?"

"Oh, you know. He'll want to see you."

"Fine."

She hung up, annoyed again. Was he matchmaking? Couldn't he see that her heart was bleeding all over the place? At least Stephen seemed to realize she was not in the mood for that sort of thing. Even as she rejected the idea, she recalled his strong forearms, warm smile, comforting presence. She sighed. Then she piled up the hooked rugs, checking to be sure each one was labelled. This is like a mini-museum, she thought. Only I have no idea what I'm doing. She'd need some help with this. But not now. Later.

On Sunday morning, Evie and James mourned the forecast together. Rain would make things anywhere from unpleasant to impossible. But they decided to go ahead with the plans and hope for the best.

Worst case, everyone would come back to the house. But the skies cleared as the day went on.

By midafternoon, James had his van loaded up with firewood. "Dad, Chad's got the wood."

"Don't want to run out."

"We won't run out, Dad. We can pick up driftwood too."

"How'd you feel if we ran out of food?"

"Yeah, that's not good. We're not going to let that happen."

"That's how I feel about the wood. We don't want things to go wrong."

"Right. Got it."

By four thirty, they headed to the beach, with Mallow and Custard in the back of the van. They scoped out their favourite spot, spread a picnic blanket, and unloaded food and firewood from the van. Soon, Dorie and Chad arrived with Alice, Chad's grandmother. Alice walked with a cane toward the blanket, and Chad brought her a chair. When Rett and Harry and their children arrived, everyone helped to move firewood, blankets, food, and toys to the beach.

James pulled eight-year-old Mason into helping build the bonfire they would light when dark fell, and Evie and Dorie spread old sheets over the two picnic tables that Chad and Harry lugged over. Rett laid out appetizers. Corinne texted James, asking for help to carry drink coolers from the parking lot, and a troop of people, kids included, headed that way.

More people arrived, bringing food and drinks, dogs and children. Dorie took a pile of kids to the water to collect shells and stones, and Rett and Corinne settled in for apparently deep conversation. James finished piling the wood for the fire and took a chair out onto the sand, sitting and gazing at the sea. Evie sat on the sand beside him.

"Hard day, Dad?" she asked.

"No, not really. I miss her every day. This day is about remembering good times together."

"We did have a lot of those."

He continued to gaze at the water. "We did. I like to think about how much she'd love to see these children growing up, you girls and Rett's little ones. Jake too, even though he's far away."

Tears prickled her eyes. "I miss her too." The waves washed in and out, in and out, on the sandy shore. Here on the bay, the water flowed gently, a benign presence on this late June evening.

"Evie!" Rett was insistent. "Come here!"

"Duty calls," she said, getting up and brushing off. "I wonder what big sister needs now?"

James chuckled. "You girls. You're so predictable."

She laughed and patted his shoulder before she trotted off to her summons.

As Evie approached, Rett said, "Stephen's here."

Her stomach gave a little lurch as she looked up into Stephen's smiling face. "Hi," she said. "Looks like you met Rett."

Stephen nodded. "Hello, Evie." He reached out and gave her a light hug.

"Stephen's from North Carolina," Evie offered. Rett and Dorie were looking at her. "He's working down at the new gallery, Leonard Fishburne's place. We, uh, we met there."

He shook hands with both sisters and then Chad, who wandered up.

"Big change from North Carolina," Chad noted.

"I like learning about places, especially small places," he said. "I like listening to people's stories."

"Oh, yeah?" Dorie said. "Chad likes filming them. You guys might have some interests in common."

Chad and Stephen stepped off, chatting together.

Dorie whispered to Evie, "Nice! Why didn't you tell me about him?"

"Stop it. I just met him a couple of weeks ago, Dorie. He's a nice man."

"He sure is," Rett said waggling her eyebrows.

"You guys. Don't embarrass me. I invited him here so he could meet some more locals. I figured there's nothing like Mum's beach picnic to bring out the stories."

"Well, that's the truth," Rett agreed. "Okay, I promise to be a grown-up about this."

As the afternoon waned, more people arrived. James returned to help Corinne greet people. Rett kept the tables full of food, and Dorie and the dogs entertained the youngest kids, along with some young parents. Water and sand were good for keeping kids busy, and food and drinks were plentiful.

"Who are those ladies?" Evie whispered to Rett. Alice was entertaining a small troop of white-haired ladies, though at least one of them had a hot pink streak in her long hair.

"Remember them? They were the food brigade when Mum was sick. I think most of them come from St. James Church, but Alice and Mum and Divya were a gang. They did the yard sale, the women's group, and that outreach to young families, remember?"

"Yeah, of course," Evie said. "But I'm not sure I know the rest of them. Maybe I should."

"Yeah, you should. Go say hi. They'll be thrilled to talk to you."

But what will I say? Evie's mind was blank, but she went to see the posse of older women anyway.

"Evelyn!" Alice's voice was welcoming. "Come and sit for a bit. We were just talking about your mother."

Evie pulled up a beach chair.

The pink-haired lady said, "It's hard to think about anything else when we're here because of Aggie." Her sadness was momentary though, as she lit up to add, "She was the most fun of anyone."

"She was pretty good at making ordinary things special," Alice agreed. "How are you doing, Evelyn? Dorie said you've moved back to Stella Mare."

Evie steeled herself. "I'm kind of in between things right now. I'm going to be doing a little work down at the new gallery."

"Oh, yes, you're the artist, aren't you?" another lady noted. "You and Jase Highborn. I went to a show in St. Stephen. Interesting."

Around the pain in her midsection, Evie ground out, "I'm not working with Jase anymore. I'm doing my own thing."

"Oh, that's good, dear," Divya said, her bracelets clacking. "A woman needs her own expression. Especially a woman artist."

Evie looked more closely. "Are you an artist?"

"Sculpture."

Alice laughed. "You didn't know that? I wonder how that got by you? You were always interested in any kind of creative project."

"When you're a kid, your parents' friends aren't too interesting," Divya noted. "I think we only got acquainted after your mum got sick anyway," she added, looking at Evie.

"That's probably right. I wish I had known that about you though."

Divya smiled. "Never too late. Come on over to my studio sometime. I can make you a cup of tea. Or a whisky, depending on the day."

Evie nodded. "Thank you. I'll do that."

"In the meantime, who's your young man?" Alice asked, sotto voce.

"Not my young man, Alice, but his name is Stephen Culpeper, he's from down south, and he's doing research on wood carvings in the Maritimes. He likes local stories."

"Oh, we've got stories," the pink-haired lady said. "Send him over."

"Stop it, Natalie," Alice admonished. "He's too young for you."

Through a burst of giggling, Evie got to her feet. He was her guest, and she probably should be looking out for him, at least a little bit. Wandering and looking, she finally located him in a cluster of people near the water, mostly men and little children. He seemed content though, deep in conversation, and she felt a little shy to intrude. As she looked on though, he glanced toward her and waved her over, so she went.

"Hi," she said.

His smile deepened. "I've been talking to Marty here about fishing."

Marty nodded. "Hi, Evie. I don't know much about fishing firsthand, but I remember my granddad's stories."

"Is he still around? I'd love to meet him," Stephen said.

"No, but my dad is," Marty said. "I can hook you up. He loves these old tales too."

"You're having fun," Evie said.

Stephen smiled. "I sure am. Thanks so much for inviting me." They walked together toward the water. "Are you having fun?"

"This event is kind of mixed for me," she admitted. "But yes, fun. Let's go eat."

The tables were laden, not only with the food brought by the girls, but with contributions from everyone in attendance. Rett encouraged Stephen to pile his plate.

"That there's potato salad with fiddleheads," she pointed out. "Local greens. You ever had a lobster roll? Danny brought some; over there. Here's a big bucket of mussels, too, from PEI."

"PEI?"

"Prince Edward Island," Evie explained. "Island province. They raise mussels there. We're more about salmon."

"Really? You can raise shellfish?"

"Oh, yeah," James tossed in, walking up. "Fishing isn't what it once was. Farm-raised this and that."

"But still plenty of people going out on the boats," Evie added quickly. "It's a mix of old and new. Not that I know anything about it, really."

"Well, most things are a mix, aren't they?" Stephen asked. "I like it all. I'm going to try these mussels and lobster rolls and fiddleheads and anything else you suggest," he added, looking at Rett.

"Well, when you get to dessert, make sure you have some rhubarb cake," she said, pointing to the other table.

He grinned. "I'll do that. I'll try to save some room."

"No worries," Rett said. "We'll be here long enough to work up another appetite. We've got sundown and the bonfire and the music yet to come."

Stephen looked at Evie with a smile. "What a nice welcome. Are you going to eat?" His plate was laden, but hers was still nearly bare.

"Yeah, I don't know. Maybe a little later," she said, setting her plate down. "I'll just sit with you. Want to go talk to my dad?"

They meandered toward James, who had gone to sit on a beach chair with Alice and her cohort. Stories were flying thick and fast, and Stephen was welcomed as warmly as Evie herself.

Stephen seemed very comfortable, but she wasn't. A weird feeling in her chest intensified as the conversation flowed. Shadows lengthened. The sky grew pink then red, deepening to magenta with dark purple clouds. This west side of the peninsula was known for extreme sunsets, but the changing light made Evie feel restless. Stephen was involved in a conversation to his other side, so she slipped out of the group and headed down the beach. As the sounds of talking grew more distant, her body settled but her fatigue grew as she calmed down. She took in deep breaths of sea air. Her traitor stomach rumbled. *Why can't I be* hungry when I'm looking at food? Or maybe I'm just too wound up to eat, with everyone all together.

She stopped walking and looked out at the setting sun. She heard the kids' excitement intensify, and James calling for caution. Must be lighting the fire, she thought absently, but her attention was on the emerging slate grey of the western sky. The distant water blended into darkening horizon, and the fog obscured the boundary between earth and sky. She floated on the sunset, feeling as if she were leaving too, along with the light, heading west to follow the sun as it set, over and over, all the world around. Sunset after sunset. Suddenly dizzy, she abruptly headed back toward the party.

"Here she is," Corinne welcomed her. "We were looking for you."

Evie squeezed out a little smile. People were gathered on the beach side of the fire, watching smoke blow toward town. It was small and carefully contained with rocks. Conversation quieted, and James stood in front of the little crowd.

He cleared his throat. "We're here because of Aggie, as I am sure you all know. Aggie loved this beach, and she loved a good picnic, and this was her favourite time of year. Don't hardly seem fair that she died in June, but she got to have a last good season before that, and I am grateful for that part. I just wanted to say thank you, Aggie, for making it a tradition to have our family and friends picnic here every year. I miss you, and I'm glad for all we had together." He stepped away, wiping his eyes.

Corinne waved a piece of paper. "Helen's not here."

"As usual," Rett murmured next to Evie.

"But she sent a letter," Corinne went on.

"As usual," Rett repeated.

"I'm going to read it, okay?" Corinne looked up over her reading glasses. "Hi, everybody. I'm sorry to miss another annual family picnic, but I wanted to send my greetings and my best memory of Mum. When I was eight, and Rett was seven and Evie five, she gathered us up and took us, three little girls, to the animal shelter for our regular visit. We collected newspapers, old towels, all the usual, and headed out to visit the kittens and puppies. Only this time was special because we brought somebody home. I couldn't believe that we finally got to have our own puppy, but Mum said now that Evie was a big girl, we could do it. That dog was Maple, and she was my best friend until I left for university. This is a memory of Maple, but it's really a memory of Mum because she brought Maple into our family.

"Mum told me that if I took good care of Maple, she would take care of me, and that turned out to be true. I learned that you have to feed the dog, even if you don't feel like it. Sometimes you have to take her for a walk and play with her, even if you would rather watch TV. These were important lessons, but the bigger lesson from Mum was that everyone in a family needs our care and concern, humans, dogs, everyone.

"I miss Mum and I'm grateful for what she gave me. Love you all! Have a lobster roll for me. Love, Helen."

Corinne turned and dropped the letter in the fire. Nobody spoke as it curled and flamed into smoke. Then she looked up.

"My turn, I guess. My sister Aggie was a second mother to me. She and James took me in when I was only seventeen, kept me for years, let me help out with the girls"—she smiled warmly, looking at Rett—"and gave me a role, and a place, and support for my education that I wouldn't have had otherwise. She loved her family, her friends, and this little town. She was a wise woman, in so many ways. I'm putting sage into the fire in her memory." Corinne tossed some leaves from an envelope into the fire. The fragrance of burning sage floated by Evie.

"My turn," Rett said, coming forward with Mason and the twins. "I remember Mum's love of the beach and all things from the Bay of Fundy. So the kids and I brought some rocks and shells that we're going to put right here." She helped the kids arrange their collected items close, but not too close, to the little fire.

Evie watched. She wondered what the little kids thought. Mason could barely remember his grandmother; he was only five when she died. And the little girls were so little. Babies, really. *To them, Mum is just an idea.*

Rett turned to her. "Evie?"

She shook her head. "Let Dorie go." There was no need to be chronological about this.

Dorie pulled Chad by the hand. "This is Chad's first time at Mum's picnic, even though Alice, his grandmother, has been every year. But Chad's moved back to Stella Mare now and I wish Mum could have met him. I think she would be happy with the work we're doing in the dog sanctuary. I'm going to miss her even more when we get married. I hope she would be proud of me." Her voice cracked and she turned toward the fire.

Chad, looking intensely uncomfortable, addressed the group. "I, uh, I'm going to be part of this family and I wish I got to meet Dorie's mum. I'm, uh, I'm not even much of a dog person, or I didn't used to be, but I do know that people can change. So Dorie and I, we want to honour her mum." He held up a wooden sign. "We're going to put this under the Best Friends sign at the sanctuary."

Dorie returned to read it aloud. "In memory of Agnes Madison and Marjorie Bartlett. Mrs. Bartlett's estate is providing a lot of our funding, so we put her on there too," she explained.

"Well, that's real nice," James said. "Nice woodworking, too."

"I didn't do it," Chad said quickly. "But I know a guy."

Dorie looked at Evie. "Now?"

"Yeah, okay. I guess so." Walking toward the fire, she gave herself a pep talk. *You can do this, Evie. These people are just family friends. You know all of them.* She turned toward the group. *Yes, just Alice and the ladies, a couple of families from the church, Dad and the sisters and Corinne. And Stephen, who was looking toward Chad and his hand-carved sign. It's okay.*

"I..." Her voice trailed away. Gazing beyond the people to the water, she saw the last of the daylight leak away. Darkness grew, flooding the beach from the ocean and from behind her on the land. She felt the warmth of the fire, smelled the wood smoke, heard a sleepy gull...

"Shh...listen to Evie," Rett admonished a chatty twin. Harry picked her up and she tucked her head into his shoulder, thumb in mouth.

Evie opened her own mouth again, but nothing came out. Everything was darkness. It was just like when Mum died; the world was dark and it stayed dark for weeks. *This time nobody died though. This time it was just me. My future died. My relationship. My career. My life. Maybe it's a good thing Mum isn't here to see it. She loved Jase. She always talked about when we'd get married. I can't say any of that to these people.*

Looking again at the firelit faces, she saw annoyance, criticism, boredom. *Why can't I do this? My sisters seem to manage it. I just can't.*

She croaked out, "I miss her. That's all." She walked away. Heading down the beach, she broke into a run.

"Evie!" She ran from Corinne's voice. She heard sounds of laughter and conversation, but she just kept running in the dark on the wet sand. Maybe the darkness would swallow her. But her legs gave out too soon. When she reached the town's picnic site farther up the beach, she dropped, panting, onto a bench.

What was that old song? Hello, darkness? She had been in this place before, but never felt like she caused it. *Mum would be so unhappy with me.* Tears slipped down her cheeks. *I've never done things right.* Didn't become a professional, didn't get married, picked a man who... Well, that thought brought cascades of images of Jase with Michelle, so she tried to steer away. Face it, Evelyn, she admonished, you're a major screwup. Mum would hate that language. She would say something about not having an adequate working vocabulary or something.

Pain everywhere. Her legs and shoulders ached. Her head hurt. Her stomach was upset, like she was dizzy or something.

What a disaster. Why couldn't she cope? Everyone else in the family coped just fine.

She immediately reconsidered that. Maybe everyone wasn't always fine. Dorie only recently got her act together. Rett and Harry had their moments, and nobody knew what really went on with Helen, since she never came home. But Evie was still certain that nobody screwed up like she did. She was the different one.

Different, yes. Not as different as Leonie.

Okay, but that's history. That's not now.

Her mind kept returning to Leonie though. She had been really different. Different language, different culture. But she made it work.

I can't believe I did that. Running away like some thirteen-year-old drama queen. How am I ever going to face anyone?

Evie lay down on the bench. It was cooling off fast, but she was by no means ready to return to the scene of her humiliation. Instead, she gazed up at the sky. *Where are you, Mum? I used to believe you could become a star when you died. Are you out there? Leonie too? Even Hannah, the diary-keeper?* The pinpricks of starlight grew brighter as the darkness deepened.

"Hey."

Stephen.

"Hey back." She sat up and looked toward him. He sat beside her on the bench.

"What are you seeing out there?" He waved toward the night sky.

"Judgment."

"Really? The stars are judging you?" He wasn't sarcastic, just interested. "Tell me about that."

She turned to him. "You don't know me. Everybody back there..." She waved vaguely down the beach. "They've all known me forever. They know the kind of person I am. But you don't, at least not yet."

He chuckled comfortably. "You're right. I barely know you. But I like you."

"Don't do that! If you knew me, you'd never say that."

"Okay. Maybe you're right. But if it feels like even the stars are judging you, it sounds like you could use a friend."

"Yeah, maybe."

"Try me. I'm the guy from elsewhere, remember? I have no reason to judge. Besides, I know a few things about not fitting in."

"Really? Like what?"

He laughed. "Have you really looked at me?"

She squinted at him in the dark. "I think so. What are you talking about?"

"I don't look like most of the people in Stella Mare, do I? My father is white. My mother was black."

"Was?"

"Yes. Unfortunately, she died about five years ago. Way too young. I know about losing a mother."

"I'm sorry."

"Thanks. I do miss her." He was quiet for a beat. "As a biracial kid, I never was really sure where I belonged. I wasn't the only one, of course. My schools were diverse: kids from everywhere really, in the Washington, DC, area. Immigrant kids and children of diplomats and regular folks."

"Different from here. I went to school with lots of indigenous kids but mostly kids from Irish and English and Scottish ancestry. And French, of course. A whole lot of white people."

"Hmm."

"It was good to go away to school."

"I bet. Probably good to come home, too."

"Well, that's where this discussion began. I never felt like I belonged."

They sat quietly. She imagined a younger Stephen, at home with his parents in Virginia. It was hard to imagine with no information.

"What did your parents do?"

"Mama was a prof. English literature. Taught me to love books and thinking. Daddy is a musician of sorts; he's from a family that has resources. He doesn't have to make a living playing gigs, if you know what I mean."

"I'm not sure I do. I don't think we have any families like that in Stella Mare."

He laughed. "Maybe not. Or maybe they're just quiet about it. Anyway, big cities like DC and college towns, like where I live now, are pretty forgiving of difference, but there still was something about being a kid in that family that meant I was not quite this and not quite that."

"Mum would say, neither fish nor fowl, nor good red herring," Evie noted.

"Yep. That's me. And it sounds like you think that's you too."

"I'm not like my sisters. You've met two of them now; what do you think?"

"Well, you don't look like Rett or Dorie," he agreed. "And Corinne, is she a sister?"

"No, she's my mother's sister. Weren't you listening?"

"Maybe I was thinking about something else," he said. "So, you don't look like your sisters. Instead, you've got this lovely, curly dark hair." He lifted a strand of curls off her shoulder. "You're not as tall. I think your eyes are a deep chocolatey brown."

"Well, that's a nice description. I've been told dirt brown and worse, but I'll take chocolate."

"Who do you resemble in your family?"

"I'm just finding out. My great-grandmother, I think. She was an Acadian woman, brought from Nova Scotia by her sailor husband who happened to be my great-grandfather."

"Acadian?"

"Yes, Maritime history. You know. Early settlers from France who were repeatedly displaced by the English. You must have heard about Evangeline, dragged off to Louisiana and all that."

"Evangeline? Like the Longfellow poem?"

"That's the one. Based in fact. But some Acadians just moved around in the Maritimes, avoiding the English, so in the early 1900s there were Acadians in Cape Breton."

"Right, of course. I did do my homework. I just didn't know that there were any Acadian people in this area," he said.

"Well, that's the issue. There weren't. She must have stuck out like the proverbial sore thumb. She didn't speak much English and there was a fair amount of anti-Acadian sentiment at that time. But really, I'm just learning about her."

"It sounds intriguing, especially if you feel a connection."

"I do, somehow. I've even been dreaming about her," Evie confided. "When I've been sleeping, that is."

"Insomnia?"

"Only since I've blown up my entire life in a single week," she said bitterly. "I used to sleep just fine."

"With an opening like that I'm likely to pry. But I am going to restrain myself and just ask, are you ready to come back to the fire?"

"Yes, sure," she said. Oddly, she felt much better. "Thanks for listening."

"Listening went both ways. Thank you." He smiled as he stood up and held out a hand. "When I left, your dad was piling on the wood and the kids were getting wilder and wilder."

"Okay, I'm ready." She let him pull her from the bench. "I like watching the kids have fun. There'll be music too. Did you inherit your father's musical genes?"

"Unfortunately not," he said. "But I am a big appreciator."

"That's my job too," she said. "We can appreciate together."

Chapter 18

That night, Evie shook the sleeping pills into her hand and looked at them. Her hot bath had been soothing, and the evening had gone okay. Maybe even well. Perhaps she could sleep on her own tonight. She dropped the pills back into the bottle and looked in the mirror.

Fingering the curls at her shoulder, she sighed. Maybe curly was okay. She peered closer to see the colour of her eyes. Chocolate, not dirt. Stephen saw chocolate.

She climbed into bed with Hannah's diary. Flipping pages, she found a recipe for bread pudding. Bread pudding. She had a faint memory of tearing bread into pieces, but then shook it off.

I'll just let it open up wherever, and that's what Leonie wants me to read.

The pages fell open at another story. Hannah's handwriting was becoming familiar and easy to read.

Mama wanted her children to know their roots, but Daddy didn't see the point. He was happy in Stella Mare, and he figured she should be too. But I remember her looking at her Bible, with some words written in it by her mother. She said her mother died when she was a little girl, but I don't know how little. She was seventeen when Daddy met her, and her mother was long gone, so she was young. I don't know if Mama realized that she'd be leaving her family forever if she came to Stella Mare. I have some recollection of her making plans to go and visit her papa, my grandpapa, and everything falling apart.

When I was twelve, a letter came from Cheticamp. A letter was a big deal, and this letter was in french, so only Mama could read it. I came home from school to find her sitting at the kitchen table, staring at these pages, cold tea in her cup. She looked like she hadn't moved in hours. The baby was crying in the cradle, so I ran over to get him. I changed him and brought him to Mama to nurse. She took him, but seemed a million miles away. I was scared. Mama was never like that.

"What's wrong? Mama?" The baby nosed greedily under her smock, and she attended to him briefly then finally looked at me.

"Mama, what's in that letter?"

She started to cry. I had never seen my mother cry, so it was shocking. "My brother, Samuel," she said. "He says Papa is very sick and going to die." She clutched a handkerchief to her face, holding the baby with one arm.

"Mama."

She seemed to come to herself then, and said, "Hannah, go change your school clothes. I need you to help me." Together we got the supper together, and when Daddy came home from fishing, we all sat as usual, but I could see Mama was upset. Later than night I heard them talking; arguing, really. That, too, was shocking. There wasn't much that Mama and Daddy fought about, but this was one thing.

In the morning, Mama and Daddy went into town to make a telephone call. She came home full of plans.

"Hannah, I have to go to Cape Breton. Can you take care here? You know what has to be done, the little ones, the cooking." Her brown eyes stared deeply into mine. "I know you can do it, ma chère."

I clutched at her arm. "You will come back?"

She smiled. "Oh, yes, I'll come back. I won't leave you with all of this." She gestured to the house. "I know what that's like. I will come back to you."

She left two days later. I remember Daddy carrying a little suitcase down the stairs. I don't even know how Mama got to Cape Breton, but I assume she got a ride with someone going that way. It's not like there were regular buses or trains. Cheticamp was far away. I remember feeling so small and scared as she left. I remembered her eyes and her words. "You can do this, ma chère."

My little brother cried for her, so I couldn't. Instead, I baked the bread, carried him around, sent my little sisters out to gather eggs and bring potatoes in from the cold space. School was not part of my day, because taking care of a home and family took all my time. I was finally starting to get the rhythm of the day, starting the bread dough after supper, making a big breakfast for Daddy and the children in the early morning, scrubbing the clothes and hanging the laundry as soon as the sun shone, when Daddy was called to the telephone in town. Most of our neighbours used the phone in the general store. A small boy, messenger from the store, ran to the house to let us know that Daddy would be getting a call later that day.

We sent him off with some excitement, but he returned heavy of foot and dark around the eyes.

"Is she coming?" I couldn't contain myself.

"Yes," he said, but there was no lightness in his voice. "She's coming. Tuesday."

The little children started jumping and shouting with joy, but I asked, "Why aren't you happy about it?"

"She's sad," he said. "Her father is gone and now she is leaving her home. Again."

"But we need her," I said.

"Yes, we do," he agreed. "We need her. So she's coming." But he still looked heavy and dark.

I was so happy to see her when she finally got home. She put her case upstairs, changed her dress, and put on her apron. She held the baby, but the little girls wanted her too, so she finally just sat down and let them sit all over her. Even at twelve, I felt the same need, but I was too grown up to ask for it. Instead, I made her a cup of tea and sat beside her.

When the little ones had soaked in their fill of Mama, they ran off to play outdoors, and she and I had a slice of my over-baked bread and our tea.

"How did you like being the lady of the house?" she asked with a tender smile.

"I'm tired," I admitted. "And I miss going to school."

She nodded. "You can go back to school tomorrow."

"Mama," I said, "I didn't do that good at being the lady. I yelled at the little girls every day, and I burned the bread on the first day, and I didn't get the washing out in time to dry."

She shrugged. "Everyone is alive. You did enough."

"I don't think Daddy thought so."

"Well, I think so. Now, why don't you go outside? I'll make the supper tonight."

I gave her a hug and ran outside, feeling lighter than I had in three weeks. Oh, it was good to be just one of the children again.

Later, I heard Mama and Daddy talking about her visit. Her Papa had died and Samuel, her brother, was living in North Sydney to work at the fish plant. He sent money home, but his wife had been caring for my grandfather and their children, and her own mother who had moved in with them. Mama's voice got louder, and I could hear her words. "It was good to talk my talk, Charles," she said. "To hear people speak my words, my language. To not always wonder what people are thinking."

Daddy's voice was muffled as it always was, his tone calming. She quieted too, and soon enough I drifted off.

Mama was different after that. I would find her staring out across the back field, or at the edge of the water, gazing toward the outlet to the sea. I wondered how hard it was to be perpetually different from your neighbours, to have a background that nobody near you could understand. Except Daddy, of course.

Evie tried to focus on more words, but her eyes were closing. Sleep. To sleep, perchance to dream. *Haven't I heard that somewhere before?*

Leonie, white-haired, crumpled, sat in her rocking chair by the stove, lap full of burlap. Hannah, tall, stately, and grey-haired, kneaded dough at the table. A youthful Agnes sat at the table, sipping tea.

Evie, hovering in the doorway, watched and listened.

"So, Agnes, who's your young man?" Hannah asked, glancing up.

Agnes reddened. "What did Mum tell you?"

Hannah laughed and looked over at Leonie. "Well, Mama, what did Sarah say? A nice man, maybe went to school, maybe knows about fish, maybe more?"

Leonie's eyes danced behind her glasses. "You tell us, Agnes. I want to hear from you. Is he handsome? Is he kind?"

Hannah dumped the dough into a bowl, covered it, and poured another cup of tea. "Do tell, Agnes. Where did you meet him?"

"At school. Well, he came to a dance at school."

"But he's not at school? Say more, Aggie, we want to know."

"He's graduated and goes to university. In Fredericton."

"Oh, a university man. Well, la di da!" Leonie giggled.

"Grandmama!"

"Never you mind," Hannah said comfortingly. "What's his name?"

"James."

"And you like him, I take it."

Evie watched Agnes redden further. "I do like him. I like him a lot. I think we're going to get married."

Hannah stiffened. "Oh, you are! Does your mother know this?"

"Shh. You can't tell her," Agnes insisted. "She wants me to wait until I'm older, but really, I'm old enough. I graduate in just a few months."

"And then what," Hannah persisted. "Babies and housework?"

"That's what we did," Leonie said. "That's what we all did, Hannah. Why not Aggie?"

Hannah looked annoyed. "Just because we all did it doesn't mean it's the best thing. Maybe Aggie would like to have a career, you know."

Agnes laughed. "Raising babies is a career, Aunt Hannah."

"It certainly is work," Leonie said with a sparkle.

"Work, yes, career, no," Hannah said. "Agnes, I know Sarah wants you to go to university too, like your James there. Why not try it out?"

Agnes looked pained. "Because I don't want to?"

"I went to Teacher's College, you know. It was a good thing too."

"But you didn't get married, Aunt Hannah. You had to work."

"You'll have to work too, you know," Hannah said sharply. "Babies are a lot of work, and then they get bigger and need stuff, and mothers end up working outside the home anyway. So you might as well get some education so you don't have to work in the fish plant."

"Fish plant? Samuel works at the fish plant." Leonie sounded uncertain. Hannah looked her way.

"Yes, Mama, Uncle Samuel worked at the fish plant."

"He's dead now." Leonie's voice grew quieter. "They're all dead now. Papa and Samuel and Charles. And Baby Michael."

To Agnes, Hannah whispered, "Michael was my brother, the first one. Died before a year, in Cape Breton."

Evie, still hovering, moved toward young Agnes, who aimlessly stirred her tea.

"Aunt Hannah," Agnes said, "do you have any regrets?"

Hannah paused. "Of course. Everyone has regrets. Anybody who gets to make decisions has regrets. At your age though, it's hard to see that the decisions you make will have lasting consequences."

"You mean like getting married now instead of later?"

"Like that. We aren't fortune-tellers, so we don't know what the future holds. We can be sure there will be consequences of actions, even if we don't know what the consequences will be."

Leonie returned to the conversation. "I came to Stella Mare with my husband. I didn't want to leave my home, but I married Charles and I had to go where he took me."

Hannah looked at her fondly. "Is that a regret, Mama?"

"How can I regret my whole life? I wish I could have been in Cheticamp and Stella Mare both, had my first family and my own family all together. It was not to be."

"Mum says I'll ruin my life if I get married to James next spring," Agnes confided.

"Sarah married at sixteen, you know," Hannah noted. "That might be influencing her opinion."

"I was seventeen," Leonie said. "Charles was the most handsome man I had ever seen, even if he didn't speak a word of French. I could see him in his eyes. He was a good man, kind and hardworking."

"So, Grandmama, was it your destiny to meet him and marry him?" Agnes's eyes were shining.

Hannah spluttered, turning to the stove.

"Not destiny, ma chère, but it was how things happened back then. Girls got married. Had babies. Worked in the house and garden, in the smokehouse and the sugarbush. Men fished, farmed, and worked in the woods. Sometimes they went to war."

Hannah turned back, impatience in every line of her body. "You have options now, Agnes. You don't have to live like my mother or like your mother. It's almost nineteen-seventy. Women have choices."

"It sounds like no matter what choices I make, I will have regrets. No escaping from regrets."

Mum! Evie tried to speak, but her hovering self had no voice. *Choose us! Choose to have us.* As she struggled, the scene faded into fog, and she sank into a deep darkness.

Chapter 19

Sunday morning felt good. Sleep made such a difference. Evie was up before James, took the big dogs out for a quick visit to the edge of the woods, and returned to dump kibble into bowls. She put on the coffee and pulled the leftover bread pudding from the refrigerator.

Bread pudding.

Bread.

Hannah kneading dough. Oh, that was some dream. Regrets either way, huh?

She mindlessly spooned cold bread pudding into her mouth, standing with the refrigerator door open. Delicious, sticky with maple syrup.

She took her coffee to the back porch. Leaning on the doorframe, she sipped and took in the exuberant pink of the crab-apple blossoms, the pale blue of early morning sky, the miniature maple leaves starting to fill up the sky at the back of the yard. The pink tree drew her, and she wandered across the dew-damp yard to stand under it, watching from the inside as the sun touched the edges of the flowers. She became aware of a sound, a humming, buzzing, chorus of vibration almost inside her head. Standing still, barely breathing, she let her whole body listen.

When she looked up, she saw them: an army of bees and wasps and various creatures, dipping into the blossoms and buzzing between them. She watched and waited. It was like an entire industry, or a city full of industry, with bees travelling quickly between flowers, no collisions, every bee with its own trajectory, its own sense of busyness, a whole world of which Evie was not a part. Every one of these creatures was doing a job, the job it was made to do. Doing it as if there was nothing else in the world. *As if my disaster of a life means nothing, and it does mean nothing to a bee in this tree right now.* With a shock, she realized that it meant very little to her too, at this exact moment of being in the tree, part of the tree.

After a while, she gently stepped out from under the crab apple and into the sun. Smelling the grass underfoot, the fragrance of the flowers, and feeling warmth on her face, she realized that now she could not hear the vibrations that were so enveloping while under the tree.

Back in the kitchen, she gazed at the crab apple from the window while she rinsed her mug. It was like a secret world out there. You had to get out of your own way to listen to what was happening.

Evie carried the diary into the living room.

"Hey, Dad, look at what I found," she said.

James, resting on the couch, sat up. "What did you find? More rugs?"

"Well, yes, but this too. This is real treasure, I think," she said, laying the book on his lap.

"What's this? A journal?"

"Not really a journal. More like a memoir, I think."

"What's the difference?"

"It was Great-Aunt Hannah's story about her mother. She wrote it after she was grown up. I think of a journal as a day-by-day thing."

"Well, look at that," James said, paging through.

"Did you know Hannah?" Evie thought about her dream.

"Oh, yes, I did. She was the one who didn't get married. Teacher."

"And writer apparently."

"Well, I didn't know that part. She died about the time my mother died, back when you girls were small. Then your grandmother came to live with us."

"And Corinne too?"

"No, Corinne came later on, when Dorie was a baby. Oh, it was wild times back then." James smiled dreamily. "House full of women all the time. I had to go to work just to get out of the estrogen soup."

"You old sexist! I'm sure you still ruled the roost. After all, that was in the 1990s."

James laughed out loud. "Yeah, ancient history. No more rugs?"

"Oh, well, yes. Lots of rugs. I was wondering if I can use the den? I'd like to lay them out, copy the designs, see what I can learn about them."

"I thought we were getting stuff out of the house."

"These are art, Dad."

He looked at her.

"Nah, I'm kidding. I negotiated some space at the gallery to store them. But I would like to have the den to keep a couple while I'm working with them."

"Well, sure. It's a little room but nobody's using it for much." He walked over and opened the door. "Oh, well. I guess I've been using it for storage."

"I think I've been ignoring it. But now I need it."

The room was packed with boxes, furniture, and plastic bins. Evie's heart sank. "Well, all this stuff has to go somewhere anyway, right? I might as well get started. Are you around to help me decide what to do with stuff?"

"Me?" James had his deer-in-headlights look. "I, uh, I trust you to make good decisions about stuff. Donate, and when in doubt, ask Dorie."

Evie frowned. "Dorie? Why her?"

James was backing away. "Because she's more hardhearted than the rest of you. She'll say dump it."

"Oh, you think so? I think she's just stockpiling stuff in Alice's barn, behind the dog sanctuary."

"I don't care what she's doing with it as long as I don't have to decide anything." With that, he turned for the kitchen, tossing back over his shoulder, "You can have the den, Evelyn. You just have to find it first."

Right. Remembering her process in the kitchen, she started making piles: trash, donate, reconsider.

By early evening she'd made enough space to lay out all the rugs. She brought in two more lamps and took careful pictures with her phone. Then she set up her laptop on the wobbly table she'd unearthed. Documentation. That was what she wanted to do. Get them documented, get the data organized, and then they could go to storage at the gallery.

The sun was sliding closer to the horizon at eight thirty p.m. when James called to her from the kitchen.

"Hungry? I'm making leftovers."

Standing and stretching, she looked around the room. The biggest, cleanest of the rugs held a glow of its own, flat on the hardwood floor full of reflected evening light. She stood over it. Was it the Leonie of her dream who hooked that rug? Or Hannah? Or some other ancestor? She had a feeling that rug hooking was something Leonie had brought to Stella Mare, but intuition wasn't fact. She had more to read in the memoir to be sure, but it had been a good day's work.

When she went to bed, Jase was back. She tossed and turned, falling into brief moments of conversation with him, with him and Leonie, a moment when Mallow and Custard snarled and bit at Michelle (she knew she was dreaming with that one), and a terrifying bit where the hooked rugs were all on fire, burning up in the den but not taking anything else with them. Leonie was standing by, watching. She turned to Evie and said, "What's done is done. No use fretting about what's over."

Evie sat up with a gasp. *Well, this stinks.* She padded down the stairs to the den to peek at the rugs. They were intact, of course, but was she?

She warmed up milk and honey and on a second thought, poured a dram of James's whisky in the mug. Sipping meditatively, she curled up on the couch and pulled a blanket over her. When the mug's contents were gone, sleep remained elusive, so she went to the kitchen. Maybe she could bake something.

"What kind of cinnamon rolls are these?" Dorie asked. "I've never seen this kind."

"What?" Evie said absently. "Cinnamon rolls?"

"Yeah, right here. I assume you made them, right?" Dorie held a pan and a tea towel.

"Maybe Corinne brought them."

"It's Mum's pan. And they're right here. And the bowl is in the—yup, in the dishwasher. Come on, Evie. Don't fool around."

"I have been doing a lot of baking. Like instead of sleeping. It's hard to remember what's real and what's a dream. But I guess I baked last night." She took a bite and said, "Oh, these are different. I've never had these in my life."

"What is this? The Twilight Zone?" Dorie was dismissive.

"You know," Evie said, poking around for the cookbook, "Mum had some old recipes in here. I was looking at this when I first came home." She pulled out the book, overflowing with bits of paper, bookmarks, and full of pencilled-in notes. "Look at this."

She held out the top loose sheet to Dorie, who burst into laughter.

"Nun's Farts!"

"Pretty irreverent," Evie said with a grin. "Some ancestor of Mum's, I guess."

James came in from the porch. "Here are my girls."

"Hey, Dad, you baking these days?" Dorie asked. "Why did you have to wait until I moved out to take up baking?"

"Baking? Nah, not me. That's Evie's area."

"Come on, Dad," Evie protested. "You made that bread pudding the other night."

He shook his head. "Not me. That was some good, though, wasn't it? Just like your mother used to make."

"Maybe we have a ghost," Dorie suggested. "A ghost who likes to bake."

Maybe, Evie thought darkly. Instead, I've been so sleep deprived I don't remember what I bake in the middle of the night. "Where've you been, Dad?"

"Doctor," James said briefly and headed to the living room.

"Wait! What doctor? What for?" Evie and Dorie followed him.

"Dr. Swami, right?" Evie guessed. "The cardiologist?"

"Cardiologist? Dad, what's up?" Dorie pressed.

James lay on the couch. "I'm a little tired, girls."

"Dad, you're avoiding." Dorie pushed harder.

James snickered. "You noticed that, did you? Don't get much past my girls." He closed his eyes and pretended to snore.

"Well, we're not getting anything out of him," Dorie observed loudly. "Where's this stuff you wanted me to look at?"

"Right here. He's going to have to tolerate our noise during his nap," she said distinctly toward the couch. More exaggerated snoring ensued.

Systematically they worked through the stuff in Evie's "reconsider" pile, adding most of it to the donation boxes. "It's hard to decide by myself," she told Dorie. "With two of us, I don't feel so weird getting rid of stuff."

"Yeah, well, I put a lot of this stuff in this room for that reason," Dorie admitted. "After Mum died and we cleared out the hospital bed and stuff, I just piled up anything I couldn't figure out in this room. I think Dad did too. That's why it's such a hodgepodge."

"I'm using it for the moment. It's a good place to look at these hooked rugs in detail. They're going to be stored at the gallery, though."

"Oooh, the gallery. You mean where that nice Stephen works."

"Stop it, Dorie. You don't always have to be the annoying baby sister."

"Oh, but sometimes it's fun. Let me look at that big one again."

They gazed together at the cobalt and scarlet.

Dorie sighed dreamily. "You know, even though I've seen that rug, it still amazes me. Who made it?"

"I'm not really sure, but I think maybe our great-grandmother. Look at how it's made. They used bits and pieces, making every scrap count."

"Like patchwork quilts?"

"Yes, and just as functional. It seems like everything had a purpose."

"And beautiful. Those women worked so hard, but they still made things pretty."

"I know, right? I can't imagine. What drive makes people do that?"

"Well, you would know better than me, since you're the artist. I wonder if those women were just aching for a way to make something beautiful because they worked so hard. I dunno."

Evie gazed at the rug. "I don't know, either, but I sure want to find out."

Later that day, she piled most of the rugs in her backseat and drove to the gallery. Cassandra was at the desk.

"Evie!"

"Hi, Cassandra," Evie said, struggling under her armload of rugs.

"Oh, let me help!" she said, coming around to take some bundles.

"We're heading for the closet," Evie explained, "but I don't exactly know where that is."

Cassandra laughed. "Well, there's only one. Follow me."

Through the far door into the office and through the office itself, the closet was exactly that. Small, but with metal shelving along one long wall, it was functional and blessedly empty.

Cassandra helped her store the bundled rugs on shelves. She'd been diligent in recording her information and labelling the rugs, especially since townsfolk had been adding to the collection. Each rug had a colour-coded label that connected it to her notes on her laptop.

"Wow, this is like a museum collection," Cassandra noted approvingly.

Evie laughed. "I have no idea what I'm doing. I'm just keeping notes on everything in case something is important. Mostly I want to make sure I don't confuse rugs from one person's attic with another."

"Can I see one?"

"Oh, sure," Evie said. "Let me find a good one. Here, let's look at this one." She shook out one of the bundles. "This one has a lot of wear."

"But look at the design. What is that, a dog?"

"I have no idea. Or a whale? You can see that this rug was used as a rug, but for some reason the family still kept it." She flipped it over. "Look at the way it's made. Some woman spent her evenings by the fire poking fabric scraps through the weave of an old flour bag."

"I'm glad I don't have to do that," Cassandra said.

"Some of them aren't about what they had to do though. This one I have at my house is more like art for its own sake." She scrolled on her phone to the images of the cobalt and scarlet creation she'd left at home.

"Wow. That's different."

"Isn't it? They all have their own beauty, but some of them seem like they were never meant to be functional."

Cassandra mused. "I guess that's true of a lot of craft. You make something functional, but the person next to you might go way beyond function to make something that is valuable for its beauty. Like pottery is functional, but a lot of pottery is art."

"I was never interested in craft before finding these rugs in my father's attic. Now it's all I think about, and the women who made them. I want to know their stories."

"You sound like Stephen," Cassandra said with a smile.

Shrugging that off, Evie continued, "I don't know how to date them. I can't tell whether the damage happened in use or in storage, and I have no idea how you correctly preserve something like this."

"Have you tried the Crafts College in Fredericton? They have a textile program."

"I didn't know that." Evie blinked and smiled at Cassandra. "Thanks."

"Show me your system. I like organization."

"Don't mistake me for someone who knows what she's doing," she warned. "This is totally seat of pants work." She opened her laptop to show Cassandra her files, but the bell jangled on the front door, calling Cassandra back to work.

Evie stepped back and admired her new space. It was small but functional. There was still room for more rugs, too, so it had a future. The rugs were out of the house, but she felt a pang as she closed the closet door behind her. She was glad that she'd kept the best rug and all the documents at home.

Cassandra was talking to gallery visitors, so Evie just waved as she headed for the door.

"Wait, Evie," Cassandra called. "Leonard left you an envelope." She handed it over and returned to her visitors.

There was a lump in the envelope. A key. She had her own key to the gallery. She felt better about leaving the rugs.

Chapter 20

Evie was finally getting some traction in her painting. By the end of the week after the picnic, she had three to show Leonard. When she dropped them at the gallery, Stephen was there. She was absurdly happy to see him.

"I brought some work," she said, gesturing with the portfolio. "Where should I put them?"

"Will you show me?"

"Sure. I guess so." He cleared a space on his desk while her chest got tight. What did she care about his opinion? But she did. She laid out her work, the largest, carefully mounted, on top.

"Oh, my," he said. "Look at this." His little smile let her take a deep breath.

"Yeah. I figured Leonard was looking for lighthouses and boats, but I just couldn't. These interest me a lot more."

"What is this? Looks like the inside of an apple tree."

Her smile deepened. "You got it in one. It's the view from underneath the flowering crab in my father's yard."

Stephen marvelled. "You can almost smell the blossoms."

"What was even more amazing was the sound. That's hard to communicate in this medium, but look closely. Can you see the insects? They were everywhere. I had to try to convey that experience somehow."

"Well, I think you were successful. Now what's this? A painting of a quilt?"

"No, of a hooked rug. One of the treasures from the attic." She looked down. "The one I haven't brought here yet. I'm not ready to store it."

"Is it really that vibrant in the original? You've done amazing things with saturation here."

Her chest warmed and she smiled even harder. "Thank you for really seeing them," she said quietly. "I wasn't sure, you know? Nobody's looked at my work for years. Well, except my father."

Stephen looked at her. "And he's your father."

"Right." They gazed at each other for a moment, until Stephen broke the silence.

"Put them on Leonard's desk. I'm sure he'll be blown away too,"

She piled them up. "That's that." She picked up her portfolio, preparing to leave, but he stopped her.

"I'm so glad you're here. Thank you again for the invitation to the family picnic."

Evie felt a wave of embarrassment. *Let it go, let it go.*

"I met some really interesting folks there."

"Interesting? Like who?" Evie couldn't imagine.

"Well, like Alice Simmons. And your father."

"Oh, come on. Alice and Dad are interesting? Really?"

His smile deepened. "Remember, I'm from away. It's all new to me. These folks you've known forever, all new."

"New eyes do make a difference," she admitted.

"I hope to spend some time with both Alice and your father, and also Natalie, the pink-haired lady, whose grandfather worked on the train, bringing rich folks in from New Yawk to see the Canadian fishermen."

Evie grinned. "Murricans."

"Yes. New Yawkers."

"Stella Mare was a destination in those days," Evie added with a grin. "If you were rich enough."

"I'm not interested in the rich visitors. Lots of people have written about that."

Evie recalled Stephen's comment about his father's family having resources. Did he come from wealth? If so, you couldn't tell.

He went on. "I'm interested in the folks who live here all year, making a living."

"Well, you hit pay dirt at the picnic because there wasn't a rich person there," Evie said.

"Probably nobody who would have considered themselves an artist either, except you," he added.

"Actually, I met an old friend of my mother's who makes art," Evie said. "But that's not who you mean, is it?"

"You get it. I'm interested in the art that gets made while making a living. Like the generations of fishermen who carved wood. They just carved. Some of what they made was functional, and some of it was beautiful and functional. I bet not one of them ever thought of themselves as an artist."

"I've been thinking about that too," Evie said. When he looked at her quizzically, she added quickly, "The rug artist. I bet she didn't see herself as an artist."

"These rugs that are in the closet were in your attic? It's probably full of treasure."

"Full of junk is more like it. I'm gathering more too, because Dorie spread the word that I'm interested. Townsfolk can't wait to empty their junk into my arms."

"Attic treasures," Stephen mused. "You haven't run into any wood carvings up there, have you?"

She laughed. "Not in the attic. You'll have to ask Dad. Wood carvings are more likely in his domain, aka the shed."

"I'd love to visit you at home, Evie," Stephen said in his oddly formal way.

"You mean talk to Dad," she said.

He reddened slightly. "Not only. But yes."

She took pity on him. "I can show you the rugs I kept at the house. How about tomorrow morning?"

She could have taken up residence in his smile. It was nice to make somebody so happy with such a simple invitation. She was smiling, too, as she left the gallery.

Mallow and Custard announced his arrival. Generally somnolent, the big dogs were awake and interested in an unfamiliar car. Evie felt a shiver of excitement as she went to the driveway to bring Stephen in through the back door.

"Come on this way. Using the back door means you're a neighbour," she explained. "Or a friend. Front doors are only for people we don't want to see."

He laughed. "Good to know."

"Coffee?" She reached for a mug.

"Sure," he agreed. They sat at the kitchen table, and she offered a plate of brown-sugar brownies that had appeared that morning. "I told you I've been having trouble sleeping," she confided. "I end up baking something or other almost every night. I don't like being up all night, but at least most mornings, there's something new here in the kitchen. My mother used to make these."

"They look great. I'm sorry you're not sleeping, but these are delicious."

"I guess. Anyway, let's go see the rugs." She led the way into the now-tidy den off the living room.

The east-facing window was bare, and sunlight picked out details on the large rug laid carefully on a sheet on the floor.

On their knees, they looked at the details. Stephen's face was lit by interest, maybe just like hers, she thought. His piney scent quickened her breath.

"Look at this," he pointed out. "Are those fish jumping out of the water? How did they do this?"

"I don't know," she admitted. "There's a level of detail you wouldn't think you could get with just rags and burlap."

"There's a story behind this," he said with certainty. "Not just the artist's own story, but a story about this fishing trip, or this house, or this place." He rocked back on his heels. "You do have a treasure here."

"That's the biggest one and they clearly preserved it. But there are more. I have a few here, but most I stored in the closet at the gallery." She pulled out another rug. "See? Mostly they were used."

"Used how?"

"I think just to buffer a cold floor. As rugs. Like beside the bed, or in the kitchen. Some people call them mats, like floor mats. See, they've been used. A lot."

"I am reminded of the story quilts. Patchwork quilts made to tell a tale, give directions, symbolize something."

"It's like a mystery," she said. "I also have these." She pointed to the diary, the memoir, and the loose papers, spread on the little table.

"Oh, now you're talking," he said, eyes wide. "A historian's dream find. Documentation!"

"Well, kind of," she demurred. "My great-aunt's stories about her parents."

"And recipes too," he noted, picking up a sheet. "Hey, what's this?" He handed it to Evie.

Curious. It was the brown-sugar brownie recipe, but in Hannah's handwriting. There was a smudge on the page. She touched it, and a bit came off on her finger. Fresh?

She looked up at him. "I thought I was making my mother's brown-sugar brownies, but maybe it was somebody else's recipe." She fingered the smudge again. *Was I using this? Why don't I remember?*

"Do you bake?" she asked Stephen. He shook his head. "Well, those old recipes were like stories. They just wrote down what they did to make the cake or whatever. Sometimes they're so specific to a person's kitchen that you can't recreate them."

"I don't understand."

"Look here." She showed him the paper. "This says to bake them in Grandmama LeBlanc's square pan. That could mean a pan of any size, but in Hannah's house the specific pan was the one from her grandmother. And the measurements are non-standard. This says to use spoonfuls. But what size spoon?" She shook her head. "I don't know how anyone managed."

"Don't you? People had community knowledge. Specific to their own community, and when you left your community, you left that shared wisdom. I bet every woman in town knew what a spoonful meant, back when this was written down."

"Huh. Are you saying that now we have standard descriptions instead of community knowledge?"

He smiled. "That's my theory and I'm sticking with it. Actually, that's really my theory. Standard descriptions are a poor substitute for the feeling and sense of belonging that comes from a shared body of knowledge. My work on wood carvings is really about the people and their shared stories. Why not the community of bakers?"

"And rug makers?" Evie looked back at the floor. What was it like for Leonie to leave her community and all the shared wisdom, knowledge, and stories? Did she feel alone and lonely? Or did her husband and children make up for being so far from home?

"I wonder about the artistry," she said. "I understand they were poor, that they used up everything they had, and rags and flour sacks could be put to use to keep the floor warmer. But what is it that compelled them to make things beautiful? Or to tell a story? Why not just make a rug and be done with it?"

"You know," he said with a smile. "You know, Evie. That creative impulse we all have. You're an artist. You know better than most."

"I'm not so sure I'm an artist," she murmured.

He looked startled. "What do you mean?"

She shook her head. "Never mind. I'm just going through a lot right now."

"Okay." His gaze lingered on her face, but then he turned back to the rug on the floor. "Have you talked to anyone about these?"

"Like who?"

"Historian?"

"Isn't that you? I'm talking to you, right?"

He reddened slightly. "Well, yes, but I was thinking of somebody I know at Mount Allison University. She would love to see these, and she might have some information for you. I'll text you her information."

"Cassandra suggested the crafts college, too," she said, but flatly. She didn't want to show anyone else her find. She felt protective, as if someone wanted to tear the rugs away from her. The brightness of the room faded as clouds drew across the sun. Evie felt a wave of exhaustion.

"You'll like my friend, I promise," Stephen said.

"Okay." She didn't look at him.

"Evie? Did I say something to upset you?"

With effort, she focused on him. "No. No, Stephen, you're fine. I'm just tired."

He tried to peer into her eyes, but she looked away. I really am tired, she thought. So tired.

As if he could hear her thoughts, he said, "Well, I guess I better get going," he said, "unless your dad is here?" He turned it into a question.

"Um, yeah, he's probably out in the shed," she said. "I'll show you." Energy rising again, she gestured to him to follow.

He followed her through the backyard toward the shabby red outbuilding. "Wait, Evie," he called to her. "Is this your tree?"

She turned to him, eyebrows raised. He gestured to the flowering crab, and her tight face softened into a smile. Oh, he'd give a lot to see that smile every day.

"You remembered," she said warmly. "Yes, this is the tree. Come stand under it. Maybe you'll see why I had to try to capture it."

He rested one hand on the gnarly trunk. "This is an old one."

"Not all that old. Mum and Dad planted it when my sister Helen graduated from college. Apples don't live as long as some trees. But listen."

He couldn't take his eyes off her face, turned up to the blossoms floating above them. The sunlight filtered through pink and mauve and magenta to touch her cheeks, giving her a glow.

"Listen," she said, eyes closed.

With an effort, he tuned in to the sounds. Cars on the street, a dog a few houses away. Then he could hear their breathing; his own and Evie's. Listening more intently, it came. Buzzing, humming, a whole orchestra of sound from low bumbly bass to high-pitched whines. When he opened his eyes, Evie was looking at him expectantly.

"Well? Can you hear it?" she whispered.

He nodded. He didn't want this moment to stop. Barely breathing, he looked up to see the musicians zipping from blossom to blossom, crossing paths right to left, top to bottom. The industry in the tree was a world apart. He soaked in the moment: the music of flying insects, the feeling of the rough tree trunk, Evie's soft scent and warmth. Whatever happened, he would cherish this moment.

He didn't know what his face looked like, but she nodded and whispered, "You see? Amazing, huh?"

He smiled. He didn't feel like he could speak, not here in this cathedral of pink. Evie led the way out.

They stood for a moment, adjusting to being beside the tree rather than under it. He looked again. "It looks like a plain old flowering crab from here," he said.

"I know. It's been there for years, and this is the first time I had any clue about what goes on. It's kind of like a factory in there, but only for a week or so, while it's blooming."

Strangely moved, he grabbed her hand. "Evie, thank you. You know, flowering trees are all over where I grew up, but I never did that before."

"What?" She turned those deep chocolate eyes on him.

"I guess I just never took the time to experience it from the inside out."

She smiled but dropped his hand. "Well, honestly, it was only because I was taking a break from clearing the house that I did. I just got lucky."

"Not lucky. You pay attention."

"I guess. Maybe somebody will buy that painting."

"It'll be a fortunate collector who gets it," he affirmed.

She shrugged. "Let's go find Dad." Still musing, Stephen followed her to the shed.

"Hi, Stephen," James said from the workbench. "Nice to see you again."

"Thank you for talking to me," Stephen said. Evie leaned against the workbench.

"I appreciate being allowed to come to your family picnic too."

"Oh, that, well..." James dusted off his hands and sat in the rocker. "Find a seat." He gestured to the wooden crates and two big, peeled stumps that served as chairs. "Yeah, the picnic is an event. I'm happy you could come." He looked up at Evie. "Don't you have something to do in the house?"

"What? Uh, oh, right." She looked at Stephen. "Dad says I'll be in the house." She rolled her eyes at James and left the shed.

James waited until the door closed and said, "It's nice for Evie to meet people here."

"I feel lucky to have met her. I'm visiting but not exactly a tourist. It's not easy to explain to some folks why I'm here asking questions."

"How about you explain it to me?" James rocked gently, hands on his thighs.

"Sure, okay." Stephen settled in on his wooden crate. "I'm a prof in a humanities department, but my background is art, art history, and anthropology. I've been studying folk art and the stories that go with it for about ten years now."

"That right? What sent you that way?"

"That's a good question," Stephen said with a laugh. "I wanted to make my own art. If you'd asked me when I was a kid, I would have said I was going to be the next Banksy, taking the world by storm and surprise."

"Did a lot of painting on walls, did you?"

"Got in trouble for it too," Stephen admitted. "Fortunately, my mother was good at seeing strong internal drive and helping me channel it. My father just saw the behaviour. It took us years to repair that."

"Takes a long time to grow up," James said. "Some of us are still working on it."

"I have hope for myself then. Not yet a finished product."

"If you're finished growing, then you're really finished," James said. "Least that's my way of thinking about it. So why stories?"

Stephen rubbed his chin. "I have a notion about communities. Our communities are held together by the stories we share. Simple stories, like the Sunshine Diner has great coffee. That's shared knowledge among coffee drinkers here."

"If you've been hanging out at the Sunshine, you know a lot of stories get swapped there."

Stephen laughed. "Yes, I have been, and I have noticed. That's been my best place so far to meet fishermen, at least ones who are currently working on the water."

"How's this relate to art?"

"Everybody creates something. Some people pick up a piece of wood and a knife and create carvings, and often those carvings either tell a story or have meaning for people who see them. When tourists come in and buy somebody's carving of a gull or a boat, they're buying a connection to the story, even if they don't know the story themselves."

"But you're collecting, what? Carvings?"

"No, taking pictures of carvings and the artists who make them. What I'm really collecting is stories. I think of stories as the threads that hold everything together."

James was quiet, looking at his fingers. Then he looked up. "Like the stories we told about Aggie at the picnic. They hold us together, and hold her close to us, even though she's gone."

Stephen nodded. "Yes. Just like that."

"Hmm." James rocked. The silence in the shed was peaceful.

"Why Stella Mare? There's probably wood carvers down south."

"Well, that's another good question. I don't know the real reason yet. On the surface, I came here because I knew I could collect stories, and my friend Leonard had a place for me to stay. I'm on sabbatical from my job, so I have work to do, but my main work is collecting stories."

"Okay, that makes sense. All except the part about not knowing the real reason. What do you mean?"

His face warmed. "It might sound a little peculiar, but it's another part of my theory. Or maybe my philosophy. Some things are supposed to happen. Ever since I heard Leonard was here, I really wanted to come."

James rocked gently. "So you think you were meant to come to Stella Mare?"

"Sounds foolish, I know," Stephen said, smiling. "Sometimes I think it is foolish. I've been cold since I arrived in March, the locals are not thrilled with my questions, and I have to work in my friend's gallery to cover my housing. But I love it here."

"And what were you meant to do, or find? Some special wood carving?"

"I don't know," he said simply. "I'm just keeping faith that there's a good reason I picked Stella Mare, except I haven't discovered it yet. My being here, now, matters."

"Kind of a spiritual fella, are you?" James watched him.

"I don't see it that way," Stephen demurred. "More like philosophical. If you believe that life matters, then all of life matters. Every little bit."

"Hmm."

"The alternative is too hard to bear."

"What's the alternative? Oh, wait, I've got it. That nothing matters."

Stephen nodded. "That's just not possible. If anything matters, then everything matters. Even small wooden carvings. The stories about the Sunshine Diner, and your wife's love for dogs."

"You believe this, don't you?" James noted.

"I don't know if it's right or real or anything, but it is a better way for me to live than to believe that nothing has any meaning."

James gave a long, slow smile. "So how can I help you?"

Chapter 21

Evie went back to the house as commanded but stared out the kitchen window toward the shed. *I should be digging around in the attic, but since I can't seem to keep myself from staring out there where Stephen is, maybe I'll just bake something. Maybe Dad will invite him to eat with us.*

She laid her mother's cookbook out on the table. Maybe she could just look at Hannah's diary. Collecting the papers from the den, she looked hard at the brown-sugar brownie recipe. It did seem very familiar. She laid it on the table and gently sorted pages and loose sheets from her mother's cookbook and Hannah's documents.

By the time James came in from the shed, she had created piles and connections.

"Well, I like that young man," James announced, filling the kettle. "Kind of deep." He sat at the table beside her. "I kinda thought I might ask him to stay for supper, but I didn't want to put you on the spot."

Evie's face warmed. It was as if her father had been reading her mind. "You mean for cooking something?"

"Well, yes, but also, I don't know how interested you are." James appraised her. "In him, I mean."

Evie spluttered. "Well, you know, I'm not really interested in anybody. Not that way. It's too soon, Dad."

"Okay, okay. No big deal. He likes you though."

She gave him a look. "I like him too, but I'm nowhere interested in dating or anything." Even as she said it, she knew it wasn't true. Dad let it go though.

He nodded and turned to her papers. "What do you have here? Looks like you've been busy."

With relief, she nodded. *Yes, let's talk about something I can manage.* "Yeah, so I had Mum's cookbook, and you know what that was like, all full of papers falling all over the place, handwritten this and that. That treasure box in the attic had all of this stuff, Hannah's diary and some other junk, but there are also recipes."

"I can see that. Pretty old, looks like."

"Very well used and hard to read for all the stains. But the cool thing is that some of the oldest recipes from the attic are also in Mum's cookbook. Some in her handwriting." She handed James a sample. "And some in other handwriting."

He compared the two sheets. "I don't know who else was giving your mother recipes, but it could have been anyone. Not just in the family."

"I know, right? That's the coolest thing. It's like these recipes are a story, or they tell a story."

James sat back and smiled at her.

"What? Why are you looking like that?" She narrowed her eyes.

"Oh, nothing," he said, turning back to the pages in his hands. "Sounds like you've got an interest in all this."

"Well, I guess I do. You know I've been baking up a storm."

"In the middle of the night, I think."

She grimaced. "That part's not so great. I'd rather be sleeping. Worse yet, I think my jeans are getting tight." She got up to pour tea for them both. "I'm really interested in those rugs, though. The women who made those rugs were probably also making these recipes. Making everyday life into some sort of art."

"Do you know what you're going to do about your interest?" James gave her a sideways glance.

"I don't know anything about anything right now," she said. "But Stephen"—she flushed as she said his name—"says he knows someone at Mount Allison University who could help me figure that out."

"In the meantime, we're still working on this house," James said easily, "and you're painting. Lots happening."

She nodded. "I am painting. It feels almost like an entirely new thing."

"Sounds to me like you're making good progress. You've only been back here a little while. Young people want everything to get sorted out right away."

"I'm not that young, Dad," Evie said. "Not really."

He chuckled. "It's a relative thing. To me you look young. I'm pretty sure that I look old to you."

He had her there. "I'm trying to be patient and maybe even kind to myself. But it's not only painting that feels new. It's like I'm starting over in a lot of ways."

He turned to face her at the table. "Isn't it great that we can do that?"

"Well, I guess," she mumbled, unconvinced. "It seems kind of late in my life to be getting started."

"Never too late," he said, patting her hand and getting up. "You've got a lot of good ideas and you'll figure things out. I have faith in you."

She watched him walk toward the living room. *I wish I had faith in me.*

Her phone rang. The number was unfamiliar, but she answered anyway.

"Evie Madison."

"Evie, hi. I'm so glad I got you."

"Hi, who is this?" She couldn't quite place the voice.

"Paul Rutledge with the Arts Foundation. Do you remember me?"

"Oh, yes. Hi, Paul. We met at the Saint Jacques Contemporary Arts Festival last winter, didn't we?"

"We did. I've been a fan of your work for a long time though."

"My work? What do you mean?"

"The way you pull people together, sort out how things fit, smooth the path for artists to function in shared spaces, and promote and publicize the work at the same time. That's not easy, as I know from my experience."

She didn't know how to respond. "Uh, thank you?"

"I know technically Jase Highborn signed off on a lot of organizing and curatorial work, but everybody knows who was handling the nitty-gritty."

"Really?"

"That's why I'm calling. This conversation has to be totally off the record. Can you agree that you never heard this from me?"

She giggled nervously. "I guess so. You're sounding very mysterious, Paul. Like a spy story."

He chuckled too. "I just needed to check out a rumour."

"Mmmm."

"Word has it that you're not working on the Peninsula Festival."

"Um, Paul," she said, "can you tell me why you need to know?"

"The Arts Foundation takes a big interest in local exhibits and productions. This is what we promote, and we want to see things go well."

"You also provided some of the funding for the Peninsula Festival," Evie said slowly.

"Right. Of course."

"Jase is the responsible party according to the contracts," she said tightly.

"Yes, absolutely," he said comfortingly. "And his funding is intact, not at risk. That's why this conversation is off the record. I just want to know if what I heard is true, that you're not running this festival."

Well, nothing can be hurt by the truth, she thought. "That's right. Jase and I are no longer working together." Her throat tightened. "And he's handling everything about the festival, along with whomever he might hire."

"Sorry, Evie, I didn't mean to poke a sore spot. But I did want to know. I've heard from a few artists who are less than happy about this development. You always made things easy for them, and they're concerned."

Evie felt a burst of worry for the artist friends she knew were planning to show in the festival. "I really don't have anything to do with it anymore," she said to Paul. "If it makes any difference, that was not my decision."

"I am sorry to hear that, and I appreciate your honesty. I guess we'll just have to see how it goes."

"I guess you will."

"Thank you, Evie. I am sorry for the intrusion."

"No, that's okay. You just took me by surprise, that's all. Goodbye."

Mornings were almost always hard. First the struggle to wake up. Then reality weighing her down immediately. No career, no home, no boyfriend. Only a bunch of moldy old rugs and a barely legible diary. *Well, and Dad, of course. And the sisters. But the me part—nothing.*

On this morning, though, the weight was there but the agony was gone. It was almost as if she had accepted the truth. Or some version of the truth.

She might not be a great artist, but she did like to paint. She might not be employed, but she had skills. Jase might not need her or want her, but that didn't define her.

I am not an artist, though. I don't know yet what I am, but I am not driven to make art like Jase, much as I hate his name right now. I am something else.

She also had Paul's voice in her head. "I've been a big fan of your work for a long time." She had never thought of managing shows and handling people as her work, but now that seemed obvious. It might not be making art, but it was still all about art.

This day, like every day, she got texts about rugs. She'd been squeezing in visits to people's home and barns, and learned to turn on her voice recorder when they told her stories about the rugs they were handing over. Some wanted them back, and some wanted her to take them. But every single one carried memories and stories.

James knocked on the den door one afternoon when she was taking pictures of her newest rugs.

"Quite a collection you've got going," he noted.

"Yeah, I know. Look at this one. Little sheep in the field, the deep green forest, a red barn."

"Nice," he said, but absently. "Evie, seems like instead of stuff moving out of this house, you're moving more stuff in."

She sat in the straight chair. "No, Dad, it's going. I have even more, but they're down at the gallery."

"Okay then. I guess these are going there too?"

"Yes. I just need to get them documented and catalogued. I'll get them out, I promise." She wondered why he was suddenly so interested.

James shifted on his feet. "I have something to tell you," he said. "Not a big deal, but there's an apartment coming up at the Gables. You know, that senior housing place."

She felt cold. "Coming up when?"

"Well, first of September."

The first of September. Like a few weeks away.

"You want to have the house sold by then?" she asked weakly.

"Well, that makes some sense, doesn't it? No need to keep up this house here if I'm living down there."

And no place for me to live. Tears started in her eyes, but she willed them away. He didn't need her to make things harder.

"Uh, yeah, okay."

"Okay?"

"Yeah. It's okay. I'll get back to working on the house."

He nodded. "Thanks."

"Dad? You're wrong. It really is a big deal." She sniffled.

"Yup. Probably." He left the doorway.

She looked around the den, more littered than she'd realized. In light of this new information, it looked full of stuff. Back to the decluttering project.

Her phone buzzed with a text and rang too. Rett. She picked up.

"Hey."

"Listen, Evie, how's Dad?"

"Funny you should ask. He just told me he's moving to a senior's apartment September first."

"Huh. Did he see the doc?"

"Why?"

"Well, he might be pushing the move up if he's worried about something. Lots of people just stay in their homes forever."

"I know," Evie agreed. "Dad's been on about not being able to keep up with the house, but he could hire somebody to do the lawn and the snow."

"I wish things weren't happening so fast. I always thought I'd come back home and raise the kids in that house."

"Well, Rett, why don't you? That could save me from having to clean everything out."

"Yeah, but Dad has to sell it to afford the next place. He won't be able to afford an apartment if he's still keeping the house."

"Is that true? I thought he had a pension and all that. Money from Mum's life insurance. You know."

"I don't actually know about Dad's finances, but I see it often at work. Folks have to sell the family home to afford the next level of care."

"Well, finances aren't the biggest issue right now, are they?"

"No, you're right. What's up with his heart?"

Evie sighed. "I'm bad at this sleuthing stuff. But I will try."

"Get Dorie to help. She's persistent."

"Stubborn as a mule, you mean."

"Well, yes, that. Let me know what you discover. I'll come on the weekend and help clear stuff out, okay?"

"Thanks. Yes, that would be a big help."

The text was another rug pickup. With a rueful glance at the den, Evie collected her notebook, camera, and clipboard and headed out. An hour later, she returned to the house with a new story to transcribe and two rugs, likely made as early as the late 1800s. Satisfied with her haul, she piled everything in her arms and backed through the screen door.

"Dad," she called. "Dad!" She dumped her pile on the kitchen table. Mallow woofed in the yard. That meant James was probably in the shed.

She picked her way through the overgrown lawn and past the unkempt garden. Maybe he was right about the house being too much. She called out again and pushed open the shed door.

James was slumped in the rocking chair, bathed in gentle sunlight. "Dad, I found..."

He was unresponsive. "Dad!" She shook his shoulder. "Dad! Wake up!" Suddenly feeling sick, she grabbed her phone from her back pocket and dialed 911. "My dad. He's here in the shed. Yes, breathing, not awake. I can't wake him."

Chapter 22

Rett met her and Dorie in the emergency waiting room in St. Stephen. "Well?" Rett demanded.

"No info, not yet," Dorie said. "We've been here a long time."

"Evie, what happened?" Rett said. "Tell me again."

"No idea. He was out in the shed doing whatever it is he does out there. I went out to tell him something and he was just sitting in the rocking chair. Just...there." Her voice caught.

Rett paced. "We don't know how long he was in that state."

Evie's hands got cold. "I guess that's correct. We were talking in the house about an hour before I found him, so no longer than that." Scary words like stroke, heart failure, syncope floated in her mind.

Rett was gathering information. "He was breathing, right?"

"Yeah, yeah. I just couldn't rouse him, so I called 911. The paramedics said his heart rate was okay, and they got him to come around a little, but they whisked him off to here."

Rett went to chat with the triage nurse and came back. "Darren Phelps. I went to school with him."

"Good to know people. The benefit of a small town, right?" Dorie said.

"And?" Evie asked.

"He didn't have any information. It's just good to have someone you know on the inside," Rett said.

Evie looked at her sisters. There was no doubt of their relationship: both were tall, lean, with a direct, clear-eyed gaze that came straight from their father, blue for Rett, green for Dorie. Two sisters. "Has anyone talked to Helen?" she asked suddenly.

"Let's wait until we know something," Rett suggested. "She'll just feel bad and there's enough of us feeling that way."

A nurse from inside the treatment area stuck her head out. "Who's here...oh, hi, Rett. You can come in now."

"All of us?" Dorie asked.

"No, just one," the nurse said. Rett got up.

"Why do you get to go?" Dorie demanded.

"Because," Rett said, and disappeared into the doorway. Dorie flounced back in her chair.

"She is the oldest," Evie reminded her.

"I know," Dorie sighed. "And she's a nurse. But I want to see Dad too."

"She's good. She'll tell us whatever she finds out," Evie assured Dorie and maybe herself.

Dorie flopped back down in her chair. "I hate this waiting around," she said.

Evie folded in on herself, arms wrapped. She couldn't shake off the image of Dad slumped over in the old rocking chair, sunlight slanting through the dusty window. Her racing heart felt like it would never slow down.

Her phone pinged, and with a guilty look at the nurse, she headed outside to look at it. Why did they keep those signs up about phones? Everybody was looking at a phone in there. *But breaking the rules makes me feel worse.* Even dumb rules.

Jase. A text from Jase. She clicked to read it.

Where are you? Stopped by your house to talk. Nobody home.

Evie felt a wave of excitement and longing. Jase wanted to see her. But why? Her excitement was followed by irritation. Why should he assume she'd be at home waiting for him to drop by?

She was trying to figure out how to reply when Dorie rapped on the glass door and gestured her in.

"What? Where's Rett?"

"Over here." Dorie pulled her along.

Rett leaned against the wall near the door to the inner sanctum, looking at her phone. "She's here," Dorie said. "Now tell us."

"Yeah, okay," Rett said. "Dad's got diabetes. Did you know that, either of you?"

Evie shook her head and looked at Dorie. "Never mentioned it to me."

"Me, either. Is this new?"

"Apparently not. He's been on meds and supposed to manage his diet since last year, and now he's got some heart complications that often co-occur. He's lucky that this spell wasn't too serious. At least they don't think there are serious consequences, but the doc is keeping him a few days to try to stabilize his blood sugar, and his cardiologist wants to do some more testing while he's here."

"Diabetes?" Evie mused. "But I've been baking. Oh, no!"

"Don't assume blame, Evie. None of us knew." Rett was businesslike. "They're going to admit him and then you can see him in his room. I'll go back down the hall here and keep him company until they find a room, but then I must get back to Saint Jacques. The little kids are missing me, Harry's on edge, and I left work in a big hurry."

"Is this good news, Rett? Or bad?" Evie was unsure.

Rett considered. "At least there's an explanation for what happened, and it wasn't a stroke, just low blood sugar. He's been good about seeing his doctors, even if he's been terrible at letting us help him. Now that we know, we can do better."

"I feel terrible," Evie said.

"No wonder he wants to move out of the house," Dorie said.

"I don't think he wants to," Evie objected. "I think he just doesn't know how to take care of everything there, plus take care of himself. He really loves it, plus it's been in his family like forever."

"But he's moving," Rett said.

"Yes. Did you know that, Dorie? He's got an apartment and a date. First of September. We're under some pressure to get the stuff out and the house sold." Evie's chest was heavy. Jase became only a faraway thought.

"Maybe it's for the best," Rett said. "Now that we know he's really not well." She looked tired.

"Or maybe now we know what's going on, we can be of real help to him and let him stay in his house." Dorie was vehement.

"Well, that's not going to be solved by us here in the waiting room," Rett said diplomatically. "We'll need a family meeting or something. The hospital will help us with discharge planning before he leaves here."

Evie said, "One of us can stay here with him."

"I really do have to go, if that's okay with you," Rett said. "The twins have really been pushing Harry's buttons lately, and I've been out of pocket due to work."

Dorie was gazing at the ceiling. "September first. That's so soon."

Evie's patience was wearing thin. "Listen, you two, you go. I'll go wait with Dad. Dore, can you stop by and check on the big dogs? I'll let you know when Dad gets to a room. Rett, go home."

She dropped her gaze to her phone, still in her hand. *Jase, you just have to wait your turn.*

Groggy, Evie heard the big dogs pacing at the bottom of the stairs. What time was it? The click of toenails and occasional whine were motivating, and she dragged herself upright. Pulling on a sweatshirt, she noted the barest beginnings of daylight as she headed down the stairs. At least the dogs woke her, instead of the other way.

"Four thirty, guys? Is this really necessary?"

The dogs pushed past her to get out the kitchen door, bounding and wagging as their paws hit the grassy lawn. They'll be soggy from dew, no doubt, she thought as she turned toward the sink to fill the kettle.

What was this? On the counter beside the sink, a plate of Mum's sunshine muffins sat waiting.

Evie backed into a kitchen chair. Muffins. When she sniffed, she could smell the fragrance of baking, and looking around, she saw the mixing bowl and wooden spoon, unwashed, on the counter.

Darn it. I'm on autopilot at night. This has to stop.

Evie absently ran water into the mixing bowl and sloshed a cloth around in it. In handling the bowl and spoon, she felt a memory in her hands, but from childhood, learning to bake under Mum's tutelage.

But was that all? She must have handled these objects recently. Why was her memory so spotty?

Abruptly she put the bowl down. When she heard scratching at the back door, she opened it to Custard and Mallow and distributed treats. She poured herself a cup of tea and sat at the table, staring at the plate of muffins.

Her phone pinged. Dorie.

Did you check on Dad yet? Chad and I are going this morning. We'll be by in an hour to get some stuff. Got any muffins?

How did Dorie know? Well, that didn't matter. What was important was Dad. Well, if he wasn't fine, the hospital would have called, she thought, still bemused by the muffins. *I do know how to make Mum's recipe. I don't have to look it up. In fact, I always said I could do it with my eyes closed.* Grabbing a muffin, she peeled off the paper and took a bite. Still warm, and so delicious. Perfect.

She finished her muffin and licked her fingers. Custard whined a little behind her.

"No muffins for dogs," she said without looking, but then relented and got them their kibble. The sounds of kibble rattling in bowls and the happy snuffling of dogs practically inhaling their breakfast were comforting. *Dad's in the hospital, I've turned into a sleep baker, and my life is still in tatters. But the dogs are happy. At least I can keep one thing going.*

Admittedly, these dogs were not too demanding. People, on the other hand... She looked at Jase's message from yesterday. She still didn't know what to say.

Her toes kicked something under the table. Peering under, she saw the big pile of new additions to her rug collection. She'd been bringing them in when things took a turn yesterday.

Dad was away, but the house still had to be cleared out, messages had to be responded to, and something had to happen with these artifacts. She finished her tea and went to get dressed.

She was photographing and recording information on the new rugs when Dorie and Chad arrived, along with Alice's poodle, Frou-Frou.

"Did you pack some stuff for Dad?" Dorie asked.

"No," Evie said, annoyed. "You can do that."

"Okay, okay," Dorie said mildly. "Just asking. Do you know where his phone is? And the charger?"

Evie sighed. No matter what, she was going to have to help with this. "Why'd you bring the dog?" She gestured to the poodle. "We've got dogs."

"Frou-Frou loves your father," Chad said. "We're going to smuggle him into the hospital."

"What? Are you kidding?"

"Chad did it for his grandmother, so he figured we'd try it with Dad too. Frou's a very good boy." Dorie gave the fuzzy white pup a fond glance. Looking at the table, Dorie asked, "Maybe some muffins too?"

Evie gave her a scathing look. "Muffins for you two, but I bet Dad's going to be on a very strict, hospital-based eating plan. Please don't help out by giving him muffins, Dorie."

"Yah, you probably have a point," her sister said. "But I'm going to have one. Hey, Chad, muffin? We might even make some coffee."

"It's way too early to get into the hospital anyway," Evie conceded.

Dorie started coffee and Evie put muffins on plates, then boxed up the rest for Dorie to take home. Dorie headed upstairs to find clothes for James, and Chad sat at the table, absently scratching Mallow's ears, which had miraculously landed under his hand.

"You okay, Evie?" Chad asked. "You found him, right? Called 911?"

"Yeah, that was me. I guess I'm all right. He's going to be okay, and that's what matters the most."

"At least he's awake and you know what's going on."

"Oh, right," Evie said. "It was last fall, right, when your grandmother had a stroke?"

Chad nodded. "Yep. I don't know if I'm over it yet, and I wasn't even the one who found her. It was a very long week in the hospital, waiting to see if she was even going to wake up."

"Does Dorie know how that feels for you?"

Chad shrugged. "Dorie knows how I feel about my grandmother, for sure. She helped me during that week. Hey, is that coffee ready? Can I get you a cup?"

"No, you sit. I'll get it."

Dorie came back with an armful of clothing, shoving everything into a cloth bag. "Coffee! Yes, please. And a muffin." She sat at the table and bit in with satisfaction. "So good," she said with her mouth full.

They were all silent for a bit, eating muffins and drinking coffee.

"So you're a midnight baker," Dorie said. "That's cool. You didn't know it?"

"No. It's weird to not remember. Sometimes I do, but other times, I just assume it was me."

"Yep. That's weird."

"After Jase and I broke up, I was having trouble sleeping and bought some sleep meds. I blamed them for the midnight baking, but last night I was just tired. No meds, but I woke up to muffins."

"There's been a lot of good food here," Dorie mused.

"Good food, but not good for Dad. Do you think this happened because I was baking?" Her throat felt thick.

"Come on, Evie. That makes no sense. None of us knew. It's not your fault."

"It makes me feel a little creepy, doing stuff I don't remember."

"Creepy, maybe, but with delicious outcomes."

"Yeah, I guess." Evie remembered the bread pudding. "Some of those recipes are Mum's, but some are even older, like from a few generations ago."

Chad looked interested. "You mean from that diary you have? I wondered what was in that."

"That and Mum's cookbook. She kept a lot of old recipes from her family and Dad's family. She made modifications on the fly, and then when she taught us to bake, we learned the modifications. Sometimes she wrote them down and sometimes she didn't."

Dorie looked pensive. "I wish I'd let her teach me to cook. I just refused when she tried and I guess she was tired out after raising you three, because she didn't insist."

"Never too late," Evie said, amused.

"I've been hanging out in the kitchen with Alice," Dorie said, "trying to learn something. But I'm not a natural at that like you are. And Chad."

Chad drank his coffee, unperturbed. "I do like cooking. I learned mostly on my own though, because Gram didn't teach me. She just fed me. I'd be happy if somebody learned how to make her fish chowder, for sure. I never mastered it."

"And pies," Dorie said dreamily. "Her strawberry-rhubarb pie is to die for."

Evie's phone rang and they all jumped a bit. So much for daydreams of pie. "Hospital," she mouthed as she picked it up. "Sure, okay. Yes, my sister's bringing them. Half an hour. Thank you."

After she hung up, she filled in Evie and Chad. "No problem," she said. "It was Dad's morning nurse. He wants his phone and some clothes, like you already figured out."

"Great. We'll get going then," Dorie said. Gathering the bag of clothes, box of muffins, and Frou-Frou, they headed out.

Before the quiet of the house could get to her, Evie finished with the rugs and took them to the car. She'd get in and out of the gallery early. Driving down the quiet streets, her phone pinged again. She pulled over to look. Another rug! Leonard's closet was already feeling small and she wasn't finished collecting yet.

Chapter 23

She used her key to the gallery, as it was still too early for it to be open. Aware Stephen lived upstairs, she moved quietly to lug in the new rugs, find places on the metal shelving, and note in her laptop where they were stored.

As she was leaving, she had a second thought. Humming to herself, she tucked one of the better rugs under her arm and closed the closet behind her. She poked around the messy office until she located some supplies. In a few minutes, she'd hung the rug across from Stephen's desk.

It was beautiful. She breathed a sigh of satisfaction and headed into the main gallery.

As she wandered toward the front door, something caught her eye; her crab-apple painting had been hung near the desk. She looked more closely. Clearly Leonard had aspirations for this piece. She'd mounted it, but he'd framed it, and very well.

She peered at the card tacked to the wall by her painting.

Summer Symphony. Evelyn Madison, Stella Mare. Watercolour on paper.

Her heart nearly stopped at the price that was listed.

She took a breath. It was the first time she'd seen her name like that since art school. And who titled that work? She knew she hadn't offered such a thing.

She stepped back for a fresh look. It was a nice piece, she thought. *But I never thought...* She fished her phone out of her pocket to take a picture of the painting hanging, and then a closeup of the information card.

Well, Leonard was optimistic, but that's okay. If he sold the piece, it would be good for both of them. She looked around for the smaller paintings she'd brought.

She found a box with a stack of unframed watercolours and looked through to see what else was there. Hers, but also a number of lighthouse and dory pieces, seascapes, and some well-done wildflower pictures. She was startled by the prices, but it was a gallery, after all, not a tourist kiosk.

Hmm. Well, good for him and good for me. If anybody buys at those prices, I'll have some cash flow in the right direction. Locking the gallery door, she bypassed her car to walk east to the Sunshine Diner. It had been a while since she'd had a good latte, and her breakfast muffin felt like ancient history. *Maybe this is good news that I'm hungry again. Or not.* She ruefully patted her hips but walked briskly toward the diner anyway.

The place was still populated by locals, some dressed to work in the woods, and some for the water. *This is an early day for me for sure.* A couple of the fishers waved at her, and she heard someone say, "James's girl, you know, the artist one." It felt good, sort of, to be known.

Cassandra, busy at the counter, nodded and smiled at her. "Evie!"

As she gazed into the pastry case, she felt a bump on her shoulder. "Stephen. Hello."

She felt a little dazzled by his warm smile. "Good morning, Evie."

"Did I wake you? I was trying to be quiet."

Cassandra gave her a quick glance. Great, Evie thought. *Now the whole town will think we're sleeping together.*

Stephen shook his head. "Were you in the gallery? I've been out for a couple of hours. Took a walk, then came here. Come and join me." He nodded toward a booth where the table held coffee, a plate of toast, and a stack of papers.

"Sure, okay." She followed him, after waving to Cassandra and mouthing "Latte, please."

"Are you always such an early riser?" she asked.

"Sunrise gets me up. I have limited time here and I have to soak it all in. I like getting up early. What about you?"

"Well, we've had some things going on, but yes, I seem to be up early. Up late too," she added.

"Up early and up late leaves something out, doesn't it?" Stephen said.

"It sure does. But I'll survive."

They sat at his booth, where he pushed his pages of scribbled notes to the side. "So, you were in the gallery."

"More rugs. They just keep appearing."

He chuckled. "That's a dream for a collector. How's James?"

"You must have been listening to the Stella Mare news network."

"Travels fast, especially if there's an ambulance involved."

"He's in the hospital. He's been faking with his family for a long time. Turns out to be diabetes and cardiac complications. He's going to need more care, more support." Her voice caught.

"Those unexpected things are so hard," Stephen said. Her chest tightened at the kindness in his voice. "Poor James. Let me know how I can help. I like him."

"He likes you too. Thanks for your offer of help."

"Do take me up on it," he urged. "My time is flexible and I'm more than willing."

"Okay," she said. "Nothing is clear yet, but I expect I'll have to accelerate cleaning out the house. He says he wants to move into a senior apartment complex."

"Do you agree?"

"Dad can do what he wants to do, but honestly, I don't think he really wants to move out of his house. He just can't take care of it and himself properly. He's lousy at asking for help."

They were silent. Then she said, "That could be a family trait."

Stephen smiled at her. "Are you that way?"

"I'm bad at accepting help. I'm not great at asking either. You had some good ideas about the rugs the other day, and I wasn't very receptive." She looked up at him. "Sorry about that."

"I didn't notice," he said loyally. "What do you need help with right now? What's top of mind, with your father's situation?"

"We need to get the house cleaned out. Even if he changes his mind about moving, the house needs to be cleared. I've been working at it all summer, but it is such a big job that it feels never ending."

"I had to clear out my mother's home after she died," Stephen said. "That was hard." He looked at the table.

Evie's eyes filled and she reached over to touch his hand. "Yes, because then you're dealing with grief too. I'm sorry."

He looked up, eyes crinkling at the corners. "It was hard, but it was good too. I learned a lot about my mother in that process. Someday I'll tell you all about her."

"You've made me think of something. We didn't have to go through that with Mum because Dad was still there. Maybe that's one reason it's so hard. Mum is part of that house."

They sat quietly for a moment. Then she sighed.

"The house has been in the Madison family for a long time. My mother's family dumped their stuff in the attic too."

"How long?"

"Like, a hundred fifty years. Maybe more."

"You grew up there, right? With all those sisters?"

"Yes. Dad grew up there too, with his siblings, and his mother lived with us until she died. I'm pretty sure Dad expected to live there until he died too."

"The home traditionally went to the oldest son, right?"

"He wasn't the oldest, but he was the only one who stayed in Stella Mare. I guess that's significant."

"And now there's no son to carry on the family name," Stephen said seriously, and she stared at him until he finally cracked a smile.

"You are kidding, aren't you?"

"I'm from the Deep South, remember? Lots of traditions."

"Fortunately, my family isn't quite as gendered as all that. Any of the daughters could have the house too, but none of us can swing it personally. I'm recently unemployed, Dorie has her dog sanctuary, Rett is established in Saint Jacques, and Helen's been in Ottawa since she finished law school. If Dad has to leave the house, then things just fall apart."

"It doesn't sound like your family has fallen apart. Maybe more like coming together."

Evie thought about that. "No, I guess we aren't any worse than we ever were. When Mum was sick, we all pulled together really well, but it didn't last."

"What about your aunt? Corinne? I met her at the picnic."

Evie felt shocked. "For the house, you mean?"

"Yes. She's a social worker, isn't she?"

"But she's not a Madison." She blushed. "Oops, maybe I'm more traditional than I realized." She giggled. "I can't believe I said that."

Stephen glanced at her. "When you sell the house to a stranger, they won't be Madisons either."

"Of course. Funny how that's not as shocking. But honestly, I don't know if anyone has thought of Corinne." Evie pondered. "I never have."

Cassandra arrived with a steaming latte and a coffee refill for Stephen. "Evie, how's your dad?" Concern illuminated her face.

Evie looked at Stephen. "News travels here," she said. "Not bad," she replied to Cassandra. "He's going to stay in St. Stephen for a few days and then he'll be back home."

"That's good to hear. Guess what? My mother has a couple of rugs from her mother."

Evie looked at Stephen. "You see? They just keep on coming."

Cassandra laughed. " Can I have her call you?"

"Yes, please. This is turning into quite a project," she said, glancing at Stephen's encouraging smile. "Everyone has a story to go with their rug, and I want to hear them all. But when I started, I had no idea how many of these things were hanging around."

"Literally," Cassandra agreed. "There's a place where I used to babysit, and they've got gorgeous hooked rugs on the living room walls. Not old though. I think the mother has a relative who makes them."

Evie's eyes grew large. "A contemporary rug maker? Oh, that's interesting. Can you give me names?"

They shared information and Cassandra left to pour coffee for other customers. Evie showed Stephen pictures of the rugs on her phone.

Stephen was smiling at her. "I think you've got the bug."

Was that true? "I thought I just wanted to find out about my ancestor. At least that how this interest started."

He raised his eyebrows.

"Okay, maybe I'm getting a tiny bit obsessed. I think about the rug makers every day. I wonder about them. I want to know what moved them. What they were thinking, hoping for. What they accomplished by making something lovely out of rags and burlap."

She looked back at her phone. "Look at this one." She handed it to him. "You're right. It's not just about the art. It's about the women. Do you know how hard they had to work?"

He shook his head, smiling indulgently. "Tell me."

"I probably don't even know. But my great-grandmother, the one who came here from Cheticamp, she had eight children who survived. Her husband fished, she grew vegetables and foraged for berries and greens, and in the fall all the men hunted for meat to keep them through the winter. They kept a cow and a pig, and my grandmother made most of their clothes, all of their food, and still had time to turn scraps into quilts and hooked rugs."

"Sounds like everyone had to work hard, except rich people who had servants to work hard for them. Not so different from where I come from. But you're describing subsistence living. Weren't there merchants?"

"Well, yes, of course. Stella Mare was a pretty well-to-do village, at least in the nineteenth century. When the tourist trade got started there were goods and services to be had. But from what I understand, my family wasn't wealthy enough to buy a lot of things. They had to make them."

"Have you studied history? Like local history?"

She shook her head. "I was never interested, but I am now. Only I'm interested in personal history. Not dates and events as much as what women's lives were like."

"It's a gross misconception that history is about dates. History is about people." He scribbled something on a scrap of paper. "I think you'd like to talk to this person," he said. "She's a prof at my home university, back in North Carolina."

"Thank you," she said. "I don't know why I'm so focused on this right now. My life is pretty much a mess. I have a lot of problems to figure out, but collecting and studying these rugs is what I want to do." She sighed and looked at the slip of paper. Dr. Jessica Woodman and an email address.

"Sometimes you get hints from the universe about where you should be putting your energy," he said. "When I was twenty-four, I was desperately trying to sell enough of my art to live on. Piecing together grants and residencies and trying to get ahead."

"Tell me about it," she said ruefully. "That's what I've been helping Jase with for the last decade or so. Getting traction is hard."

He nodded. "The best part for me was meeting older artists and talking to them. Then I started to think about art in a broader way; not just art made by self-described artists, but art forms that showed up in everyday life."

"Like wood carvings."

"Exactly like that. When I talked to the people who made them, I learned so much. I learned that I wanted to know more about those people and their art, much more than I wanted to struggle to try to make a name for myself in the art world. Capturing stories and pictures was just, I don't know, it was more important. To me."

"So..."

"Well, so I had to figure out how to turn that impulse into skills, and ultimately how to feed myself with it."

"You became a professor of, what? Art? History?"

He laughed. "You just jumped over about twelve years of my life, but yes. My appointment is in humanities. I've studied a lot of different things though."

"Are you saying I have to go back to school?" That didn't sound very good.

He shook his head. "You don't have to do anything. You said you've got a lot of current problems to solve. I'm just telling you a little about my path. At least my path so far."

She smiled up at him. "So far? More goals?"

"Well..."

"What?"

His face darkened. "Things are uncertain back home. I'm not sure that there's going to be a job for me to go back to."

"Really? Why?"

He shrugged. "It's a complicated mess of university finances and them trying to be more efficient. But there's a chance that my program will be cut."

"I don't really know what that means, but it doesn't sound good."

He laughed. "No, it really doesn't. That doesn't mean much right now, because I'm here for the full year, I have my funding for this project, a place to live, all of that. But I'm a little uncertain about the future."

"That's rotten," Evie said. "Unfortunately, I can relate."

"You can?"

"Yeah, well, I haven't told you why I'm here, but it's kind of the same. I lost my work and my home all at once."

His face held a question.

"A breakup."

"I did hear something," he said cautiously.

She snickered. "Of course you did. This is a very small town."

"Not so painful?"

"Oh, very painful. When you run your partner's business, write his grants, sell his product, and do his publicity, breaking up is harder than the usual."

"Evie, I'm so sorry."

She swallowed. "I think it was for the best, but I still can't quite find my way into the future. My dad keeps saying to do the next right thing, and that's working so far, but I like to have my life organized. Know where I'm going. You know?" Tears pooled in her eyes, but she looked at Stephen anyway.

He handed her a paper napkin. "I do know."

She mopped at her eyes. "Sorry."

He looked out the window. "I was married before. To a sculptor, more self-involved than I realized, and we were able to part amicably enough, but I felt at loose ends for more than a year. It took that long for me to realize I would be okay without her, even though I was much better without her than otherwise." He turned back to Evie. "Another story I'll tell you sometime. If you're interested."

She smiled. "I'd like that. But how do you function without goals?"

"I try to hold them loosely. Not get stuck or locked into a future that might not suit me."

They both drank coffee. Evie liked how she felt with Stephen.

"Not get stuck but not be flailing all the time, right?" she asked.

"Grounded and clear. That's what I aim for," he said. "Please note, it is an aspiration. I don't always get there."

She smiled. "I left something for you to see at work," she told him.

"Now I'm intrigued."

"See my Cheshire cat smile?" she asked. "Consider it a surprise. But now, I've got to get home, check on Dad, and clear some space. You don't need any old furniture, cracked china, or stray socks, do you?"

He chuckled. "Plenty of junk of my own, thanks. But I can help you move it anytime."

Chapter 24

Dorie called with an update. "He's good. I can tell he's feeling better, because he's so annoyed about the diet they're prescribing for him. But he's staying for a couple more days."

"Do you think he's up for more visitors? I'd like to see him, but I also know getting the house cleared is important."

"I think you should go. We need to carry the load for Rett. It's only a half-hour drive for us, but it's a lot farther for her. And harder, with the kids."

"Good point."

"Dad's going to be getting bored, and that means no good," Dorie said, amused.

"How did it work getting the dog in there?"

"No go. They saw him right at the front door. Guess that's a late-night maneuver only."

"Well, nice try anyway."

"Yeah. Listen, I can come over this afternoon for a couple of hours to help with the house. Yes?"

"Sure. Come before four, when I'll go to visit Dad."

Despite the coffee, Evie was overwhelmed with drowsiness and lay down on the living room couch for a little catch-up nap. Midnight baking took a toll.

"I cannot stay here," Leonie said to Charles, her voice faltering. "You don't know what it is like."

"This is our home. My home," rough-voiced, Charles also spoke French. "You can't just leave."

She reached for his hands. "All of us. Please, Charles. I cannot stay where I am so hated. How can I raise my children in a place where nobody will accept them? How will our daughters find husbands?"

He frowned. "It's not that bad, Leonie. It just takes people time."

Dropping his hands, she turned away with a sob. "You cannot understand. I have nobody here except you. I need to go home to Papa and Samuel and my village."

He sat and pulled her into his lap. Leaning against his shoulder, she continued to sniffle. "I thought I could do it. That Mother Mary would give me strength."

"Can't I give you strength?" Charles asked. "You're my wife. We agreed to be together, before God and your family. I need you. The children need you."

She turned to face him, dark eyes brimming. "Yes. And I need a friend. Just one friend, Charles. Just one woman who doesn't whisper about the French girl, who will smile at me in church. Only one."

"I didn't know it was that hard here," he said sorrowfully. "I just didn't know."

A commotion at the door made them both jump up. "Mama, Daddy, come and see!"

Evie yawned and stretched, tried to turn over and realized she was on the couch. Poor Leonie, she thought, and dropped back into sleep.

"Mama!" Hannah called out from the garden where she was tending cabbages. "Mrs. Smyth is here."

Leonie brushed the flour off her hands on her apron. "Bonjour, Sally," she said to the woman who came through the door, and the two smiled at each other.

"Tea?" Leonie asked.

"Yes, thank you," Sally replied. "I'm here to bring you an invitation though."

Leonie put two cups on the table and sat. "An invitation? That's exciting."

Sally leaned back. "Well, maybe not. Wait until you hear it."

Leonie smiled. "Now I really want to know."

"I hosted the Ladies Circle from St. James Church last week. One of the ladies saw the rug I made, the one you helped me with, and she was most interested. She wants to meet you."

"Peasant craft?"

"Oh, Leonie. No. She's not like that."

"Well, some are."

Sally's brow furrowed. "I know. Some people have been, well, not very nice."

Leonie raised her eyebrows. "That's the least of it."

Sally shook her head. "I know, peasant craft, peasant food, peasant garden. Some people are just nasty. But this lady, Mrs. Harrison, she's not like that. She wants to learn and she thinks other ladies would also like to learn. I almost brought her today."

"What? Don't do that, Sally! Tell me before you bring those English ladies around."

"Mrs. Harrison isn't English. She's Irish, like your own Charles. You'd like her, I'm sure."

"If you're certain, then I agree," Leonie said finally. "Do you want to see what I'm working on now?"

Evie's eyes opened suddenly. These dreams were too much. It was like reading a serial. What would happen next? She squeezed her eyes shut, hoping for another glimpse of the past, but the time for napping was apparently over.

It was good to know Leonie figured out how to make a home here though. She had lived in a time when she didn't have a lot of choices. As Evie was musing, her phone buzzed.

Jase. Jase! She sat up and clicked to answer in one smooth movement.

"Hey."

"Evie. Finally. I've been trying for two days. Where've you been?"

"Yeah, sorry about that. Um, Dad's in the hospital. I'm, uh, busy."

"Sorry to hear that. Is he okay?"

"We hope so."

"Good, good. Listen, Evie, I really need to see you. I've realized some things, and I need to talk to you. In person."

Her heart leaped. *It finally happened!* Just when she'd given up, or almost given up.

He went on. "I stopped by yesterday, and you didn't even reply to my text."

"Right. Dad..."

"Yeah, okay. But can I see you? Today, maybe?"

Her stomach was doing flips. "Not today. I've got to visit my dad."

"Well, where is he? In St. Stephen, right? Can't you stop by?"

Her jaw tightened. "No, Jase, I can't stop by." *You dumped me, idiot. I'm not dumping Dad for you.*

"Okay then, I'll come to you. Tomorrow. You going to be home in the morning?"

Where else would she be, Evie thought despairingly. "I guess so." *Unless Dad gets worse.*

"Okay, I'll come by your house about ten. Okay? I've got some other meetings in Stella Mare after that."

"Wait a minute, Jase. This meeting with me is for what?"

"I just really need to see you, Evie," he said warmly. "I've been thinking a lot, and I need to talk to you." Her stomach did that flip thing again. What was really going on?

"Okay," she agreed. "Ten a.m."

She was on her feet, pacing and thinking. It was about time he came back. Her mind raced with possibilities. When could Chad get her stuff back to the loft? Was he going to propose? What was going to happen?

Her internal braking system squealed, telling her to remember other things, but she ignored it. Jase was back. Everything was going to be back to normal.

Rett was coming out of Dad's room when she arrived at the hospital.

"Hi," Evie said. "I thought Dorie and I had this covered. You don't need to drive all the way down here."

Rett was pale and her hair was escaping its bun into tendrils around her face. "Hi," she said, grabbing Evie by the arm and pulling her down the hallway. "Come with me. They kicked me out."

"What's up?" Evie demanded.

"They're trying to get his sugars stabilized. He's just had another big low. It'll just be a few minutes."

"I have no idea what that means," Evie said flatly. She wasn't sure she wanted to.

"He's just not managing well," Rett explained. "His body doesn't remember how to keep things stable. It overreacts to some things and underreacts to others."

"I can relate," Evie said. "But you don't mean emotionally."

Rett chuckled. "No, I really don't. They don't want visitors in there right now because they're doing stuff, but you'll be able to see him soon, I think."

"You look tired."

"I'm not surprised. Callie was up half the night with nightmares."

"Oh, poor kid."

"Yeah, and Mason's beside himself with worry about his grandpa. Harry's preoccupied. Nobody's doing very well at my house." Rett looked preoccupied too.

"You're here plus keeping things managed at the care center. You might need a break."

"I'm thinking about taking some time off," Rett admitted. "I don't know how I can keep up the pace." She sat heavily in a hallway chair.

"I feel like a slacker," Evie said. "I don't even have a job to go to and I'm exhausted."

Rett said, "Exhausted goes with breaking up, I think."

At her words, Evie felt her stomach do that flip again. "Jase wants to talk. Say's he's realized some things. He's coming by tomorrow morning. I think he wants to get back together." She watched Rett's face.

Rett was expressionless. "Oh?"

Evie spluttered, "How do you do that? Poker face? I know you have an opinion or six."

"It's not my job to react, just to listen," Rett said. "That's the face I put on for complaints from families."

"Well, you're really good at it. He wanted me to come over after visiting Dad, but I said no."

Rett nodded but said nothing.

"No sisterly wisdom?" Evie prodded.

"Oh, if you're asking, then yeah. I've got a ton of sisterly wisdom," Rett said. "You've done a lot for that guy. Has he done as much for you?"

"But I love him," Evie burst out. "At least, I think I do."

Rett was impassive. "They're a lot easier to love when you're not living with them," she said. "Don't forget the cheating part. Forgiveness might be divine, but you have to be sure people don't take advantage of your good nature. They'll walk all over you if they can." She stood up. "Let's see if we can get into Dad's room."

Eyes downcast, Evie followed, mind swirling. Jase, Dad, Leonie and Charles, Stephen, Leonard, even Rett's pale face and shadowed eyes. *Nothing is the way it's supposed to be, me least of all.* Her chest tightened as she entered her father's hospital room. Her gaze glanced off his face and moved around the room. Oh, flowers.

Rett went to the bedside while Evie investigated the flowers in order to arrange her face. When she turned to her father, she hoped she appeared composed. "Hey, Dad," she said, approaching the bed.

"Evie." His voice was crackly, like he hadn't used it much. "How you doing, kid?"

She took his hand. "I'm fine."

"Sorry to leave you with the dogs and all."

"No worries, Dad. The dogs are fine. We're fine. You just need to do what they tell you to get better, right?" She surreptitiously wiped at her eyes. Rett glared at her and shook her head slightly.

"Everything is fine, Dad," she said more strongly. "Do you need anything? Dorie brought a bunch of stuff, right?"

"Yes." He sighed like talking was too much effort. "Reading glasses."

"Okay," Evie agreed. "I'll make sure you get them. I see the newspaper arrived."

He grumbled, "No good without my glasses."

Rett was watchful. Assessment mode, Evie guessed. *No matter what, Rett was always a nurse. And what am I? What a selfish thought. This isn't about you, Evie.* Feeling annoyed with herself, she pushed her thoughts away.

"What did the doctor say, Dad?" Rett asked.

He gave a dismissive gesture. "I'm here for now, that's all I know."

"Hmm." Rett stood up. "I'll see what I can find out." She left the room.

Standing by the bed, Evie watched her father fall asleep, body settling into the bed, face relaxing. It was strangely intimate to see him this way. She didn't like it. Usually if Dad was sleeping it was in the recliner in the living room, not grey-faced on a hospital bed. She suddenly recalled her mother lying in a rented hospital bed in the den, unrecognizably pale and thin, balding from cancer treatments. *Oh, this isn't good.* She turned away to look out the window.

Rett returned to the doorway, gesturing for Evie to come out. Evie returned to her father's bedside and whispered to him, "Bye, Dad. I'll bring your glasses tomorrow." Then she headed to the hallway.

As she left the room, her tears overflowed. Rett, waiting for her, wrapped an arm across her shoulders. "Come on," she said. "Coffee."

Evie shook her head. "No, I don't think so. I'm okay. I'm just really tired."

"Listen, Evie, he's going to be okay. I know it's hard to believe."

"Rett, aren't you the one who said it was impossible for a man his age to be okay?"

"That was months ago. I was overreacting," Rett said. "I just got caught up in thinking about Mum."

"Oh," Evie said with relief. "I guess that's what happened to me too. It's hard to avoid remembering."

"I don't want to stop remembering," Rett said, "but I need my brain to remember that just because she died doesn't mean Dad is going to die too."

"Blunt, Rett."

"That's how I roll," Rett said with a grin. "It's not a joke even though it sounds kind of funny. Your brain makes these associations. We're probably all experiencing that a bit."

"You're a nurse. You know people don't always die in the hospital."

"When it's your own family, your brain loses that professional edge. Things get confusing. Blurry. Difficult."

"Okay," Evie said, shaking her arms and hands. "I need to keep my memories in check."

"I think Dad will be back home by the end of the week, actually," Rett said. "He might need some extra attention."

"He's not that easy to help, you know," Evie warned.

"I know. That's why we were all surprised by this crisis. Things are going to have to change though."

Evie felt even more exhausted. "I don't know."

"Nobody's asking you to do anything. Not yet. There'll be a discharge meeting and we can figure stuff out then. Let's just all keep an open mind. Okay?"

She nodded and they parted.

Stephen rapped hesitantly on the back door. Big barks announced him, and he peered through the glass for signs of human life. A moment later, Evie came to the door.

She looked surprised, but no more surprised than he, to find himself at her door.

"I came to help," he announced.

"Help?"

"With the house-clearing project. If that's what you're doing while James is in the hospital, I can help."

"Really?" But she held the door open for him. "Do you want some coffee?"

"No, I mean it. I'm here to help."

She laughed and sat at the kitchen table. "Well, don't think I don't appreciate it. It's just that you might have caught me doing something different. I know I said I was working on the house but…"

"But?" He sat beside her.

"There are things that keep calling for my attention. More compelling than clearing out old junk."

"Come on, Evie," he said. "What could be more compelling than that?"

She hesitated, but then grinned and got up. "I'll show you. Come on into the den." She led the way.

He followed her, noticing the light glancing off her dark curls, the gentle sway of her hips as she pushed open the door, her giggle as she waved her hand over the desk for him to look.

"You've been painting!"

"I have. I've been trying to make sense of these rugs. Look here," she said, laying a large watercolour next to a rug. "I'm trying to fill in the spaces where there's wear, so I can see what the original designs looked like."

He looked from rug to painting and then at all the paintings covering the desk. "This does seem a lot more interesting than hauling dusty junk out of the attic. But what if you find more treasure up there?"

She laughed. "I think the treasure part has been exhausted. Most of the new rugs I've been working with don't even belong to me. Have you seen how the pile is growing down at the gallery? Oh, what did you think of my surprise?"

Smiling, he said, "I like seeing it and thinking of you." He liked the rug, but he also liked that she had thought of him when she hung it.

She reddened slightly. "It's a pretty good one," she said. "They vary a lot. I think my ancestor's rug is the best though, and I don't think I'm too biased."

"Which one is that?"

She pulled out a painting. "This one. This was protected when it was stored, and I bet it was kept out of direct sunlight forever. It was my first find, and so far, it's still the best, both in terms of preservation and craftsmanship."

"Listen to you now. You're starting to sound like an expert."

"No, not me. But I did get in touch with your Jessica, and a woman at the Craft College like Cassandra suggested. I've got a reading list now. I've been studying up."

"All you have going on, and you're still studying up."

She looked at her painting. "Obsessed might be more like it. I have a lot of things to think about, and this work lets me stop thinking about them. Besides, I keep thinking there's a message about my future somewhere in this." She waved her hand across the desk.

"Painting?"

She shrugged. "Maybe. Maybe creating a space to display these rugs. Maybe something that brings together the old recipes and the old handicrafts."

"Evie," he started, putting his hand on her shoulder. She flinched, and he pulled his hand back like he'd been burnt. "I'm so sorry," he said.

She shook her head. "Overreaction. I'm just a little tense, and even when I'm working on this stuff, part of me knows I should be doing something else." She led the way back to the kitchen, carefully closing the door. "Dogs," she said over her shoulder, by way of explanation. "They don't discriminate between antique hooked rugs and dog beds."

"I did come to help," Stephen reminded her. "Is there something I can do?"

Evie considered. "Well, maybe you and I could make a little headway in the shed while Dad's away. We've got that giant dumpster in the yard. We might as well make use of it."

"Great."

"Let's do it. Only an hour though. Let's see what we can pitch in an hour."

Chapter 25

Evie slept that night, tired and relieved that Dad would be okay. She had a warm feeling about Stephen's help in the shed. She was pretty sure they'd disguised their progress so James would not realize anything was gone, but they'd pitched empty paint cans, broken sand toys, and rusty garden tools.

Going to sleep was one thing, but when she woke it was with the intense awareness of Jase's impending visit. Five thirty was early. What on earth would she do until ten a.m.? She hoped tea would settle her stomach.

The sun was peeking up already and the big dogs were certain that the day had begun. She let them into the yard, put on the kettle, and turned on her phone.

Message from Leonard.

I sold a painting. Electronic transfer to your account. Can you make some more?

Message from Rett.

Try to get some sleep. We don't have to figure everything out right now.

Another message from Rett.

Don't fall for anything this morning.

Evie felt slightly comforted, but then annoyed at herself and Rett. *Of course I won't fall for anything. I can take care of myself.* But it was still kind of nice to think of Rett sending that message at what time? Oh, four a.m. Kids must have been up again.

She poured her tea while checking her bank account. Her fee for the consigned painting would be a nice bump in the balance. She stared at her phone as she tried to make sense of what she saw.

The deposit was there. It was minuscule, but there. That's barely coffee money, she thought, enraged. *I'm sure I didn't agree to that.*

She started her reply to Leonard, but the dogs at the door stopped her. While she fed and watered them, she decided to wait. It wasn't even six a.m. Nobody would expect an answer this early. Besides, Leonard had been nice. Maybe it was a misunderstanding.

She brought her laptop to the kitchen. She'd not had time to log yesterday's dreams about Leonie. When she was tapping in her recollections, an email came through. Maybe a lot of people were up before six.

It was from the textiles prof at the craft college, Rachel, checking in. She'd sent a link to a new display of heritage textile art at an Ottawa museum. Evie sent her a quick note of thanks and dug in.

The museum rugs were breathtaking and the notes about each one fascinated her. Apparently, she wasn't the only person who thought women's arts and crafts were important. According to these sources, they shed light onto the lives of women in the past and made a political statement as well.

Armed with her new knowledge, Evie went to the den. She pulled out Leonie's cobalt and scarlet creation and spread it across the worktable. The colours were still vibrant, the shapes clearly defined, the story right there in the picture. It was easily as good as the pieces in the museum.

Amazed and gratified, Evie gazed at the rug. This is important art, she thought, and not just to my family. *Thank you, thank you, Leonie.*

A gust of air brushed her shoulder. She smiled at the jumping fish and tossing boats on the rug and folded it back up.

Returning to her laptop, she was filled with a sense of something she couldn't name. Something that felt good, right, and like movement forward. Opening an empty document, she started to type. Bullet points helped her think.

Notes to myself:

- Leonie and Hannah are here with me, in some way I can't understand. There's a door right there, behind these rugs, and while I can't see it yet and don't know where it leads, I need to trust the process. Do the next right thing like Dad says.

- Leonie left her home, family, and culture to live with Charles in his hometown. Nobody spoke her language or knew her family.

- I don't think I can relate. Not really.

- Leonie had few choices, except in certain domains. She was queen of the garden, the kitchen, and textiles, clothing, blankets, quilts.

- Sovereignty.

- But within limits. The limits imposed by social expectations, husbands, and finances.

- Making beautiful things out of very little is, in itself, an art form.

- Leonie's art is important. Domestic crafts made life possible for people, but they also made room for art. Harsh lives became more beautiful when there was art, and women who were tasked with keeping everybody else alive needed ways to express their creative selves. Even when they gave up almost everything for others, they still had that spark.

- Could that be true? Can I say that creating a beautiful home using scraps, leftovers, even burlap bags, is a form of making art? Domestic art?

Evie closed her laptop. *What does this mean for me?* She thought about her life with Jase, feeling pain like an arrow to her heart. Some women still jumped to a man's demand. Maybe she was one of them.

Once thought, she could not stop thinking it.

Leonie didn't have choices, but she did. Even with her lack of choice, Leonie turned her life into a work of art. What might Evie do with all her opportunities?

That felt like a burden, not a gift. *My life is just a mess. I could never do what she did.*

That gust of air touched her shoulder again, but she ignored it. She didn't feel like an artist, or really like anything.

Mostly she felt a nagging dread about Jase's upcoming visit.

She got up and stretched, fists in her lower back. *I feel weird, like only half here. At least I didn't bake anything last night.*

She opened the laptop again to send Stephen the link to the museum, and before she thought better of it, sent the entire file of rug pictures to Rachel at the crafts college. Maybe it's time for Leonie's art to see the light of day, she thought fiercely. She needs somebody on her side.

It was still hours before Jase would arrive. She leashed up the dogs, put on her sneakers, and headed out for a long walk.

By ten a.m., she was on her fourth coffee. She'd texted to her dad, sent his reading glasses to the hospital with Dorie, and was working on sorting the accumulation from the hall closet when Mallow announced Jase's arrival. Dusting her hands on her jeans, she headed out the kitchen door. From the edge of the porch, she could see him check his phone, swipe at his hair. Then he opened the car door and stood up in one smooth move. She appreciated his feline grace, and when he saw her watching, his smile was brilliant. Her face was warm, her stomach fluttered, and her heart pounded. *Jase. Finally getting it. I had really given up, but here he is. He's here. Finally.*

She wanted to jump into his arms, but something held her back. Instead, when he reached for her on the porch, she deflected his hug and said, "Come on in. I made coffee."

She put his mug on the table. He sat, looking around the room. "Where's your dad? His truck's in the driveway."

The heat of anger blazed through her. "He's in the hospital. Remember?"

"Oh, yes, right. How is he?"

She stared at her cup.

"Really, Evie, I just forgot. How's your dad?"

"Not great," she said shortly. "But that's not why you are here."

"You're right," he said. "I like James though. I hope he's feeling better."

She nodded. "Thanks. We hope so too."

"So, Evie," he said, reaching across the table for her hand. "You were right."

"About?"

"You said I would reconsider. That I'd realize some things after you were gone. You were right."

She felt the steel in her gaze soften. "I was?"

He nodded. "I really need you, Evie."

"You do?"

"I do. I want you to come back."

"Come back home? Is that what you mean?"

He shifted in his chair. "I need your hand on the wheel, so to speak. It's been what, three weeks? Four? You've been here doing nothing and I'm missing you."

Doing nothing? She moved those words around in her mouth but decided to let them go. "You're missing me."

"Every day." He gave her his winning smile. "It's so good to see you."

She felt herself thawing. "Are you missing me like you've reconsidered your position?"

His smile dimmed. "Which position is that?"

"Married. A baby."

He pulled back from the table, dropping her hand. "Uh, not that position. What I mean is that I need you."

Across the table, she could see him clearly. Bits of grey in his hair, crow's feet around his eyes, a receding chin that suddenly looked weak.

"Let's get clear. What, exactly, do you need me for?" She felt frankly nauseated now, her stomach feeling exactly as it had when long-legged

Michelle had climbed down from their sleeping loft. If she did throw up, maybe it would land on his shoes.

"Listen, Evie, I can't do this festival alone. Michelle—"

"Oh, yes, dear Michelle. She's not working out?"

"She's great," he said simply. "But she isn't you."

"Wait a minute. Are you still seeing her, this Michelle?"

"Yes, of course I am," Jase said. "But she's an actor. She has no idea about the business. She isn't making any headway on the festival contacts either."

She wondered briefly if he knew how many artists had already pulled out.

"Time is getting short. I need you back, Evie. I'm willing to make you a very good offer."

"An offer. You make me believe that you want to reconcile and now you're making me an offer. On a grant-funded program that I got for you. Does something seem a little off to you?"

"Listen, I never said anything about getting back together. That's all in your head. You misread me."

Had she? Maybe.

"What's this very good offer?"

"I'd like to hire you as my assistant. I can't pay very much but you'd be back on the festival staff."

Evie blinked. "Did you just offer me a job as your assistant?"

"I did. You were right about everything you did. I didn't realize that before. Now I know that I need you as my assistant."

"What did you pay me before, when I was 'assisting' you for the last ten or so years?"

"Well, see, that's why this is better. You'll actually get paid."

What an idiot. He was still looking hopeful.

Leaning back, she folded her arms. "You can't possibly pay me what that work is worth. Not if you're taking a cut." She liked the sharpness in her voice.

He recoiled.

"Do you have any idea why I did all of that? Why I gave up my own art practice to support yours?"

He stared helplessly. "No. Did you give up your art practice? You were still painting, weren't you?"

"Not possible. The work I did was more than full-time. There wasn't time for me to paint and promote Jase Highborn Art."

He looked aghast. "I didn't make you do that, you know. Nothing could make me give up my art."

"I know that. But I gave up mine. No, you didn't make me. I did it for love and to make our future together. I thought love meant you sacrificed for each other. I thought you would love me if I gave up my own interests to promote yours. I was a fool."

"Evie..."

"But I'm not enough of a fool to do it again. Maybe you didn't respect me because I didn't respect myself. But guess what. That's over."

She stood up.

"I'm glad you understand what it takes to run your business and the festival. Put your little girlfriend on it. Maybe she'll let you take advantage of her."

"She's not you, Evie. She doesn't have your skills. Or your work ethic." He looked near tears.

"Are you kidding me right now? You're not improving your position."

"I'm really at a loss here." He got up and paced the floor. "I don't even know how to get in touch with some of the artists for the festival.

We've already missed a deadline, and the San Francisco contact has cancelled our contract because I didn't get the work out on time."

She felt a small twinge of sympathy that wanted to become guilt. She firmed her jaw. "That's not my problem. I am sorry you're struggling, but I'm not bailing you out."

He squared his shoulders and stuck out his chin. His little chin, she thought. New strategy. Watch what he does now.

"This has implications for you too, you know. You wrote that grant. You agreed to make the festival happen."

"Get mad, Jase, go ahead. But a month ago you reminded me that my name wasn't on the grant, the contract, or in your business. I was out, totally out, and with nothing. It was all you, all the time."

He leaned against the sink, arms folded, frowning.

"Remember? You were ready to do it all. You thought you were doing it all. Your failure does not implicate me in the least."

He dropped his arms and took a breath. "Evie. Please. Don't do this. I'm in trouble here."

She could feel a tiny wavering. *Evie, be strong.* "You made your decision. Now I've made mine. It's time to go." She held the kitchen door open for him.

He gave her an imploring look as he walked out. "Please reconsider. Please."

She was careful of the old glass, but the door still slammed satisfactorily.

Gravel rattled as he spun out of the driveway. As she leaned on the old door, she began to shake. *What have I done? Did I just give up a job?* She wobbled to a chair.

I can't believe he just said that.

I can't believe I just did that. What is a woman worth? A wave of righteous anger made her pick up her phone. Watch out, Leonard

Fishburne, she thought. No, I'm going in. Dropping the phone in her pocket, she grabbed keys and headed out. *Grandmother Leonie, give me your strength today.*

Chapter 26

She pushed into the gallery, walking briskly. "Hello?"

A few browsers walked the main room and Stephen sat at the desk, gazing at a laptop. "Evie!" he greeted her with a kiss on the cheek. "What's going on? Your face is red. Been running?" He guided her toward a chair.

"Not running. Is Leonard here?" Her gaze was caught by a watercolour behind the desk. Yes, another one of hers, well framed. She squinted at the price.

"Leonard? No, not right now," Stephen said. "Evie, I wanted to talk to you about the rugs."

"What about them?"

"Can you sit down? You seem agitated."

She tried to relax her shoulders and allowed him to pull out a chair for her. "He's out?" She scowled. She needed her anger to keep her going. "He's sold a painting. The crab-apple one."

Stephen smiled. "Oh, yes. That's wonderful. Good news."

"You know, I didn't really pay attention to the terms. I used to handle consignments for my—my ex-partner, but I didn't really think..."

"Evie, what's the matter?"

"I think he's cheating me."

Stephen's eyes were wide. Maybe it was her tone. But she didn't care.

"Why do you think Leonard's cheating you?"

"He texted to say he'd deposited my cut for the sale of the crab-apple blossom painting. I know what he was asking but look what he gave me." She held out her phone with the bank deposit on it.

"Oh, Leonard, you idiot."

"The place is littered with idiots. I did not agree to that. This is robbery, and I'm sick of people taking advantage of me. I'm not going to let this happen." Her face was hot, and she couldn't remain sitting.

"No wonder you're agitated. There must be a mistake. I'm sure he'll fix it," Stephen assured her.

"He better," she fumed.

"He'll be back," Stephen said soothingly. "Can you sit down?"

She was vibrating. "I'm not sure. I just had it out with my ex too."

"Oh. Okay."

"I might need a minute." She paced. "Maybe I need more than a minute. I'm going into the office."

"Okay."

She marched into the messy office. When she caught sight of the rug she'd hung on the wall, she finally exhaled. It really was beautiful. She gave herself over to gazing at the details, feeling her agitation settle with each breath. In a few minutes, she went back into the gallery. The visitors had gone.

"Sorry about that," she said to Stephen.

"You don't need to apologize," he said. "We're good. I wanted to talk to you about the rugs."

"I don't know. I'm still pretty mad."

"You are. But not at me, right?"

She softened. "No, of course not. I'm not mad at you."

"About the rugs. I think they might be very important, more important than we realized."

She smiled at him. "You said 'we.'"

He shrugged. "I'm invested in your project." Then he tipped his head down to look into her eyes. "Maybe I'm invested in you."

Her face warmed with pleasure. "That's nice. But I also appreciate your help with finding out about the rugs. In a way, women who made everyday objects into art were working inside a system that kept them down. Making art was a way of standing up for themselves."

"Subversive. Makes you think differently about things."

"I guess so. The whole thing is making me think hard about women's place in the home, in history, and even today."

A wave of anger hit again. That friggin' Jase, thinking she wanted to be his poorly paid assistant. *Oooh, I could spit nails.*

"Evie?" Stephen brought her back to the present.

"Right. Sorry." She recovered herself. "Do you remember I told you about my great-grandmother, the one who didn't belong?"

"I remember that conversation well," Stephen said.

"She made a place for herself by helping other women find their art. To subvert their social positions." She grinned. "This is not a conversation I could have with my father."

Stephen grinned back. "Don't underestimate him. Speaking of James, how is he?"

She sobered immediately. "Getting ornery, so it must be time to come home. We don't know how much care he'll need though."

"That's hard." His eyes were soft and warm.

"Yeah. On the good side, he's still alive. When I think about that, I'm more sympathetic to his grumpiness."

Stephen nodded. "Good. What are you going to do about these rugs?"

"I don't know. After I talk to Leonard, he may tell me to get them out."

"No, I don't think so. He's a hard case, but he's not mean. But Evie," he added, "he's also interested in your rugs."

Taken aback, Evie said, "They're not my rugs. At least not all of them."

"Aren't they? You've taken them on, collected them, you're documenting what's known. Don't discount what you've put into this. That's your work, your time, your thinking."

She looked at him skeptically. "You really are an academic, aren't you? As if my thoughts could be valuable."

"Leonie might have said the same thing about her rugs. But somehow I doubt it," he said. "I get the impression she knew her worth."

And I don't? "What do you mean, he's interested in rugs? You say it like it's not a good thing." Before Stephen could reply, Leonard entered from the rear.

"Hello!" he called out. "Steve! Eve! Hey, that's cute."

"Leonard," Stephen said easily. "Evie was looking for you."

"That's excellent. Come on back here, and let's look at those rugs you've got in the closet."

Evie tossed a look at Stephen over her shoulder, and he gave her a thumbs-up. She followed Leonard into the back room.

"You sold my crab-apple painting," she said.

He gave her a wide smile. "Yes, isn't that wonderful? Did you get the payment?"

"I wanted to talk to you about that. It was a lot less than I expected. Less than we agreed on."

"Evie! I would never cheat you."

"Of course not. I just thought there might be a calculation error."

"Well, let's see." He sat at his desk and opened the computer. "I sold it for four fifty, and you got paid... Oh." He looked up at her.

"That seemed a little low." She watched his face.

"Well, what did we negotiate?" he asked, looking for another file.

"I think we were pretty, uh, informal," she said. "But informal or not, fifteen percent is too low."

"How much did you make when you sold them before?" he asked.

Not much, she thought. "Circumstances were different then. I was a student, and they were tourist bait selling at a kiosk down on the landing. Now you're selling art."

"Hmm. What would you consider to be fair? Remember, I have to make a living here."

"Fifty percent." Evie was firm. "Standard terms."

His face registered shock. "Fifty! I can't possibly. Forty."

I am so glad I didn't say thirty. "Forty-five. I paint them and bring them to you complete, you know. You're not even hanging them."

He looked faintly annoyed. "Except I did hang the one I sold."

"True. It looked great up there, by the way."

"It did," he said, with some pleasure. "I was very pleased with your work, Evie."

"You even gave it a title. That was a little weird."

"Not me, not at all. Steve."

What? Stephen had come up with *Summer Symphony?* She reminded herself not to get derailed.

"We're still talking about terms, Leonard."

"Done. Forty-five percent. Less fees."

She narrowed her eyes. "No fees. You're not even putting them on the wall. Come on, Leonard. I'm not a kid," she said.

"Well, if I decide to frame and hang it, that's going to come out of your commission."

"But I get to approve which ones you hand sell, and which land in the bin."

He released a theatrical sigh. "Okay, Evie. But we're going to have to talk about those rugs. I can't be storing them for free."

"I'm already teaching an August class for you in exchange for space. What else do you want?"

"I know a guy," he said, just as Stephen walked into the back room.

"Leonard, you're starting to sound more and more like a local," he said affably.

"A guy?" Evie prompted.

"A guy who might be interested in your rugs. If I broker a deal, we can set some good terms, like twenty percent for you."

"Wait, what? A deal to sell the rugs? They don't even belong to me, at least not all of them."

"Well, you think about this," Leonard instructed. "In the right hands, that could be a decent display."

Evie was sure her dismay was visible, but when Stephen walked behind Leonard and rolled his eyes, she giggled. "Well, I'll think about it, yes," she said. "In the meantime, you owe me some money."

"Ah, right. Yes. I'll have my accountant get on that."

"We both know your accountant isn't paying me," she said. "I can bill you if you like. In fact, I can bill you in advance of the sale. Then you'd have inventory instead of consignment."

"No, no, that's okay. I'll adjust the payment later today."

"Good. So, I guess I'll see you later." Head held high, she stalked out of the room and through the main part of the gallery. She was so intent on the door she was surprised by Stephen catching up with her at the door.

"Hold on. Do you, that is"—he was a bit breathless—"good work in there, and do you have time for coffee?"

"I'm, uh, I don't know. I could just fall apart any second here."

"I get it. Come on. Let's go for a walk instead."

They started off briskly toward the beach, but Evie's steps slowed the farther they got from the gallery. Soon she was strolling. Stephen matched her, step for step. The beach, mercifully, was nearly empty.

"Better?" he asked her.

"I think so. Yes. It's been a morning."

"You took him right on. Good for you." She felt the warmth of his approval.

"Not too pushy?"

"Not pushy at all. He was taking advantage. You just said no, unacceptable."

"I want to tell you about this morning. When Jase came by."

"Oh, the artist. Right." Stephen looked across the bay.

"I thought"—she gulped—"I thought he was coming to make up, to reconcile." She felt her throat tighten. Sniffling, she added, "I can't believe I'm telling you this."

"Did you want to reconcile?" His voice was so tight she turned to look at him. He was pale and his eyes dark.

She shrugged and turned away. "Yes? No? I couldn't tell, honestly. But now I'm very clear."

Gently taking her shoulder, Stephen turned her toward him. "Well?"

She stared at the sand at her feet.

"Evie? This is important to me." Tucking his finger under her chin, he lifted her face so she gazed at him. "Evie?"

She shook him off and walked on. "Well, isn't it obvious? He had another agenda."

He followed her. "What agenda?"

She wiped her sleeve across her eyes and faced him. "That rat bastard wanted to offer me a job as his assistant to manage the Peninsula Festival that he already stole from me. Ugh!" She shook her fists. "That slimy good-for-nothing. I was all sad and depressed before, but now I'm just hopping mad. First Jase and then Leonard. Taking advantage. Men!" She glared at Stephen.

"Whoa, there!" He held up his palms. "Don't blame an entire sex."

She could feel the steel in her back and fire in her eyes. "I'm done. I've bent over backward for men and I'm finished. No more. Nobody is taking advantage of this girl any more."

"Good for you." Stephen shook a fist in solidarity. "But Evie, do you think I'm taking advantage of you?"

She appraised him. "While I'm being all honest and stuff, I will say that I've wondered why you're so nice to me. Whether, maybe, you want to grab those rugs too, and turn them into some research project or something." She held his eyes.

He flushed slightly.

"Oh," she said, anger rising with her interpretation. "So even you, Mr. Nice Guy from North Carolina. Man, this stinks." She turned and marched off, back toward town. When she sneaked a glance over her shoulder, she saw him gazing out to sea, hands in pockets. Good. He should be ashamed. She stomped on home, fuelled by righteous anger and adrenaline.

Stephen returned to the gallery, shaking sand off his shoes.

"Where've you been?" Leonard asked irritably. "I thought you were in until Cassie gets here. I need to go out."

"Okay, I'm here now," he said mildly. "Go ahead."

Leonard gathered some things and got up to leave the office, but Stephen was in the way, leaning against the doorframe, arms folded. "You upset her."

"So? I fixed it already. It was just an error."

Stephen said, "Okay. We can let that be. But trying to take those rugs from her. What are you doing?"

Leonard frowned. "Running a business. I'm in the business of selling art, as you well know. Sometimes that means works that hang in the gallery and sometimes I broker deals for other work."

"Do you always take eighty percent? That's a pretty sweet deal for the broker."

"That would be good for Evie too," Leonard explained. "She doesn't have a job, so any money is a plus."

"Come on," Stephen said. "I don't think she's going to let you take advantage like that."

Leonard made a sound. "Based on what happened here this morning, I suspect you're correct. She pointed out that she's not a kid. I forgot that she used to manage Jase Highborn's practice."

Stephen was on a tear. "Evie's in a bad way right now, and I don't think she knows the value of what she's uncovered. I don't like this at all. I think you're trying to manipulate her to your advantage."

"Manipulate! I don't manipulate people. I help people buy and sell things they want and need to buy and sell. She would never be able to find a buyer for those rugs on her own."

Stephen slid toward his desk, narrowed eyes on Leonard. "She's not looking for a buyer."

"Stephen, you're overreacting. I just offered her an opportunity. One she wouldn't otherwise have."

"Yeah, like you selling her paintings and paying her less than the materials cost is giving her an opportunity."

"Friend, watch yourself," Leonard warned. "I made a mistake and I have rectified it. You don't get to crucify me for that."

"Right. Yes, you're right. I'm sorry."

Leonard's voice was still raised. "I might ask you to clarify your interest in Evie Madison. You're pretty involved for someone who's only here on a sabbatical."

Stephen's face warmed. "I can relate to her. She's struggling to find her place. Doesn't really know where she belongs. Not an artist, but not yet sure what she is."

"You think she belongs with you? Maybe you're the one taking advantage."

"Knock it off. You know me better than that. Besides, this is not your business."

Leonard lifted his chin. "How I run my business isn't your business either, Stephen. We're done here. I'm going."

Stephen thumped into his chair and opened his laptop but noticed Leonard's brisk progress across the gallery and out the front door. The bell jangled as he shut it firmly behind him.

"That was unpleasant," Stephen muttered to himself. Trying to shake off the nasty interaction, he turned to email, but the wave of new messages was overwhelming. Sighing, he got up and poured a cup of Leonard's weak coffee. He thought about ignoring his email, but his responsible side prevailed.

More drama from the department, but nothing that was actual news. Everyone was on edge, but nobody knew any more this week than last. There was a note from a journal editor, too, and he clicked on that with some optimism. Oh, a rejection. Great. This is just not the day for good news, he thought drearily.

He pulled up Jase Highborn's website again. Glancing at the artist's picture, he felt distaste. But in rereading the copy, he recognized Evie's style and her voice. Her descriptions of the man's work were compelling.

Evie Madison has more going for her than she knows. Maybe more than anybody knows. He thought of the crab-apple painting, now hung carefully over the unused fireplace in his upstairs apartment, and the day she'd taken him on a tour of the inside of the tree. Getting up, he carried his coffee to the harbour window and gazed out.

Instead of seeing the docks and the visitors, he visualized Evie's hair curling in the morning fog, her overflowing eyes, and heard again the disappointment in her voice.

He sat back down and pulled up a browser window.

Chapter 27

Later that morning, Evie pulled into Alice Simmons's driveway. A cacophony of barking greeted her. She stuck her head in the barn door and heard her sister's voice. "I'm coming!"

Dorie and Frou-Frou emerged from the back of the barn while Evie was helping herself to coffee.

"Hi, sis," Dorie said. "What's up?" She looked worried.

Evie shook her head. "Nothing about Dad," she said quickly. "But I've had a terrible day and I need to talk to someone."

"Terrible day? It's only eleven thirty," Dorie said, pouring her own coffee. "Here, sit down. The dogs are fed. I'm not quite finished with the cleaning, but I can talk."

Evie poured out her morning to an attentive Dorie.

"Eeww, what is wrong with Jase?" she said at one point. "He must really think he's the center of the universe."

Evie grimaced. "I think I helped him develop that fantasy. I treated him that way. I'm furious that he would even consider asking me to work for him, but I can also see how I trained him to think that I might agree to it. Then Leonard at the gallery, trying to get away with paying me practically nothing for my work, and wanting to sell the hooked rugs at a huge profit for him. It's been yucky."

"But listen," Dorie said, "it also sounds like you told them off. In a nice way."

"Not really very nice," Evie admitted. "Mostly angry. I wasn't too nice to Stephen, either."

Dorie looked very serious. "Nice is overrated. You don't have to be nice. What's going on with Stephen?"

"Maybe I just threw him in with Jase and Leonard because he's a man," Evie admitted. "It just felt like every man I know was trying to get something out of me."

"Stephen seemed really lovely," Dorie said. "I was hoping you two might hit it off, you know."

She shrugged. "Now that I'm a little less mad, I can think better. He seems interested in helping me with my rug project, and maybe friendly in general. He hasn't been a jerk, but he calls Leonard his best friend, so maybe that's why I'm wary."

"Or maybe you've just had a terrible day on top of a terrible week and month, and it's hard to trust any man right now."

"You're getting smart in your old age," Evie said, smiling at Dorie. "Not just the baby sister."

"I had to grow up sometime," Dorie admitted. "I do reserve the right to act like a kid without notice though."

"Thanks for being a good listener. I don't feel so bad about standing up for myself. The weird part is, now I don't miss Jase at all. For weeks, part of me has been waiting for him to want me back. My life was on hold because I was waiting for Jase to come to his senses. Turns out I'm the one that had to get my thinking straight."

"You're not feeling all sad about the breakup?"

"It's amazing. Right now, I am grateful to Jase for being such a jerk. He made everything perfectly clear. Even without a job, a home, and living with my father, I'm better off without him."

Dorie looked thoughtful. "Better off without him, yes, but are you better off without that grant you were working on?"

"I'm not going to be Jase's assistant anything."

"Of course not. You put a lot into that project though. It's a shame to get nothing from that."

"Well, I guess I can say I got experience. Like life experience, nothing that can go on a resume. I made contacts with some interesting artists, started to create connections." A tiny idea began to take root. "I'd like to see it through, actually, but not as anybody's assistant anything."

Dorie was gazing into the rafters of the barn. "What if Jase was your assistant?" She laughed suddenly. "I like imagining stuff. Silly, but fun."

Evie was intrigued. "Serve him right. What kind of a boss would I be?"

"Oh, mean, very mean," Dorie laughed. "To Jase, anyway."

"Well, I don't think Jase would ever let someone else be in charge. He always has to look like The Man. Honestly, I think I'd rather be in charge of something of my own." She rinsed her mug in the little sink. "Thanks for the coffee and clarity," she said to Dorie. "And the fun fantasy. Call if you hear from Rett, okay?"

Dorie hugged her. "Yes, and maybe we can go to visit together this evening."

"Sure. I'll text you."

The big dogs were ecstatic upon her arrival at home. "You guys miss Dad, right? Well, me, too. Nothing feels normal." She ruffled Custard's neck fur and opened the door for both to go out. Mallow threw himself down in a patch of sunlight. Custard paced the fence and then sat gazing back at the house.

Steeling herself, she went into the bedroom where Rett and Helen had spent adolescence fighting with each other. Throwing open the closet door, she jumped back as stuff tumbled out onto the floor. "Oh, great," she breathed, and pulled a plastic trash bag from her back pocket.

Ninety minutes and three trash bags later, she'd cleared the closet. She posted the boxes of clothing online for donation and trundled the full trash bags out to the shed.

She pushed the door open gingerly, but the shed was empty even of her memories. She hauled the bags inside to await pickup day. A shaft of sunlight fell on Dad's rocking chair and her throat caught. *He's going to be fine. Home by the end of the week,* she heard Rett's reassuring voice in her mind.

Only last week, Stephen visited with Dad here in the shed, talking about who knows what. She hadn't been really paying attention, she thought, ashamed. *So caught up in my own misery, I didn't even notice things right in front of me.* Like Dad's problems.

That was over.

Tools scattered the old workbench, something that would never happen with Dad at home. She matched each to its carefully silhouetted place on the pegboard and put it away. At least the shed would be tidy for his homecoming. Well, tidier. She shook out the pillow from the seat of the rocker, replaced it, and turned toward the door. Good enough. She left without a second glance.

Returning to the house, she made tea and curled up on the couch. What would it be like to run the Peninsula Festival? She'd always imagined Jase welcoming artists and audience from a platform, herself running around in the background with a clipboard or something. What if, instead, she was the one doing the welcome?

Nope. She cringed from the image of being in the limelight as artists withdrew, venues failed, and audiences stayed home. That was not for her. No wonder Jase was upset. He'd let things go for too long. No, she would not be bailing him out. It was too late for any of that. Instead, she let her mind wander to another fantasy, where she greeted a group of women artists and they gathered around a big table, sharing food and ideas, with hooked rugs displayed all around. Ah, that felt better.

That was enough. Shaking her head, she let go of that scene and picked up Hannah's book where she had left off.

> Mama made my wedding dress. Sally helped her design it. It was red, a gorgeous deep red colour and I dyed my shoes to match. I loved how the chiffon overskirt swirled around my calves. I'd been waiting for Robert to get home; we considered getting married before he left, and when I realized he was stationed close to Sydney, near where Mama was from, I thought about going up there to meet him and get married. But instead, we decided to wait until we could be married in Stella Mare with all our families around.

Because of Robert being in Cape Breton, Mama's stories about her and Papa during their early days flowed freely. Papa was in the Merchant Marine with Uncle Samuel during the Great War and disembarked in Sydney. He followed Uncle Samuel home and fell in love with Sam's baby sister Leonie. Mama made jokes about Robert coming home to marry me, and my younger sister Sarah teased me about him falling for her. Instead, though, he was killed during part of the Battle of Saint Laurence. He didn't come home, I didn't wear my red wedding dress, Sarah married a local boy too young to fight, and before long they were having babies. I was still at home with Mama and Papa, and glad of it, too, because Mama was busy with her rugs and rug classes and the household needed seeing to.

I missed Robert so much that I couldn't be bothered to meet anyone else. When Alex Deschamps wanted to go walking with me, I told him no. I got a reputation for being "unable to move on" from Robert and I liked it that way. However, when Sarah was having babies, I loved to spend time at her house, rocking, carrying, feeding, and later teaching my little nephews and nieces about, well, everything. I especially loved sweet, funny little Agnes. I was blessed to teach children in school and blessed to be another mum to Sarah's children. Mama never went back to Cape Breton after that one trip. She buried her father, and when word came that Samuel was ill, she phoned and wrote letters, but didn't suggest going back. My Papa didn't want to return, and I think Samuel's illness was so painful for him to think about, they didn't even talk about it. Uncle Samuel died when I was twenty-three.

His name was never mentioned again.

Mama is near eighty now, old in face and figure, but her hands can still make anything: baked goods, those rugs that everyone raves about, and she can change a diaper, grow a garden, and sooth a fevered brow. Papa died twelve years ago in a fishing boat accident; one of those things that we wish would never happen but seem to be inevitable. Maybe the sea has to take some of us for her own. Anyway, Mama wants to move in with Sarah and her tribe, but they have a houseful already. Mama and me, we just keep on. When she has a place to go, then I'll travel, first to Sydney to see where my Robert was lost, and then maybe to Cheticamp to see where Mama's family comes from. I know my Stella Mare roots, but I don't know about these Acadian people, my forebears, my mother's people. I want to know who I am.

Me, too, Hannah. I want to know who I am, too. Evie felt the words wrapping around her heart. She lifted her chin and dropped the book onto her lap. The loose papers and pictures slid onto the floor. Grabbing them up, she peered at the grainy black-and-white images. Two women, six kids of various sizes, probably sometime in the mid-fifties? Sixties? Evie wasn't sure.

The back of the photo carried some writing that she finally made out to say the picture included Sarah and Hannah, with Sarah's children. She held the photo under the lamp to look at the tallest girl: her mother Agnes, at ten or eleven years old. Hannah and Sarah both looked far older than Evie would have expected. Hannah was probably only my age, Evie thought, early thirties, but maybe life had taken a big toll. Losing her lover like that, maybe it makes you old before your time. Six babies in about eight years probably aged a woman too. And it would be more years before Corinne arrived.

Sarah, my grandmother. Hannah, my great-aunt. Both daughters of Leonie, my Acadian ancestor. Women of Stella Mare. Courageous women, like their mother.

Evie leaned back against the couch and held the photo to her heart. Did Hannah ever get to Cape Breton? Did she ever get to see Robert's grave? Evie tried to find memories of Hannah and Sarah, but could only recall Grandma Sarah, old, a little frail, and often cantankerous.

Corinne. She would check with Corinne. Corinne might know.

As soon as Cassandra arrived to take over the gallery, Stephen put on his running shoes and left. He walked first, down Water Street. Then he picked up the pace and headed toward the end of the peninsula. Stiff and tight, it took some time for his joints to soften and his body to settle into the rhythm.

Past the campground, he veered off the road to the running trail, cool trees overhead contrasting with the sweat trickling down his back. Pushing his speed, all thought left and there was only the pounding of his feet and the sound of his breathing. When he slowed to a walk, it was because he didn't have any choice.

He pulled off his shirt and wiped his face, panting and walking. He wasn't even sure where he was, but it didn't matter. All that mattered was the flow of air into his lungs and energy through his body and the blessed relief of slowing to a walk.

As his body settled, he tuned into the sounds around him; rustling leaves, his footsteps on the cinder trail, a squirrel complaining at his interruption. Beneath it all was a deep silence.

He bent over and stretched, then reached over his head, taking big breaths. The silence was there, despite chittering and squawking animal life. It was big, holding all of them together: squirrel, trees, man. As he looked up, a breeze touched the canopy of white pines, rustling the needles, reminding him of his favorite running trail back home. There, though, he ran under loblolly pines, but they made the same sound in a breeze. Comforted, he started a slow jog back in the direction from which he'd come.

Running was good for the body and the soul, he mused. Now he could think more clearly.

The way back to the gallery seemed longer, but of course he wasn't running like a wild man all the way. Hoping to see no one, he slipped through the back office door and upstairs.

An hour later, watered, showered, and fed, he was down in the office at his laptop. It was quiet in the building; Cassandra had left after closing. Leonard could be anywhere. But *he's not here right now*, thought Stephen. He enjoyed the creaking of the old building and the sounds of the evening harbour through the window, and right now, he didn't want to talk to anyone.

After scrolling around for an hour, though, maybe he did. After getting a return message from someone he knew at the university in Saint Jacques, he called.

"Stephen." Trent sounded welcoming. "I didn't know you were in the province."

"Yes, since March. I'm sorry I haven't been in touch. This project keeps me busy, plus I have a little gallery gig and the weather, man, that took some getting used to."

Trent chuckled. "I remember my first year here. It was not what I expected."

"I've not even been here in real winter yet."

"Just wait."

"I've been warned," he said, smiling. "Got my parka and boots at the ready."

"Are you still at Mountain View University?"

"I am. My first sabbatical."

"There's a lot of talk about what's going on there. Are you getting burned by that?"

He sighed. "Everyone is getting burned. There's no escaping. That's part of the reason I called."

"Oh, man, I'm so sorry. Right after you got promoted too," Trent said sympathetically.

"Nobody's predicting anything on the record," Stephen said cautiously. "I'm trying to be proactive."

"What's the worst case?"

"They shut down our program and my colleague and I both lose our positions. Nobody is protected under that circumstance." Stephen thought for a moment. "It might not be that extreme."

"Well, I don't think I'm a lot of help, frankly," Trent said. "We're not likely to have any tenure-track openings for a few years."

"That's okay," Stephen assured him. "I wasn't really looking for a job. Just trying to keep my information up to date. I don't even know what I'd have to do to work for money in Canada. I'm only working for rent right now."

Trent laughed. "You don't have a housing stipend?"

"Leonard Fishburne charity, you could call it."

"How is Leonard, by the way? Still looking out for Leonard?"

Stephen chuckled. "He's doing well. You should come to Stella Mare this summer. See his new gallery."

"Maybe we'll do that. In the meantime, we are going to be seeking sessional instructors for winter term. I think there's a class in art history. Are you looking?"

"Oh," Stephen was surprised. "Well, sure. I'd like to get my feet wet, in a manner of speaking. I really like it here. It wouldn't be a bad thing to get acquainted with your school and colleagues."

Trent laughed. "You're thinking about moving here to the land of ice and snow? What's captured your attention?"

Stephen pondered. "That's a good question. Work is going well." *And I've met the loveliest woman, but I think I'll keep that to myself.*

"Getting much written?"

"Lots. Accepted is another question. I feel good about the work, though, despite what certain journal reviewers think."

"That would be reviewer two?"

"Isn't it always? Anyway, that part of work is going okay. I'm surprised at how much I like the life here. The people too."

"If they accept you, it can be a wonderful place to live. Danica and I have enjoyed it. You should come up for dinner sometime."

"I'd like that," he agreed with pleasure.

After they hung up, he went down the street to the fish market and the liquor store. Bay scallops and chardonnay in hand, he headed toward Leonard's house on the water. Leonard was wrong to take advantage of Evie, Stephen thought, but I was wrong to be so harsh. I own a part of all of that. It's my job to make it right.

Chapter 28

Pondering Hannah's diary, Evie called Corinne for more information, but Corinne had her own agenda.

"Hi, Evie. How is James?"

Evie was startled. *Oh, right. Of course, she thinks I'm calling about Dad.* "He's the same. Rett thinks he'll be home later this week."

"Not worse, at least."

"No, not worse. Doing okay. But I need some help. I've been digging through the house, and I have questions."

Corinne chuckled. "I bet you do. Fire away."

"I'd like to talk to you in person. Can you come to the hospital with us this evening? Dorie and I are going to see Dad. We'll pick you up and then we can talk on the way."

"Aren't you efficient! That's a great idea. Tell me when to expect you."

Dorie drove so Evie could talk to their aunt. "Thanks for being my source this evening," Evie said. "Okay if I record you? I've been recording stories all over the peninsula."

Corinne looked surprised. "How formal. But sure."

"Thanks. Okay, so, Grandmother Sarah came to live at our house when I was about four, I think. Is that right?"

Corinne counted on her fingers. "Close, anyway. Your Grandmother Madison owned the house, and she stayed in the little room off the kitchen, the den, until she died. I think that happened when you were a baby, or at least small. Then my mum—your grandmother—moved in. I remember because so much was happening all at once. I was close to finishing high school, Dad died, your Grandmother Madison died, Mum needed company, and your parents had a room available. Mum was capable, but she hated being alone, and I was heading to Fredericton to university. The timing was right."

"She wasn't with us for long, was she?" Evie struggled to recall the old woman who lived in the den. Her two grandmothers blended in her memory.

Though driving, Dorie threw in a question. "Why don't I remember any of this?"

"No, you wouldn't," Evie said. "You weren't born yet."

"Right," Corinne said. "I went away to school, then Mum got sick. Instead of her helping Aggie with the kids and the house, she was another person Aggie needed to take care of."

Evie had a vague memory of white sheets, the smell of medicine and disinfectant cleaner, and her mother shushing her while she played dolls on the stairs. "I really don't have any clear memories," she admitted. "It must have been a hard time."

Corinne laughed shortly. "It got harder when Aggie got pregnant at forty. But she and Mum had a good laugh about the whole situation."

"Really?" Dorie said. "What was funny about it?"

"Well, Aggie was doing exactly what Mum had done. I came along years and years after the so-called last baby."

Evie grinned at her. "Just like Dorie."

"I know you remember when Dorie came. You were pretty old then."

"I do remember that. You came to help Mum and you stayed like three years. You got stuck with us."

Corinne laughed. "Well, Aggie had her hands full. I only stuck around until I got into social work school, and then I left again. Aggie and James were my family. Your house was my home base."

"Still before my memory," Dorie said. "But I guess if I was the baby, that's why."

"That's why," Corinne said comfortingly. "I'm looking forward to seeing James."

"Dad's house is kind of like your family home too, Corinne. Is that what you meant?" Evie questioned again, trying to understand.

"I didn't grow up there exactly, but I spent a lot of time there after Aggie and James got married. I knew your other grandmother well. When Mum had to move out of her house, though, I was at a loss, except for Aggie and James. You know how when you girls went off to school, you could always go home? That's what your house was like for me since Mum didn't have a house anymore."

"You might have some thoughts about Dad selling it. Some feelings."

Corinne said, "Thoughts, yes. I wish James could stay in his own house. I also understand how moving into a different kind of place would be attractive to him. He doesn't want his family taking care of him."

"But why not? He and Mum did it for both of their mothers. Why not him?" Dorie asked.

"You're right, Dore," Evie said suddenly. "That what's felt wrong about this whole plan to sell the house. I don't think anyone in our family has left their home to go into care. It just hasn't happened."

"Are you offering to take care of Dad?" Dorie asked. "I can tell you from my recent experience, it isn't all that much fun."

Evie shook her head. "I wasn't planning on it. But..."

"Nobody in this family is easy to help," Dorie interrupted. "We all think we can do everything on our own, but it just doesn't work."

Corinne jumped in. "I think James's desire to move is because of the house. He wants to be able to keep things as nice as they were when your mother was alive, and to be frank, he's been slowing down for a long time."

Evie was stung. "You mean we haven't noticed it."

"Maybe. I see this all the time in my work with older people. It's hard to notice something that's going to turn your world upside down."

"Until you find your father slumped and lifeless in the shed," Evie said with heat.

Corinne nodded. "That does get your attention. How are you doing with that, anyway?"

Evie shrugged. "Okay. I've been back in the shed. But it was scary to find him, and I admit, I'll feel better once we know what to expect."

"I expect we'll all feel better. James most of all," Corinne said. "His health situation has made all of us take notice. Let's see how he is, and maybe you girls and Rett and I can find some time to talk. I can help you make some plans."

James was sitting up in bed, and Rett's husband Harry was there with their son Mason. Mason and James were playing Go Fish on the bed. Harry moved away so they could get close to the bed.

"Hi, Dad," Evie said, her voice thick.

"Girls! Nice to see you." His voice sounded strong, but there was an edge to it. "Mason's about to beat me." He turned to the little boy. "Right, Mason?"

Mason nodded enthusiastically. "Grandpa, do you have any tens?"

"Oh, you knew it! Here you go." James handed over his cards. "And that's the game. Good one, Mason." Mason gathered his cards up and slipped past his aunts to hover beside his father.

"We didn't bring any entertainment," Dorie said. "It's a good thing for this family that we have Mason." She and Evie both turned to look at the boy, who squirmed with obvious pleasure at her acknowledgement.

Turning back to her father, Evie said, "All we brought is us."

"I guess that'll do then." He gave her a tired smile.

"We're going to head out," Harry said. "Mason needed to see you for himself, James. He's been a bit worried."

Mason skipped over to clamber back onto the chair and give James a kiss on the cheek. "I'm glad you're okay," he said quietly. "I'll bring my Old Maid deck next time."

James dabbed at an eye. "You do that, Mason. Only I think I might be going home soon. Maybe we can play Old Maid at my house."

"Good," Mason said. "You and me and Mallow."

James chuckled. "You and that dog. Well, maybe I can beat Mallow, because I know I can't beat you." He smiled and watched Harry and Mason as they left.

"Mason's not the only one who needed to see you," Evie said. "We brought Corinne."

"Yes, I wanted to see you with my own eyes, like one of the kids," Corinne said. She poked through the get-well cards that adorned his table. "Look at this," she said. "You've got a fan club, James."

"I dunno how everybody knew I was in here," he said, sounding aggrieved. "Nobody has any personal business anymore."

"Oh, Dad, you love it," Evie said. "People care about you."

Dorie plunked herself in the other chair. "Speaking of caring about you, what does the doc say? What's happening next?"

James pushed himself back up out of his slump. "Well, cardiac rehab is one thing."

"Rehab? Did you have a heart attack?"

"No. But they've been poking around in there and they think the rehab program would be good for me. Preventive, maybe."

"What's involved?" Evie asked with interest.

He gave her a look. "Exercise. Diet. Mindfulness." He spat each word out as if it held a bad taste.

Corinne burst out laughing. "Curb your enthusiasm, James. Lots of people manage health conditions that way."

"Aw, I know," he said, "I just hate being told what to do all the time. No wine. No whisky. No desserts."

"That does sound pretty grim," Evie agreed. "Are you sure they said you can't have any of those things?"

"Well, that's how it sounded to me." Listening, Evie thought her dad sounded like an old man.

"Maybe it won't be that bad," Dorie intervened. "If you do what they say and you feel better, it'll be worth it, right?"

"Oh, right, says the queen of leftover pizza," James said.

"Are you teasing right now, Dad, or are you mad?" Dorie asked.

James sighed. "Probably both. This whole thing makes me mad, but I guess I have to listen. Did you see what they wanted me to eat for supper? Jell-O. Jell-O, ladies."

They chatted a bit longer, but soon James looked exhausted. Evie elbowed her sister. "Uh, I guess we'll let you get some rest," Dorie said.

"Will you be back tomorrow?" he asked plaintively.

"Hopefully you'll be coming home soon," Evie said. "I'm working on getting the house cleared out, but I'll come tomorrow evening if you're still here."

"Good night, Daddy," Dorie said, leaning over him. Corinne patted his hand, and the three trooped out.

Once they were in the parking lot, Dorie said, "Well, that was not easy." As they headed for the car, she suggested, "Ice cream?"

"Oh, yes," Corinne agreed.

"I'm really tired," Evie complained. "Does every hard thing require ice cream? Can't we just go home?"

"No, we cannot. We need ice cream. Don't you have a story to tell? Didn't you talk to Jase today? Corinne needs to hear it."

"Yeah, that's why I'm so tired," Evie explained. Had her meeting with Jase really only been that morning? "I had a whopper of a day. I really need some sleep."

Dorie laughed. "She's been baking up a storm at night. I wish I could be so productive."

"It's kind of disturbing actually. I'd rather sleep. When I do sleep, my dreams are weird, like seeing a movie about our ancestors. Like Grandma Sarah and Great-Aunt Hannah, and their mother."

"Oh, right," Corinne said. "My Grandma Leonie. The French one."

"See?" Evie said impatiently. "That's how everyone, even in her family, thought of her. The different one."

"What's wrong with that? She spoke French, she came from a different place, she was different. Different isn't bad, you know." Corinne was firm.

Evie subsided. "Feeling like you don't belong isn't good."

"No, that can feel terrible," Corinne agreed. "But people can be different and still belong."

"Leonie hated being here. She missed her family. She felt shunned by the women of the town because she was Acadian."

"How do you know this?" Corinne wanted to know.

"Well, Hannah's memoir says it. But you know, Leonie barely had any English when she came here, and she was one of the first Acadian people to live in Stella Mare. The English and French had struggled for centuries on both sides of the Atlantic, and I expect that played a part in the prejudices. From what I read, I think Leonie really struggled to find her place." Evie stretched her arms up and then yawned. "Oh, yeah, I am feeling it. Tired. What a day."

Dorie wasn't finished. "Without Leonie, none of us would be here."

Corinne laughed. "She gave the family a good start, with her seven children."

"Seven surviving children," Evie corrected. "I don't even know what happened to some of them. You're right, she gave the family a good start, but she also made a difference in the town. She taught women how to make those hooked rugs I've been collecting. She knew how to make do with very little."

"I think many women were good at that, back in the day," Corinne said.

"True, but Leonie literally taught. The textile artist from the craft college pointed out to me how you can see her style showing up in the later rugs from here."

"You showed her?"

"Well, I sent her pictures. She thinks there's a possible museum kind of collection there. At least the start of one."

Dorie stared. "Come on. Those old ratty rugs? They belong in a museum?"

"Well, maybe. Some of them. There's a rug museum in Cheticamp, where Leonie was from. Plus there's a collection in the archives of the Museum of History in Ottawa."

"No kidding," Dorie sounded amazed. "Junk from the attic for the win."

"Not junk," Evie corrected. "I already had an offer to buy them."

"No!" Corinne and Dorie both turned to her. "Really?"

"They're not mine, and besides, I think they mean something to Stella Mare." Evie felt a rising excitement in her belly. "Maybe they do," she backpedalled.

Corinne eyed her and wrapped an arm around her shoulder. "Looks like you have a project in mind," she said, smiling.

"Maybe," Evie said, grimacing. "I'm still figuring stuff out."

"You'll do it. You're good at figuring stuff out," Dorie said stoutly. "I'm starving though. Aren't we supposed to be getting ice cream? Come on."

"You're like a bulldog about that ice cream," Evie said.

"Yes, I am. I'm not letting go," Dorie agreed.

"Maybe you can tell me more about Sarah, Hannah, and Leonie over ice cream," Evie suggested to Corinne. "Chad showed me where to get moose tracks."

"Moose tracks!"

"But I want vanilla."

"Boring. You're just boring, Dorie."

"Vanilla with chocolate sauce, chocolate sprinkles, whipped cream, and a cherry. That's not boring."

The three piled into the car in search of sweet solace.

Chapter 29

The dogs announced a visitor the next morning. Coffee in hand, Evie looked out the kitchen window to the driveway to see the florist's van. She intercepted the delivery person who was heading to the front door.

"Back here," she called from the kitchen porch, slipping into her shoes.

"Ms. Madison?" asked the delivery driver. When she nodded, he handed her the arrangement, covered in cellophane. "For you."

"For my dad," she corrected, looking at the flowers. "Thank you!" she called to his departing back before she went in and put the flowers on the kitchen table. She pulled off the cellophane and left the card for James to read later. She snapped a picture and sent it to Dorie, Corinne, and Rett.

Evie: Hope Dad's coming home soon. Flowers are accumulating.

Dorie: Who sent Dad flowers? Helen?

Rett: I don't think so. Who sent them?

Evie: I thought Dad would like to open the card himself.

Corinne: Just open it. He won't care.

She pulled the envelope out of the arrangement and the card slipped out.

To Evie.

Hooray for clarity.

Xoxo Stephen.

She dropped the card on the table and stepped back. Then she leaned in to look at and sniff the arrangement: hydrangea, tulips, and baby's breath. It was gorgeous, really. She picked up the card and read it again. Then she sat down, hard, eyes on the flowers as if they could speak.

Her phone buzzed.

Dorie: Well?

....

Dorie: Evie? Who sent them?

She tapped a moment.

Evie: Actually, they're for me.

Dorie: Jase? Don't let him sweet talk you.

Rett: No flowers make up for what he's done.

Evie: No, from Stephen.

Rett: Ooohhhh.

Corinne: That man who came to Aggie's picnic? He was nice.

Dorie: Speechless, I am. Very nice. Send another picture.

Evie complied, and even added a selfie, exaggerating her expression of surprise. Then she added, *Okay, I'm going now. Got to clean out another closet. Who is checking on Dad this morning?*

Rett: I'm calling the charge nurse at ten. Will text later.

Evie: Got it. Bye!

She was headed toward the target closet when her phone rang. Jase. This can't be good, she thought. But oh, well. "Hey, Jase."

"Evie, hi. Um, I have a question."

"You think I should answer your questions?"

"Come on, Evie. I'm sorry about yesterday, and I know you're mad, but I'm feeling pretty desperate here."

She sighed. "Okay, what?"

"I can't find the artist files, and I know we have contracts to get out."

"What do you mean? I left everything right there on your office laptop. The whole directory system is set up to make things easy to find."

"Well, easy for you, maybe."

"You're probably going to have to hire a project director, Jase. If you can't figure it out, find somebody who can."

There was silence.

"Maybe I'll just cancel the festival," he said quietly. "I haven't spent any money yet so I can just send it back."

"Actually, you can't send it all back. You owe me for about eight months worth of work on this project."

"I do?"

"I created all those files, made all the contacts, set things up. With the expectation that we'd get funded, and I would be on salary for the summer and fall."

"Riiiiight."

"Not to mention writing the grant proposal to begin with."

"Nobody gets funded to write proposals."

"True. But if you have hired help to do your writing, you pay them." This feeling of steel in her backbone was unfamiliar. But she liked it.

"If I pay you, what will you do if I have to cancel? Return the funds? I can't pay you out of pocket, you know."

He's wondering if I'll sue him, she thought, amazed. She waited, gazing at the cluttered closet.

"Evie?"

"You do owe me, Jase. I'll send you an invoice."

"If I send the money back, I can't pay you!"

Evie thought about Helen. What would her lawyer sister say about this? "You know, we have a lot of financial loose ends to clean up."

"What? No, we don't. This, maybe, but nothing else." He sounded scared.

"We lived together for a long time, had shared assets." She realized she was just parroting her sister. She didn't even know what that term meant, for sure. It was time to end this conversation.

"But about the festival, maybe returning the funding is the best thing to do. If you can't pull it off and do it, well, just give up."

"Geez, Evie, you're not helping here."

"Why should I help, Jase? You told me this is not my project. I don't need to be helpful."

"Yeah, I know," he said tiredly. "I'll probably never get anything funded again."

"All the artists, too, Jase. They're counting on the festival for income, and sales and visibility. You'll be disappointing a lot of people." She kept her voice firm but was glad he couldn't see her gleeful expression. "Except for the ones who have already pulled out."

"Yeah."

Silence again.

"Hey, how did you know anyone pulled out? Are you undermining me?" His voice was louder.

"Calm down. A couple of them called me. Undermining isn't my way." *Even if it is yours.*

His voice dropped. "Yeah, I know. It's upsetting how many people have left."

There was silence.

She could almost hear him shift gears.

"Evie, sweetie, you're being a tad bit unreasonable here." He was using his cajoling voice. She suddenly felt very tired.

"Stop it, Jase. You can't manipulate me anymore. I'm not being unreasonable. I am being extraordinarily helpful for a recently cheated-on and dumped girlfriend. I'll bill you for services rendered and have my lawyer get in touch with you."

He snickered nastily. "You mean Helen."

"I mean my lawyer. Goodbye." She clicked the phone off and tossed it onto the couch. "Woohoo! Go me!" She shook her fists in the air and ran in place. "Yah! Way to go, Evie!"

The big dogs tumbled out of the sun porch and circled her excitedly. "You guys, you won't believe it. Was that really me?" Mallow nudged her with his big head, and she crouched down to hug his hairy body. Custard bumped into her too, wanting pats. "Did you hear your Auntie Evie? I told him a thing or two." She sighed with satisfaction, and the three headed to the kitchen. That was a good day's work, right there, and it's still early, she thought.

She gazed into the kitchen at Stephen's flowers. What a lovely man.

The ping of an email notification sent her to retrieve her phone. A bank deposit; what was this? She opened the account page to accept the deposit from Leonard and saw his note. "I regret my actions that damaged your trust in me. I hope this adjustment meets your expectations."

The figure was exactly correct. "Yes!" She headed back to the kitchen.

The big dogs were sitting patiently, angling for treats. "You guys. So predictable." She pulled two biscuits from the treat jar. They looked expectantly from her face to her hand.

"Just listen to my morning," she said, waving her hands around. "I've vanquished Jase, gotten flowers from Stephen, and money and an apology from Leonard. The world is back on track."

Her companions were rapt but drooling. "You're such good listeners," she said, "at least when I'm holding a treat." She handed out the goodies. "You guys are so gross. Now I have to wipe up dog slobber." They ambled back to the sun porch, Custard chomping immediately as usual, and Mallow carrying his biscuit back to his bed.

Dogs. She was smiling even as she wiped slobber from the floor. The drool was her fault for making them wait, but how else do you get a couple of huge dogs to listen to you? The fragrance from the flowers deepened her smile.

This day was better than she'd hoped.

Time to turn this energy to good use: tackling the next closet. She gathered her trash bags and donation boxes, and then tied her curls up in a kerchief. *I look like those old pictures of Grandma Leonie, back in nineteen-whatever.* Popping another of her mother's CDs into the player, she bopped her way to the big hall closet and got started.

Two hours later, with an empty closet and boxes full of potential donations, she called a break. Taking her tea and her phone to the kitchen porch step, she revelled in the sunshine and scent of new-mown grass from the neighbour's house. Breathing deeply, she tapped out a text to Stephen. Her phone rang immediately.

"I'm so glad you like the flowers," he said.

"You really surprised me. I assumed they were for Dad."

"I had some thinking to do yesterday. I'd like to tell you about it if you have time today."

Uncertain, she said, "We're still waiting to hear about Dad. He might be coming home, so I have to keep my time pretty open."

"Oh."

There was a brief silence. Was he disappointed? "Maybe you could come over here?" she suggested. "I'm clearing out closets. It's very exciting."

"I can help you. Is it okay to come now?"

She thought about the untidy kitchen. "Uh, sure, if you keep your expectations low."

He laughed. "I don't have expectations. Hope, of course, but no expectations."

When he arrived, she was digging through the last boxes left in the den. He called to her from the kitchen screen door. "Evie? I'm here."

She emerged, shushing the dogs, tripping over the detritus in the hallway and feeling dusty all over. "Come on in!" She saw him push the screen door open, his face a little worried but then crinkling into a smile when he caught her eye. Her heart beat a little faster, and she pulled off her kerchief to shake out her hair. His eyes widened.

"See the flowers? They smell wonderful. Aren't they gorgeous?" she asked, gesturing to the sideboard. "I don't think I've ever received flowers before."

"I'm honoured to be the first," he said. "You should always have flowers."

"What a nice idea," she said.

"Comes from my mother. Something about women should have flowers to share their space."

"I like that idea," Evie said.

"My mother would have liked you," he noted.

My mother would have liked you, too. "I do really love them. Do you want to sit down? I can get us some coffee." She pulled mugs from the cupboard.

"Thanks." As she walked behind him, she smelled his piney scent. Like he'd been out in the woods. Like fresh air.

Coffee in hand, they both spoke at once. Evie pulled back. "You go ahead. I was just wondering why the flowers?"

"I was just going to explain," he said. "You asked me yesterday what I wanted from you." He glanced into his mug. "That really made me think."

"Well, I don't know…"

"No, please let me explain. I didn't think I had any expectations or wants where you're concerned. I didn't think I was even hoping for anything."

She tried to listen, but her heart was pounding.

"I understood that you were feeling pressure. Your ex and Leonard both tried to take advantage of you."

"Tried?"

"You're right. They did take advantage of you, and both in the same morning. No wonder you asked whether I had the same kind of agenda." He looked up. "I was a little offended by the assumption, though."

"Should I be sorry? I don't feel sorry." The words jumped out of Evie's mouth. That steel was still there in her backbone. *Oh, man. What happened to being nice?*

Stephen didn't sound offended when he responded. "No, I don't think so." He looked very serious. "I think you were on point."

"Really?" *I can't wait to hear this.*

"Yeah. I'm not proud of this. Later, I had a talk with Leonard. I called him out on his behaviour with you."

"Your best friend."

"My best friend, but what he was doing wasn't okay. The conversation was hard, but Leonard and I have had hard conversations before. In the process, he challenged me to check my own expectations."

"What do you mean?"

"He accused me of having an agenda where you're concerned."

Her heart was still thumping. "Is it true? You have an agenda?"

His face crumpled. "I don't want to be the kind of guy that takes advantage of anybody. So I tell myself that I don't have any agenda. You and Leonard made me look harder. Deeper, I guess."

She waited.

"I don't want to steal your work or get you to do my work for me. I don't want to turn you into my assistant. I don't have an agenda like that."

"Good. Besides, those are already taken."

"Yes," he said ruefully. "I was happy to witness you standing up to that kind of treatment. It's not okay." His eyes held pain. "There is something though. I have to acknowledge my own interest in you, though, and try to clarify it."

Evie's ears pricked up. He was interested in her? What? "That's very, uh, thorough of you. Analytical."

He looked even more miserable. "It's who I am. Thorough. Analytical."

Her fingers twitched against the seat as she gripped it. "What did your analysis turn up?"

"I tried to look objectively at myself, which is like doing your own dental work. It's pretty close to impossible."

She couldn't help her smile.

"I made a list. I like you. I like spending time with you. I like hearing your excitement about your attic finds, the stories and the artwork. I can imagine a professional future for you where you discover things about yourself you never knew. I'm amazed and delighted with your paintings."

"Well, thank you. I appreciate your help, connecting me with the university, and pointing me in the direction of the crafts college."

"That's very comfortable for me. I like helping students, and I could see you as a sort of grad student and me in the advising role. That came to mind immediately, but it's a bit of a smokescreen, I think."

"What do you mean, smokescreen? I really appreciate all the advice and suggestions you've offered me."

"You're welcome, and I'm glad to be helpful. That's not all though."

The pause lengthened.

Finally he looked at her eyes. "I have to be honest with myself, and honest with you. I think about you, a lot, and not in the abstract."

"Oh?"

"Like a man thinks about a woman." He looked, what, scared? Embarrassed? "I know you're recovering from a breakup, and I'm not exactly Prince Charming. In self-analysis, I'm a geek who is overly fond of listening to people, good coffee, and you."

It was hard to know what to say. "I'm not in the market for Prince Charming." Or anyone else, she thought a little bitterly.

"I know you've been through a lot," he added.

She grimaced. "I kind of planned to swear off men."

"Forever?" There was a hint of a smile in his voice.

"Forever seemed like a good idea," she said. "I could make myself a world just for women, you know. Study women's domestic arts, read and write in women's studies. Get myself connected to a place where I can study women's lives, you know. All of that."

"There's so much in that I want to talk about," he said. "But first"—he took her hand—"let me say that I don't expect anything at all. I only needed to be perfectly clear with myself and with you."

"I don't feel clear yet," she admitted. His hand was warm and strong. "What are you really saying? Do you have an agenda or don't you?"

"Fair enough. My problem is I didn't let myself realize how much I like you. I like you a lot."

Barely breathing, she waited.

A long moment later, he added, "I would like to take you out. Have dinner, go for more walks, clean closets. Whatever it takes to spend time together. See if there's a spark."

She stayed still. He wasn't finished.

He gave her a tentative smile. "I should add that there's more than a spark on my side. More like fireworks."

Matching his smile, Evie said, "In the interests of clarity."

"Right. Honesty and clarity."

She exhaled. "My turn for the honesty and clarity."

She gazed toward the window and spotted the crab-apple tree, now in leaf and bearing small green fruit.

She turned back to look at him. "Even though I think I want to swear off men, something inside me keeps saying 'but not Stephen.' Like you're in a different category or something."

"Not a man? I'm not sure how I feel about that." He was smiling though.

"Definitely a man. Oh, no question about that." She took in his shoulders, his strong hand holding the mug, his warm eyes. "But a man that can be trusted." Unaccountably, her eyes filled.

"Thank you." He waited.

"You're different."

"Yes, that's my calling card," he said with a smile.

"No, not that way. I mean, I don't know people—men—who make a point of clearing up when there's a spat or disagreement." She sniffled.

"I don't sleep if I'm not on good enough terms with people I care about," he admitted. "There's blazing self-interest in that."

She shook her head. "Doesn't matter. You did offend me yesterday, a little, and you showed up to apologize. To talk it out."

"Is that working?"

She smiled through her tears. "In the interests of clarity and honesty, I'll admit to a spark too. That's why I couldn't swear off all men. That spark is burning pretty bright right now."

She reached across the table to take his other hand. They smiled at each other until Evie said, "Okay, so what now?"

Stephen chuckled. "Oh, I don't think anything much has to happen. I just wanted to let you know where I stand."

"Well, it sounds like maybe we're standing in the same place," she said. "At least about this one thing."

"I'll take it. In the meantime, can I help you with something today?"

"I'm practising taking help, so I won't say no to that. If you help me get this hallway cleared, maybe I can get the den ready for Dad just in case they let him come home. While we work, I can tell you about what just happened."

"I'm all ears. Let's get busy."

After the hallway and den were cleared to Evie's satisfaction, they took a break for a late lunch and glass of tea.

"Sweet or unsweet?" she asked with a grin.

"Look at you! Regular southern gal, right here in the Maritimes. Sweet for me, please." He smiled at her. "Next thing you know, you'll be saying y'all."

"That will be a while," she said. "Let's take lunch to the back porch."

After their immediate hunger was sated, Stephen said thoughtfully, "So, no festival this year."

"Nope, no festival." She crunched her chips.

"And you feel…"

She shrugged. "I'm more interested in my rug project, to be honest. I really don't know what it's going to be, but I'm not as worried anymore."

"You're painting too."

She smiled dreamily. "I am, and I had forgotten how that is. I do love it. How did I ever let go of something I love so much?"

"That apple tree..."

"I am a little sorry that's gone. It's like the beginning of a new chapter. I love doing these studies of the rugs, but that tree was like a rebirth."

"Every time I look at it, I remember what it was like to stand in that blooming, buzzing pink with you," he said, smiling at her.

"What do you mean every time you look at it? It's been gone for a while."

He continued to smile.

"Oh, you didn't. Did you buy that painting?"

"I did. You'll have to come see it. It hangs over the largest of the three non-working fireplaces in my apartment."

"Really." She wasn't sure how she felt about this.

"Did you know that another one sold yesterday?"

"No. Why didn't Leonard tell me?"

"He probably didn't know. Cassie sold it. She's a big promoter of your work, you know."

She pondered. Maybe her paintings were good enough, not just for a friend to buy.

"Do you know which one?"

He shook his head. "I suspect that whatever you create, there will be someone who loves it."

"Yeah, right," she scoffed.

He nodded. "Believe it."

"You're biased, as you already said," she pointed out. "But maybe I should get busy on the next group for the gallery."

"Never a bad idea. I've got to get back to work or Cassie will be looking for me."

It was late afternoon by the time Evie got back to her laptop.

The new mail notification was glowing. She was excited to see another note from Rachel, the textile artist at the crafts college in the capital. Evie read it. Then she started over from the top.

Twice through and she was still unsure, so she called Stephen. "Can you look at something for me?"

"Something? A draft of something?"

"Uh, no. Somebody just sent me a, I guess a proposal, and I don't know what to make of it. I'll forward the email, okay? Can you look at it now?"

"Yeah, sure, go ahead. Okay, I've got it. Do you want to hold on while I read it?"

"Please."

During the silence, Evie tapped her fingers on the desk. When she realized what she was doing, she squeezed her hands together. Then discovered she was tapping her foot. Finally, Stephen said, "Wow."

"Wow?"

"Yeah, wow. I think they're offering you a show, or something like that. For the rugs. It sounds like this person, this Rachel, her department wants to sponsor a show for you to display the rugs, do a talk about the artists. Wow, Evie. Pretty impressive!"

"Is this a real thing though? Is it someone else trying to, you know, take advantage? I don't know enough to tell."

Stephen said, "Oh, no. This is legit. They're recognizing the rugs as art and as historical artifacts at the same time. Look at what she said about it...'domestic arts as a subversive activity, bringing empowerment to women who lived otherwise disempowered lives.' She gets it."

"Those are my words," Evie said. "I've been writing back and forth with her for a little while. She's been helping me to formulate my thinking about the work."

"So that's excellent. She's not stealing anything. She's offering you a way to highlight and share what you've found.'"

Evie suddenly felt shy. "It is a wow kind of thing then. I'm kind of overwhelmed."

"It is wonderful news. Maybe you can just enjoy it."

"Maybe."

"This calls for a celebration. What do you think?"

"I feel like I have a lot of things to celebrate. But I don't think it's time yet."

"No?"

"Let me get Dad back home, and then we'll celebrate. I promise."

She could almost hear his slow smile. "I'll take it. In the meantime, will you come to visit your crab-apple painting? I'd like you to see my place."

She didn't have to think twice. "I'd be delighted."

Chapter 30

Friday at noon, Evie and Dorie were waiting with the dogs in the yard for Rett to arrive with James. After exhaustive internet research and a phone consult with a dietitian, Evie had filled the refrigerator with things she thought her father would like to eat that also fit into his new guidelines. Dorie, on the other hand, brought a bag of chips and lemonade to celebrate his homecoming.

"That's not really helpful," Evie admonished.

"Yeah, but he needs a reason to live, you know. You can't just be perfect all the time," Dorie explained. "I understand the need for a good diet, but moderation, right?"

"I thought if apples were closer for him to grab than chips, he was more likely to eat apples."

Dorie frowned. "You know our father. He's more likely to order pizza than eat an apple. Chips, well, maybe they're just symbolic."

"Symbolic of what?"

"Oh, I don't know. Maybe I'll just eat them." She tore open the bag and tossed a chip into her mouth. Custard immediately leaned on her leg. She looked down and said, "Thanks, bud, I've got this." The dog wandered away.

Dorie crunched. "So, Evie, you had a date. Tell all. Stephen invited you over and then what?"

"You are a brat," Evie said sharply.

"Come on. I'm just *interested*."

"Oh, the way you say that just grinds my gears, baby sister," Evie said with a growl. Then she relaxed and smiled. "But okay. Only because I want to."

"Do tell." Dorie looked expectant.

"He lives above the gallery, right? The place is cool, old woodwork, but a nice bathroom. A bunch of fireplaces, but none of them work. Oh, he has one of my paintings hanging over a fireplace."

"Ooh, that's promising."

"A little uncomfortable for me, but that's okay. The apartment has a weird little kitchen that nobody could cook in."

"But he did, right?"

"Well, kind of. He made a salad. With cold shrimp. French bread."

"Will you get down to the good stuff? I don't really care about the menu."

"What do you want to know?" Evie knew she was teasing, but she couldn't help it.

"Come on," Dorie implored. "Dad's going to be here in a minute and I'll never get to know. Did he, you know, kiss you?"

At that moment, Rett's car drove into the yard. Evie wasn't interested in sharing the very personal details of her evening with Stephen. Certainly not with Dorie. "Saved by the big sister," she said with a grin.

"Darn it."

The car ground to a halt and the girls converged on the passenger door.

"Okay, okay," James said, smiling, as he climbed out. Leaning against the car, he grinned and shaded his eyes against the late morning sun. "Girls and dogs. You guys look pretty good to me."

Evie reached to hug him. "You look pretty good to me, too, Dad," she said, but his chest felt a little fragile to her. She handed him off to Dorie and helped Rett get his belongings out of the car.

"So, how's he really doing?" she asked Rett, sotto voce.

"Not bad," Rett said, pulling things from the backseat. "He probably feels better right now than he has in a few weeks, now they've got his blood sugar stabilized."

"That sounds good. We just have to keep things that way."

"Yes. I have a long list of discharge instructions, and we'll figure it out. Let's get this stuff inside. He probably needs to sit down."

"You girls talking about me?" James asked. "I'm old but I'm not deaf, and no, I don't need to sit down."

"Well, I do," Rett asserted, and they all trooped into the kitchen. While Dorie made tea, Evie warmed up soup and sliced bread, and James settled down at the table like he'd never left.

Rett laid the discharge planning sheets out on the table, and they scrutinized them while they ate lunch. "So, this says you go into St. Stephen three times a week for rehab," Evie noted.

"Yep. That's the exercise and meditation program," James said. "I started going this week. Had a session this morning, in fact. Some pretty nice people there."

Dorie and Evie looked at each other. "That sounds good," Dorie said. "Is this a thing you need a ride for?"

James frowned. "No, I can drive myself. I just can't stop for doughnuts and a double-double on the way home. The dietitian says some of that stuff has been why I've been so tired lately."

"Tim's will probably have to close, Dad," Dorie said.

"I know," he agreed, deadpan. "I've been keeping them in business for years. Dunno what they'll do without me."

"So, I did get the den all cleared out, Dad, in case you need to use it for a bedroom," Evie offered.

"Stairs are part of my program," James explained. "I appreciate all that hard work, but I can stay in my own bedroom. I'm going to keep climbing stairs as long as I can."

"I cleaned that out for nothing?" Evie was dismayed.

"Not for nothing," Rett reminded her. "We're still working on clearing the whole house, right?"

"We are," Evie said. "Stephen came over to help."

"Ooh, Stephen," Rett said. "Are you guys, you know, an item?"

"They had a date," Dorie said helpfully. "Hey, Dad, did you hear that Stephen sent Evie flowers?" She chortled.

"Shhh," Evie said. "He was a big help."

"A date," Rett mused. "Imagine that."

"Nice young man," James said.

"Dorie, knock it off."

"I haven't been much help with the house, I know," Rett said. "Maybe I can go through some stuff while I'm here."

Evie put a hand over Rett's. "You're forgiven. You're so busy. But if you have time today to pull out items you want us to keep, that would be very helpful. Dad, it sounds like you really do have things under control."

James shook his head. "I've got to be careful of that, Evie. Thinking I had everything under control is what made me lose consciousness out in the shed that day. They teach in rehab that you need to let your family help you. We have to be able to count on each other."

"I'm here, Dad. You can count on me," Evie said, throat full.

"I know. I'm mostly talking to myself. I'm not good at asking for help."

"Family trait!" the three daughters said at the same time.

Rett said, "None of us are good at that. We all like to help other people, but we are notoriously difficult to help. At least Harry says that about me."

James went on. "To your point, Evie, I can drive myself to rehab, I can sleep in my bedroom, I know how to test my blood sugar. But I need to let you girls know about my doctor appointments, my diet needs, and stuff like that. I'm going to try to do that."

"We're still not finished clearing out the house," Evie said.

"It looks amazing, but I'm sure there's more to do," Rett commented.

"Like I said, if you guys can pick over the boxes on the porch, I'll get the rest of the stuff to the donation center," Evie said. "I think I've done every closet. Except Dad's."

Dorie asked. "Maybe I need to try to get over here more."

"About that," James said. "I told the Gables Center to give that apartment to somebody else. Now that I'm feeling better, I don't want to move right now. I'm sure the time will come, but it isn't going to be this fall. Maybe next year."

"Dad! That's wonderful!" Dorie exclaimed.

Evie exhaled. "Oh, that feels good. Like we have a little more room to maneuver."

"Maybe a lot more room," James said. "I'm optimistic."

"The job is so much bigger than it sounds like," Evie said. "I didn't realize how much work is involved. How many decisions."

"We still need to clear out, but we have more time. Is that right?" Rett asked.

"Well, it's more of a 'want-to' than a 'have-to' at the moment," James said. "This summer is the first time anybody ever tried to clear it out. Mostly we've brought stuff into the house. No wonder it's hard. It's kind of like making the tide turn around. It just won't go until it's the right time."

"Dad, how poetic," Dorie said. "I like it. Maybe we just need a big flood tide to wash all this stuff away."

"Well, there's a lot more room here than I realized," Evie said. "The house always felt so small and filled up, but now"—she gestured—"there's space. It feels spacious. Room to move."

"I like it," James said, looking down. Mallow put his head on James's lap and Custard nosed Evie's knee. "Even these big lugs don't seem to take up as much space."

Rett's phone buzzed. "Oh, I've got to get to work. Harry has a deadline, the girls' daycare lady is sick, the dog needs his shots, and life just goes on. Love you, Dad. I'm so happy to see you back home where you belong." She kissed the top of James's head. "Let's figure out how to keep ourselves connected and organized," she said to her sisters. "Life gets ahead of us."

"Yeah, it does," Dorie agreed.

"Sorry, Evie. I can't go through stuff today. I'll call you, okay?"

"Sure. But maybe, can you all come for a cookout on Saturday? Next Saturday. Get the whole family? Is that okay with you, Dad? I'll do the cooking," Evie offered.

"Family cookout, check. Sounds good to me," James agreed. "Diabetic-friendly food, right?"

Dorie grinned. "I'm going to have to learn, too, Dad. Celery sticks instead of potato chips."

Rett liked the cookout idea. "I'll check with Harry, but sure. Daytime though, right?"

"Sure, or you can spend the night."

"Evie, I love you for the idea but there are five of us plus a dog. You have plenty going on here. Better if we wrap up before the twins' bedtime and head home." Rett sounded firm.

"Okay then, early cookout supper next weekend. Healthy food options!" Evie declared.

"Only if they taste good too," James added.

"Right, Dad," Dorie agreed. "No Jell-O. I'm going to go too. Chad had a project he was wrapping up and the dogs, of course, need attention. We're available on Saturday too. I'll help with the food." She looked at Evie. "No chips. I promise."

James grasped Dorie's arm as she headed to the door behind Rett. "Thank you, girls," he said. "You don't know how much you mean to this old guy."

"Oh, Dad," Dorie admonished, dropping a kiss on his head. "We mean the world to you, right? We know that."

He rolled his eyes. "That's what I get for being sentimental. Get out of here." He swatted at her as she flounced away.

"You girls," he said, looking at Evie, the only one left in the room. "You're good girls, always have been. A little messy and chaotic, but good."

"Oh, watch out, you," Evie warned. "I've been cleaning up mess all through this house. Watch out who you're calling messy."

"You're looking good," James said. "Things getting better?"

"Does it show?"

"Something is making you happy."

"Things are better. All around."

He raised his eyebrows and waited.

She went on. "I'm really done with the whole Jase thing. Ready to talk to Helen about a lawyer. He owes me."

Her father smiled.

Evie nodded. "You know what? I've sold some art. Leonard wants more, and now somebody wants me to do a show with these rugs."

"No kidding. Somebody's interested in our junk."

"Treasure. Mum used to say, one man's trash is another man's treasure. Now I know exactly what that means."

"Well, that's all pretty good," he said.

The silence was comfortable, but he was looking at her expectantly.

"I did have a date with Stephen, and he did send me these flowers."

He nodded, satisfied. "He seems like a good man. Going back down south though."

She shrugged. "Maybe not. You know, we artists and our artsy-fartsy lifestyles. Things change."

"They do."

"About Jase. I needed him to need me. I thought if he needed me, that was enough."

"Hmm."

"Stephen doesn't need me for anything. He can take care of himself."

"Ummhmm."

"But he wants me. That's the difference."

"Sounds like you know your worth."

"I think I've struggled with that a lot. I'm learning. It's a process."

He smiled at her. "You're a good girl, Evelyn. Your mother would be proud. I'm proud."

"Thanks, Dad. I appreciate that." She stepped back. "Now do you need a nap? Water? Help with anything?"

He scowled. "I'll let you know when I can't get my own glass of water, thank you very much." He grinned suddenly, and she giggled. Dad was home.

Chapter 31

Evie was busy all week. First off, she negotiated menu items with Dad.

"I don't have to eat green stuff at every single meal, Evie."

"The dietitian said…"

"I don't care. I'm doing what they told me. No wine, no sweets, and watch out for the potatoes. I don't have to eat broccoli for breakfast."

"Dad, you're exaggerating. I'm not suggesting that."

"No, but what did you put in that smoothie to make it so green?"

"Never mind. I'll leave you to fix your own breakfast."

"Thank you."

Next, she had to see what a lawyer might tell her about her situation. She asked Helen for a referral.

"Lawyers are expensive, you know."

"Yeah, obviously. I was just wondering if there's some way to get information about whether it's a good idea to hire one."

"Sure. Let's talk and I can point you to some local resources, too," Helen agreed. "You know, I'm glad you're doing this. It's important to take care of yourself."

"I guess that's been my life lesson for the summer. Thanks."

"Evie, in case I haven't said it enough, thank you for everything you're doing at the house, and with helping Dad."

She put painting on her daily schedule of the "next right thing." Painting was soothing and exciting at the same time, and it had the lovely benefit of potential income thanks to squaring things with Leonard. She spent a few hours every day in the den with her colours and her favourite rugs.

Hanging out with Dad was good, too, but there was only so much time. One afternoon, she was in the den, working, when he stuck his head in.

"I was just wondering if you'd like to come out for a walk with me and the dogs. I got to get my steps in today."

Evie smiled. "No, I can't. But thanks. Have a good walk."

Soon she heard the jangle of leash hardware and the closing of the kitchen door, and the house grew still. Her phone pinged.

Stephen: I hear we're having a party on Saturday. How's the planning going? Can I help?

Evie: I was going to invite you, but somebody beat me to it.

Stephen: Dorie. She said I could bring chips. I said I wouldn't think of it, as I am perfecting my mussels in white wine recipe. What do you think?

Evie had to laugh. Mussels in white wine, indeed. Dear Stephen. When did he have time to practice recipes? She felt like she'd been running full tilt.

Besides Dad and getting her financial life in order, she started planning for the winter show in Fredericton. Leonard convinced her to have a fall preview for the Stella Mare families who had contributed their ancestors' work. The ideas were exciting, but she also felt pressure. There was pressure to create something for the families of the rugmakers but also honour the challenging lives of women in the past. Too much thinking left her feeling frazzled, so she just jotted notes as they came to her.

The next right thing, she thought. It will all get done.

Maybe she could just concentrate on the family gathering that was coming up. She had a menu, Dorie apparently managed the guests, and it was all fine. No stress. Just a family barbecue. The forecast was even good.

She pushed away from her desk and headed to the kitchen. *When in distress, bake. Or at least, eat.* The refrigerator held fresh fruit, vegetables, leftover soup, and sourdough bread. Nothing to eat at all, she thought. *Where's the toffee pudding? Nun's farts? Sunshine muffins? Where's my midnight baker when I need her?*

She felt a lot better now that she slept instead of baking. But sometimes an apple just didn't feed the need. She settled for dipping her apple slices in peanut butter, pouring a cup of coffee, and calling Stephen.

"So, mussels in white wine."

"I'm almost there. One more practice session and I'll be ready for Saturday."

She giggled. "They sound delicious. There are reasons why I like you."

"Mmm. Reasons why I like you too. I wish I could tell you in person." His voice grew husky.

"Well, I'll see you at the party for sure."

"Maybe we can sneak off like a couple of teenagers. I don't think I ever did that in my misspent youth."

Evie laughed. "Can you imagine? With the eagle eyes of my family everywhere? We'd have trouble living it down. But it might be fun to try."

By Saturday, Evie was ready for a party. She opened all the windows, ran the vacuum through the downstairs, and made sure the refrigerator was cleared out. James got ice in the big ancient cooler, and together they found the horseshoes and cornhole games stashed in the shed.

"Well, it is easier to find stuff now that we cleared so much out," Evie said approvingly.

"I have to admit I like it better too," James said. "Not so much risk of losing your head every time you open a closet door."

"Losing your head?" Evie was amused.

"From stuff falling on you. You did a good job getting things organized. You even got me organized, and that's a big feat."

"It was a job and a half, but look what we got! All this space. We get to see the beautiful floors in this house."

"Probably made by my great-grandfather on the Madison side," James said. "It's a nice old house."

They were interrupted by the scrabble of dog toenails on the floor as Custard and Mallow hustled to greet Frou-Frou. Dorie burst in, laden with bags and boxes of food. Chad followed, solicitous of Alice, who carried a cake box.

"Looking like a party," James crowed, peeking in Dorie's boxes.

DOMESTIC ARTS

"Get out of there," she said, gesturing with her head. "Open the fridge for me, please, instead."

James complied, while Chad went outside to put the drinks on ice. Alice put her cake box down and headed outside, where the sounds of children indicated that Rett, Harry, and their family had arrived. Another car arrived and Leonard and Cassandra got out.

James headed outside, calling to Mason to come play horseshoes.

"Well, Dad's going to get his exercise today," Evie said to Dorie.

"What?" Dorie asked absently. "Oh, right. Yeah, we all will, probably. Can you help me sort out what needs to go on the grill?" They looked together in her boxes of food and tried to get it organized.

Chad was on the kitchen porch managing drinks for the guests. He called through the screen door. "Evie, Steve's here."

Evie's stomach gave a pleasant flip. She looked up from her task to see him come in, carrying a big stockpot. "Hey," she said.

His smile warmed her. "Hey, yourself. I'll put these on the back burner, okay?"

"Sure. I don't think we're ready to eat yet, so don't turn them on."

Moving past her at the counter, he kissed the top of her head. Then he put the pot on the stove. "That was nice," she said.

"A hands-free greeting," he said. "Now my hands are available, but you look busy." He gestured toward the packages of chicken, sausage, and burgers she and Dorie were sorting.

"Oh, go," Dorie said, with a jerk of her head. "You did the menu. I can handle the food from here. Go have a good time."

"Okay, I'll take you up on that," Evie agreed. "Come on." She tugged at Stephen's hand. "I've been sprung from the kitchen. Let's go see what's going on outside."

The party kept improving, Evie thought. James and Chad cooked the barbecue items. "Why do the men cook when it's outside?" she asked Stephen.

"I don't know," he said, "but maybe I should be bonding with them over the grill. What do you think?"

"Maybe it's a guy thing," she said. "Yeah, I think you should try it. See about that bonding. Report back later though."

He laughed and headed toward her father. Callie called for her to come and draw in the driveway with sidewalk chalk.

"Evie makes the best pictures," Callie said to her twin, Maggie. "Evie, can you make us a unicorn?"

"Sure," Evie agreed. "But you have to draw too."

"I want a mermaid," Maggie insisted.

"Unicorns and mermaids. Let's do them together. What colours do you want?" The three of them covered the upper part of the driveway with rainbows, fairies, and magical creatures of all sorts.

"Mum, come look!" Callie demanded of Rett, who strolled over while sipping her drink. "Mum, Evie makes the best pictures. Did you know that?"

Rett smiled. "As a matter of fact, I did. Evie is an artist, Cal. She could draw anything when we were kids. I was always jealous."

"No, you were not," Evie argued. "I was jealous of you. And Helen."

"Well, maybe we were all jealous of each other. That could just be a normal part of being siblings," Rett suggested.

"Helen was never jealous of any of us," Evie persisted. "She was always perfect. Everybody loved her."

Rett said, "Maybe. Or maybe you remember things the way they felt, not necessarily the way that they were."

"I never considered that. Probably true." She got up from the driveway and dusted her hands on her jeans. "Cornhole?"

"Your guy, there, looks like he's a champion cornhole player. How'd he learn about that?"

"Maybe they play cornhole everywhere. Even in North Carolina." She looked across the yard, now mown and tidy, to see Stephen graciously celebrating his victory over Mason, Cassandra, Harry, and Corinne.

Dorie brought a tray full of food to one of the picnic tables, and Chad followed with a platter of meats from the grill.

"Time to eat, everyone," Dorie said, but nobody moved toward the table. "Come on, guys," Dorie said. "The dogs are going to grab this stuff if you don't."

Evie got up to put the dogs in the house. Stephen put his fingers in his mouth and whistled.

"Sorry to be so loud," he said, a little abashed when everyone stopped what they were doing to look at him. "Dorie's trying to say something."

"Come eat!" Dorie said. Finally people flowed toward the tables.

When everyone had a plate of food, James stood up. "I want to say something," he started and then cleared his throat. "I'm grateful to be here, grateful to have all of you in our family, and so happy we have this day together."

General cheers went up and people started to eat.

Evie filled her plate and went to sit with Stephen.

"Hey," he said. "My mussels were a hit, except for the kids." He wrestled a sausage into the bun and took a bite. After swallowing, he said, "Good party. Are you having a good time?"

"Oh, yes," she said. "Dorie did a lot of the work. I might have to clean up, but I think I'll get some help with that."

"You know I'll help," he assured. He slid an arm around her waist. "Any time."

"That's dangerous," she pointed out.

"Why?"

"Somebody could steal your food while your hand is busy," she said with a straight face.

"You put the dogs inside though," he joked back. "I trust your family, the human members, anyway."

As they put away their plates, Dorie called for everyone to come into the house. The living room was mercifully cool because the blinds had been drawn since early morning. Chad was messing around with the television.

"What's going on?" Evie asked Rett, who shrugged.

"Helen. Dad wanted everybody here for a few minutes."

Helen's face appeared on the TV screen. Evie and Stephen were on the couch, but others stuck their faces in front of the camera to say hello. It was chaos.

James waved his hands for attention. "Everybody got a seat, or near enough? Okay. It's been a big summer, since our picnic on the beach for Aggie. A lot of things have happened, some good and some not so good."

"That's for sure," Dorie said, leaning over the back of the couch.

James gave her a look, and she subsided. "Sometimes things that look not-so-good have better consequences. That's the kind of summer this has been. Because of my health scare, I learned new ways to take care of myself and I feel better than I have in years. Because of, uh, some problems, Evie came home and cleared out the house and that looks better too."

"Hey, Dad. I didn't do that single-handedly, you know," Evie protested. "Everybody helped."

"Yes." James was moving on. "This summer we got Chad as a permanent member of the family"—there was cheering—"and Stephen is here now too." Stephen also got cheers.

"Nice to meet you, Stephen," Helen said.

"A parent's greatest joy is seeing their children step out and make their own place in the world. I've been blessed to see this happen with all my children. Now I have something for you to watch on the TV. Right, Chad? Can you let Helen see it too?"

"Yeah, no problem," Chad affirmed and clicked away.

A disembodied voice came from the television. "In a moment, we'll talk with artist Evie Madison, a whiz at finding treasure in people's attics."

"Oh, no," Evie said. "How did you find that?"

"You can't keep secrets from an internet-savvy guy like your father, Evie," James said with amusement. "I don't know why you didn't just tell us. We could have watched you on the broadcast news. Now we're just looking at a rerun."

"Evie! That's Evie," Mason called out, pointing.

Evie put her face in her hands but peeked a little bit. She had avoided watching her interview, but she couldn't avoid this.

Stephen had his arm around her shoulders, and he gave her a comforting squeeze. "It's a good one," he whispered to her.

"You saw it?" she whispered back, incredulous. "Oh, no."

"Leonard told me they only talked to you. Good for you."

She grimaced. "I was happy to have him with me though."

"Shows growth on his part, not hogging your time," Stephen said in her ear. She glanced across the room at Leonard, chatting with a little girl.

"I understand you've been collecting attic art, some might call it," the interviewer said. "Look at these designs."

The camera panned to the half-dozen rug paintings encircling Leonie's cobalt and scarlet creation. Leonard had jerry-rigged the display while Evie was getting makeup put on. Who knew they used makeup even on the news?

"Yes, I've discovered some wonderful hooked rugs made by Maritime women about a hundred years ago. It's become a community project because so many people have old handicrafts like that in their attics."

"You take attic junk and turn it into art?"

"No, not at all. People find objects in their attics that turn out to be art. All I'm doing is looking at them differently."

"Is this kind of like that Antiques Roadshow, where you never know what you'll find?"

Onscreen, Evie laughed, and everyone laughed in the living room.

"Shh!" James said.

"I don't think anyone is going to find a fortune, but I hope to bring visibility to women's domestic arts, in the sense that they are really art. Kitchen, living room, garden, and barn, women have made art in all their domains. We plan a show at the Fishburne Gallery"—the camera cut to Leonard, who tugged at his lapel and smiled—"in the fall."

"If people can't get to Stella Mare this fall, will there be another opportunity to see this display?"

"Thanks to the Arts Foundation, we will have a show at the New Brunswick College of Crafts and Design in Fredericton in the winter."

"Don't miss the trash to treasure art show," the interviewer said.

Evie cringed. *Really?*

The interviewer continued, "Watch this space for updates on the upcoming Domestic Arts show in Stella Mare and Fredericton. My thanks to Evie Madison for sharing her passion project. Now everyone, go check your attics!"

The interview had been edited to a merciful minute.

The screen went blank. Evie didn't dare to move her head. What was everyone thinking?

"Hey, that was great," Dorie said. "Passion project! How cool."

"Not so bad, huh?" Stephen asked, giving Evie a squeeze.

"Good job," Corinne said. "I can't wait to go see this show." There was a general buzz of conversation as people responded to the video and Helen reluctantly signed off.

Evie had finally started to breathe again when James's phone rang. He handed it over to her.

"Helen? Why are you calling me on Dad's phone?"

"First number I found. I wanted to catch you before you started playing cornhole or something."

Evie laughed. "No worries about that. I think cleaning up is the next thing."

"Well, whatever. I wanted to talk to just you," Helen said.

"Really? Me?"

"I know we don't talk much. My fault, that one. But I wanted to tell you how proud I am of you. You know, without being all gushy. Dad said you took charge of clearing the house. Now I hear that you've got a new project that is taking off. That's comeback stuff, you know."

"What do you mean 'comeback stuff'?" Evie asked.

"After all that happened with Jase. We've only talked about the legal parts, but what happened with you and Jase, that's kind of like losing a limb at first."

"That's a good description. I did feel like I was walking around with a gaping wound for some time."

"You've come back from that. That's what I mean."

"I'll say I'm still a work in progress. But I am seeing changes. Thanks for noticing."

"I noticed. What you've done takes guts."

Evie demurred. "Mostly work, but thanks. When are you coming home? I want you to meet Stephen."

Helen's voice warmed. "You really like him."

Evie smiled to herself. "I really do. He's not like anybody I've ever met before. Being with him, well, it's still new. But so good."

"Oh, Evie, I'm so glad."

"He likes me even when I'm a wreck," she said. "I wouldn't say this where Dorie could hear me, but he takes my breath away. You know?"

Helen chuckled. "I can't say I do, but it sounds wonderful." She sighed.

"Dad can't say enough good things about Stephen. He's made a big impression," Helen said. "I can't wait to meet him. And Chad, too."

"They're both pretty great. Different from each other," Evie added.

"New family members. It's like the family is moving ahead and I'm missing it." She sighed.

Evie agreed. "It's true that things are changing here. Sometimes too fast. It'll be good to see you at home again. You said you'd come for Dorie's wedding."

"Yes, but they're slow in setting a date. I don't want to wait. I'm going to come for your fall show. The one in Stella Mare," Helen said.

Flushing with pleasure, Evie said, "Helen. Thank you. It will mean so much to have you here. I'll send you the date as soon as we know."

"Great. In the meantime, congratulations on so many things, Evie. You know I love you."

Evie hung up, bemused. She found James to return his phone. He looked at her, a question in his eyes.

"I don't know what's up with Helen, but she said she was proud of me. That's so weird," Evie said.

"I'm proud of you too. Your mother would be overjoyed."

Her eyes spilled over. "I don't know why I'm crying. Thanks, Dad."

He patted her shoulder, then pulled her in for a hug. She sniffled against his shoulder for a moment, then pulled back to say, "Guess what? Helen's going to come home when we mount the fall show."

"Really?" James's face lit up. "That's great."

Rett and Harry were gathering kids, a dog, and their belongings. "End of the day for us," she said to her father and Evie. "Baths and bed. Day camp tomorrow." She hugged her father and added, "So Helen's coming. That's going to be a big event."

James was glowing. "It'll be so great to have all four Madison girls here together."

"You're really happy about this, aren't you?" Evie asked.

"You can't imagine," he said. "Hey, Corinne, all the Madison girls in Stella Mare at once. What do you think about that? You think we can get a photographer guy to come take a portrait?" He walked off, chuckling.

"Well done, Evie," Rett said. She patted Evie's shoulder, then swept her tribe out the door into the waning afternoon. Corinne followed, and Alice, looking tired, got a ride from Chad and Dorie.

"I'm sorry about leaving some clean up," Dorie said to Evie. "I know I promised."

"I'm on the job," Stephen assured her. "No worries. This is my best thing."

Between them, Evie and Stephen handled cleanup quickly. As the sun slipped farther from the sky, James went upstairs to rest. Evie and Stephen leashed up the big dogs. As they walked, Evie held the dogs in one firm grip, and Stephen held her other hand, equally firmly.

Night fell, and a nighthawk screeched noisily from above the soccer field. The large orange disk of the moon crept over the far horizon. Dogs snuffled comfortably. Low tide scented the air.

"Nice party," Stephen said.

"Mmmm," Evie agreed. "Nice evening after the party."

"That too," he conceded. "It's a good night to savour what you've got."

"Savour?"

"Soak it in. I love what you've got here. The way your father is with all you girls."

"What do you mean? He's always giving us grief about something."

"He'd do anything for his girls. His family is the light of his life. And you're the same way."

She shrugged. "I guess that's one of those things that you don't see clearly because you live it. I never thought about that being unusual. It's just Dad."

"It's not my experience, for sure."

She knew so little of his family. "That's too bad."

"It just is," he said, a little pained. "I'd love to connect more with my father, but it's never seemed possible."

"Dad really likes you," she said. "He's added you to the family already, if you hadn't noticed."

He smiled in the dark. "Yes, I noticed. I like it."

"I like it too." She squeezed his hand.

"Today was a celebration for sure," Stephen said.

"Yeah, having Dad home and feeling better is wonderful."

"It wasn't just that," Stephen said. "It was about you, too. I hope you're able to take in all the love, the fun, the acknowledgement."

"I'm trying. There was a lot of all of that today."

"All richly deserved."

"Thank you." They walked along without speaking for a little while. Then she said, "So, how's that spark doing?"

He stopped, and she stopped too. He turned toward her. "That spark has been in conflagration mode all week. How about yours?"

"Full on fireworks. Maybe we should do something about that."

"What a good idea," he murmured, as he pulled her into his arms.

Gratitude

I learned so much working my way through this book, and I want to acknowledge some very important sources.

First, cookbooks. I enjoyed both *A Taste of Acadie*, but Marielle Cormier-Boudreau and Melvin Gallant, (Goose Lane's translation, 1991) and the Trueman's *Favourite Recipes from Old New Brunswick Kitchens* (Nimbus Publishing, 1994, 2011). Several of the recipes that Evie makes were inspired by these books.

Further, it was my joy and pleasure to find a wealth of sources about Acadian people in New Brunswick and Nova Scotia at the Fredericton Public Library. If you want to know something, go to a library. If you want to know more, ask a librarian. They are the keys to the universe.

The idea that women's work in and around the home, including creation of textiles, is simultaneously art, craft, and political expression, was not original to Evie, though she found it a remarkable reframe on her personal experience. I expect she'll be learning more and perhaps contributing to future discourse on the subject.

My own thinking about women's work has been influenced in myriad ways. I want to thank my many sources, including my mother-in-law, Marjorie Grout, many years a quilter and quilt appreciator, Rachel MacGillivray, a textile artist from the New Brunswick College of Craft and Design, and Dave Lombardi and Linda Young, for sharing the story of their Grenfell Mission hooked tapestry.

As always, gratitude is due to my editor, Lara Zielinski, my Saturday workshop group, my cover designer, the sterling Claire Smith of BookSmiths Design, and my Monday evening women's fiction group. At home, I've been supported by my beloved partner in life and crime, who tells everyone about the "other woman" living in our house – that's what a pen name will do for you!

About Annie

Annie M. Ballard writes about women and family ties in small villages we can all imagine as home. A New Englander by birth and Maritmer by heritage, she's a people person who digs into the lives of her characters. When she's not writing, she's happily baking, gardening, powerlifting and trying to make friends with every dog in her neighbourhood. Annie's stories include strong women living real lives, good men trying to do better, and always a happy ending.

Find her webpage at anniemballard.com
She's on FaceBook and Instagram, too.
Subscribe at https://www.subscribepage.com/newsfromannie

Also By Annie M. Ballard

Published by Devon Station Books

A Talisman of Home

Angels in the Architecture

A Heart for the Homeless, Sisters of Stella Mare, book 1

A Home Out of Ashes, Sisters of Stella Mare, book 3

Available at your favourite book retailer.

Made in the USA
Middletown, DE
26 October 2022